LANTERN'S PASSAGE

The Lessons of Life Remembered

Published by
Sunrise Glory House
San Diego, CA

Printed in the United States of America

Lantern's Passage is a work of fiction. Names, characters, places, and
incidents are a product of the author's imagination or are used
fictitiously. Any resemblance to actual events, locales, or persons,
living or dead, is coincidental.

ACKNOWLEDGEMENTS

To my wife, Lynne, and daughters, Isa and Kate, for their love, patience and encouragement during the writing and publishing of this work.

To the millions of talented un-published authors with so much to say.

LANTERN'S PASSAGE

The Lessons of Life Remembered

BY

Andrew L. MacNair

Prologue

There is a photograph that stands at the corner of my desk. The frame is a simple band of painted blue. The subject, in subtle strokes of black and white, is, at first glance, unremarkable. It shows a large, weathered cottage on a low rise of sand. The camerawork lacks professionalism; the lens tilts with childlike simplicity, but looking more closely an imaginative viewer detects something more. There is a face there, wise and lined with years. It is the face of the great cottage, and it is there to remind me of two summers long ago; a time when death entered my life for the first time, and I learned that love is the most powerful force there is.

I need only glance at that photograph and close my eyes to recall every detail of those surroundings. Truly. Every detail. Not merely the fleeting images of morning sunlight slanting through a front room, or the deepening gray of the sky before an afternoon storm. No, all of the details are there, the sounds, the smells, the tiny bits and pieces that are drawn moment by moment, day by day through all of the senses when we are very young. And in this polished office so many years away, surrounded by my books and my art and the accumulated dross of my life, I merely close my eyes to hear the sea oats. They stand tall, swaying on the low dune beneath the open window of my childhood. They are tapping and clacking like castanets in the night's breeze. I feel the coarseness of sand in the bed sheets, the grainy remains of another day of barefooted exploration. I taste the salt in the cooling air. And I feel the ocean, always there beyond the window where the sun rises. I feel each vibration, each wave slapping in rhythmic patterns upon the sand. I feel the sweetness of fatigue and the sentinels of sleep.

It was the place of my summers, the home base in the great games of tag, an area of mystery and lesson and self-designed exploration. It was a place of awesome power and gentle tranquility, and I am now certain it was a place created just for children to absorb some unseen, but always felt energy. We knew it. We felt it because we were children. It came into us through the soles of our bare feet. It poured in through the crowns of our heads. It emanated from the sand and the waves, and the wind, and it filled us through our skin.

It was the familiar spot from which I always ventured a little nervously, a little boldly, and it is the secure space to which I always return. Even now, so many miles, so many years away, I return there with ease.

And it was the place where Maggie Silver shared the secrets of the world with me.

Gentle Breeze

The first time I noticed Maggie Silver, she was crying. I had seen her before, of course, all the children of Nags Head, or any of us that were not drinking age adults, knew each other, but I had never really SEEN her before that moment. She was six years older than I, and a girl. She didn't create forts in the sand the way we did. She didn't play tag, or crack the whip. She had just been over there somewhere, two cottages to the north. I remember that she always seemed alone, and it was as if she had, up to that point in my life, simply been a part of the scenery, an invisible player who had not yet entered the stage of my awareness.

When I first saw her she was standing on the side porch of the Silver cottage in cut-off denims and a faded purple t-shirt. I had just run full tilt around the corner of the Harris cottage--which lay between Maggie Silver's and mine--when I heard a loud clatter of metal and shattering china. I dropped instinctively to the sand and scurried into the shadowy haven of the pilings below the Harris place.

"Putrid pustules! They're Satan's fruit, an I hate 'em." The voice I heard was high pitched and shrieking. It was radiating through the darkened screen of a window next to where Maggie was standing, and it was, at that moment, scaring the pants off of the ten year old boy hiding in the shadows thirty feet away.

"You tryin' to hide raisins in this pile of godawful crap. I know what you tryin' to do an' I hate 'em, goddamnit." A thud resonated sharply against the wall where Maggie stood. I peeked tentatively around the piling.

Beyond the space of sand between the cottages she stood with her arms folded tightly across her chest, and she was shaking. Her eyes and cheeks were wet. From my hiding place I watched as a single tear slid along the crease of her nose and dropped like the tip of a warming icicle onto her faded t-shirt. That was the first time I truly saw Maggie Silver.

"Wicked girl." The voice was losing intensity now. "Never give 'em to me ever agin'."

"I won't, Momma. I promise I won't." I watched as her shoulders sagged forward and her chin lowered to the tear-stained spot. It was the unspoken signal that we children knew all too well. The indication that no more blows should be thrown, no more teasing should take place. It was the sign of the wounded and beaten.

She was barefoot. Her hair was dark and long, and with her head lowered submissively it hung in thick drapes across her face. I wanted at that moment to see her better, to see that face, and I didn't want her to hurt anymore.

Then her chin came up and she shivered as if a ripple had moved through one side of her and out the other. She closed her eyes, and when they opened again her shoulders rose and I knew. It would be okay for her.

"You get in here and clean up this mess, girl."

"Yes, Momma." Her voice was soft, but not meek, and I didn't hear affection in it, just compliance.

"And don't you never try to hide them evil little things in my oat meal agin, you hear."

"Yessim, Momma."

Maggie Silver then did something that I can recall as easily as the sound of sea oats or the salty tang of the Nags

Head air. She stretched out her hands. She stretched them in a long graceful movement towards the ocean and then drew them very slowly back towards the salty tear spot on her blouse. Her arms were curved, her fingers loose, and it looked to me as if she were gently pulling on some invisible tree. Her hands came almost to her chest before she turned them over and pushed them slowly out towards the ocean once more. And then she turned, and with the most beautiful eyes I had ever seen, looked directly at me. And smiled. With that turn of the lips, with that mere crinkle of sinew and skin about the face, with that began the greatest, and most mysterious, odyssey of my youth.

***

I knew what we were having for dinner that evening well before I touched the rusted handle on the screen door at the back of the cottage. The familiar smell of boiling shrimp drifted out to me ten feet beyond the first of the five steps. I smelled the bay leaves and onions near the third plank, and then a clean scent of artichokes as I bolted through the door.

"Rinse your feet! And don't you slam that…" Too late, the screen smacked like a small firecracker against the door jamb, bounced out a foot and popped again. I had once more forgotten the two most important rules for re-entering the great cottage. I halted, annoyed at my forgetfulness, quietly re-opened the screen and plunged my feet one by one into the dish bucket of sandy water set conveniently on the top step.

In the kitchen, over near the stove, Nina May loomed with a fierce expression on her face. That kitchen was her domain, and sand was not welcome there one bit. I

tried on my best smile. She could grumble at me for the
tiniest of infractions, but never for very long. I was the
youngest of the three MacLaren boys and for that reason she
might reprimand me for sandy feet in her kitchen, but also
the reason her annoyance never lasted overly long. I was
still a child, and in her weakening eyes, small enough to be
wrapped into her huge apron and hugged like one.

"Where you been all day, Master Little?" She was
smiling back at me now. A wide smile below the thickest
glasses and biggest nostrils a ten year old could imagine.

"I went with Pooh up to watch Jethro set his nets this
mornin', Ma'am. Then we went on up to Jockey's Ridge
for most of the day."

Nina May was large. My ten year old arms couldn't
circle her middle by half. She was the darkest woman I had
ever known and had raised me a good part of my life; not
that my Momma had relinquished any of her own
responsibilities in my nurturing, rather that Nina May had
just taken on a portion of those disciplines as a personal
commitment to decency and love. I'd gotten warm treats
from her oven, layered thickly with sensible wisdom, and
sprinkled with the good dash of southern manners—the kind
a young boy required. She'd seen to it that I'd learned those
manners well, my occasional transgressions resulting in
ample smacks on my bottom until I'd learned it all properly,
or she couldn't catch me anymore.

"You two climbed all the way to the top of that pile
of sand? What in heaven's name for?"

"I like it up there. You can see to both sides AND
see the lighthouse down at Hatteras. We had a jumpin'
contest in the sand at the top. I won." I added this last part

just to let her know that I was tough. I thought for a moment and then asked, "Nina May whyn't you come on up there with us some time? It's as pretty as a postcard, you'd like it." It just seemed important to ask her.

She chuckled at the invitation. "Child, my 'thritis has me bent like a willow most days now. I can barely walk up these steps to this here kitchen. A mountain of sand? No, Master Little." She laughed and placed a wide hand on my hair. "I guess I'll just have to listen to you tell me about it." She stepped back and eyed me curiously as if I had somehow changed during the day. "You know, I think you is taller today. Your hair sure is blonder. Those curls are closer to white than yellow." I liked the idea of both of those changes, but especially the notion that I might be getting taller. A boy needed that.

I'd forgotten about dinner. "Nina May, are we havin' shrimp tonight?"

"Yes, Master Little, in 'bout ten minutes. You need to get on up there and get yourself washed." I'd made it home just in time again. The rules were pretty simple for the MacLaren boys in the Outer Banks, be home before sunset. Be cleaned up for dinner. Be seated at the table on time-- with a clean shirt. Obey the adults. And of course, rinse off the sand and don't slam the screen door. I managed to remember most of them pretty well.

I climbed to the upstairs bathroom through the secret passageway. That was how we all referred to it, an odd architectural feature in the back part of the cottage. Father said that it had been an eccentric notion of the builder who'd been out in The Banks hammering away on our cottage before most of the others had even been staked out. I figured that man simply had children, because the passageway was clearly too steep and tight for adults, being a narrow flight of stairs that rose from the kitchen to the upstairs hallway where it came out next to the bathroom. At each end there were short doors with no handles on the outside, just dangling strings to lift the inner latches. When the doors were shut the passageway was inky black, which made perfect sense for the amusement of children.

I washed off the sweat and fine grit of the day with the tap water that always smelled of old eggs and had just finished toweling the dust from around my ears when the dinner bell tolled with a single note that rose like evaporating mist into the furthest beams of the cottage. It was a genuine ship's bell, solid brass, and had hung next to the ocean-side window of the dining room since my grandfather had bolted it there in 1910. I had one minute.

The table was set, and my family seated in their customary places when I slid in next to Donny, who whispered, "Cuttin' it kinda close aren't you, Peckerhead." Hey, I was there, and my shirt looked clean. His did not, a point I might just let slip out casually during some lull in the dinner conversation.

The entire room smelled of shrimp. The windows were steamed up with it, and the table, which could comfortably seat twelve, now had just the four of us clustered at one end. It was partially covered with two layers of newspaper. Small bowls of melted butter and squeezed lemon were placed within arms reach. A platter of artichokes was steaming up the air at my father's elbow. It was the typical Nags Head feast.

Heads were bowed and we all intoned, "Come, Lord Jesus, our guest to be, and bless these gifts bestowed by thee."

That came from the Moravians. I really didn't know who the Moravians were, or what their grace meant exactly, but I liked it. It was short and rhymed. I did know those Moravians, whoever they might be, made good cookies, thin spicy ones that we ate at Christmastime back in Burlington, and those were good enough reason for us to use their grace at our table.

I was pulling apart my fourth shrimp, the whole pink ones transforming into a translucent mound of empty ones on the newspaper in front of me, when my father wiped the juice from his chin and said, "Drew, Nina May said you were down watching Jethro set his nets this morning. Did you see his catch this afternoon?"

"No Sir, we didn't. Pooh and me went up to Jockey's Ridge and then I played around here some before dinner. Did you go?"

"'I'" It was my Momma. She was frowning at me like Miss Holt, my fifth grade teacher. "Take Pooh out of the sentence and see how it sounds. Did me go up to Jockey's Ridge?"

"No, ma'am, I did." Momma, being an English major some years back, was persnickety when it came to my speech.

"Well, your father and I went up to watch." She was sucking on the right end of an artichoke leaf, eyeing me over the top a little disapprovingly, as if Jethro's net haul was something that had been penciled onto the calendar for the whole family to attend. "We strolled up this afternoon, and I thought I might find you with the other children. We had a beautiful walk, and I found two whole sand dollars for our collection."

I wanted to explain that I wasn't five years old--the age we started our shell collection--but instead asked, "Was there anything different in the nets today?"

"Just one of the oddest creatures I've ever seen. It was some kind of eel, and bless me if he didn't set his heel on it and then grab it in his bare hands. I was certain it was going to wiggle around and take his fingers off, but he just tossed it back into the waves like it was a piece of rope."

Jethro Sorrini was legendary in that part of The Banks. He was a year-rounder and had lived in Nags Head forty-two of his forty-three years. His father had been a fisherman in Portugal, as well as every other relative Jethro could recall, but the older Mr. Sorrini must have decided at some point that the catch was better on this side of the Atlantic, because one day he simply left his patch of ocean near Lisbon and brought his wife, one-year-old Jethro, and all his hopes to a small cottage north of the pier.

Jethro was also the Pied Piper of Nags Head. Children followed him everywhere, moving about him like one of his great flowing webs, spreading in front, drifting behind, some in silence, most chattering and asking every sort of question all at the same time. The littlest ones, for whom time was still a mysterious measurement, were certain he was an authentic pirate. The piercing eyes, massive beard, limp, ragged scars, and his amazing manner of speech, convinced most of them that he'd walked the decks with Blue Beard and Morgan.

The afternoon hauling of the catch onto the beach was, for most, a combination marine biology lesson and a social event not to be missed.

Around the table, the dinner conversation had finally weaved through the labyrinth of our individual days to a quiet lull. I asked the question that had been pestering me since I'd seen Maggie standing on her porch. "Father, who are the Silvers?"

"Well, they're Baptists," my mother slipped that right in. She said it as if that summed everything up.

Donny coughed into his napkin and I clearly heard, "Weirdos."

My father arched a bushy eyebrow at my brother, indicating that he had also heard the comment, and said quietly to me, "They're a nice family, Son." My father never seemed to say bad things about anyone. "They've come through some rough times here and there. Why do you ask?"

"I was just wondering about them. I mean I know about Skeeter," I hesitated and asked what had really been inside my head. "But is Mrs. Silver sick or something too?" We all knew about Skeeter. He could be seen on the Silver porch pretty much all the time. He'd gotten polio when he was four, and now he had to push himself with his hands around the sides of the Silver cottage on a flat board with little caster wheels. Momma called it a poor man's wheelchair. I thought it looked kind of fun for awhile, but I also knew he never got to go any further than those three porches. I didn't really know what polio was either, but Momma told me I wouldn't get it because I had that dime-sized scar on my shoulder. I was glad of that. I didn't want to have to roll around our porches like Skeeter did on his.

I saw the look float between my mother and father, and I knew my question was going be answered in my father's slow, considered way when something was serious.

"She has an illness, Son. It makes her...." his speech slowed to a crawl... "not right in the head at times."

I took this in and nodded energetically as if I understood. I didn't. What illness? What was not right in Mrs. Silver's head?

"What's the matter with her?"

"Nobody knows what it is, or what it's called, Little. She hasn't had it too long, and we're praying she'll get over it soon." My mother added this. She had now moved beyond the shortcomings of the Silvers being Baptists, and was beginning to answer a little more of my burning question. "She just gets sick sometimes and needs help, has to stay in bed for a period. The girl...what's her name, John? She cares for the boy and Mrs. Silver."

My father dipped the final pink shrimp into the coagulating butter in front of him and replied, "Margaret, Jean Gray," He looked at me and then added what I already knew, "but they call her Maggie. The father left some years back, so it's just the three of them living there. Mrs. Silver grew up in The Banks, been here her whole life."

"And not much to show for it either. She's got small money coming in from what her mother left, but not much else."

Donny was slyly circling his index finger around the side of his head, which I was pretty certain he meant for the Silver family and not our mother.

The smoldering coals of my ever-present curiosity had been fanned by all the partial answers, but I knew from ten year's of such things that I wasn't going to learn any more of what I really wanted to know that evening. It fell under that frustrating phrase, "We'll talk about it more when you are older."

As Nina May entered to remove the empty bowls and glasses, and Donny and I began the fun task of rolling up the empty shells and artichoke leftovers into big, fat newspaper cigars, I mentioned in a voice just loud enough to be heard by both my parents, "Is that a new shirt, Donny?"

The arrest came like all those events that we assemble under the vast roof of tragedy. It swept in at an hour deep in the night, not quite beyond the threshold that would have pushed it into morning, and like all tragedy, it was an event that should never have occurred. Though anticipated by many, it arrived quietly, like a tiny puff of wind, and with it all of our fine layers of complacency were blown far into the air.

The arrest was made by Sheriff Jack Brennan, who came in the old model Pontiac that the citizens of Dare County had raised money for. He arrived in the darkness with no lights spinning, no howling sirens to disturb the natural rhythms of the night. And Mr. Brennan came in his uniform, gun and all, looking far too official. It was, I remember, part way into the second summer, during that week when everything dissolved and the world that I had known so well got torn apart. I was eleven and she was seventeen, and I remember that it happened the second night after the most violent storm of the decade thundered across The Banks, the one the locals eventually came to call Big Leo because it arrived precisely on the cusp.

Rising Wind

I felt the change the following morning before I opened my eyes, before I pulled the covers back or stepped onto the polished planks of the floor. I couldn't feel the regular rhythm of the waves under the eastern windows, and the air about my bed felt as if it might crackle like a wool sweater at the slightest inclination. The sunlight wasn't streaming in to light up the boards on the opposite wall, and the curtains, the short white ones on the north side, were angled like prayer flags. Outside, the air whistled through the shingles like a tuning of reeded instruments, so I knew immediately that the wind had changed. It was all blowing from the opposite direction, and blowing hard.

I padded over and wrapped a hand around a curtain to keep it from slapping at my face and peered out. Dark clouds boiled in menacing shapes in every direction. The sky looked like burnished steel. The ocean's shade was the same, just darker. The wind was gusting from the back of the house in bursts that rose and diminished with slight deviation and I knew from my ten summers of forecasting that it would be that way all day--a steady blow with no change, and in the afternoon it would rain hard and only then would the wind begin to drop.

This would be a day when I would stay close to the great cottage. I wouldn't seek new routes to the dunes, or over to the sound. I wouldn't swim in the waves or construct fortresses or castles. I looked at the ocean and saw that it was too windy to cast a lure for the greedy bluefish beyond the breakers. It would be a day of comic books, crazy eights, and simple distractions. The storms, even the smaller variety, kept me instinctively close by the great cottage.

I swept a few grains of sand from between the sheets, pulled the covers to the metal head frame and lay my pillow across the top. The smell of frying bacon drifted up along with a strong aroma of fresh coffee, and I knew Nina May was again moving about in the realm of her kitchen.

I tip-toed down the secret passageway hoping just once to sneak up on her, but what Nina May had lost in her eyesight she seemed to have gained in her hearing. I just couldn't surprise her like I could my mother. Her wide back was towards me; bent over the stove, but Nina May was pretty much always bent over. It came from what she called her 'thritis. I knew that whatever it was it hurt her, because she complained about it to me and no one else. It made her fingers curl and ache, and even though I wanted to, I never knew quite what to do to help her. My hurts usually felt better after a small spray of Bactine and some form of bandage, but her 'thritis didn't seem to be that kind of hurt

Without looking up she said, "Good morning, Master Little. You sleep well?"

"Yes, Ma'am, like a stone in the wizard's palm."

I was the first down for breakfast again, but that wasn't unusual. I was young, and my room was on the ocean side where the sun demanded early attention. I was usually up, and after a few minutes of sensible conversation with Nina May, out the screen door in the back before anyone else had even come down.

As Nina May was setting a bowl on the scarred metal table tucked into the nook in the kitchen, my eye settled on a gull hovering just above the north window. The bird was struggling against the wind a few feet above the edge of the roof and seemed to be eyeing my freshly poured Cheerios with hungry purpose. Gulls often looked a little dim-witted to me, and they pretty much always looked greedy. This one was looking both right then. He was flapping into the wind, eyes turned toward the window, and he was going nowhere. I think he must have finally figured out he was doing something wrong, and that my Cheerios were somehow beyond his beak, because, with what I was sure was a wink; he lifted one wing, spun, and blew like a strip of paper in the opposite direction. I contemplated this seemingly trivial event and knew that it was an omen meant just for me. My plans were instantly set.

Cereal, orange juice, a slice of Canadian bacon, and I was done. A hug for Nina May and I was out the back door, where, at the last instant, I remembered to close the screen softly.

I stepped onto the plank at the top of the steps and peered across the empty highway toward the dunes. To the right, far up on the crest of Jockey's Ridge, the sand was peeling off in a high rooster tail. It would be impossible to see, or even move up there. Nearby, blades of dune grass were bent into flat ribbons and humming like harmonicas. Conditions were perfect. I sucked the air deep into my lungs, chest puffing out in proper super hero fashion. It was, in my opinion, a perfect day for flying.

During my previous summers in The Banks I had been a pioneer in many disciplines. I'd dabbled as an alchemist, creating glittering gems from common pebbles. I had been a zoologist, assembling the finest collection of sand scurrying creatures the world had seen; a philatelist;

bee keeper; glassblower; archer; and a daring mountaineer setting crayoned pennants atop the loftiest peaks of nearby sand. Of course, I had also been an English sea dog with vast quantities of Spanish gold. Each of these endeavors had shown varying degrees of perseverance and success.

Being a superhero, however, that was an aspiration that never waned.

The building behind the cottage functioned as a boat house, storage shed, and sleeping quarters for Nina May; three separate spaces, two of which I was permitted to enter whenever I wished. I ran to the middle door and searched under the steps to find the rusted screwdriver that we used to pry on the salt encrusted hasp. I slid the screwdriver into place and pulled with both hands. The hinge held momentarily, and then with a groan snapped back. Inside, a mass of buckets, brushes, and rusty cans that would never be opened again lay in piles reaching to the rafters. Somewhere near the middle I found them, two paint smeared sheets.

From the rear of the cottage the wind was blowing steadily across the porches and out to a white-capped ocean. Hugging my bundled sheets, I made my way to the front corner along the right side. The weathered rocking chairs were rolling on their curved pedestals as if guided by the hands of ghosts. I looked carefully at the sand below. No sharp sticks were in view, no burs or shells. My landing zone was free of the usual perils, so as I'd seen in the movies, I wet my finger with my tongue, raised it analytically into the air to check wind speed and direction and stepped onto the bench that ran the length of the porch.

As I stepped up to the wide railing, I decided that the same clever builder who'd designed the secret passageway had also created the perfect launching pad for small super heroes. Steadying myself against the post, I tied the lower corners of my sheets onto my rope belt and grabbed the upper corners with both hands. Decades of the MacLaren cottage paints were splashed proudly across the surface. My flying spinnakers were ready. I would be lifted across the wild peaks of the Atlantic to the distant shores of France. Taking a breath, I stepped off, throwing my arms apart like a statue. The sails snapped open, filling like bowls, and I shot outward with a yell that surely roused any human still asleep that blustery morning.

I was airborne, pulled outward and upward by the rising drafts circling the cottage. My flying machine worked in spectacular fashion, a perfect harmony of invisible currents, old sheets, and my ten-year old body. I was flying, and undoubtedly the same jubilation that filled old Orville as he drifted above his own airstrip just up the road, now filled me. I fluttered twenty feet beyond the corner railing and dropped, rolling and laughing, into wet lumps of sand.

I raced back up the front steps to the railing again, and this time I did not merely step off, I jumped with all the strength my small legs could express. The sails pulled me instantly into the gray beyond. I dropped four feet further out than my first flight, and I was certain that I had, just for an instant, seen the beaches of France that Father had once described to me.

"Hey Peckerhead. Pretty good jump." Donny stood leaning into the door frame at the end of the porch, arms folded in a classic, tough guy stance. He'd had to shout some into the wind, but I heard him clearly. His compliment, rare as a royal jewel, settled on me like a crown, and my grin widened considerably. Sharing a flying experience with an older brother, even one like Donny, was ever so much better than describing it in the past tense.

I scrambled back up to the porch and pushing the wads of cloth toward him said, "Donny, you've got to try it. It's just like, like Batman, or Superman. You could get back on the railing and get a really good start. You'd go forever with a good jump. I want to make a cape. You want to help me make a cape?" Instantly I realized I'd made a critical younger brother mistake—being overly enthusiastic.

Donny, at fourteen, was always working towards a single goal, looking cool. He practiced. A lot. He imitated the best of our times, matched their moves, their detached expressions, through careful study. Elvis, Audey Murphy, and James Dean all nodded indifferently back at him from every mirror in the cottage.

The only times I'd seen my brother lose any of his well-rehearsed cool was on those occasions when his asthma had struck. He'd turned the blue of a pre-dawn sky during those attacks, and the fear I'd seen in his eyes scared me silly. It had sounded as if he were sucking for his life through a drinking straw, and once, after an exceptionally severe one, he confided that it had felt like he was drowning in his own special pool. Most days, however, Donny was the perfect image of fourteen-year-old North Carolina cool.

"No, I don't want to make any stupid cape, you stupid Peckerhead." The look I got withered me more than his well-turned phrase. Grabbing the knotted sheets he shot me his best Jimmy Cagney sneer and said, "Let me show you how to really fly. Sit back and watch, Turdferbrains. You better go get the boat, cuz I'm gonna land myself ten yards into the ocean."

I looked towards that water. It was whipped into a bowl of quivering foam, black driftwood and seaweed. The waves weren't peeling across the sandbar in neat, green rows. They were looming like trucks, crashing violently from every direction. It all looked deadly dangerous to me, and I hoped my brother's flight didn't pull him out there. He was a stronger swimmer than I was, but even Jethro hadn't taken his boats out that morning. It was that rough.

Donny balanced on the railing, neatly measured off six paces to the post and pushed off with the force of Superman clearing an upper-story window. He ran and leapt majestically towards the clouds, spreading the sheets like a bent kite, and then dropped six feet from the corner of the cottage, crumpling to his knees. The sheets flapped insignificantly around his middle. It had been the equivalent of an aerodynamic belly-flop.

I knew better than to start laughing. This had been a serious big brother miscalculation. I watched him mentally re-constructing the flight, adjusting. Bigger sheets. More surface area. And then I saw that he'd reached the same conclusion I had. His slightly pudgy fourteen-year-old body was designed for tackle football, and clearly not meant for sheet sailing. It dawned on me that there were still a few advantages to being ten-year old small.

For a moment I thought Donny was contemplating another flight, or worse, he was considering climbing the steps and smacking me a few times, that being a favorite pastime. There was a lot to prove on his part, and clearly, quitting this early held risks to his image. I wasn't sure if he was ready to accept defeat so quickly, but he did. Very casually, he untied the knots at his belt and stood. Without looking at me directly he patted off the sand, sauntered up the steps and dropped the sheets onto the floorboards. He sort of sniffed and asked indifferently, "So, how many seconds do you think I was up there. Five? Six?" I had to be careful here. I really didn't want to get pounded on that early in the morning.

"More like seven, Donny. You hung up there a long time."

"Yeah, later Peckerhead."

After my fourth ascent to the stratosphere I landed a little more roughly than I intended and finished face first in the sand. I was cleaning off the shell pieces and coarse pebbles sticking onto my cheeks, glad that nobody had seen my substandard landing, when I realized that somebody had. My flight had taken me just far enough beyond the corner of the Harris cottage to be in line with the porch along the sides of the Silver place. There, kneeling on his flat board with caster wheels, Skeeter Silver was watching me. He was peering like an inmate through the balusters that lined the front, and he was swaying back and forth as if listening to some personal incantation that no one else could hear.

I hesitated, not knowing what to do, frozen in jumble of embarrassment and confusion. My awkwardness didn't come from my less than perfect landing, rather from the realization that I had ascended my own steps so easily and jumped with super-hero agility into the air. It embarrassed me that these were movements so natural to me and far too alien to the smaller boy watching me from behind the balusters. I was, in that tenth summer, still young enough to feel the magic of childhood flight, and just old enough to sense the peculiarity of what had occurred. I had floated like a seedling, while Skeeter had watched secretly from his knees.

I wasn't aware of what caused me to close the distance of space between Skeeter Silver and me; it wasn't that so many yards separated us, but a chasm much wider. Perhaps I was driven by my curiosity. "Who are the Silvers?" Perhaps it was something else, but at that moment I knew it was something I must do.

Skeeter stopped swaying as I walked up the slope towards him. I knew he was younger than I, perhaps eight or nine. Somehow, as children of Nags Head, we just knew these things, like some great hierarchical numerical system that we were all keenly aware of. He had on tattered shorts faded to deep pink. His hair was nearly as white as mine, but less curly and longer. Coming closer I saw that he had the greenest eyes I'd ever seen. He was white as a clam shell, which made the wild spattering of freckles around his face appear more numerous and prominent. I looked at his hands and saw that they were covered with frayed gardening gloves. They were the only other clothing he had on besides his shorts. He must have noticed me eyeing them because the first thing he said to me was, "They keep me from getting too many splinters." Pure North Carolina drawl. I nodded as wisely as I could.

"Yeah, I hate splinters too. Are they slippery? You know, like on the boards?"

Skeeter grinned. In his smile I saw that one of his front teeth was missing, the permanent substitute pushing in an odd rectangle about half way down from his gum. He pulled off one of the gloves and grinned again. "Yep, they are, but when I want to go fast I take 'em off."

I stood at the corner of Skeeter's cottage, awkwardly digging my toe into a carpet of sand. Like ours, it was raised on pilings so the outer lip of the floorboards was just above my eye level. Skeeter turned and looked apprehensively down the side porch towards a screened door at the back and then looked at me again. "You want to come up for a bit?"

I wasn't sure. Those five steps looked like lofty peaks in some mythical land, and climbing them was going to take me into unexplored territories, but from some compelling curiosity I had crossed the space between his cottage and mine, and for the same reason I decided to cross the threshold to Skeeter's confined world. As I bounded up the steps, he lifted himself with a practiced ease from his rolling board onto the bench below the railing. With one hand he pulled his legs up by his ankles and tucked them like twigs beneath his thighs.

My first impression of Skeeter Silver when I sat down next to him on that bench was that he was skinny. Really skinny. I could've counted that boy's ribs if he'd raised one arm above his head, and with his longer hair and half tooth he looked just plain odd. But his eyes said something else. The green shone like ocean water on a sunny day, and his smile sparkled shyly with wholesome warmth right at me.

For a few seconds it felt strange sitting there. I was pretty sure asking more questions about his gloves and how he rolled around on caster wheels wasn't really good manners, or for that matter, how I had flown with sheets and he hadn't, so I asked what I figured was the next best thing. "Hey, you like comics?"

"Yeah," His green eyes lit up like lanterns. "I like The League of Heroes? They're my favorites. But Batman, he's second best. He can fly over a mile in one leap, you know, just stretch out his cape and glide all over Gotham. He can go all over the place like that."

"Wow! They're my favorites too. I like Captain America, the way he can throw his shield like a weapon and cut right through bricks and stuff."

"And Superman, the way he can see through things."

And so it went. We sat on the bench for nearly an hour that morning, Skeeter and I, rating our favorite superheroes and their amazing powers, neither one of us noticing our own limitations, or rating each other in any way. We journeyed to other worlds where champions flew, where gargantuan objects were tossed about with astonishing strength, and where villains were always done away with before the final page.

Sometime later I felt the wind strengthen to just below a howl, and an idea came to me. "Hey, Skeeter I know something we can do. Wait here, I'll be right back." As I raced down his steps and across the sand towards my own cottage, I realized it sounded a little dumb to have told him to wait there. He'd probably been waiting on that porch most of his life.

I managed to get up to my room and back out before anyone knew I'd come in. A minute later I was back on his bench opening the small paper sack with my treasures. Skeeter looked at me strangely, as if I was an oddity he'd never encountered. I was a friend who had returned to his porch.

"Here," I said, "blow this up." I handed him a deflated, blue balloon, still coated with fine packing talc. He frowned, not understanding my design yet, but took it between his fingers and set to inflating it. For a moment I thought he wasn't going to be able to do it. The balloon fluttered limply at his lips, his cheeks puffed out like a blowfish and then the balloon sagged again. His eyes became determined, fiercely so, and on the second try it expanded slowly and evenly into a basketball sized globe. I patted his knee and said, "That's it, now tie it off at the end." That part defeated him completely. He stretched the nippled end around a single finger and tried four times to thread a knot.

I realized, somewhat puzzled, that my new friend had never knotted a balloon before, so I showed him how to wrap it around two fingers and push the end up through the space between. In a moment we had a large blue balloon and a green companion tied, and ready for aeronautic ventures into the upper reaches of the atmosphere.

I pulled a stick from the crumpled bag in my lap. It was a smooth driftwood piece that I'd carefully selected from the tide line the previous summer. My best kite string was wound in a neat spool around the middle. And finally, I drew out my last treasure, a five inch curved, folded fishing knife.

"Wow, that's cool." Skeeter's green eyes locked onto the mother of pearl handle like it was a glowing blob of kryptonite.

"Yeah, it is." I accepted his compliment just like that, because I knew the knife was cool, and because I was more proud of it than any comic book I owned. "My dad gave it to me last year on Fourth of July," I boasted. "I use it a lot for fishing. You know, like when you have to cut a snagged line or something." I stopped. Skeeter was still looking at the knife, but his eyes had changed. The sparkle that had graced them seconds before was gone. My father's words returned to me from the previous evening. *It's just the three of them living there.*

He looked up from the knife handle and down the length of the porch towards the dunes. "I ain't got no daddy," was all he said. "An' I ain't never fished before." And that was as peculiar to me as anything, because I didn't know many kids without a father and just about everyone, except my mother, knew how to fish. He hadn't said it resentfully; there was no spite or malice, just a second of quiet sadness between us before I said, "Well, maybe I can show you how sometime. I've got three surf rods." Skeeter chewed on his lower lip and mumbled skeptically, "Uh huh."

While Skeeter silently watched, I unwound two long sections, cut them with my knife, and tied the ends to both our balloons.

"Now we just let them fly up to the moon, Skeeter. Let the string out slowly, and whatever you do, don't let go of the end or it'll be out over the waves in about two seconds." I showed him how to tie it onto his wrist, and I figure I must've been a pretty good instructor, because that boy had that balloon drifting up into the wind thirty feet before I could get my knife folded and back into my paper bag. He laughed the whole way, not like a little set of the giggles either, he laughed deep down between those skinny ribs the entire time. His shoulders shook with it. That balloon and Skeeter were both flying into the clouds. He felt every tug, every subtlety of the wind, every drift of current and movement. Skeeter Silver was no longer on his porch in his world of rolling wheels; he was flying into the blue beyond.

Sometime later I tied the longer line from the driftwood onto the end of his string. He spun it out the entire way and that blue balloon got smaller and smaller, until it looked like a tiny speck on the dark gray of the clouds. Skeeter didn't stop laughing until the string was wound almost all the way back down and the balloon was bouncing in the air a few feet beyond the corner of his porch.

As Skeeter's fluttering balloon descended just enough for him to reach out with his skinny fingers and grasp it, I sensed the slightest motion behind me. Even as the wind whipped about us, and the first telltale drops began to splatter onto the sand, I felt the change, a ripple of movement in the air. It might have come from her breath or a vibration about her hands, but I knew she was there. I turned and saw Maggie Silver. She was standing quite still on the long porch silently watching her brother and me. The wind was tossing her hair about her face, but through the strands I saw her eyes and the smile, the same one I had seen the day before. In that instant a bolt of jagged lightening pierced the sky above the ocean, and Maggie's eyes widened. She didn't look surprised, she looked as if she was trying to pull the electricity from the air.

"They call you Drew, don't they?" Her expression didn't change. Her voice sounded like pecan pie, soft and inflected in the slow Outer Banks style.

"Yes'm." I replied, because right then she didn't seem like one of us, like a child, so I used my abbreviated version of Ma'am.

"I'm Maggie, Drew." It was a plain statement, but woven inside it was the command. I wasn't to call her Ma'am. Then she said, "That's a pretty sound, isn't it?" I wasn't sure what she was referring to. The thunder had just rolled in like a kettle drum above us. The wind was whistling around the porch, and the sand was rasping against the pilings below. There were a few too many to choose from.

"What?"

"My Skeets, laughing like that. It's such a pretty sound." She came towards her brother in one step, placed her left palm on his head and smoothed his wind blown hair back down. "We don't hear it much around here."

Skeeter sort of flapped his balloon shyly against his other hand, where it gave a little squeak, and said, "We've been flyin' balloons, Maggie. I got mine up so high it looked like a pencil dot in the clouds. And Drew's got some of the same comics as me. And he's got a fishin' knife with a pearl handle. His Daddy give it to him. An' he's got a giant ball of string wrapped on a driftwood stick." Skeeter's green eyes had lit up again and his sentences were bouncing around like popcorn.

Maggie sat on the bench between us, while Skeeter kept right on talking about how he'd learned to tie his balloon and how it had flown so high. He called it

Superman, he said, because it was the same color blue. The rain began falling heavily, big drops that formed wide divots in the sand. It felt good sitting there listening to the patter of rain. It smelled fresh and clean, felt safe and protected on that porch with just the three of us. And Maggie Silver was surely the prettiest thing I had ever seen.

"Skeeter, think you can go and fetch us some iced tea? I imagine Drew is getting somewhat thirsty with all this flying." Maggie slid her palm along the side of Skeeter's face in a tender enticement. I was startled. I didn't see how my new friend was capable of getting anything for himself, much less bring us all glasses of tea, but he just nodded cheerfully with a, "Sure thing Maggie," and lowered himself onto his small board. He scooted the length of the porch, caster wheels spinning and twirling roughly as he came to the screen door and disappeared through it.

Maggie must've known what I was thinking, because she whispered, "I move a lot of things down low in the cabinets and ice box for him. He'll do just fine."

"I was kind of wondering," I replied.

She smiled, and her eyes seemed to drift away. "He doesn't get many visitors, Drew. What you did was sweet.' And then the eyes focused on me again. "I get the feeling that's something that kind of comes natural to you."

"I... guess so." Like most compliments I received, I hadn't learned yet quite how to respond to them. "It was fun." Then I boasted, "I knew the wind was just about perfect for it because I'd been sheet-flying earlier this morning."

Maggie smiled with a puzzled expression. It was the first time I'd seen her look like she was one of us, younger.

"Really? Tell me how you fly with sheets." So I explained how I'd launched into the rising winds around my porch and how I'd hovered and seen the beaches of France on the horizon. Maggie asked me questions here and there, and after a few minutes she looked towards the ocean and the dreamy look I'd seen earlier came back into her eyes. Then she looked at me as if she'd reached a decision of some importance and said, "Drew, there's someone I'd like you to meet sometime." And then added, "But only if you'd like."

I hesitated. "Sure, I guess that'd be okay." I wasn't sure. I was, in truth, nervous as I could be. I was thinking right then that she wanted me to meet the woman who'd been screaming and throwing bowls of raisin oatmeal at her. The prospect of that introduction didn't appeal to me at all.

Skeeter rolled back through the door with three glasses of sweetened tea covered with plastic and rubber bands all set in a small wooden box hooked to the front of his rolling board. Maggie's invitation was forgotten as we each drank from our glasses and watched the storm quicken and the rain begin to drive in at sharper angles. Pretty soon we had to move back from the bench in the front as the drops began to angle in on us.

As we sat, I watched Maggie sip her tea. She seemed to delight in the flavor as if the drops contained a blend of ingredients that she alone could taste. Her hair was thick and black, and in those moments it danced like sea grass in the wind. She was tall and thin, but not bony like her brother. Like all the children of the strand, she wore a thin coating of sand and dust upon her bare feet like delicate beige socks. She had high cheekbones, and lips that reminded me of apples in the fall. It was Maggie's eyes, however, that were exceptional. They were proud pools of cobalt that dared you to guess what went on behind them. She raised her glass to her lips, and the light shimmered like crystals through the hair on her forearm. Up near the elbow, I saw a nasty scar that looked like a triangle of melted plastic.

I glanced around at the outside of the cottage. The porches, like ours, stretched around three sides, but the posts were unpainted and had long, ugly cracks. There were missing shingles around the perimeter of the front door, and the screen on one window was torn and flapping like a wing with each gust of wind.

"Maggie? Honey?" A voice drifted through the back window near the door Skeeter had just come through. I sat up with a jolt. It was the same voice I'd heard the day before, the one that had been shrieking about putrid pustules—which I still needed to consult Mr. Webster about--but it sounded different now, soft and a bit sleepy.

"Yes, Momma?" Maggie's tone snapped to flat compliancy.

"Could you bring me some of that iced tea, Honey? And maybe some crackers? I'm thirsty as can be."

"Yes, Momma."

She took a breath and sighed as if her rest was over, then reached down to gently squeeze my hand and say quietly, "Come back over again, Drew. We can talk some more." As she walked the length of the porch I watched the way her hair swished back and forth. Then she was gone through the darkness of the door.

Skeeter was swaying again, like I'd seen earlier. He looked at me shyly and then whispered, "My momma's havin' a good day."

It was an odd thing to have told me, and I didn't know how to reply. Yesterday the voice had sounded like the wicked witch of OZ, and my imagination had spun most of the evening like a tornado with cows and trees all whirled up in the air. Sitting with Skeeter right then I was trying, without much success, to keep warty noses and pointy hats from spinning across my movie screen.

The rain was falling at a steady pace now. The top layer of sand was dark and saturated; the wind was dropping to a light breeze. Suddenly, it all felt peculiar being there, like the scary parts in a movie just before something bad happens. I didn't want to be sitting on Skeeter's porch anymore. I wanted to be in my own house, up in my own room.

I lifted my paper bag and stood quickly. "Skeeter, you keep Superman here and the string too. I gotta go now." I paused and as an afterthought added, "I'll bring over some of my comic collection tomorrow. Okay?"

As I ran around the side of the Harris cottage I glanced back. Skeeter was rocking gently to his personal rhythm once more, looking at me through the balusters of his porch.

Sand

The following day blossomed bright and cloudless, only to be marred a few hours after breakfast by one of my least favorite activities, the choosing of teams. The big games of boys in the sand necessitated such things, coming from the need to form groups, display dominance, establish superiority, and, in my case, inferiority. And, as always, I was obliged for unexplained reasons to join.

We were on the beach a half a mile south of the cottage near the old Beachcomber Hotel. There were thirteen of us standing in a cluster, eleven if you removed the two self designated captains who were standing in self-righteous positions twenty feet away. They were looking at us younger, and seemingly lower quality, cattle, and Donny, as usual, was one of the captains. He was glancing coolly my way, but purposefully avoiding eye contact with me. I didn't exist, and he was taking a long time choosing the next member of his team. Clearly none of the remaining candidates was even remotely capable of understanding his genius plays at quarterback. I had, at that time in my life, come to despise the game of football.

Georgie Marovich was two inches shorter than Donny, and three months older. At fourteen he already had the dark shadows of a mustache lining his upper lip. He used that bit of hairy growth to his advantage at every opportunity. He knew it made him look dangerous, so he was always stroking the thing with his thumb and index finger, and by default that mustache made him the other captain. Most of the younger, facially and otherwise hairless, boys whispered that he enhanced the thing with small amounts of black shoe polish, but none of us dared state that publicly.

Georgie looked pretty much like what he was, a truck driver's son. His arms stuck down through a torn t-shirt that had stenciling of some kind of race car on the chest. The biceps looked like they lifted fully packed boxes of machine bolts for a living. With his black hair cut like a landing strip on top and buzzed around the sides, he had the only perfectly square head I'd ever seen. He vacationed in a cottage his mother's family had owned for two generations. It was half a mile south of ours, beyond the Beachcomber. His father drove a big truck up and down the Eastern seaboard, which was the reason Georgie spent his summers in The Banks. His mother was bored nine months out of the year and subsequently took pleasure in her summer friendships with the ladies of Manteo and Nags Head.

He and Donny were best friends, and over the years had been responsible for more unexplained explosions in the dunes than anyone could count. They were masters in the art of dissecting firecrackers and repacking the powder into every conceivable container. They spent hours searching garbage cans for shrapnel and spent goodly amounts of their allowances on tape and wax. Had Georgie not eaten lunch and dinner at our house a dozen times over the years, and had he not built the sturdiest sand forts from the lumber around our cottage, I would have been totally terrified of him. As it was, I was just mildly so.

Donny was looking at us now, sort of sighing and shaking his head lightly, as if he were standing in front of Mr. Jensen's produce bins looking at ugly heads of lettuce. I counted. Five of us remained. The Morley twins, both twelve, Sean Tyner, little Pooh Hutton, and me. I did the calculations and the sinking feeling hit me. I knew what was coming.

"Ricky." Donny pointed with a limp finger.

"Jason." Georgie didn't even point, and the Morley twins were split to the two teams, which were now evenly matched and numbered.

Donny grinned, a wide toothy grin, looked directly at me and said, "Sean, you're on my team."

"Shit." Georgie waved a pair of fat knuckles towards Pooh and me. "Bottom of the barrel gets two. You guys are over here." Pooh and I, it appeared, equaled one player. We weren't even worth choosing, we were half choices. I hated football.

Georgie immediately started in with his captain's orders, brusquely telling all of us where to line up and what to do. I was instructed to place myself in front of Ricky Morley and block, which was just fine with me. Ricky and I liked each other and had formed a pact. In previous matches we'd agreed to act tough, look tough, and not bump each other hard at all. Besides, neither one of us really wanted to try to tackle Donny or Georgie anyway. The two of us crossed our arms like small barricades and fenced harmlessly with our elbows while the great designs of the bigger players went thundering around us.

"Huddle up!" Georgie was barking seriously now.

"You want some gum?" Ricky's hand was extended towards me as we crossed over the invisible boundary between our two teams.

"Bazooka?"

"Yup, an' I got some Pixie Sticks and wax juice in a bag over there if you want 'em." Ricky, though older than me, was always nice, which was one of the reasons I liked being around him. The other was that, like me, his name had been changed to something he liked more than the one his parents had given him. They called him Eric, a name he didn't like too much, so he made sure everyone else called him Ricky. I didn't mind being called Andrew that much, except when my mother connected it to my last name. When she used it that way, I knew I was in trouble for something.

I popped the pink block in my mouth, pocketed the waxy cartoon for later, and headed towards the mysterious gathering called "The Huddle." The sugary flavor tasted fabulous and I grinned and nodded appreciatively over my shoulder at Ricky, unable to thank him with the wad and saliva working overtime in my mouth.

I hadn't paid too much attention to the game details, like which team was actually winning, but learned as the seven of us formed our sloppy circle that we were now tied at twenty-one.

"Listen up!" Georgie was down on one knee with his palm out like a map and getting more serious by the second. "We're gonna fucking score here, all right?" Our captain swore before, during, and after every play. I think he believed it was either going to help us win, or help his mustache grow, which he was now rubbing with his finger and thumb, making him look as if he were immersed in deep thought. "I got a good play thought up." He looked at me, and my stomach suddenly felt like hamsters were running around inside it. "Marty close the gap 'tween you and MacLaren, so those jerks can't see in here." Marty Brenner moved an inch closer to me and spread his elbows to keep the far-sighted spies from seeing Georgie's open palm.

"Marty, you line up like you're going to hike the ball as usual, but Robbie's gonna be standing next to me like a halfback. You hike it to him. You got that?" Georgie was using three fingers like pointers on his flattened palm to show us the secret play he'd obviously been thinking about for some time.

"Yeah, Georgie, no problem. What's the count?"

"Hike it to him on forty-four, Marty. Forty-four. Pooh, you just stand next to Marty and do nothing as usual." Pooh Hutton was even smaller than I was and didn't mind doing nothing, and right then he looked even smaller, because he'd taken his glasses off which made his eyes appear miniaturized on his face. "Wink, you sprint a post to the left corner, right to the goal line. Donny's gonna go with you to cover." Another finger showed Winston May running down to the left on Georgie's palm. Winston Ewell May III, we all knew, was the richest kid in that part of the strand, his granddaddy having founded one of the big hosiery mills in Greensboro, and Wink liked to act snobby about it most of the time. He was another one that didn't especially like his first name. He was a tall as Donny, but skinnier, and as our best receiver he caught the ball whenever Georgie decided it was the right time to pass.

Georgie's eyes and palm now swung in my direction, and I knew I was in trouble, deep trouble.

"MacLaren, you block Ricky for two seconds, just two, and then you walk down the sideline over there like you're going to help yourself to a Pixie Stick from Ricky's bag." How he knew about Ricky's candy I didn't know, but it was the least of my concerns. "You walk right on past the bag to the corner of the goal and stand there. If Wink is covered, the ball is coming to you. None of those dicks will ever expect it." While his eyes locked on mine, Wink May kind of sneered at me as if I was incapable of catching a cold much less a football. I also had my doubts. "And MacLaren, you don't drop it no matter what." I didn't hear a single word of the last of Georgie's great design.

The other team knew something big was in the works. The signals had been sent all too clearly when our captain had dropped down to one knee and spent nearly a minute pointing to locations all over his hand. My stomach now had the same hamsters and at least three new rodents jumping up and down in it. My breath was coming in shallow gasps. I really didn't like Georgie's big secret play; there were a few too many flaws in it by my reckoning.

"Hup, thirty-three, sixty-six, ninety-nine, FORTY-FOUR." The ball sailed in a wobbly arc back to Robbie Neidermeyer. Winston May sprinted straight down the middle of the beach and banked left. I fenced with Ricky while my brain counted, *Mississippi one, Mississippi two.* And then I was walking. Alone. Casually. Pooh Hutton sat his small body comfortably down in the sand, well out of anyone's way and did nothing.

Behind me, Robbie had run forward eight steps, stopped, and pitched the ball underhanded back to the waiting hands of our illustrious captain. A Flea Flicker. It was one of the only plays I recognized, because, like the Statue of Liberty, I liked the name. Beyond Ricky's paper bag of sugared treats someone's torn t-shirt was pushed into the sand. The goal, our goal, was ten feet in front of me. I looked to the left and saw Winston May running in small circles waving his arms wildly in the air. Donny was moving casually next to him. I turned and there, in the air, framed in bright sky blue, was the most terrifying object I could imagine. The football. It had reached the pinnacle of a graceful arc and was now spiraling directly towards me. Georgie had not only designed a good play, he had lofted the perfect pass, which was now curving directly down towards my feebly outstretched arms.

Please let me catch this. I won't slam the screen door, please. PLEASE! The brown oval sloped gently down; I could see the stitches, the laces spinning like a gyroscope. I spread my arms. That ball was mine. I would wrap myself around it like a boa constrictor.

Donny's shoulder struck the center of my back one second before the ball reached me, instantly knocking every particle of air from my lungs. I heard him grunt as he pounded my face into the sand and rolled on. Grains of coarse grit pushed into the side of my mouth, into my ear and eyes, and then the complete terror of not being able to take a breath struck me. I tried to yell, tried to pull something, anything into my empty chest. Nothing worked and I was momentarily lost in a pool of sheer fright, certain I had been injured beyond repair. Finally, I sucked in a small spasmodic breath, then another, and struggling to my hands and knees, pulled a full, glorious lungful all the way down to my stomach. Then I puked.

"You can't fucking do that, Donny. It's illegal." I heard Georgie arguing our team's case somewhere up above me. "You can't hit him before he's touched the ball. We get it on the one yard line. It's the rules." Donny was calmly objecting, and nobody seemed to be noticing that I was near death, wearing puke and sand all over my shirt and crying.

I stood up slowly, tears mixing with the grit and salt around my nose and mouth. I reached up to touch a raw spot on my cheek and discovered the wad of sandy gum pressed into the hair just above my left ear.

"I didn't hit him early. He touched the ball. It was perfect timing." Donny was proudly justifying nearly sending me to the hospital.

The argument continued as Pooh Hutton squeezed through the circle of larger bodies and came to my side. He saw that I was crying, and whispered in his slow, quiet way, "Sorry you got hurt, Drew. Weren't right what Donny done to you." Above all the noise and cussing Pooh's small comment caught Donny's ear. He spun the small boy around with a quick jerk.

"What do know, you little turd? You know anything about football? You know who Johnny Unitas is? Huh? Do you? You know who Y. A. Tiddle is? You got any idea, you little shit." Pooh's small eyes immediately found the sand between his feet. His head began rolling back and forth like a fishing bob, and then his shoulders started shaking and tears welled up and dropped onto his toes.

Up to now nobody had paid much attention to me, even though I happened to be the subject of the ongoing argument. I wiped the snot from my nose onto the shoulder of my sleeve and screamed at the top of my lungs, "You shut up, Donny! You just shut up. Pooh doesn't need to know about your damned Wahyea Tittie. None of us do. You're an asshole." And then everything stopped. Every voice died away and an unnatural quiet settled over our group. Drew MacLaren had cussed and nobody, not a single boy on that beach, had ever heard me cuss before. I just didn't do it. Up to now.

My older brother knew that he'd gone one step too far, and for a very long three seconds he just stared at me as if I had grown a pair of red wings. "Asshole?" he said it kind of quietly, with a fraction of a smile touching the sides of his mouth as if I'd just been passed one of his batons of sophisticated coolness.

"That's right, Donny MacLaren, you're a damned asshole." And I almost added "and so's your family," but then I remembered I was screaming at my brother.

"Whoa, Peckerhead. That's pretty tough language. For a little shit. You best be careful, because if I don't pound you down into this here beach sand the Chink Lady's gonna get you. She likes to boil foul-mouth little brats like you. Eat you for dinner."

"There ain't no such thing, Donny." Ricky Morley had reentered the discussion. "She don't exist neither, and you know it. You quit making things up to scare the little kids." Ricky was sort of in between the older boys and us younger ones. He was standing up to Donny, but looking a little unsure of himself either from his lack of height, or the secret belief that maybe, just maybe, the old witch did exist and liked to suck the flesh off foul-mouthed kids on occasion. We had all heard of her, of course, The Chink Lady--and most of us were pretty certain we'd seen her in those dreamy moments just before sleep swallowed us. She was out there listening. Somewhere. And she knew, in some mysterious way, when we swore, and if we did it too much or too often she would steal through our windows during the night to carry us away for her ghastly feasts. Like most of the cloudy myths and legends that we'd come to accept as fact in the Banks, none of us really knew the origin or the validity; we just held them as truths until someone older or wiser set us straight.

"She does exist, Ricky. I've seen her."

"Bullshit, Donny. If you know so damn much, you tell us where she lives."

Donny wouldn't lose; his cool image far too important. If he'd had a cigarette right then he would have casually blown smoke in Ricky's face and turned his James Dean collar right up around his own ears. He spoke authoritatively with a tone of fourteen year-old wisdom. "She's got one of them clam shacks over on the Sound. It's hidden, buried right down near the water in the reeds and mud, so none of you turds could ever find it, but I know where it is." His voice dropped to a whisper. "She sneaks in and takes the littlest runts cuz they're easy to lift up and carries them there to boil up like potatoes in her stew pot. The young meat's softer, by the way." He sneered at Pooh, then me. All eyes were on my brother now, his audience listening intently, everyone except me. I knew my brother was lying. I knew he didn't know a thing about the Chink Lady, and I knew she wasn't real. She was imaginary, a story made up by the older kids to scare us younger ones. Or maybe some stuffy adult had created her specifically to keep our mouths in check, but she wasn't real. I was certain of that.

Like many of the boy's games we played in the sand, we often preferred them to end in ties. No one actually won or lost that way, and the opportunity to take up the epic struggles existed for other days. So it was with this one. After my outburst of profanity everything sort of dissolved into the salty air as we each wandered away for lunch, or simply to sit in the shade of our own porches with a favorite comic. But from that game each of us carried fresh and well-formed opinions of each other. We also carried our individual beliefs in the existence of the Chink Lady of the Pamlico Sound. Sometime later, I would realize that my life had veered slightly in that single instant when my breath had vanished, and from that moment on, the great games of boys in the sand became far less consequential in my life.

Father knew that Sheriff Brennan's Pontiac would be coming down the highway at that hour so late in the night. He was dressed and waiting patiently on the back steps of the Harris cottage for Mr. Brennan's arrival. He'd brought the big flashlight he used for night fishing with him, and unlike any of the rest of us, he knew that Mr. Brennan would be arriving for her right at that time.

Donny watched it all from own bedroom window near the front and heard a lot of the conversation between Father and Mr. Brennan. Afterwards he tip-toed to my room and told Skeeter and me what he'd heard. While Skeeter cried softly, he told us that Father had to climb up over the smashed in porch steps to help Maggie down to the sheriff's car.

Mr. Brennan told Father that Frank Curry was still unconscious in the hospital down in Manteo, so the sheriff was the only one able to check on folks. Father asked if the highway was still torn up. The sheriff replied it was and that the landing at the inlet was ripped up so badly the ferries couldn't cross from one side to the other. Father offered to would help in any way he could, and then he whispered something that Donny couldn't hear, but whatever it was made Mr. Brennan answer respectfully and shake Father's hand.

Right after Donny snuck back to his room, Skeeter told me where to find the letters.

***

"Nina May?"

"Yes, Master Little?" I was in between mouthfuls of tuna salad and salty potato chips when the question seemed to rise up out of the nasty ache between my shoulder blades. I was sitting at the metal table in the kitchen while Nina May was rubbing her tender fingers and popping the ends off snap beans piled up in her apron.

"Did the kids in your family ever pick on you when you were little?" I knew she'd come from six brothers and three sisters, which always amazed me when I thought much on it. I knew her family'd owned a small farm once with two other families in the mountains near Blowing Rock and that one of her brothers had been sent to prison for robbing, but that was about all I knew.

Nina May's forehead creased into a wrinkle of memories. "Well, of course, they did, Master Little. I think that's part of almost every child's story. It just comes with playing and growing up. But my momma, she watched us like an ol' hen most of the time, and if any one of us got too mean she got right mean herself. Mostly though, we looked out for each other. We had to." She looked at the scrape on my cheekbone, laid one of her big hands on the center of my back as if knowing that I was precisely where I was hurting and said, "And by the time we'd grown we'd learned to be real kind to one another."

Sometimes I could tell when Nina May was trying to give me something to think about--like a lesson--without really telling me outright what it was. She was doing that just then, wanting me to forgive my brother. But I was mad, and I'd decided I was going to stay mad until I was at least a foot taller than he was.

That evening, just before dinner, I wandered over to the Silver cottage and found Skeeter sitting with his legs pulled up beneath him in the same spot on the porch. I handed him the five loaners I'd selected from my collection. The best of the group lay proudly on top with scarlet letters stretched boldly across the cover. "This one's brand new, Skeeter. Thought you might want to borrow it for a bit. Look here. See, it's The Flash. He's brand new." Around us the sky was china blue and warm to the skin, the sun dropping slowly into the tall dunes beyond the highway. The uneasiness that I had felt at the end of the day before had dissolved with the storm, and we were once again discussing comics, and that always created a comfortable feeling between young superheroes.

"I've got some for you, too, Drew." I realized he must have been waiting there most of the afternoon for me to come over. He smiled shyly with his half tooth and pushed a cloth sack towards me. I peeked inside then pulled out three tatty issues of Batman, and a brand new one of Superman and Lois Lane--a true gem in my opinion.

"Oh, neat, I haven't seen this one." I flipped to the first page, the blues and rich reds of skyscrapers and super capes stared back. Above the railing of the porch the sky was now a bruised shade of purple, and I thought of how nice it felt to sit there, how tackle football seemed a great deal less fun than watching the colors of the sky.

Suddenly behind me I heard Maggie's soft accent, "Drew, it is good to see you again so soon. I had hoped you might come over today." She sounded like one of Momma's friends making a kind remark at a dinner party. I turned. She was barefoot and in a dress the color of the horizon at midday. Her hair was pulled back with a thin pink ribbon, and her eyes were bluer than any of those other shades.

Skeeter started chattering before I could say a word. "Look, Maggie, Drew's brought me a new one, The Flash." He held the comic up next to his face like a framed award for her to see. "Looka here. See how fast he can move. He got streaks flying behind him everywhere he goes."

"That's real sweet of Drew, Skeets. You go on inside now. I've got dinner just about ready for us. And take those with you." She jutted her chin towards the stack of comics I'd brought over. It was a quiet command that Skeeter obeyed without argument, and I knew it was that way between them. It was like Nina May had said, they had to look out for each other.

Maggie turned and whispered conspiratorially, "I was hoping you might come and meet my friend tomorrow." Instantly my fear with all its warty noses and pointy hats returned. Mrs. Silver's shrieks rose in my ears. Then I thought of how she had phrased it, a friend of hers, not the nasty witch that lived behind the screened window and slung bowls of oatmeal against the wall.

I hesitated. "Sure, I guess," and then I asked, "Who's your friend?"

Maggie smiled as if something were secretly quite amusing to her and leaned in closer to me. In a whisper she said, "Her name's Mai Lin, but I believe you call her The Chink Lady."

The Dunes

That night my imagination kept me awake for a very long time, and after all the lights in the great cottage were finally off, I got up to make certain that my windows were tightly locked, again.

I had been certain, absolutely so, that the old witch had been a myth, a children's tale created to prevent us from swearing too much. That night, however, I lay awake picturing her in fine detail. I knew exactly what she was going to look like, how her boiling cauldron, the one that I would fit so nicely into, was going to feel. Her house, of course, was dark and mildewed, half buried in a damp sump within the reeds. Her very large cat would be guarding the door with a single open eye. Shelves of black spices, prepared to flavor my young flesh, would line the walls. And the wart upon her pointy nose would extend just beyond the brim of her pointy hat.

A little before sunrise I got up, deciding that I had seen one too many horror movies during the previous year, and slipped on my long pants and wool sweater. I needed to talk with someone, maybe get some advice; the type that I knew would not come from my family.

Entering the kitchen from the secret passageway I found something I hadn't expected at all, my mother. She was sitting at the metal table in a green robe, one leg primly crossed over the other. She was sipping a cup of sugared coffee and reading quietly aloud to herself--one of the big anthologies of poetry from the shelf next to the fireplace in the living room.

She straightened herself in the chair and closed her eyes to the pre-dawn light. "I'll tell you how the sun rose- a ribbon at a time." The stanza rose from memory. "The steeples swam in amethyst, the news like squirrels ran."

The door latch clicked. She turned at the sound, and seeing me, set the volume upon the table and spread her arms in a motherly invitation to climb into her lap. She just didn't understand that I was almost eleven and far too big for such things. Instead, I stretched my neck forward for a hug and messy kisses along my hairline.

"Good morning, my sweet Little."

"Morning, Momma. You're up early." I reached into the cabinet for a bowl and then rumbled through the drawer for a spoon.

"Yes. Well. I didn't sleep that much last night and decided some Dickinson might be just the way to start the day. Would you like me to read you something? You've always been so appreciative of such things, my little bookworm."

I thought a better way to start the morning was with Cheerios and an adventure of some sort, but didn't say so. "Sure, Momma." I nodded agreeably. "Read me one of your favorites."

She pushed her hair back with her fingers and after searching the index of first lines, opened the volume to the proper page.

"O world, I cannot hold thee close enough!" She started in a whisper. "Thy winds, thy wide gray skies! Thy mists that roll and rise!" and on she rolled, swaying to the rhythms of Edna St. Vincent Millay, and in the last stanza she looked just like Skeeter peering out from the balusters of his porch. When she finished tears were welling into the curves of her eyes.

"Momma?"

"It's okay, Little. I just…" She folded the book dramatically and pushed her hands deep into the lap of her robe and smiled at me sadly. "I miss Alex today. I wish he were here like the old days." The old days being last year. The impact of my oldest brother's decision to remain in Washington for the summer had been felt by all of us. For Momma it had been hardest.

As she sniffed lightly and dabbed at the side of her eyes, I decided that it was probably better to wait until a different morning to ask her to stop calling me Little. And our hug, the one just before I raced out through the screen door, lasted a very long time.

The pier was a ten minute walk north of the cottage, a gathering place for fishermen, crabbers, shell collectors, and a few early risers. A hundred yards beyond it, Jethro's longboats were nestled high up on the sand. From the front of the cottage I could just make out a single gull perched one-legged on the pier's railing and two men in folding chairs at the end trying to hook some flounder before the sun came up. Below, in the darkness I saw a lone figure milling about the pilings and smiled to myself. Pooh Hutton was up.

"Hey, Pooh." I ran the last twenty feet in the sand and hooked the index finger of my left hand together with his and pulled it apart in our secret handshake. We grinned at each other. Pooh's round glasses were, as usual, either grimy or covered with some film of salt or dust. I used to wonder how he walked about like that, until I realized he moved so slowly in his own world that he didn't risk bumping into too much. "You going to watch Jethro head out?" It was a silly question; other than fishing, there weren't too many reasons to be at the pier that time of the day.

"Well, I got showed how to mend the nets yesterday. Angelo showed me." Pooh spoke slowly, and as usual with him, there was no bragging, just an understated self-assurance. "and I wanna practice some more this morning."

Pooh, being my closest summer friend, told me things he didn't tell anyone else. I knew, like so many of the other boys in the area, he had an unspoken wish to someday, or perhaps sooner, become a member of Jethro's small crew. I also knew he was probably the most likely to do so. Like Jethro, Pooh was year-rounder and at nine he knew more about fishing than most of the rest of us put together. It was just one of those things that he was good at, learned from his dad who ran a charter north of the pier. I'd seen him trick a lure and pitch it perfectly into a school of blue before I could get my reel unlocked. Like me, he couldn't cast too far yet, but he knew all about knots and lures and bait, and more importantly, when and where the sea bass and pompano ran. He was learning about the big nets now from a few of Jethro's boys who'd taken a genuine liking to him. As usual he was quietly pulling it all in and storing it. Pooh also had something else, another quality that made him a good fisherman; just like me, he didn't mind being alone. Most of the time he seemed to like it that way.

"Angelo? Wow! Did he take his shirt off? You see the scar?" Angelo's shirt almost never came off, and having never seen it, I was hoping for some detailed description of the legendary purple stripe.

"No, but I seen it last year. He told me it's no big deal, but he still don't want no one to see it" The scar, however, was a big deal to us. We whispered about it, as most of us were pretty sure it was the longest in the state, maybe the country, because it ran from below his neck, down his backside, to the top of his butt. Local folks who knew him well knew that Angelo Bertolli wasn't embarrassed by the size or color of the scar, but from the fact that it came from an all too-common mistake, being inattentive. That was what really made him self-conscious.

Two years earlier he hadn't been watching the nets well enough and had gotten his pants caught in an outgoing cork line. While one of the big winches played out the net, Angelo had been dragged over the gunwale as a rusty bolt tore an inch wide ribbon out of him. He'd floated in the water for long time until the drift boat had gotten over to haul him out. He kept telling the others that he was too old for that kind of a stupid mistake.

The scent of all that blood in the water kept the blue sharks nosing around for a few days, but they were usually hanging around the big nets anyway.

Pooh touched my shoulder lightly with his fingertips and asked gently, "Does your arm still hurt? Donny hit you too hard. I seen it."

He must not have seen it quite that well, maybe with his glasses over on the sidelines, because I almost told him that the hurt was in the center of my back and not in my shoulder. But Pooh was my best friend, so I fibbed, "Nah, it's not so bad," It did hurt, but it was manly to say it that way, and right then I really didn't want to talk about it with anyone.

Above us, moving across the planks, I heard whistling--the Toreador tune from Carmen. I recognized the melody immediately because my father loved opera. He listened to it on his hi fi most evenings while he tapped away on his typewriter. Every Sunday he would tune in the live broadcast from the Met and sip Old Fashions or Mint Juleps and research. As I was growing up I would ask him to tell me the stories, especially if there was a swordfight involved, and though I liked them a lot, I thought most of them seemed kind of sad.

I knew it was Jethro whistling up above, because he loved opera even more than Father and always seemed to have some tune or aria spinning around in his head that percolated out as a whistle or a hum.

Pooh and I sprinted up the bank at the foot of the pier and onto the planks. Jethro's massive back was moving away from us towards the gas pump on the lower dock out near the end. His limp made him to pitch in even movements side to side, but he always rocked with such smoothness that he appeared to be standing in one of his long boats drifting over the swells. His right hand was wrapped loosely around the handle of a big red gas can, and perched, like a small bird's nest on the back of his head, was the Portuguese fisherman's cap that we children were certain Jethro slept in, because it seemed to be permanently affixed to that spot.

"Jethro!" No one called him anything but Captain, Captain J., or his first name, which Pooh and I both called out at the same time. We took off running towards him, flustering the one-legged gull who squawked, pumped into the space above the railing and then resettled, eyeing us irritably.

"And who's this?" Jethro's head flew around, his long hair and beard spinning outward like a carnival ride. His voice boomed across the planks in loud speaker fashion. "Ah, a couple of fine buccaneers. First Mates MacLaren and Hutton come to visit. How be ye, lads?" This was Jethro, big as the horizon. He was to us, the Honorable Captain J. of the Spanish Galleon, Estrella y Luna. It was how we knew him, and evidently, how he pictured himself. No one was ever certain if it had evolved from his own imagination or from the children that sought him out, but those who walked with Jethro for any length of time realized that it was, in a strange way, a true part of his dreams. Somewhere, lifetimes ago, the Estrella y Luna had sailed under his command, and at some point in the future the ship would return. He would leave his long boats near the pier and step aboard his vessel to retake the helm once more. It was merely a matter of the right tide and winds, but the great sails would be raised again.

Jethro set the gas can on the pier and held out two large hands for us to latch onto. We swung like small pendulums out and back, and then skidded to a squeaking stop on the splintered boards. One of the men reeling an empty lure over the railing frowned our way as if our ruckus was driving his flounder to deeper waters, which it probably was. Jethro looked at him with a smile as wide as the pier and defused the man's irritation instantly.

"I want to help Angelo mend the nets again," Pooh stated slowly, a habit he maintained even when he was excited.

"Well, there's a right fine fisherman for you. Quick hands and a quick mind make less work, Mr. Hutton, and my Angelo tells me you have both. And you, Mr. MacLaren?" Jethro eyed me curiously, perhaps sensing that I harbored a question or two and needed counsel. "What is your business today? Come to chat?"

I didn't want to come right out with it, not with Pooh there, so I said, "Oh, I just wanted to help, too, Jethro." But he knew.

"Mr. Hutton. There are some sweet, fat fish waiting to swim into our nets this morning. It will be of no use if the nets are full of holes. Run and find Angelo. He'll be up at the lot." He laid a large hand on the back of Pooh's head and gave him a gentle push. Pooh happily scampered down the beach towards the longboats.

"Do you want me to help with the gas? I can carry the can for you." I was trying to act casual and be a dependable first mate.

Jethro looked at me again. He had unusual eyes, deep blue like the waters of the banks, and they glowed from the middle of a strong, gentle face. It was all surrounded by the biggest tangle of black hair and beard anyone had ever seen. On the rare occasions when he was serious, those eyes looked right into you, which they now did. His resemblance to the legendary Ben Cherry, alias Blackbeard, was not entirely coincidental.

I hadn't come to Jethro for much beyond good chatter and his endless knowledge of the sea and local lore before, so when I came that morning with a greater need, he knew it. And being Jethro, he would do his best to help.

"Mister MacLaren, you may indeed carry the gas can, but it might do well if you haul it down the ramp and I back up. It tends to get heavier on the return trip. So tell me, how is your family? John and Jean Gray are well?" Jethro thought everyone but the children should be called by their first names. He always asked about my parents, and Momma, for all her formalities and decorous manners, adored Jethro. She referred to him as that silver-tongued Portuguese gentleman.

"They're fine. Momma's getting set for her big party in a couple of weeks. Your coming, aren't you?"

"If there is ice cream, Lad, I'll be the first."

"Great! Father's making homemade again. Anyway, he's been working on *The Hopeshefloats*. There's a crack up in the fo'c'sle which isn't holding a patch so well." Our twenty- two foot sloop hadn't left the garage for the entire summer.

"Hmmm..." He tugged on the side of his beard. "Why don't you tell John I'll drop by Sunday afternoon. We'll see if we can't do a bit of work on that. Tell him to have the tools and cloth ready. Make sure that big radio of his is set up. Aida's on this week." He mentioned this as if it were a broadcast all of humanity would be tuning into. "We'll sing in loud, ugly voices and patch that ill-named boat together. And how're your brothers? I haven't seen Alex at all this summer"

We'd arrived at the gas pump on the lower dock. Old Mason Farrow rose grumpily from a low stool where he'd been sitting with his legs stretched out, silently took the empty can from me, and with a practiced motion stuck the nozzle into the hole and cranked the handle on the pump.

While the bell clicked off the measures like a metronome, I answered, "Alex stayed up in Washington this year. He's got a girlfriend." That, I figured, was answer enough. "And Donny's doing all right." Without thinking I frowned and added, "I guess."

Jethro looked at me and nodded in understanding. "Uh-huh. So, your brother's been rough on you lately, has he?"

I chewed on my lower lip.

Jethro pulled two folded bills from his pocket, looked at the numbers on the pump and handed them to Mason. Twenty-seven cents would be credited to next week's filling.

He lifted the can as if it were a basket of folded clothes and limped up the ramp. As we walked towards the foot of the pier, he set his free hand on my shoulder and said almost secretively, "You know, Lad, brothers have a way of changing. I'm certain it will be that way with Donny. Brothers are like flatfish. They start off swimming one way when they are young, seeing things all in one direction, acting sure of themselves, and then the eye begins to move across to the other side. Then the fish turns and swims flat. A mystery of God, no? After that, the whole world looks differently to him. And at him. Donny will change. You will see."

"I hope so. I mean, I know he's my brother and all, but he's nothing but a bully sometimes. Not anything that my folks would get really mad about, but..." I stopped. I wasn't ready to say that I hoped Donny's eye did move

around to the other side of his head, or he got struck by a
giant bolt of lightening or a pack of wild dogs bit his toes
off. But I wanted something to happen; I just wasn't sure
what it was. I was picturing some small cataclysm that
would magically transform him into a kinder brother.

At the end of the pier I asked my question, "Jethro,
have you heard of the Chink Lady?"

His big head swung around sharply, and he eyed me
with a mixture of grin and serious frown. For an anxious
second I thought he was going to set the gas can down and
face me directly, but then he turned and walked down the
beach staring straight ahead. "Lad, you have heard words
used for people, words that aren't especially nice?"

"Like when Donny calls me a little peckerhead?"

Jethro laughed deeply. "Aye, a bit like that, but
when they are used for a group of people?"

I knew what he meant. And I knew the words too,
but I didn't use them. My parents had taught me well in this
area. I was never to use them. Once, just once I'd made the
mistake of calling Nina May an old nigger because, in my
defense, I didn't know any better. I'd heard most of the
older kids say it all the time. I thought that it was what I was
supposed to say. I got my bottom smacked more times than
any other day in my life, and they weren't soft ones, but it
wasn't the sting on my fanny that hurt for so long, it was the
disappointment that I saw in the circle of faces above me.
Now it was just like swearing; it didn't come naturally to
me. I'd watched my share of war movies, where Krauts and
Japs were bad, but I didn't use those names either. I'd heard
older boys, like Wink May, use words that I didn't even
understand. Kikes. Spics. Wogs. He called just about

everyone some kind of name, but just like those Moravians who made spicy cookies and short graces, I had no idea who they were.

Jethro switched the gas can over to his left side, put his right hand on my shoulder, and spoke in an uncharacteristically slow manner. "Lad, when my father came to this place, the other fishermen called him a Wop and a Guinea. He spoke very little English then, but he knew their intent, if you know what I mean. I think those other fishermen were really jealous because my father caught a lot more fish than they did." He smiled at this thought. "Both of the names for him were wrong. He was Portuguese and a proud man. He loved where he came from, and even though those names were meant for an Italian, my father never forgot them and never forgave those fishermen for the cruelty. It made him angry and sad, and ate at him slowly. This word Chink, it is not such a good word."

I was puzzled. "So, what does it mean?"

"It means Chinese, someone from China."

"That's it? She's a Chinese lady?"

He smiled at me and said, "Yes, Lad, and I do know of her, and I know very well that she doesn't eat wicked children for dinner, she eats rice and fish just like you and me. I also know that she is quite kind to the boys she allows herself to meet. Or the young women." He grinned slyly at me, bent down almost to my level and said, "Anyway, who would want to eat the children from this place--their meat is far too tough." I grinned right back and thought of Donny.

We arrived at the longboats, and I held the funnel while Jethro poured the gas into the big oval cans strapped below the outboards. I was proud to be helping. While he concentrated on pouring carefully, I was thinking about all of it, what he had told me, his father, people from other places, people with different languages and colors, and I was wondering why people used ugly names. I thought about those seconds when I'd gotten so mad at Donny I'd called him a name. Then I wondered what group of people I was in and if someone had made up a bad name for us.

The longboats rested in the soft sand near the steep rise that lead to the lot. On the bow, in hand painted, neat red letters, I could read <u>Nina</u>, <u>Pinta</u>, and <u>Santa Maria</u>. Jethro loved anything Italian, Portuguese, or even remotely connected to the Iberian Peninsula.

His boys came strolling down the rise towards us, laughing and jostling into one another. He called them his boys, though they were actually five grown men of various ages and size hired to set and haul the nets. As far as we knew, Jethro had no children of his own, though a few of the older kids said he'd been married once. That was why I figured he called those men his boys. He just loved children.

There were jokes and laughter as they stowed their bags and thermoses, and then all of us, including Jethro, set to pushing the longboats down the bank to the water's edge. Angelo Bertolli heaved on the port bow, I on the starboard. He had a few days of moldy stubble growing on his cheeks and even from a yard and half distance I could smell the overpowering odor of garlic. His linguini, and the resultant perfume on his breath, was as legendary as the scar we were all hoping to get a peek at some day.

Jethro patted me on the back like member of his crew and boomed, "It has been a delightful walk this morning, First Mate MacLaren, and I am indeed pleased you came. As always, I'm grateful for your help." He looked at the sky and announced, "This morning is a gift of God, no?"

With sweat dripping from his hair and beard, his eyes shining like blue coals, he jumped over the gunwale and took the tiller in his powerful hand. The bow popped upward through the first wave, and I saw him still smiling, grinning like a pirate in his little cap. He looked at me as if we held the secret location of some immense treasure between us. Perhaps we did.

***

At seven that morning I met Maggie on the dune side of Ensign Bill's house, though it probably doesn't deserve to be described that way. It was really a single room, a flimsy construct of thin boards that had been so beaten by the winds and time that it would surely crumble into the sands with a push of a single finger. Ensign Bill happened to be the name that children had made up for William Sotherby, the ancient Navy man who, though still the rightful owner, no longer lived there. The windows had long ago been shattered out by the smooth shell pieces that we considered our best slingshot ammunition, and there were no doors or floors, just weathered vertical boards, three rotten steps, and a tattered shingle roof.

I remember the hour well, because it would be precisely when Maggie and I would meet most days but Sundays and storm days over the next two summers. As she told me, "Momma sleeps every morning for an hour and a half and nothing wakes her. It's my time." She'd confided this as if those allotted minutes were viciously guarded and precious possessions.

I'd told Nina May that I was going crabbing at the pier and felt bad about fibbing, especially to Nina May, but the only people I had any desire to know where I was going were Maggie and I.

I crossed the highway a half a mile south of the cottage, feeling nervous and tingly. Ensign Bill's shack was set down in a low bowl between two of the smaller dunes, impossible to see from the highway. Looking towards it as I reached the ridge I saw no one. A tremor of panic swept through me. Had I made some mistake? Gotten my instructions wrong? Where was she? But then, through the vertical spaces of the gray boards, framed in the upper square of vacant window space, I saw her.

She was gazing towards the western dunes, swinging her arms in front of her and behind, sinking and rising, rocking gently on her heels and toes in a single fluid motion. It looked odd, but in a curious way, natural. It was a smooth, practiced movement with no blemishes or jerkiness in the transition. My breath came more rapidly.

To that point in my life I had not done much that was overly secretive or stealthy. My world had been open, one which I willingly shared with my parents. I had, of course, played the simple games of childhood concealment and dare, tasting the small forbidden fruits and illicit candies, like the first puff of a cigarette, or jumping from the high landing above the inlet. But when asked, I had always been truthful. Walking that morning to meet Maggie, a girl five years older than I, however, felt more an act of disguise than any I had ever committed. And that is why my breath came rapidly, that and the fact that her hair swayed in soft ripples as she rocked backwards and forwards.

She must have heard me, my breath or the pounding of my heart, because before I had made my way completely around to the back side of the shack, she said excitedly, "Can you feel it?" and as usual with Maggie, I didn't immediately know what she meant.

"Umm?"

"The air, Drew. It is so full this morning." Maggie stopped her rocking motion and smoothed her hair back behind her ears.

To me that air felt like most other mornings, a strengthening breeze with the dunes beginning to emit shimmering mirages along the crests. I certainly didn't know what she meant by full. It felt nice, warm in the shallow where we stood--but little different from the day before. Not wanting to seem contrary, or unaware of the quality of the morning's air, I replied, "Yep, it feels great to me too. Nice breeze, today." And then with the confidence of a young meteorologist, I added, "though I bet twenty nickels we get rain this afternoon."

"Do you really think so?" She was grinning at my prediction.

I nodded with conviction. "Sure, see the way the clouds are boiling real low over the ocean. That's gonna make rain this afternoon." I saw Maggie look to the ocean side and then back at me with an amused expression of respect for my young forecasting skills. Then it dawned on me that she'd lived in The Banks her whole life and probably knew every signal of change the winds and clouds could offer.

She started walking at a rapid, purposeful pace, and I had to follow behind at a careful trot. We were weaving through a maze of low dunes, an area not traveled by any but small animals that foraged on whatever meager foods might be found among the shrubs. No tourists wandered these paths. There were no vaulting hills of sand, no historic lighthouses or monuments to men and their flying machines. This was an area of scratchy plants and obscure paths that ran in a winding labyrinth over to the sound. Here and there, on the opposite side, were stretches of stinky mud laced with glossy oil patterns upon their surfaces. Even I, who took pride in such things, did not feel comfortable wandering through the area.

"Watch the burs here." Maggie glanced over her shoulder and skipped like a ballerina to the left, avoiding a wide oval patch beside the path. The wind had blown a dusty cover across them, so they lay camouflaged, waiting patiently, I thought, for my foot to embed themselves into. They were like all of the concealed hazards, razor shells, and shards of glass, rusted cans, and the occasional strand of wire that we instinctively searched for wherever we walked.

Ahead, Maggie was singing quietly to herself. Nothing understandable, no meaning that I could make out, just simple tunes that drifted from melody to melody and sounded like a child's nonsense rhymes. It occurred to me that she sounded as if she were walking in her own peaceful daydream.

I, on the other hand, was still nervous. Since the previous evening I'd been drafting images, watercolors, that rose in smoke and mist and drifted away, only to rise again in other forms. I had painted the sands on our path, the grasses, and the ridges along the dunes. I had seen the shape and size of the Chinese Lady's house. The Chinese Lady. Her portrait had been painted a dozen times in my mind, her face shifting like the wind. After my conversation with Jethro, however, the palette held softer colors. The face before me now was gentler, and even though there wasn't a single wart or pointy hat to be seen, I was still nervous. After a few minutes I called out, "So Maggie, how did you meet...what did you say her name was?"

"Moon and wind, her name's Mai Lin." She sang it back, and just then I felt a shift in the breeze and knew we were nearing the sound.

"Rrright..., so how did you and Mrs. Lin meet?"

She slowed and began to skip sideways in a little crossover step that made her hips and shoulders and arms all turn in ripples like dancing twine. She shook her head and laughed, "No, not Mrs. Lin. She's just Mai Lin. Or just Mai, and we met when we were walking."

"Where were you going?"

"Nowhere special. You know how sometimes you just walk. I like to walk when I get my time," And I guess sing, because that's how she was sharing this first meeting with me. "and Mai Lin does too. She likes to collect things along the shore, so we met one morning and started walking together. I've been coming over here since."

"Does she live alone?"

"Ever since I've known her."

I wanted to ask her where they were when they first met, and where they went, and what they talked about, and how old she was then, but quite suddenly, I knew we were there. I didn't know why or how. There were no visible clues, no house or gate, nothing but scrub pine and bamboo, lots of tall bamboo, but something had changed. For a moment I didn't know what it was, and then I understood. The sounds were different. Barely discernible, jingling softly in the breeze I heard small pieces of wood and glass and metal. And I heard water, not the soft lapping of shore waves, more like the trickling of a stream.

Maggie walked directly at the bamboo, turned and grinned mischievously at me, and then, like a magician, disappeared. I halted in total confusion, and for the few seconds that it took me to gather myself and arrive at the spot where she had vanished, my imagination went right to work. I began to wonder, and then totally convinced myself, that I'd been lured into a well-designed practical joke, something that Donny had been part of. I was sure I was going to be left out there. I would be abandoned on the other side of the strand, and nobody would know where I was. I would wander in that labyrinth of dunes forever. The idea resurfaced that the sinister Chink Lady really did eat foul-mouthed brats who swore at their older brothers. They had all thought it up together, and I wondered forlornly who was going to miss me as I slowly wasted away.

I'd been in a fifth-grade play the year before. Cinderella. I'd been the Prince's messenger and had to wear tights and a floppy hat with a feather and carry the glass slipper for the girls to try on. The slipper was really Julie Proxmire's mother's shiny dress-up shoe, and wearing the tights was the most embarrassing thing I'd had to endure to that point in my life. I remember how the big velvety curtains felt and how they overlapped, so you could walk right out onto the stage and back, appearing magically in front of the audience. That was what I now stood in front of, tall bamboo curtains that overlapped, so you could slip right through and back.

Maggie stood grinning, humming her unrecognizable tunes, just inside the wall. She reached out and pulled me into the inner garden. I looked around, and the most popular word in my summer vocabulary came out very slowly. "Wow."

The garden was crafted from a dream. It wasn't fancy like the rose arbors of my grandmother or have any of the bright colors of my mother's pansies or periwinkles. The garden inside the bamboo curtain was small and designed for more than the eyes. Every sense had been carefully and subtly considered. Wind chimes hung in the branches, all made from collected bits and pieces from the shoreline or the dunes. Tinkling sea glass spun on threads and refracted the morning light deep into the shadows. Strips of painted tin curled like water spouts were hung at just the proper height. But the pieces of cut bamboo were clearly the most beautiful instruments in the garden's symphony. They were sliced at shallow angles, some long, some thin, some short, and each had its own hollow tone that resonated with the slightest breeze.

In the center there was a single tree, very low, speckled with ripening cherries and a plain wooden bench beneath it. The air smelled of honeysuckle and mint.

A small stream of water played over dark cobble stones into a shallow pond, and I knew, without seeing them, that goldfish swam there below the water plants. Gravel paths curved symmetrically around the tree and pond and joined at the foot of the steps to the backside of the house. Her house. I was in the garden of the Chink Lady, and it was as far from what Donny had described to the boys on the beach as it could possibly be.

She stood on the small porch above us, wearing what appeared to be shiny black pajamas, and I saw the woman was not tall. It was the first feature that I noticed, her height. She was what my mother might have described as petite, though something about her seemed strong and it had me wondering if someone had helped her with her garden the way my grandmother did. She didn't look extremely old. I guessed that she was near my mother's age, but there was an agelessness that made it impossible for me to determine.

The next feature I noticed was her eyes. They were curved like dark oval buttons, and flashing. They seemed to be laughing, even though she herself was not. Her hair was short and brushed straight back with no part.

Without any introductions she beckoned us with a wave of her hand and called out, "Come quickly. The egrets are leaving. Come, come." So Maggie, without saying a word, pulled me by the elbow up the steps and through the kitchen, where I glanced to the right and saw a large cooking pot that, thankfully, I was a bit too large to fit in. I saw a small table and lots of cooking utensils and jars lining the walls. And then we were through and onto the back porch.

"There, there. You see. They rested, now decide to leave. Those are the lazy ones. Come late. Leave late. Lazy. Lazy." She was shaking her head as if disappointed by this idleness on the birds' part. The flock that Mai Lin was referring to was now beginning to flap and run and lift in a low arc above the smooth water of the sound.

I had seen egrets on their migrations before but hadn't paid much attention to them. Mai Lin, however, was so delighted by their movement that it felt like my fifth grade teacher when she was demonstrating a new way to add fractions and got really excited and the whole class knew they needed to be paying attention. So I quietly watched.

The three of us stood at the railing, and I saw how the birds rose and tucked their legs like ski poles behind them and flapped in a straggly line up the coast. Maggie and Mai Lin followed the flight, and it was an uncomfortably long time before anyone said anything. Then Maggie touched my shoulder and said, "Mai, this is my friend Drew MacLaren. Drew, this is my friend Mai." The introduction sounded a bit strange when she said it, sort of formal, but I liked it. Friend. That made me feel like I had been invited into their party. I was a member of the club.

"Welcome, welcome." Mai bent lightly at the waist and touched her fingers together in a quick movement that made me want to do the same thing. Quickly she said, "Tea, yes tea. I make us some tea. No work today. We talk" Her voice lifted and fell like one of Jethro's cork lines on a windy day. She dropped words from her sentences like missing pieces of a jigsaw puzzle, and it all came with an accent that clearly wasn't the North Carolinian drawl I was used to. "Sit, please."

I looked about the deck where we were standing. To the left there was an empty space with no chairs; on the right there was an enclosed area with screen, lathing and door in the center. I didn't see any chairs there either. Maggie walked to the enclosed part. I followed and saw flat, brightly colored cushions propped neatly against the back wall. I smiled. Sitting on the floor, now that was my kind of sitting.

Maggie sat down and silently patted the cushion next to her as an invitation. I plopped myself onto the pillow, pulled my legs in and waited. I expected something, an explanation or offering of some sort. I had a dozen questions ready to ask about the woman fixing us tea, and just as many about Maggie herself, but she looked silently out at the wide flatness of the sound, closed her eyes and began to breathe. Really breathe. Deeply and slowly, like one of my big county-fair balloons expanding and deflating. Since there was nothing for me to do, I looked around.

We were perched in a cove a few feet up. Small waves rippled onto a narrow band of sand a short distance away, and beyond that, the sound stretched out endlessly. The scrub pine and most of the reeds had been cleared back from the beach just enough to see to the north and south. It was secluded. And like so many secret spots, it had a feeling of peace and incredible beauty.

After a short time Mai Lin scurried in with a small round tray and a wide smile. As she set the tray on the floor of the porch, Maggie opened her eyes.

Mai patted my knee. "I make tea for us the way I made it for Colonel Albers. He like milk and sugar. So I make it that way. Tea good for you. Sugar maybe not, but good tea." I almost started giggling. She spoke so quickly in this manner, and with such animation, that it made me want to laugh from it. I didn't laugh, however, and showed my well polished Southern manners by responding politely, "Thank you very much, Ma'am."

She patted my knee again. "Oh, Drew. I'm not Ma'am. I'm Mai Lin. You call me Mai, if you please. Very easy to remember." She had strength in her voice, a force just below the surface.

"Okay, Mai," I replied uncertainly. I wasn't accustomed to addressing adults with such informality. Except Jethro, every adult I spoke to had a title of respect, whether I actually respected them or not. Mai, however, didn't seem to be speaking to me as if I were a boy; she was speaking to me as if I were an equal and that puffed me right up and made me want to act that way. I would be dignified, hold my cup just the way Donny had instructed me to hold Coca-Cola bottles, with the pinky extended at the proper angle. Then I noticed that my cup had no handle. It was round and a little too hot to pick up.

"Mai, the tea is delicious." Maggie was taking her first sips and blowing across the rim, caressing her cup with both sets of fingers. She savored the drops as she had two days before with her iced tea. I picked up my cup and felt the temperature. It was dropping just enough to take a sip, and I decided that someone had figured out a pretty good method to keep from burning your lips, unlike the handled mugs of hot chocolate that always seemed to leave me with a scalded tongue.

The tea was delightful, not that I had tasted much tea in my time, but the flavor was rich and sweet, and I complimented our hostess the way I had heard my mother and her friends talk to each other on social occasions.

Mai Lin had yet to pick up her cup, and I wondered if that came from manners practiced where she came from. I wondered exactly where that was. When she did pick it up, just before she sipped, she closed her eyes and bowed her head slightly. I was pretty certain she didn't use our Moravian blessing because she bowed her head too quickly. I think she saw me watching her because she whispered, "I say thanks for the tea. It taste better that way." I nodded in serious agreement.

Mai was unquestionably unlike any other woman I'd encountered in my harbored existence. Beyond her short, blackish-gray hair, shiny, black pajamas, and unusual features, she moved and talked with what can only be described as genuineness. There was sureness in her movements, her laughter, and indisputably in the light of her eyes.

She asked me undemanding questions about my family and what I enjoyed doing, and with each answer I settled more comfortably into my cushion. She seemed to be studying my face, at times peering closely at my forehead, my cheeks, mouth, and chin. When I told her how I loved to ride the waves that rolled across the sandbar at low tide, she clapped her hands together and laughed with delight. "You ride waves? I have never seen this. It is much fun?"

My hands and head immediately began moving in enthusiastic swimming motions, imitating the art of body surfing. "Really fun. Like flying, but in the water. My father and I do it together all the time."

"I must see this. Very clever. To be in the ocean is good. The water there gives much good energy."

I didn't know about energy. That sounded a bit like Maggie's comment on the air being full that morning, but I said, "Well, if you want, I can teach you. I'm pretty good." I realized that it sounded a bit like boasting, but I wanted her to know that I would be a good teacher.

"You need teach me to swim first, Drew." Her eyes wrinkled into laughter.

I was amazed. I'd never known anyone in the Banks, except Skeeter, who couldn't swim. Even my mother paddled about with her pink hair cap on calm days. Water was everywhere. It surrounded us, and swimming was as normal as walking in my world. Mai lived twenty feet from the Sound, how could she not know how to swim?

"Well, sure. I could teach you," I said. "It's not that hard."

Mai Lin turned from me to Maggie, and touching her knee gently, asked, "How is practice, Daughter?"

Maggie nodded, "It's good, Mai. Better than last week. I've felt more of the tingling in the fingers the way you said, and I think I have gotten my feet set right now, but I think my knees still push out too far."

"Good, good. Remember, see picture, but not try to force picture. Let it flow in like soft river. It will come."

Suddenly I felt totally left out. What was Maggie practicing? What was the matter with her fingers and knees? My desire for answers overcame my ability to listen. I raised my hand, pushed it up slowly until my elbow paralleled the deck. There were habits that came from being a cultivated Tar Hell boy at that time. The tendency to call all adults sirs and ma'ams was coupled with the requirement to raise one's hand to ask questions. Teachers demanded it.

"Umm…what is the matter with your knees?" Maggie had the smile, the dreamy one that rose from inside. She had just drifted into her own secluded world again, some area of obscure mystery like a place in one of my comic book stories, so it was Mai Lin who answered.

"Daughter has learned a practice, Drew. Old teaching from my country, very old." A short silence followed when I had to resist the temptation to raise my hand again.

Finally Maggie came back from wherever she had drifted and clarified some of my confusion. "Mai Lin has taught me to breathe and move in a different way, Drew. It's traditional, sort of like an exercise, or dance, and when I move I have to make sure my knees are bent correctly." I didn't understand completely, or even remotely. It sounded like something my gym teacher had told us when we played basketball, a game I had learned quickly, I was even less skilled at than football.

"Do you have to practice a lot?"

"Every day." There was pure resolve in her voice.

Mai Lin reached for our empty cups, and her eyes locked onto mine. "You learn this also, Drew, if you wish. But must work, like young bird with new wings." And then she said what I didn't want to hear. "And parents don't mind."

My parents. I had thought of them briefly during the walk through the dunes but had conveniently pushed aside any of their reactions to my visiting with a complete stranger.

I glanced shyly at Maggie. She was gazing across the water, the wind tossing her hair across her face. I didn't understand a thing about what she was learning from Mai Lin, but I knew then that I wanted to learn it with her. It felt special, like an unwrapped gift, or a folded note in school. I imagined us walking through the dunes, sipping tea, and standing on the deck above the water. I would learn to bend my knees properly, just the way Mai instructed. I looked at the sand on Maggie's feet and knew right then I wanted to learn all of it.

I told Mai Lin so.

Maggie and I carried the tray and cups into the kitchen to wash them. As I set them on a narrow shelf next to the others, I saw the big cooking pot on the stove. It looked much smaller and friendlier now. The herbs and powders lining the walls seemed now like an expanded version of the spice-rack in my own cottage. I saw a small room to the right of the kitchen and a door beyond that I guessed lead to a bedroom and bath. The walls in the sitting room were lined from ceiling to floor with books.

We stepped onto the back porch, and I saw that the pond below did have goldfish, big ones. Mai Lin gave a quick bow again and touched her fingers together. "Thank you. Wonderful visit, my friends. I see you tomorrow, Daughter?"

Maggie nodded. "Yes, Mai. Tomorrow."

"And you, Drew?"

A little too quickly I replied, "Yes, Ma'am," Then simply, "Sorry, I'll remember. Just Mai"

She laughed and held out two tangerines for our walk back through the dunes.

***

"So, does she fix tea every day during your lessons?" I was trotting, Maggie skipping, along the sandy path back towards Ensign Bill's and the highway. Between questions I was spitting tangerine seeds with unerring accuracy into the burs and grasses along the edge, and both of us were flipping our citrus peels like Handsel and Gretel.

"Not always. Most of the time we get right to our work."

"Work?"

"That's what she calls it. Energy work. You'll see."

"She talks kind of differently, huh?" I was curious about it, and hoped my comment didn't sound rude.

"She's from China, Drew, and like us, she's got her own accent." I pondered that for a moment and thought about a family from Maine that had rented one of the cottages near the pier the previous summer. I'd heard them talking a few times while they were baiting their hooks. They had talked differently, too.

Maggie slowed to a walk, and I started setting my smaller feet into the footprints she created ahead of me. I had to give a little hop to reach each one, but it was a sweet amusement, and I was certain there were no burs there. Maggie grew quieter as we neared the highway and stopped talking completely as we parted and made our way north towards the cottages, I along the ocean and she beside the road.

I didn't understand many things about that first journey through the dunes with Maggie or my first meeting with Mai. I didn't realize that my lessons, in truth, had already begun. Or that my energy work, as they referred to it, had also already begun. I didn't feel the depth and strength of Mai Lin's garden or the power of sitting on that deck. And I didn't understand at all why Maggie grew so quiet, and her step so heavy as we reached the dividing line of asphalt in the sand.

But all these things I eventually came to learn.

The Sheriff put her in his patrol car and drove her down to the station at Manteo just before midnight. He put her in the back seat, and likely because of the agreement that he and Father had made, he did it with respect and didn't use any cuffs on her. With all the driftwood and sand still strewn across the highway, it took a lot longer to get there than it should have.

When Mr. Brennan brought Maggie to the station he made her sit in front of his big desk in the office while he sat in his tall chair on the other side. He asked her a lot of questions, none of which she answered, so he had no choice but to put her in one of the cells they used for drunks and the occasional young thief they arrested for breaking into the vacation cottages.

There weren't any drunks or petty thieves in the station that night, just her. Later she told me that the worst part wasn't the harsh questions the Sheriff asked, the ones she couldn't answer, or wouldn't. She said the worst part was how the air had felt and how it all smelled.

***

My father was a tall man, strong, and easy to recognize from a distance. As I trotted along in the sand, making my way north along the beach, I could easily see him walking from our porch towards the ocean. His height, in addition to giving me a clear visual marker, also provided me with continual aspirations that, at any minute, I would sprout to similar heights and with some luck tower over my older brother. As yet, it hadn't happened. I saw that my father was dressed in his dark green trunks which signaled that he was preparing for his morning ritual. He had years ago begun referring to it as, "My Own Holy Communion," a phrase my mother declared verged on blasphemy, but nonetheless, it was his unvarying routine. He would walk to the water's edge in his slow, methodical manner and pause to survey the waves for a time as if peering across the bow of the troop carrier he'd served on in the Pacific. To me he always appeared wisest right then, sort of all-knowing or at least fully aware of the subtle distinctions he saw in the rising swells. He would rub his hands together, retie his trunks, test the temperature with his toes, and then carefully select the ideal wave to jackknife over. On bigger days it would be a dive under or through one, but always with the same prologue. It was his ablution, and I knew that he believed honestly that his soul was purified from that communion with the salt water.

My father had taught me about the ocean. He wasn't an avid fisherman or an exceptional boater, so my knowledge of lines and lures was less than many of my peers, but he was a master at riding the waves. I was his protégé. He didn't merely catch and ride the surf with his body; he perfected it into an art form. He had tutored me each summer, flavoring our lessons with selected phrases that returned whenever I entered the water. "Placement and timing, Son, those are the secrets. Position yourself at the peak. Feel how it is going to break and when you decide that it is yours, swim with all your strength." Over the years I had learned how to dip my shoulder, turn, and slide like a torpedo through liquid tunnels. I'd become expert at flipping, spinning, gliding on my back, and at the beginning of that summer I had felt a sense of mastery that only large storm waves could diminish. My confidence had grown, and being overly confident in the ocean, as I had been reminded by my father on many an occasion, was foolish and dangerous. "The ocean is patient, Drew. It will wait and always win."

Our wave-riding time together had shaped the bond between us--more than most other events of our lives-- because it was a mutual adventure and always performed with passion.

I peeled off my shirt and sprinted the last few yards, arriving just as he was entering the temperature-testing phase of his ritual.

"It's warmer than yesterday, Son." The slow pronouncement and accompanying smile were invitations for me to join him in Holy Communion.

"So that mean's the Gulf Stream's in closer?" I was trying to show off what I'd learned.

He nodded slowly. "Yep, or the sun's just heated up the water inside the bar. We haven't had any big swells stirring up the bottom for awhile, just that little storm the other day. The shape's pretty good. See the left coming in?"

I looked to the sandbar some forty yards out and saw a sweet, medium-sized crest peel across on a flawless tangent. From years of experience we both knew precisely where to place ourselves. It all came down to knowing the bottom. It dipped quickly away from the beach and then rose gradually up to the bar, where I could actually stand in knee-deep water as the waves crested. At dead low tide it was often too shallow to ride, and I had come up on more than a few occasions with raspberry abrasions from collisions with the bottom.

My father's feet found the rise well before mine, and as he turned and took my hand to pull me further up the rise, the motion triggered a whisper of memory. It swept me back to when he'd first taught me to swim, pulling me through the water as I kicked my small legs in resolute flurries.

I wanted a little time before I broached the subject of visits to Mai Lin's. A few good waves together would create the appropriate mood, but as we neared the top of the bar, he asked, "So how are things going? You and Donny getting on all right?" He always seemed to know when we weren't.

I dove under a wave, found my feet on the sand and stood. "Yes, sir, sort of. I mean, I guess."

My father looked towards the horizon to make sure nothing was coming and said, "I noticed you two didn't have a lot to say to each other at dinner last night."

"No sir, we didn't. We're not talking so much right now." I was truthful with my father, even on sensitive matters. It was our way together, because unlike my mother, he rarely reproached me for my missteps in life. Over the years we had developed comfortable formalities, ways of addressing each other, approaches to delicate subjects, and I had come to trust his counsel completely.

"Is he picking on you too much?"

"No, Sir. I kind of got hurt playing football. Donny tackled me a little hard. That's all."

Father nodded, and without saying anything stroked into a rising peak. His timing, as usual, was perfect. I watched as he tucked one arm along his side and thrust the other stiffly in front, and through the back of the wave I saw his lithe body speed like a porpoise inside the wall of water. In waves he always seemed to move with smooth acceleration and velocity. On land his motions were slow and carefully measured.

I claimed the next one. The swell rose steeply as it crossed the shallow bar, and I stroked and kicked with all my strength. As the peak began to fall, and I with it, I heard Mai Lin's voice whispering in the spray, "The water there gives much good energy." I dropped my shoulder, stretched and kicked and flew across the face, suspended, half in liquid, half in the air. And, as always, I whooped. As loudly as I could. My father hadn't taught me about whooping, that had been one of my own embellishments.

"Mighty fine wave, Son, mighty fine." He was grinning at the ride, my abilities, his teaching, and our common love for it.

"Father?"

"Yes, Son?"

"Would you and Momma mind if I went to visit a woman over on the sound?" I hesitated for a moment. "She's Chinese."

He looked at me carefully, his forehead creasing into small wrinkles of reservation, and I became nervous that I hadn't asked it quite right, and he might not allow me to go.

"Is this someone you know?"

"Yes, Sir, her name's Mai Lin, and she wants to teach me Chinese exercises, and I told her I'd ask you first. Maggie Silver knows her, and she's really nice." I was in rapid approach, wanting to layer all the positives as quickly as I could. "And she has a garden with wind chimes."

My father saw the good things in people, always had. People had to prove to him that they weren't good before he would accept it. He didn't take enjoyment in rumor or gossip, and eventually I learned that those were the qualities that my mother so loved in him, that and the fact that he was tall, athletic, and an exceptionally good chef. He wrote cookbooks, Southern and very popular ones and told me once that he and Momma were liberals and intellectuals, which were words I didn't understand at all, but it sounded as if he were saying they were kind and smart. That, I already knew.

"Well…What kind of exercises does she want to teach you?" Father liked exercise. My opening had gone well.

"It's a breathing exercise, I think. I mean, I don't really know all about it yet."

"Well, exercise can't be bad for you. I'll make you an agreement. You let me know when you're going and what you're learning, and you can go whenever you like." And just like that, as we stood in waist deep Atlantic surf, he granted me permission.

After a few more fine waves my father wrapped a long arm around my shoulders and said slowly, "You know, Drew, I don't know what it is about our ocean, but whenever we swim like this, I always feel so… alive. Maybe it's being together, but it just feels right. Doesn't it?"

"Yes, Sir, it does."

We shared his towel to dry, and Our Own Holy Communion was brought to a finish. Walking up the sand towards the great cottage, he said quietly, "We're all going for barbecue this evening." That was to let me know to be home a little earlier and have on a cleaner shirt than usual.

"Nina May, too?"

"That's why were going. It's her birthday tomorrow. We're going down to Piggly's for dinner." I knew it was one of her favorites, all of ours, but it wasn't something we usually did together. I tried to remember when Nina May had come out with us before and couldn't.

Father squeezed my shoulder and said, "By the way, you won't need to ask your mother about these visits of yours. I'll talk to her about it." This meant that he would discuss it in his own way, in his own time, and I was free to go. He patted the back of my head and added, "And I expect you probably don't want your brother to know where you're going either."

"No, Sir, I really don't"

"Well, I can understand that. Your Uncle Thomas used to treat me kind of roughly when we were younger, if you can believe it." I couldn't, because my uncle was just about the kindest man I knew, next to my father. "Son, your brother will learn who you are soon enough. He'll change. You'll see." Adults kept saying that, and I kept hoping it was true.

***

The simple lessons of cause and effect come effortlessly to us when we are young. We learn how the wind whips the sand into the air and stings the eyes; how the sun bakes that sand and scorches our feet; how Cheerios with sugar and milk taste better than Brussels sprouts with any amount of butter. They are the uncomplicated lessons that are easily absorbed and brought swiftly to the surface when we are young. They are the lessons of the senses. The more obscure lessons of cause and effect, however, take longer to comprehend. Those that involve the emotions lie in a mysterious category, hazy and unclear to ten-year-olds. Cruelty, for instance, is a complex, irrational act, and not easily understood at that age. In that summer I was to begin learning that for some people meanness came as naturally as breathing.

Our evening began with a song. It was Nina May's birthday eve, and in my mother's belief system any such event warranted a celebration to be extended over long periods of time. In our house Mother's Day began in April and continued until Father's Day commenced in June. We celebrated May Day, Summer Solstice, both equinoxes, and there had been some discussion of including Boxer Day until Momma determined it might interfere with Christmas. So she gathered us all into the kitchen that evening, Donny and I keeping a safe three people between us, and led us in Happy Birthday song to Nina May. After which came presents and spice cake that my mother had baked at the Morley cottage in order to keep it a surprise. No one seemed particularly concerned with the curious sequence of cake before dinner, because no amount of dessert could spoil a good plate of barbecue.

Nina May stood in the center of her kitchen, her glasses trapping tears along her cheeks. She beamed and laughed. "Lord a mercy, Mrs. MacLaren, you outdone yourself. There was no need to go getting' anything for me."

My mother politely disagreed and handed Nina May our gifts one by one.

She had purchased them from local tourist shops north of the pier and written cards from each of us. There was an embroidered pillow that smelled of balsam from my father and her. From Donny she had found a beaded glasses case, and from me a small wooden box, delicately carved with our favorite bird, a pelican. That one prompted a smothering hug for me.

Not quite understanding the sensitivity in such things, I blurted out, "Nina May how old are you going to be?"

She chuckled, "Master Little, I don't celebrate birthdays much like I used to, and truth is, I stopped counting a few years back. But I believe I be sixty-eight this year. I like that number, so I think that's what I'll be." I'd never known anyone who didn't count their birthdays. I was going be eleven at the end of the summer, and if my mother wanted to start celebrating that a month early, it would be just fine with me.

It was a wonderful celebration, with six candles, one for each of us, including Alex. There was laughter and tears, and sweet spice cake. My mother announced that we would have one slice before dinner, and if appetite allowed, a second one later. The presents were perfect and afterwards there was laughter-filled drive down the highway for what Father referred to as "the best barbecue in North Carolina, and therefore the world."

The air was clear and sweet after the short rain. I hoped Maggie remembered that I had predicted it.

Piggly's was a diner set perpendicular to the highway, long and narrow, with six booths and pink Formica tables with a maze of tiny lines swirled through them like splattered paint. The counter had eight stools, big puffy ones, that still tempted me to spin on them like I had when I was four. The air hung heavy with the smell of pork and hickory, and although there were seven sandwiches listed in little white letters on the menu board, no one ever ordered them. You came for "the plate"-- coleslaw, hush puppies, pork barbecue, and iced tea. If you wanted any variation on that, you ordered lemonade. And of course, they had a jukebox.

All five of us were laughing as we entered Piggly's, some silly joke my mother had told that had prompted Donny to add an inappropriate, but funny addendum. For a Friday evening it was quiet, still early, and only one car was angled into the five-space lot that was submerged under a thin blanket of drifting sand. Father guided us through the door and into the first booth, calling out over his shoulder to the short woman behind the counter, "Evening, Millie. We haven't had the whole family here for almost two weeks now, and that's just too darn long not to have the best barbecue in North Carolina. So, we're back."

Millie Martin was standing behind the counter on a peach crate. She was an eyelash taller than I was, so she kicked the box along the floor behind the counter all day to fix and serve everything for her customers. She was also about as round as the cartoon pig they used on all the signs and menus around the diner which made that peach crate sag and creak like it was begging for mercy.

I liked Miss Millie a lot, and had known her for as long as I could remember. She had asked me to call her by that when I was two, and she in turn had called me Drew Drop. Miss Millie would let me spin on her stools in front of the counter until I was dizzy, while she'd fix the best chocolate shakes in the history of the world--even when I didn't have anything in my pockets but sand. I'd twirl and listen to her stories of the old days when there was a lot less out on The Banks.

She was our self-proclaimed historian and photographer, and she hung black and white, and color photographs all along the walls of the diner. There were watercolors of old ships and pirates--always my favorites— and the bathrooms had nautical charts from centuries ago. It was an odd assortment of significant and trivial events, and local people, and it covered every available space above the height of the booths There was one photograph, a wave twice as big as the great cottage taking direct aim at the end of the pier, and near the door, there was one of Miss Millie herself that you always saw as you left. In that picture you could tell it was a sunny day, and she was skinny and in shorts; she was holding a King Mackerel on a fishing line. She had told me once, with a far-away look, that she was seventeen in that picture.

My parents had been coming to Miss Millie's long before I was born, and Father had dedicated four glowing paragraphs to her diner and its succulent barbecue in his first book. What he didn't mention in those thirty-two lines was that Miss Millie was as close to being a card carrying communist as Nags Head had ever seen. Nobody had ever been brave enough to ask her to open her wallet for verification, but she loved to rattle on to anyone on either side of the counter about Dwight's industrial military complex fomenting evil about the world. She would whip up orders and hash out comments like, "the man has the intelligence of potted palm, John. Look at his vice president. That dunce Nixon's still kissing away at Joe McCarthy's backside, even now. Look at the crap going on in the Congo for God's sake." My Father would nod his agreements and I would pretend like I understood one iota of what she was talking about, which I didn't.

Miss Millie had been firing up the brick oven in the back for three decades. She'd had a friend named Clara who worked the cash register and lived with her for a long time. Clara was gone now, died three years ago from a disease in her heart, and I knew that Millie's own heart nearly died that year just from the sadness. I asked Momma once why Miss Millie hadn't ever married and was told that, "she just isn't the marrying kind." Momma told me Clara was only thirty-nine when she died. Now Miss Millie ran the diner by herself.

I slid in next to Nina May and across from my brother, giving me a full view of the length of the diner, tables, counter, and the restrooms at the end. On one of the stools in the back I saw Mr. Brennan sitting with an empty plate and a pile of wadded up napkins in front of him. There was another empty plate in front of the stool next to him. I really didn't know Mr. Brennan all that well. I knew he was our sheriff, but he didn't have any uniform, or handcuffs, or gun sitting there in the diner, so I had my suspicions as to whether he was really a sheriff.

My father sat next to me, nodded politely towards Mr. Brennan who was staring in our direction in what my mother would have said was less than mannerly way.

Momma turned and called, "Millie, we'll have five plates of barbecue please," and after a quick count around the table, added, "and three shakes, one chocolate, two strawberry, and two ice teas." It was Nina May's birthday eve after all, so the shakes were a treat for her and Donny and me.

Miss Millie, setting two pieces of chocolate pie down near Mr. Brennan, called back, "Sure thing, Jean Gray, be a couple of minutes for those shakes."

Nina May, maybe from habit, was straightening the plastic place mat and silverware in front of me when I saw her hands stop arranging things and start to tremble. They moved slowly away from where they'd been above my fork and down into her lap, and I saw her begin to rub them as if her 'thritis was bothering her.

The door to the men's bathroom had just opened, the long, skinny spring at the top giving out the familiar squeak that no one had ever bothered to fix. I saw young Frank Curry walk out zipping up his fly and buckling his wide belt. Now he looked like a sheriff, all done up with khaki pants and shirt, black shoes, and a gun at his side. When he looked up from his belt buckle and saw us, he stopped and sort of stood up as tall as he could make himself, which wasn't all that tall. He looked at me and Nina May and my father on that side of the booth with a cold, nasty stare. His head tilted back an inch or so, and he sniffed.

Donny was flipping through the jukebox cards, most likely searching for Elvis tunes, and Momma was just asking Nina May a question about her sisters in Raleigh, when Mr. Curry, who was settling himself back down on the stool on the far side of Mr. Brennan, and couldn't have been more than nineteen-years-old, said in raised voice, "Millie, I don't appreciate having my fine dinner spoiled by the smell you allow in here." Instantly I felt my father tense. Differently. It wasn't the same kind of tension that I felt coming from Nina May on my right. She was looking down at her hands, not moving a thing, but I saw the muscle in my father's forearm twitch and his expression get hard. I'd only seen that look once before, when he was talking with a man who'd driven his car off the road and over our mailbox in Burlington and stunk of beer.

Frank Curry took a first bite of his pie and cleared his throat so everyone could hear him. "Good way to ruin a plate of fine barbecue and this silk pie if you ask me, Millie."

"No one did ask you Frank." Miss Millie was working hard to get the blender going, probably so no one could hear anything with the whine of the motor. She clapped the metal lid emphatically onto the blender and said, "Frank, you got an ugly mouth and a little too much resemblance to one of Mussolini's boys with all that khaki you're wearin' today." Frank looked like he was perplexed by the statement or preparing to take on Miss Millie with more of his lip.

Mr. Brennan, without looking at anyone in particular, said quietly, "Shut up, Frank." That was the first law enforcement command I'd witnessed, and it made Frank Curry eat the rest of his pie in sulky silence.

At that age I had begun to neatly place my mother and father in their own roles. They did things differently, each in their own way, and I thought that I could foresee with my young clairvoyant powers, their reactions to most things, such as when Donny or I were in trouble, or when I was going to ask for something they might not like the idea of. I thought I was pretty good at it. It was why I had, that very morning, chosen to ask my father for permission to visit Mai Lin. I was sure, before we dove through our first wave, how he would respond. Sometimes, however, one of them would surprise me beyond measure. That evening, it was my mother.

Maybe it was from her social outing being spoiled, but in truth I knew there were certain things she just wouldn't stand for. She stood up from our table, her napkin sliding with none of its usual etiquette, from her lap to the floor. She looked like someone had simply misquoted one of her favorite English poets and needed a little correction, nothing more, and with that expression of a teacher preparing to discuss a student's lapse in judgment, she walked right up to Sheriff Brennan, didn't even acknowledge his sulky deputy, and said, "Jack Brennan, you know I'm the President elect of the Women's League in this county, don't you?"

Mr. Brennan wiped his bald head with the palm of his hand and said wearily. "Mrs. MacLaren, I do know that, yes."

"And do you know I also lead the garden club for the ladies of Manteo and Nags Head, even though not one of us can actually grow a single rose or a marigold in this strip of sand?"

Mr. Brennan sighed quietly at that and replied, "Well now, Mrs. MacLaren, that I did not know."

My mother lifted her chin and looked down at Sheriff Brennan with a searing look and said in the iciest voice I'd ever heard her use, "Each of those women voted you into the office you now hold, Sheriff, and if you want to perform the duties of that office for another year or two, you will keep your foul-mouthed, immoral, adolescent brat of a deputy on a very tight leash from this moment forth." She then smiled sweetly at Miss Millie, the way she would when she spoke in front of an audience, and said, "Millie, I apologize, but we'll be taking those orders to go this evening."

Millie replied unhappily, "Well, I can certainly understand that, Jean Gray. The atmosphere has sort of deteriorated with our little journey through the Reichstag this afternoon." She shot Mr. Curry a glance that with a light breeze behind it would have knocked him right out the back door.

I looked at Father and knew what he was thinking. He wanted us to eat our dinner right there in that booth. He was waiting to hear if Mr. Brennan or Frank Curry was going to say anything at all, and I could tell that he didn't like the idea of us leaving Millie's. But I guess he understood why Momma wanted us to, or maybe he glanced over and saw what I saw. The rims of Nina May's glasses had trapped a small pocket of tears again. They weren't like the ones from the presents and cake and songs we'd enjoyed earlier. I knew that, and I sat there feeling a bit helpless and unintelligent, because I didn't know what it was that Mr. Curry had meant. I just wanted whatever was hurting her to go away. All I wanted was to hug her, so I did.

The evening had begun with a song and ended with a child's embrace and an early drive home. Donny sat in the front and talked nonstop to Father about the Yankees and the Braves and whether there might be a chance of them meeting in the World Series again, and he moaned on and on about how good his hush puppies and strawberry shake smelled in the paper bags. I didn't listen. I kept thinking of the moment when Nina May was fighting her tears back and how behind her thick glasses she had looked a little bit like Pooh Hutton on the beach. Scared and hurt.

Breath

Maggie started out the next morning before I rounded the corner of the old shack. She walked ahead of me silently with long, purposeful strides that I couldn't keep up with no matter how hard I tried and didn't want to for fear of stepping on some peril in the sand. The day before she'd maintained a brisk pace, but nothing like this. Her silent resolve had me guessing if she was angry with me, which made me feel uncomfortable. I had looked forward to going to Mai's again and selfishly wanted our walking time to be simple, with the same uncomplicated delights of the previous day. I wanted to talk. I wanted ask her about all sorts of things I wanted to ask her what she knew of meanness, which seemed to be revealing itself in my life more and more. I wanted to tell her about the scene in the diner the night before. I hadn't thought it all out, but I knew I wanted to talk.

Maggie, however, walked rapidly, with no conversation, and I was learning that when Maggie set herself to stubborn silence, nothing changed her, so after a short time I started a dialogue with myself.

"You know, I think my legs must've gotten shorter overnight. You do? Yep, I do. That must be it, all right. They shrank. Cuz I can't seem to walk nearly as fast as yesterday. Is that so? Yep, I'm probably going to need new shoes now to fit over my shrunken feet, maybe new pants too. If they keep on shrinking I don't know what I'm going to do. I'll be walking around like a beetle and need a whole new set of clothes." Then I added, "Geez, I sure hope my head hasn't shrunk, too." I heard a giggle in front of me.

"Course, you know it might be that my legs didn't shrink at all. Might have been that breakfast this morning. Momma always tells me not to put all those iron shavings on top of my cereal. That could've weighed me down a bit."

Maggie patted her pockets, pretending to look for something, and laughing called back, "I could've sworn I put my horseshoe magnet in here somewhere."

"Yeah, well, I wouldn't be able to keep up even if you strapped me on a bicycle and had a magnet the size of these dunes." She stopped, not just slowed down, but stopped and turned, and then I saw why she'd walked ahead with her back facing me like a shield. Maybe she hadn't wanted me to see it, which didn't make much sense, because I would have soon enough, or maybe she just wanted to hurry away from the ocean side of the strand, but her eye was bruised a dark purple and swollen like a plum. I could see that it hurt her in more ways than physical. I stood there staring, feeling more uncomfortable by the second.

"It's all right, Drew. It was just an accident, a little one."

"Doesn't look so little to me." I wanted to add that it didn't look like any accident either, but I figured an explanation would come when she was ready.

"It was Momma. I was feeding her some of her medicine last night." She hesitated and I could see in her expression that she was finally going to tell me. "She's sick, Drew. Got a disease in her brain. Had it 'bout six months, now and sometimes it just… sets her off. It's like she's not there when it happens. She's not my Momma then."

"What kind of disease?"

"Nobody knows. We only got one doctor, and he sure doesn't know."

"Do you have to take care of her all the time?"

"She does some things for herself, just like Skeets, but I've got to be there mostly 'cuz she gets so tired. Neither one of 'em can manage much on their own." She managed a shy grin and said, "I've gotten to be a pretty good cook, though," and in a quick motion, flipped an invisible pancake into the air and caught it in an invisible frying pan.

I tried to picture how it worked inside the house I'd never set foot in, and the first question that came to me was the obvious one. "Do you have to stay there during school time, too?"

We stood facing each other, and I could tell that the answer was as painful as the swollen eye. "I had to quit the last month of the year, and I don't expect I'll be finishing up with the others."

I moved away from that. "So what happened to you last night?"

"Well…there's times when she just plain doesn't want her medicine, or she doesn't want me fooling with her. Heck, I don't think that stuff helps her anyways." Maybe she thought that was answer enough, but I stood there looking at her with that big question mark over my head, just like in my comic books, until she said, "She kind of swung her elbow up at the wrong time."

"Oh."

"Knocked me right to the floor." She attempted another grin, and with the swollen eye she looked both beautiful and absurdly silly at the same time.

We started walking again, winding along the curves more slowly now. Trying to make her feel better, I told her about the wind being knocked out of me and how that had felt. Her voice got serious. "You couldn't breathe? Really?"

"Nope. It was only for a couple of seconds, but I couldn't breathe at all."

She slowed a bit, and beyond her shoulder I could see the high screen of bamboo shielding Mai Lin's garden in the distance. She said something in a far-away voice, something that puzzled me at the time and remained with me always. "That's horrible. Really horrible. I can't imagine not being able to breathe. That's our gift, Drew, our key."

We entered the gap in the green curtain without any of Maggie's shenanigans of the day before, and above us Mai Lin stood waiting in the same place on her back porch. "Come, come. Little time. We begin." But as we neared the steps she saw the bruising around Maggie's eye and appeared to bob her head in a calculating way, as if this had happened before. She scurried through the door into her kitchen.

"Sit, sit, Daughter." Maggie obediently plopped herself down in one of the only two regular chairs in the cottage, nestled beneath the small table in the kitchen. It puzzled me that Mai Lin didn't ask any questions and Maggie didn't offer explanations. Mai merely lifted jars, stirred and mixed, looked at the bruise closely, and stirred and mixed some more. The mixture became a brown and mucky-looking paste with an odor like the vapor rub Momma put on my chest when I had a winter cold.

With a practiced technique Mai spread the mixture around the bruise with a flat stick and wrapped a narrow band of soft cloth about Maggie's thick hair. She slipped a folded piece of puffy gauze over the eye and smoothed her hair back gently. "You be a pirate while we work today," which is exactly what she looked like with the patch, and when I screwed up my face into a scowl and grumbled a paraphrased line from one of my books, "Aargh, Mateys, who's hidden the lady's tankard o' rum", all three of us broke into the giggles.

After that, according to Mai Lin, it was time to begin. We moved to the porch above the sound, where Maggie promptly stepped into the screened area. I was left uncomfortably alone with Mai Lin. I had pictured all three of us doing the mysterious exercise of bent knees and tingly fingers together, and it was made worse when Mai Lin just looked at my face again for a long moment. She just stared, took my hands and looked at each one carefully, turning them over and back, peering closely at the palms. I stared at the door where Maggie had disappeared.

"First lesson is to relax. It is work, but it will come." Now, relaxing had never been too hard for me before--most times I felt like I was pretty much an expert at it, and it certainly hadn't ever felt like work. But I was ready to be an apt student and just like multiplication I would practice until perfect.

"Okay, I'm relaxed."

"No, no, no talk now. Just listen. Do same as I do." I watched. She began to breath, and her hands began to rise, drifting up from her waist level and settling gently back with each exhale. I tried to follow. "Breathe like balloon filling slowly. Slowly." I took that breath in like a furnace fan, my hands going up and down like gull's wings. "Too fast. Take the air deep down, Drew. Make tummy round and fat." I almost started laughing again at that one. "Breath come in slowly, go out slowly. Let hands rise and float. Listen, hear my breath." I listened and heard her soft inhale, slow and deep, then the gentle hissing as she exhaled. Her hands lifted and fell in precise harmony. I imitated, trying to match her rhythm.

"You breathe own breath now, not like me. Fill slowly. Be like a young tree."

I let the air fill my lungs gently and deeply. It felt like sand in the egg timer, and slowly it became my own pulse, a rhythm, a pattern, like the waves at night. "Remember tummy fill round and fat with air. Close eyes to halfway. Now, now we try to relax. Let mouth and neck go loose, like empty cloth." I closed my eyes part way and felt my mouth and tongue and cheeks empty and soften like a sail with no wind, and the thought came to me that Mai Lin was right. It took practice to relax.

I don't know how long I stood there breathing, my hands drifting and falling, but I slipped deeper into her voice, listening to her tell me to ease my shoulders and chest. My stomach filled and emptied like a round billows, and I forgot about everything but my breath.

"Okay, we have tea now." The pattern screeched to a stop, and a small part of me felt like my mother had just told it to get out of bed when it was so warm and cozy under the covers. The very same word that came to me the previous day when I saw the wind chimes now returned.

"Wow." Mai Lin stood there grinning at me, eyes sparkling. She took one of my hands and looked at the palm again.

"Good start, good relaxing. Knees all wrong, but good start. You like Song of Rising and Falling Hands? What you hear?"

"Wow"-.There was that word again-"Very much, Mai. It sounded like the waves at night."

"Good, that is good sound, good song for you to hear. You do this well." Instantly, I was proud, not sure exactly what I had done to be proud of, but the compliment felt good.

When Mai Lin returned with three cups of tea, a small bowl of steamy water, and a folded cloth on a tray, Maggie stepped quietly out from the enclosed area. Her uncovered eye was bright, and the glimmer of pain that I had seen when we had walked through the dunes had been replaced with a quiet calm.

"Okay. You not be pirate now. Medicine work quickly. We remove patch." Gently, she unwrapped the cloth and lifting the towel and bowl, cleansed the oval around Maggie's eye. The paste had hardened and was now the color of creamy peanut butter. She rinsed the cloth in the warm water and swabbed gently in both directions. The skin around Maggie's eye was now pinkish and showed no signs of the purple bruising from earlier. The swelling had vanished.

As she was dabbing at little flakes stuck along the eyebrow, Mai tenderly brushed Maggie's hair back with her other hand and whispered, "Daughter feel better now." Maggie reached up and held the older woman's hand against her cheek, holding the palm like a baby's blanket. Mai Lin gently kissed the crown of her head.

"Yes, Mai. It's better." And when she looked my way and smiled, I saw for the first time the child in her eyes. I saw Maggie Silver as a little girl.

"So, Drew," she sighed, "Now you see why I come here." I didn't know if she meant the lessons, the companionship, or the time away from her agony on the other side of the strand."

"Drew good student. Work hard. Not much dust to clean off." Mai handed me my tea, then Maggie's, and I asked her what she had meant about dust on me.

"Well, Mr. Student, when we are young we have little dust, like clean chalkboard in school. As we grow, we have more…what do we call them, little drawings, like in schoolbooks?"

"Doodles?"

"Yes, yes, doodles. Doodles need to be cleaned off."

My questions faded for the moment. It all felt so peaceful. I just wanted to sit there. Forever. There was no urgency, no hurry to anything. We were simply there.

As we set to leave, Mai handed us two tangerines again and said, more to me than Maggie, "Tomorrow Sunday. We work day after. I wait to see you."

Then she whispered something to Maggie that I just barely heard.

We walked the trail, I spitting seeds and sending pieces of tangerine skin in curving trajectories like bottle caps, and Maggie humming quietly. The air was warm and felt different, tasted different, and thinking about it, I smiled to myself. It felt full.

Nearing the highway I asked, "Maggie?"

"Hmmm?"

"Is your Momma going to get better?"

She stepped to the side of the path so I could walk next to her. She was looking into the sand, and I could see her frowning, not at my prying. She was looking at some reflection, like an answer that might be buried there.

Her voice came harshly. "I don't know, Drew. The damned doctor doesn't know neither. He says it's a degenerative neurological condition, which sounds like a lot of gobbledygook, if you ask me."

"What's degenerative mean?"

"He told us it means it's getting worse, and he told us we'd need a bunch of tests done in some hospital up in Boston, which we sure as heck don't have enough money to do. I can barely get our groceries each week." With that simple admission I knew why Maggie had never played the games in the waves and sand that we other children had played. I understood why Skeeter had never fished or flown balloons. And I realized why Maggie's ninety minutes of independence were as precious as hidden treasure to her. I was just happy that we had shared those minutes that day and that I had made her giggle just a bit.

As we were crossing the highway, Maggie grew quiet, her expression distant and somber. I recalled what Mai Lin had whispered as we had left, "Be patient, Daughter. Give love, even when none given back."

***

"Jesus Christ, Peckerhead!"

"Momma doesn't like you to say that and you know it. I don't want to play and I don't have to if I don't want to." Donny stood in front of me with Wink May, looking like he wanted to twist my arm up around the back of my head, his usual way of convincing me that he was right and I was wrong. We were standing on opposite sides of a submerged sand fence to the south of the cottage, and a hundred yards further down, I saw clusters of boys and girls, two energetic dogs, and one nervous-looking cat perched on MaryEllen Brewster's shoulder. MaryEllen had just turned thirteen and carried that cat like a newborn baby all over the place. She wrapped it in a small blanket, and most of us now thought the cat was permanently affected, because it was scratching and peeing in the sand about once every minute.

"Come on. Look down there. We've got everybody playin'. It'll be the biggest game of Capture the Flag in the history of the world. Don't be such a shithead."

"I've got other stuff I'm doing right now, Donny. I just don't want to play. All right?" But inside, I knew it was going to be a fun game. They usually were when there were lots of us running and screaming all over the place and full contact tackling wasn't involved. Suddenly, I regretted the commitment I'd made.

I had my surf rod, the big red one, with the heavy test line and a four inch silver lure all tricked up and ready to go.

"Hell, Itsyprick, there aren't any blues running until the evenings anyways. That's what my dad says. What are you going to try to catch, crabs?" This was from Wink May who made the comment sound like a dirty joke. He had started hanging around with Donny more and more, and more and more, I'd begun to dislike him. With a nasty tone he added, "You got no sense, Dickbrain." He had his left hand on his hip, and he looked down his nose at me like I was some type of bug. A big gold ring with a purple stone sparkled from a finger on that hand.

Wink had one of those faces that most folks would call handsome, with a straight nose and high cheekbones, but set right in the middle were a pair of dark eyes that looked like they took keen enjoyment in twisting the legs off crabs and watching them try to make their way back to their holes. He had wispy hair and thin lips, and he seemed to always be sneering at something.

"Bluefish don't wear watches, Winston." I was trying to out-talk him so I used his real name just to annoy him a bit. "They were biting earlier this morning, and Pooh landed four in one hour, so you and your dad don't need to tell me when they are going to bite. Besides, I'm not out to set a record. I'm teaching a friend how to fish." And as soon as I'd said it I wished I hadn't. I knew it was a mistake. They didn't need to know a thing about my plan, but too often with Donny these days, I was saying things I wished I'd hadn't. I knew he and Wink would pry it out of me, torture me slowly, until I told them.

Donny snickered. "You teaching somebody how to fish. That's a good one, Peckerhead. That's the funniest joke I've heard in a long time. Just who're teaching today, Oh Wise One? MaryEllen's cat?"

"Shut up, Donny. I'm teaching a friend, that's all."

"Well, Itsyprick. It's gotta be some kind of dumb-shit girl, because my dad says every Tar Heel boy knows how to fish in these parts." Winston May was really beginning to get on my nerves.

"It's not a girl, Wink. I'm teaching Skeeter Silver if that's okay with you," I pumped up the sarcasm to a dangerous level, "And it's okay with your dad."

I saw Donny look at me strangely. He didn't say anything. There was no cutting remark, no joke; he just stared at me kind of thoughtfully. Winston, however, didn't miss a beat. His tone was incredulous. "A crip? You're gonna teach that shriveled-up little white trash crip how to fish? No fucking way."

That hit me like a wave, a big powerful one, right in the gut. I was mad, spitting mad, probably as mad as I'd ever been in my entire life. I was ready to try, at all personal risk, to kick or punch or scratch someone nearly twice my size, but Donny, still looking at me thoughtfully, said, "Be quiet, Wink."

"What the hell, MacLaren? You taking his side?" Wink seemed as astounded as I was. He had his hand on his hip again, but this time he was looking down his nose at Donny.

"No, I still want him to play, Wink, but if he wants to go show Skeeter Silver how to fish, that's his business. And don't call him any more names or Skeeter neither. That boy didn't ask to get that disease, so don't call him names about it, okay?" Wink was dumbstruck, glaring at Donny like he was a pure traitor to the great cause of name calling and bullying, and for half a second I thought he was going to make the mistake of taking a swing at my older brother. Fortunately for him, he didn't.

I picked up my surf rod and started stomping through the sand along the fence line, glad that I wasn't walking the other direction to play in the biggest game of

Capture the Flag in the history of the world. I didn't want to be around any kids right then. I didn't want to be around Donny, or Wink, or MaryEllen Brewster and her damned cat. I didn't particularly want to be around Skeeter for that matter. I just wanted to be alone. The only place I really wanted to be was sitting on Mai Lin's porch watching the egrets.

I heard Donny call out, "Hey, Drew"

I looked over my shoulder and saw him standing alone, Winston May's lanky body sauntering petulantly off towards the crowd down the beach. "What?" I almost yelled it.

"Tell me later how many you guys catch. Okay?"

For the first time that summer Donny didn't look like James Dean or Audey Murphy, or Elvis. He looked just like Donny. Maybe it had been seeing my mother stick up for Nina May in the diner. Or maybe his idea of what being cool really was had changed a little, but for the first time that summer he'd stuck up for me. And for the first time that summer he'd called me Drew. I smiled, at little weakly at him, and nodded.

"Yeah, sure thing, Donny."

The sheriff questioned Maggie over and over about what she'd done during those long hours at the height of the storm. He asked her why she'd left the cottage and her mother lying there in bed alone. With the winds ripping the shingles from the roof, and the waves pounding under the pilings and buckling the floorboards, she should have stayed. But she had left.

The sheriff was convinced Maggie had done it, absolutely certain. No one else had a reason to commit that murder. And he knew for a fact that it was murder. The coroner had phoned him. Suffocation. And now, like an open telegraph line, all Dade County seemed to know it.

Nothing valuable had been taken from the cottage, not that there was anything of value in that old place. The sheriff asked Maggie a lot of questions that she didn't answer. She didn't say a word or even look at him, and that just made the sheriff angrier.

Angelo Bertolli called Mr. Brennan just about the time the sun was coming up. He told him about the boat, so the sheriff put Maggie back in the holding cell that smelled of urine and vomit and drove back up the coast.

He motored out in one of the longboats with Angelo, just beyond the pier. The only reason they'd found the boat, Angelo told him, was from the cork line that had floated up like a wiggling finger out of the hull.

None of them wanted to dive down to find out what had gone wrong. The water was like gray lead with jagged white caps and was far too cold from being stirred up by the enormous surge. But in the end, Angelo took off his shirt, showing that purple scar to all the people gathered on the pier. He dove down, and it was a very long time before he came back up.

From the water, where he held on to the bouncing gunwale of the drift boat, he whispered to the sheriff. Nobody on the pier heard his words, but everyone could see from the expressions that something had gone terribly wrong, and for a long time, the only sounds were the waves and the quiet weeping of all of those people

***

I pitched the silver lure way out in a long, looping arc. It spun and twirled and sparkled in the mid-day sun and plopped softly into a green ocean. I always loved the sound of the whirring, like a droning of mad bees as the line played out. I spooled it by hand, feeding it out through the eyes, and walked slowly backwards up the slope towards Skeeter who sat patiently in his familiar seat on the porch. He was fascinated by the whole process and hadn't stopped chattering about it until I'd asked him to.

I was regretting my obligation to instruct him, which was turning out to be more complicated than I'd expected. Most times when I was by myself, I would cast the lure and reel it back in a simple rhythm from a favorite 'lucky spot' at the water's edge. This was different. I had to cast the lure and then carry the rod backwards up to his porch, being careful not to trip as I walked. Sand could ruin a reel quicker than salt.

"Here, take the butt end of the rod and hold onto it until I get up there." There was a slight edge to my voice from the desire to be doing something other than hauling a surf rod up and down the slope. Skeeter lifted the pole tentatively over the railing and waited quietly as I made my way up next to him.

"Flip the bale down and reel the line in slowly." I took his left hand and positioned it on the cork handle above the reel. As my fingers slid across his palm, I felt the roughness. He had a callous lining that felt like the bottoms of my dress shoes. Those hands were his feet, and that simple thought both alarmed me and made me kind of happy that I was there showing him how to set them on a fishing pole. Everything softened right then, and the meanness of the morning melted away. I smiled at my buddy and lifted his other hand up to the oval knob on the handle. "Now just reel it in slowly. You can kind of pull back on the rod and then reel on it." I showed him the motions.

"Wow. It feels like pulling in Superman out of the clouds, Drew!" We both glanced over at the blue balloon tethered sadly to the nearby post. Superman looked like he'd had a lot of recent exposure to kryptonite. He was sagging low, a mere shadow of his once-proud self.

"The trick is to make the lure kind of skip under the water. Not too fast, but you don't want it to sag either. It's got to look like a minnow to the other fish."

Skeeter's green eyes scrunched into a question, freckles merging into the creases. "What's a minnow?" I noticed his half tooth was now almost whole and the grin pretty much standard-Carolina boy.

"A minnow's a baby fish, Skeeter. There's thousands of 'em out there." It kept amazing me the things he hadn't seen, so I told him how they moved like clouds speeding by in the shallows, how they streaked and swerved and crowded together in groups. I could see him picturing the whole thing. I told him all about fishing being something you had to feel, not see, how the lure had tugs and prances that you sensed through your hands and forearms all the way down into your stomach.

The lure was nearing the shore now, and I needed to do the whole thing again in reverse. Skeeter handed me the pole, and I reeled in the slack as I walked down the slope.

My cast was farther this time, and the walk back up seemed easier. As I was coming up the steps a long, ugly groan filtered out through the screened window at the back. It sounded like a different movie this time--Frankenstein was in there, arms stretched out, bolts and scars sticking out all over the place, but it was scarier because it was close and somehow much bigger.

"It's my Momma, she's kind of…up and down right now." Skeeter looked nervously at the window and then at me, and suddenly felt I like I didn't want to be there again.

The quiet returned, and Skeeter began to reel the lure in. He pulled gently and spun the handle, getting the hang of it pretty well. Then I saw the spasm, the tiny vibration at the tip of the long rod. The lead eye jumped twice and then bent down softly towards the ocean. It wasn't a blue, that was for certain. It was smaller.

"You've got something, Skeets! Reel it in slowly, but don't let it go slack. Keep it steady." I wanted to take the rod from him, but knew better, because I remembered my own first catch. You did it on your own. It was part of the rules.

"What do I do? Am I doin' it right? Do you think it's a big one, Drew?" He was looking down the long line that disappeared into the ocean. Whatever fish was down there, it'd opened up a chatterbox on the porch. Skeeter started giggling like he had when our balloons were flying. It was pure delight for him and for me, because I knew exactly how he felt.

As the angle of the line came near to shore, I ran down. The water was about ankle deep where the line dipped in. I grabbed it in one hand and lifted. I felt the fish flipping near my feet, and then I had it dangling in the air around my knees. It was a perch, skinny and round, about two hands big. It was silvery, small, and it was Skeeter's.

"Reel the line in as I walk this little guy up." I had to yell a bit, but he understood how it all worked now, and in a minute he was looking at his first catch flopping back and forth, and like every kid who every landed his first, he had no idea now what to do.

In the slowest drawl I think I'd ever heard, Skeeter said, "Can I touch it?"

"Sure. Just watch the hooks."

He poked a tentative finger at it, then another, and finally grabbed at it just to have it squirt right back out.

"Here, grab him like this." I wrapped my hand around the perch's head and tightened the line until it stopped squirming. "It's a perch, and we're going to need a bucket or something."

"There's one around the back near the shower and the mop."

I ran around to the back. The Silver cottage, like ours, had a tall outdoor shower with a raised row of thick planks right in the sand for rinsing off salt water. The head, also like ours, was stained solid with green oxidation. Below it I found a rusty bucket, which I filled halfway and lugged back to the front porch.

"I'm going to show you how to take it off the lure, but you got to do it yourself. It's part of the rules." Skeeter nodded seriously.

The perch, I saw, had caught itself on one of the four hooks hanging along the bottom. It had somehow snagged a gill as it swam beneath the lure, probably more out of curiosity than any attempt to swallow the thing, because the lure was nearly half its size. It was just poor luck.

One thing Skeeter had was strong hands and arms. They were like cables, and when he wrapped his fingers around the perch a second time, it was like a small vice. He slipped the hook out of the gill and dropped the perch into the bucket like he'd done it a dozen times before. We watched the fish swim in quick circles around the bottom of the bucket. Skeeter looked at it like it was a shiny blue ribbon he'd won. As I watched him for a moment, I realized, totally astounded, that it was the first time he had ever done anything that he felt like he could be truly proud of. And that wasn't right. I remember him bringing us iced tea the first day we'd met, so I asked, "Skeeter?"

"Yeah?" He didn't look up, just kept grinning down at the fish flashing around the bottom of the bucket.

"How'd you learn to lift yourself up like you do? Up on the bench and down onto your board?"

He stopped looking at the bucket and looked up at me, frowning. The greenness in the eyes wasn't mad. It didn't hurt from my question. It hurt from his memories.

"Well...I had to work at it is all. Don't remember the first times so good. I was pretty young. I do remember my arms not wanting to do it at first, 'cuz I was too small. I guess I just grew bigger and learnt how." He hesitated a moment. "Why'd you ask that, Drew?" The pain of the memory had left his eyes, replaced now by one of embarrassment.

"Well, Buddy, the way I see it, it's darn near the bravest thing I've ever known anyone to do."

He looked at me like I was crazy, disbelief brimming. "You don't believe that."

"I do. It makes Captain America look weak, if you ask me, and I mean that."

He looked at his fish again and touched the side of the bucket, stroking the metal gently. He started to grin bigger and bigger and then looked at me. The glimmer of light was back in his eyes. "Drew, do you think we oughta let Charlie go?"

"Charlie?" I laughed.

"It's the best name I could think of. He's Charlie."

"Well…" I hesitated, "he's not really big enough to keep anyway, but it's up to you."

"Can you do it for me?"

Charlie reentered the water and headed home faster than any fish I'd ever caught, and I came back up and told Skeeter exactly how he'd looked as he left.

In the early afternoon we caught three large blues and let them all go, and the entire time Skeeter laughed harder than I'd ever seen.

***

"Momma?"

"Hmmm?" The answer was sleepy.

"Are you up for a little company? I've brought a friend over." Maggie's voice had that steely sound to it, like she was trying to be nice but didn't really feel up to it.

"Is it a young man calling?" Now, I didn't really think of myself as a young man quite yet, a grown boy, daring adventurer, superhero maybe, but not a young man, though the idea wasn't all that displeasing.

Maggie had come out onto the porch right after we'd sent the last of our bluefish back to wherever they called home and asked me to come in and meet her mother, who she told me was alert enough to have a visitor right then. I wasn't sure why she wanted me to, and the idea terrified me. It was only from the trust that had grown between us that I was able to step across the threshold into the dark room. By that time Maggie could've asked me to walk barefoot on hot coals and I would've agreed.

"It's Drew MacLaren, Momma. You know John and Jean Gray a couple of doors over. Drew's their son."

The woman opened her eyes and blinked a little at the light, which sort of surprised me because it was as dim as the Batcave in there and smelled like moldy newspaper and sickness. If I had worn any boots right then, I would have been shaking like Skeeter's perch inside them. I tried to think of when I'd been more nervous in my life and couldn't.

Clarisse Silver pulled herself slowly up against the pillows on the headboard and straightened her hair, gown, and the covers in a meticulous way. Company had come to call.

"Do come in. I... must look something terrible." Her eyes settled on me, focusing slowly in blend of confusion and embarrassment. She had long hair, gray and blond, flowing like waterfalls down almost to her waist. Her skin was ashy pale, and like Skeeter, she was bone thin and had soft green eyes. At that moment those eyes were looking at me in total bewilderment.

I looked around the room nervously. It was the messiest thing I'd ever seen. No. Not messy, just so full of knickknacks that it looked messy. There were photographs in fancy frames, porcelain figurines, dolls, jars full of buttons, brushes and combs with silver-backed handles, glass candle sticks, books, and things I couldn't see or probably name had I been able to see. The only semblance of order were the photographs, which appeared to flow in a lazy chronological order from left to right around the perimeter of the room. Perched like a haughty conductor above it all was a cherrywood mantle clock ticking away the seconds.

"Well, Bless me. Child, I remember you now. You were just a baby when I last saw you. Look at you now, all grown up. And handsome as a movie star, too."

This was definitely a compliment I couldn't react to. I tried to think of something witty, and the only thing that swam up through my panicky brain was, "Thank you, Mrs. Silver."

"You can call me Clarisse, Child. I've gotten less conventional with age." She sort of waved her hand about as if that explained away the room and all her appearance. "Come closer. Let me look at you." I stepped nearer to the bed with an effort, my feet feeling like they were pasted to the floor. Maggie's mother reached out and, with the lightness of a butterfly, rested her hand atop my own and smiled. There was a light tremor to her touch. The skin was warm and dry like birch leaves in the sun. It felt oddly like my grandmother's and for the first time in our meeting, my fear began to melt away. Up close I could see that she had been beautiful once. It was like wax paper covering her features now. I could tell she wasn't that old, maybe my Momma's age, but the grayness of pain had descended in layer upon layer across her face, obscuring the features of the woman that now held my hand so gently. Her green eyes were dim, but sweet, like Skeeter's.

Maggie pulled a chair over, and I sat near the bed. Clarisse asked me questions about my family, whom she seemed to know plenty about, and as she talked I learned that she knew plenty about other families in The Banks as well. Just like Miss Millie she had lots of tidbits about folks all tucked away in her head.

"You know I used sneak off to go dancing with Millie Martin down at the Beachcomber back when they had the pavilion. Miss Millicent and Miss Clarisse, they called us." She raised a thin, gray smile at the memory. "We had different last names back then, of course. Those boys would line up to dance with us, and I remember catching a lashing from my Poppa the first time he came to find out about it. That wasn't the last time, though. No Sir, he was a minister, you see. Didn't like any of that carrying on. Only music he tolerated was gospel. You like gospel, Child?"

"Yes, Ma'am, what I know of it."

"Well, I liked it until he told me it was the only music we could listen to. I just couldn't see how you could dance to gospel the way I liked, and Millicent and I, well, we did like to dance." The thin smile returned.

Clarisse talked on and on about the past, and slowly I noticed a change begin to creep into her eyes. They were focusing harder, more intently, and yet she didn't seem to be aware of what she was looking at. They began to twitch and dart to different objects about the room as if she was trying to find something but just couldn't figure out where it was. I looked around at the clutter, wondering what she was trying to find.

On the dresser two photographs caught my eye. In the first, Clarisse was cradling a baby in her arms, and I knew instinctively that it was Maggie. In it Clarisse was astoundingly beautiful, like Guenevere in one of my books, and the photographer had captured precisely the pride she felt holding her newborn, yet, in the eyes there was the tiniest suggestion of something that I couldn't quite establish.

The other photograph was of Skeeter when he was really young. He was standing at the front of a chapel that I knew was just a few miles south of where we were. He wore a coat and tie, and with his hair cut short and neatly combed, he looked like a little man. It was odder to me than any picture I think I'd ever seen.

Clarisse let my hand slip away from hers, and Maggie tugged on my shirt at the shoulder and I knew that it was time to leave. I said the only thing I could think of. "Mrs. Silver, I hope you get better soon."

"We're praying for that, Child. Praying every day. God will enter this house and drive the demon out. Satan will be thrown down." Her voice was rising with each word.

Maggie pulled my hand towards the door that lead to the kitchen and whispered hurriedly. "You'd best go now, Drew. I'll see you tomorrow, okay?" There was a sense of urgency in her voice.

"Sure, Maggie. You bet." The air had suddenly changed inside the room. I felt it, just like the morning of the storm.

"Drive the demon out!"

Clarisse's voice was getting louder.

***

Jethro could speak Italian, Portuguese, and of course, English. He knew a lot Spanish, too. He liked to tell the children that walked with him that it was because he wanted to order every flavor of ice cream in as many countries of the world as possible. His passions were evident to those who knew him. He wore them proudly, talked of them, sang them, and shared them with any person who would listen and often those who did not. He loved the ocean, opera, and ice cream in no particular order. A cold beer or two was also an acceptable pleasure on now-and-then occasions. There were a few passions, however, that Jethro kept as hidden as stolen gold.

Captain J. had walked to our cottage, that being his favorite mode of transportation on land. Most days, once his nets were set and he was back on land, he could be seen alone, or with a passel of children, strolling along some stretch of shoreline or highway.

But today was Sunday, a day of opera and beer. No nets would be set or drawn, and time would be stretched comfortably to accommodate the obligations of good friendship.

We were in the converted boathouse. Father had hired a young carpenter to add three feet of planking onto the end of the old garage a few years back, extending it just enough so our twenty-two-foot sloop could fit snuggly inside and the wobbly doors folded and locked. The width allowed for ample space on each side of the hull, but none in the front and back unless the doors were swung open, which they now were. There was a warm spray of sunlight to reach half-way to the back wall.

The boat rested on saddle horses, and above it in rafters, the aluminum mast and rigging criss-crossed the beams. Jethro and Father were leaning forward on wobbly beach chairs near the bow on the left side. Both men were shirtless, in ragged shorts, paint splotched tennis shoes and peering like surgeons at a splintered section of fiberglass about eighteen inches long. They were in their sanctuary, the habitation of men and boats. Brushes, tools, and empty beer bottles were spread about the floor at their feet. The big Magnavox on the shelf was turned up to near-deafening levels, and the dark strains of Verdi's Aida were bouncing through the rafters. The two men looked as happy and content as they could be.

Jethro reached for a can at his feet and said, "John, this is the finale. Aida enters the burial crypt in the next act. It's where she sings 'O Terra Addio' with Radames. It is, in my humble opinion, the saddest and sweetest aria ever written. How can a person create such beauty? My heart tightens like a reef knot every time I hear it." He looked to the rafters and said without joking, "I should warn you that you will probably see a grown man weep when they finish together."

"That will make two of us then." My father looked up at me and winked. He was carefully snipping cracked fiberglass around the opening with a pair of tin shears. Jethro was stirring up a pungent mixture of resin, and I was on the bow, wiping the hardwoods with teak oil, enjoying immensely how the grains and rich color were coming instantaneously back to life under my authority. Unlike the mundane chores we performed about the great cottage, caring for <u>The Hopeshefloats</u> was a pleasure that I never tired of, and working with my father and Jethro was, in all ways, pure delight.

Jethro handed me a long rectangle of measured cloth and masking tape saying, "Young MacLaren, if you would be so kind as to lay this cloth across the back side of our hole and tape it, then we can set a good coat of resin across her. After she dries we'll fill her from the front. Make it tight there, Lad." I, being the proper size, could easily wiggle into the fo'c'sle to tape the cloth, but one of the adults would need to apply the gooey, noxious resin. I tapped and stretched the cloth like a seasoned apprentice, and after my part was done, Father maneuvered himself into the opening and holding his breath, layered the sticky mixture onto the cloth.

Returning topside he took a deep breath, and from his dizzy look I could tell the fumes had been powerful in the cabin. "That ought to do it, Jethro. Good mix. It's already beginning to harden."

"Aye, well, that's my secret, John, always use a few more drops of the catalyst than it calls for."

"What's a cat list?" My curiosity was awake again.

"Catalyst, Son." He spelled out the letters one by one and said, "A catalyst is something that comes in and changes what it's been mixed into, like water in cement." Father was always quick with good definitions. "It sort of stirs up all the other ingredients and causes a chemical reaction." I attentively filed this, as if it were an important item of information I would need for the future.

On the radio a man and woman were beginning to sing in dramatic style. Jethro started humming along with them, tapping a dry paint stick on the hull in precise rhythm. Then my father began to hum, tossing his head back and forth with the sad melody. Jethro started singing and our garage suddenly became a grand operatic symphony hall. The music built, the voices, all of them, swirled into an intoxicating crescendo.

Jethro, I heard instantly, did not have the loud, ugly voice he had described to me, but a resonant and beautiful one, deep and powerful like his face, and though I had no idea what any of the words coming from the radio or the men around me actually meant, I could feel the sadness in every note. Without understanding, I also knew that all the music pouring out of our garage and reverberating across the dunes that Sunday afternoon was about death.

True to his word, at the finale, tears were rolling down Jethro's cheeks into his beard. Looking over I saw that my father's cheeks were also moist.

"Bravo! Bravo!" My father was clapping vigorously, so I began clapping, and then both men bowed to a vast audience concealed somewhere in the sea oats.

"You are a very fortunate man, John." We were now outside the garage on the north side. The Hopeshefloats was patched, seaworthy once more, and needed only to have the fiberglass scar sanded and painted before it took to the waves again. I was wrapping newspaper around a paper cup of congealing resin, inspecting the tan of the new planking on the end of the old building, noticing how out of place it looked next to the gray of the older ones. Jethro was cleaning a sticky brush with thinner, while Father scrubbed his fingers with a cloth. There was a savory mixture of oils and salt drifting into the air about us.

My father opened the last bottle of beer and handed it to Jethro. Grinning to himself, he replied, "I think I've known that for quite some time now, Captain, but tell me, why do you think so?"

Jethro took a long pull at the bottle, and in an unusually quiet voice replied, "Your treasures, John. They are so easy to see. Fine sons, a beautiful wife, and so much love about you. You are a fortunate man.

My father, sensing the change, said kindly. "Well, I suspect we're both rather fortunate, Jethro. We each have our riches, our friends, good food on our tables, those great arias we love to sing, and we have that." His long fingers swept in an arc towards the ocean. Our eyes followed. The horizon looked like a painting in a marbled museum. Bruises of peach and lavender plumed above the water, and light winds swirled it all about with fine brushes.

Two doors to the north a single word pierced the breeze. I didn't know the word, didn't know its meaning, but I felt every ounce of the venom as it shrieked. "Slut!" There was a crash, a table or a chair, and then it grew eerily quiet. Both men, as soon as they heard it, jerked upright, sucking the air about them sharply into their lungs. Jethro exhaled slowly and lowered his head into his chest as if in prayer.

"It is getting worse with her, John?" From the way he had asked it, I couldn't tell whether it was a question or a statement.

My father nodded. "Most days are quiet, at least we don't hear much, but this… yes, it's happening more." He motioned with his eyes towards the window. "I wish there were something that we could do for her, for the girl and boy. You've known her a long time, Jethro. You know how tough she is. She's been a fighter her whole life, but this. It just seems… so unfair."

Jethro raised his eyes to the screened window. Then looked directly at me, but asked of no one. "And the girl, this must be more difficult for her with each day?"

Father nodded. "It must be," was all he said.

I wanted to scream about Maggie's swollen eye, scream at them about her tears and silent walks back from Ensign Bill's, but it felt as if it wasn't mine to tell, it was Maggie's

I always knew when Father reached one of his decisions, and I knew he'd arrived at one just then. He wrapped his arm around my shoulder and said to Jethro, "We're heading back to Burlington in a few weeks, but I'll talk with Jean Gray tonight. Maybe we can be better neighbors in the time left, help with something. Bake some foods. Something."

Listening to my father and Jethro talk about Clarisse while the sky shifted like desert sands, I pictured her in her darkened room of cluttered memories. She was leaning against the carved headboard, as I had seen her that morning, long hair flowing across her gown, green eyes set into a gray face. Almost instantly a second picture transposed itself on top.

One of my earliest gifts had been a bound set of Scribner's Classics. They were, like my fishing knife, possessions of great value. I polished the spines, arranged them in my own order, changing them whenever I felt inspired. Treasure Island, Kidnapped, The Boys King Arthur, Robin Hood and half a dozen others. At first, my parents had taken turns reading to me, but then, as I'd grown, I'd ventured through them on my own. The illustrations--painted by N.C. Wyeth at his commissioned best--leapt out at me in fine detail and sumptuous color.

From hours of intent gazing, I knew every turn of muscle, every flight of arrow, and glint of steel. I could recite the captions below each plate from memory, and one in particular always, always drew me to it. It was of Robin Hood dying. Death, like cruelty, was a mystery that I had pondered with no understanding.

In the illustration Robin was leaning against the headboard drawn and gray. His hair was long. He was preparing a final arrow to be launched through an open window beside his bed. There was no target, simply a last flight of feather and shaft deep into the forest, but there was something in his face though, a look that I figure Mr. Wyeth must have drawn and redrawn a lot to have gotten it so perfectly. Robin knew. It was his time, and with that arrow his spirit would also fly.

Right then I pictured Clarisse sitting wizened, but dignified, in her bed. She was preparing herself the way she had that morning, smoothing her hair and bedcovers, and the metaphor I created as I stood with Father and Jethro was crystal clear. I saw her dying, just like Robin Hood. Very soon she would launch her own form of arrow and her spirit would fly, and with it all the bitter cussing, the bruises, the anger and pain that Maggie felt, would also fly away and never return.

But I would be wrong with that metaphor. She was not ready. Maybe it was what Father had said, Clarisse had been a fighter her whole life. I hadn't seen it in her face in the dim light of the room that morning. The shadows had obscured her resolve.

Cranes

My first days of lessons with Mai Lin were like the wooden doll from Russia that my mother kept upon her dresser in Burlington. The doll was simple in appearance, a peasant in plain clothing, babushka and sack dress, but upon pulling it apart from the middle, one found tucked within another and another, an assortment that lead deeper towards a mystifying center. So it was with my lessons. Plain and simple in appearance, they pulled me further into my own inner spaces. At every curve of the path Mai's directives remained clear in my memory.

I also began to understand exactly what Maggie had meant by work. Mai took my education seriously and kept me moving at a brisk pace from the moment we arrived each morning to the moment we finished and tea was ready. Then everything slowed to a tempo that paralleled the unhurried water and air about us. We would sit on our own pillows and Mai would tell of birds and wind and imperial China.

"Six movements you learn first. Same breath, different movement. Three pushing, three circles. Very easy. You already learn Song of Rising and Falling Hands. Need only to learn other five. Must relax in all of them. Not think. Keep knees bent, not go over toes. You ready?"

"Okay, Mai. I can do that," I responded with as much optimism as I could muster.

"Okay, show me what you learn the other day. Very slow." I tugged on my memory, set my feet apart, and closed my eyes halfway. I drew the breath deep into my belly, pushing it out into a ball as my hands rose.

"Let fingers go loose." After a few breaths the pattern began to fill me again, and I floated along with my rising and sinking hands. "Good, now let body rise and sink with breath." I straightened up, making myself taller and dropped into a crouch. "No, no, body too stiff and drop too low. Feel like balloon drifting up and down with hands."

I tried again, concentrating, wanting very much to get it right, trying very hard to relax, which I was beginning to understand was not a good way to actually relax.

"Okay, Mr. Student, next lesson. Now we learn to push tree over. Very easy. You watch." Mai lifted her hands with a deep, slow breath and pushed slowly against an invisible tree, sinking lightly. When her arms were fully extended, I realized where I had seen the movement before. Maggie-- in those first moments when I had spied her on her own porch, and that is why it flowed so easily for me that morning. It was already etched in memory. I imitated Mai perfectly.

"You fool Mai? Do this before? You professional?"

"No, Ma'am." I grinned and was instantly sorry that I'd forgotten how to address her again.

"Not <u>Ma'am</u>," But I heard the laughter in her voice.

"I know, Mai. I remember."

"Okay, so you do this now like Mr. Professional. Relax body, close eyes and only feel feet. Feel streams of water bubbling up from ground into feet. You understand?"

"I think so, Mai." It was a strange picture to imagine when she instructed me, but when I closed my eyes and slipped after some minutes into the slow echo of pulling the little tree towards me and pushing it away, the sensation was there. At first it was merely a tingling, a mild, almost imperceptible pulsing, but with each breath it grew, until it felt like tiny currents of warm water percolating into my feet, through my legs and out to my fingertips. I tried to give my attention over to it and think of nothing else.

I could never tell quite how long, how many cycles of breath, I drifted through in those first days and lessons with Mai. In the beginning my mind flickered with myriad objects that I became better at snaring with my butterfly net and hauling away. And each day my breath drew me like a siren into its caverns until I succumbed gently to its sounds and rhythms. Then Mai would announce that tea was ready.

After filling balloons and pushing trees, I was taught how to draw invisible strings from the air, push columns to the side, polish tall mirrors, and finally, on the sixth day, to hold, oh so lightly, a small ball that I circled like a magician's globe in front of me. Each of the movements carried with it the distinctive sensation of flowing current and was sung to the entrancing tune of my own breath.

Near the end of the week, I began to feel an odd sense of privilege. The knowledge that Maggie, Mai, and I were sharing something so honored and old made me feel special. I was also pretty certain not too many other Carolina boys had learned these things, and with that pride came responsibility. I would do it well.

Each lesson was followed by a familiar routine: Mai would bring our cups, and the three of us would chat about whatever presented itself beyond her deck. Some days she would offer glimpses of her life in China-- gathering squash from the fields in the fall, planting seeds in the spring, and drying fruit in the summer sun. Mai was a superb story teller, and through her curious version of English I learned of General Tsao, The Yellow Emperor, and the great Shaolin Temples of the past. My first excursion to another country came through Mai Lin's eyes and voice.

One morning Mai even attempted to explain how molecules of electricity worked, but from her accent and my lack of chemistry, the lesson remained unclear.

Afterwards Maggie and I would wend our way back through the dunes with sweet tangerines, occasional laughter, and casual conversation. It was there that I learned more of the chapters of her life: How her father was a curdled memory of alcohol and neglect, how he had abandoned them when Skeeter was born. I learned that the triangular scar on her arm came from him demonstrating in a drunken rage how to iron his shirts correctly. I listened to how Skeeter had fallen one day and not gotten up, and how Maggie cared for her family by herself. Each walk added fragmented answers to my self imposed question, "Who are the Silvers?"

On Friday, after I had been taught the last of what Mai called, The Six Winds in the House, Maggie and I were walking through the dunes and I asked her what she did in the screened space while I was learning my lessons.

She answered with pride, "Well, I'm learnin' my own lessons. Right now, I'm doin' the Eight Strands of the Brocade." That sounded mysterious enough and stirred my ever-present curiosity. In truth, I was hoping she might show me some of it. Feeling like a veteran, I reasoned that if I could learn my own six movements, then eight shouldn't be that hard. I also wanted very much to be sharing anything with the girl walking along the path next to me.

"Okay, so what's a brocade, and is it hard to learn?" I shot a tangerine missile wickedly close to her ear.

She tossed another in an arc over her head, not looking back to see if it found its mark. "Well, a brocade is a beautiful piece of cloth, and I've been working on it for about six months now. I still have a few problems getting it right." That stopped me mid-stride.

"Six months? You've been doing eight little movements for six months? How long does this stuff take to learn?"

She turned and looked directly at me with a serious expression. "Drew, Mai has been doing this her whole life and says she still finds small things that she needs to correct. And you can't think about your mistakes cuz' you're trying not to think. You're always working to get it right, but not thinking on it. Kind of a puzzle, huh?"

"Kind of an impossible puzzle, if you ask me. I don't get it at times. I mean, if I think about not thinking about it, like when I'm supposed to be relaxing, then I remember that I'm thinking about it."

We rounded Ensign Bill's and I skipped up along her side. She looked at me and told me the secret that I was just beginning to understand. "But if you let yourself go, if you just drift into it like a stream, then you don't have to think at all."

Suddenly I knew that being in that place--that tranquil stream where she didn't have to think, where pain was forgotten, where her drifting moods melted away and warm currents flowed, where no one shrieked at her--that was where Maggie truly wanted to be.

***

For the first time in more than a week Donny and I were sitting at the kitchen table having lunch. I'd managed to eat at different times and quickly enough to avoid having to share that meal with him over the course of the last seven days. Dinner was a mandatory social function that neither of us could ever miss, even with the best of excuses, but lunch was something we could come in and fix ourselves, or politely ask Nina May for, if she was there and in a good mood. We'd both happened into her kitchen at the same time, and Nina May being in good humor, prepared two egg salad sandwiches, chips, and milk for us.

Donny hadn't been exactly nice to me over the week, but ever since he learned that I was teaching Skeeter to fish his picking on me had become a lot less physical.

"Where the heck have you been cuttin' off to every day, Squirt?" I wasn't sure whether Little Peckerhead had become an appellation of the past, or my older brother didn't want to incur Nina May's wrath right there in her kitchen, but Squirt was certain more pleasant to my ears-- especially since I'd summoned up the courage to ask Georgie Marovich what a peckerhead was, and he described in full detail what body part I'd been called all summer.

"Nowhere special, here and there." This was my version of it's my business and not yours, the original version being a bit too dangerous to say outright.

"Yeah, so where exactly is here and there? You've been leaving and coming back every morning just in time to swim with Dad." And I had been doing just that because I'd contracted to tell all that I'd been learning at Mai Lin's. It was part of our agreement, and I wanted to share it with him. I also wanted to catch every wave possible that was forming over the sand bar in the days that we had remaining.

"I've been playing with Pooh, and Ricky Morley, and visiting with Jethro, that kind of stuff." Donny was usually pretty good at figuring out not only when I was fibbing, but how to torture almost anything out of me. This time, however, he looked at me with his tough-guy expression, trying to bore holes through me with his eyes, and I just stared back. I saw my hands pushing against a small tree, my breath filling into my stomach, and Donny sure as heck couldn't tell what I was thinking about.

"You boys finish your lunch, so I can get to finishin' my pie." Nina May was scowling seriously, neutralizing any intentions Donny might have had to torture me. Both of us took huge bites, and through mayonnaise and egg mumbled, "Yessim," in unison.

Nina May was rolling out a bottom crust for a pecan pie when Donny asked her something I'd wondered about often enough myself. "Nina May, did you really have nine kids in your family?"

"Yes, indeedy. I did." The pride was easy to hear. "They's only six of us now, though. Three's with Jesus."

Donny nodded, chewing on egg salad and Nina May's answer at the same time. "How'd they die?" Being older, I guess, made Donny a little surer of himself so he could ask such things.

"Well, two of 'em was older'n me and 'jes died of bein' old, and my brother Timothy died long time ago." It grew quiet in the kitchen.

"How'd he die?" Donny asked.

I saw the rolling pin slip with a small twitch. She left it on the counter and pushed both hands into the small of her back to lift herself up and face us. She pulled out the third chair at the end of the table, sat down with a small groan, and looked right at us.

"You really want to know, Master Donnell?" Nina May, and only Nina May, got to call him that one.

"Yes, Ma'am, I do." Both of us did.

She took off her glasses, and in turns, rubbed her eyes with her knuckles as if to clear away a layer of fog that had settled there. She exhaled and sort of drifted inside herself. "Well…my Timothy was younger'n me by three years, an' I think it was about when I was five, I'd decided that he was mine to raise. We all sort watched over each other, but Timothy was special to me. I helped feed him, an' bathe him, and helped him get his clothes on 'til he learnt it himself. An' nobody messed with that boy because they knew how I could get." She pursed her lips up in a sly smile because she knew that we were both quite aware of how she could get. "He was a smart boy and laughed all the time, always getting' in trouble with pranks an' tomfoolery, but he minded me."

"We had a farm up near Marrotsville back then, up in the mountains. We worked it with two other families, so there was kids and yard animals everywhere, all the time. I remember mostly the dust in summer and it bein' awful cold in the winter, but we was thankful 'cuz we had a good house an' no leaks.

"Well, one year, after Marshall Hudson asked me to marry him, an' I gave him my yesses, a bad thing happened." Nina May stopped and looked at her hands, which shook slightly as she rubbed them slowly in her lap. "I guess I must've been about nineteen, cuz Timothy was sixteen, I remember that. I was livin' bout two miles away in a cabin that Marshall'd built, little room made out of logs. That man was about the worst with tools as you'd ever see. Cabin had holes like my flour sifter. Well, that fall we heard there'd been problems over in Marrotsville. Someone'd broken through the back of Barman's Supply an' made off with a bag of barley an' two of rice, an' word got round that my Timothy'd been in on it. He was always cuttin' an' jokin' with folks, so he was first to catch blame for things, but I knew it wasn't him. He didn't do that kind of stuff. He was a good boy. An' everyone knew a man would've needed an ox to haul off those three sacks and Timothy sure didn't have no ox.

"One evenin' Marshall an' I heard they were comin' to talk to him about it an' so, bein' a bit skinnier those days, I ran over to the farmhouse fast." Nina May stopped, and the only sound was the shortness in her breath and a small wave that pitched itself up the slope along the beach.

"When I got there, they'd already tied his hands. His head was all busted up an' bleeding, an' they were pushing him into the back of their car. It gets kind of hard rememberin' it, but I know I ran at them screamin'. I tried to scratch one of em' with my nails an' got my fingers smashed for it." I glanced over and saw Donny gripping the lower ledge of the table like he wanted to rip it off and start hitting things in the kitchen. It scared me seeing his face that way.

"They took my Timothy away." Nina May stopped. Her eyes had lost their focus.

"Did they have a trial and send him to jail." This came from me. I asked it as nicely as I could, but I had to know. I pictured it like I'd seen in movies and television.

Nina May's eyes focused gently on me, and she said very evenly, "They told us a week later that he hung himself in his cell that same night."

None of us talked. Donny didn't want to ask any more questions, and though I wanted to ask if her hands had shaken at Miss Millie's from those memories, I knew I couldn't. Nina May lifted herself slowly back up and went back to her dough. I could tell that Donny was sad and angry. I think we both wished right then that we could fly around the earth and turn the time back--just like Superman did for Lois Lane. We wanted to change it all somehow. Nina May bent to her crust. Just before she pressed it into the pie tin, she rubbed her fingers, trying to get the current flowing through them once more.

Jack Brennan stood up in the longboat, swaying back and forth with the ragged swell. He swore a blue streak to himself when he heard what Angelo'd found thirty feet below the surface. Then, like the crowd on the pier, he almost started crying. That would have been for the first time in forty years, he thought.

It seemed like it was all happening too fast, spinning with too much velocity inside his overly-tired mind. Two people. Two friends he'd known his whole life, one of whom he would miss like family. His deputy was busted up like a rag doll in the hospital, and he'd been driving around the whole damn county helping terrified people and checking damaged property for way too many hours.

Shit! Another thought sprang into in his tired head. How was he going to inspect something thirty feet under water? Probably meant the State Police would need to be brought in. Equipment he didn't know a thing about would need to be trucked down; photographers, reporters, and a huge goddamn mess. He wiped his head with the palm of his hand and then swore again, this time right out loud. Maybe, with some luck, they could get the gears into neutral on that thing and haul it out on those big wheels.

Goddamn that girl. She closes her mouth tighter than a goddamn clam.

Then Jack Brennan remembered something else, a small detail he'd overlooked with the storm, and the deaths, and his damned deputy. 'Christ! She's got a younger brother.' He'd forgotten about the boy completely. 'And he's crippled. Goddamn sonofabitch!' He'd need to send someone around to get him into foster care, and that meant more paperwork. He swore again.

The sheriff didn't realize that he needn't have sworn so much about Skeeter being neglected. While he stood in the longboat beyond the pier, Skeeter and I were in my room. We had just finished reading the letters together.

***

In addition to wind, sand, and water as expected events in Nags Head, there was Jean Gray's end-of-the-summer party. They were as annual as her petunias, and she tended to them with more care than any flower she'd ever stuck in the ground. In truth, though the name implied that those social events were solely hers, she always shared the credit with Father. Rightfully so, because he created the most delectable foods imaginable, and each year attempted to outdo the previous one with greater gastronomic prowess.

Father, as a true Southern Gentleman, believed that a man's refinement was measured by how precisely he mixed Mint Juleps and how thinly he sliced a Smithfield Ham. My mother, I had come to understand, really enjoyed the autocratic power of assembling her guest list almost as much as the event itself. She believed that any person who mistakenly crossed her at any time during the summer deserved the social homicide of not being invited to her grand event. She would scribble and scratch off names for hours and anticipate the mailing of those invitations with a sort of malicious delight.

For Donny and me The Party of '58 was an event fashioned from bittersweet ingredients.

Our impending departure from Nags Head was something neither one of us was looking forward to. It never was, but this summer was the worst. We each had our different reasons: I had been walking with Maggie each morning to Mai Lin's, and the notion of leaving that euphoric setting to return to the mundane world of sixth-grade was weighing heavily on my young spirit. In my comings and goings I had also failed to notice a shy, but blossoming, infatuation with MaryEllen Brewster on Donny's part, and that was his reason for not wanting to leave. His infatuation wasn't easy to see. First, my brother hated cats, and was so coolly independent, that the image of him strolling along with MaryEllen and Sir Peesalot,--Ricky Morley's name for it, not mine-- was as foreign to me as curried shrimp. In any case, neither of us wanted to leave.

It was Saturday, and the grand party was to take place the following afternoon. It was also the tenth morning that I would skip along through the dunes and be taught some new manner of moving and breathing. As usual, I was greatly excited at the prospect.

The dawn sun hadn't poured in through the eastern windows to awaken me that morning. It was windy and gray, and I had slept later than usual. My mother, on the other hand, was already up and swirling about in a nervous frenzy. As I padded sleepily towards the bathroom, I met her hurrying along the upstairs hallway in her robe peering out windows, shaking her head, and saying fiercely, "How dare it get cloudy." I smiled, and as reassuringly as I could and forecasted that it would be beautiful the following afternoon. I could tell that only helped her mood minimally.

"It has to." This sounded like one of Moses' commandments. "We have forty-three guests, two bartenders, two servers, a huge tent, and four Mexican mariachis arriving at three o'clock.

"Mexican what?"

"Mariachis. It was your father's idea. Musicians. They're coming all the way from Florida with guitars and instruments and who knows what." She was in a tizzy.

"Wow. That sounds neat."

"Neat is not what I want, Little. I want traditional. I want roast beef and lobster and martinis. I want Benny Goodman. Your father is in some new cooking phase and has decided mariachis and margaritas are somehow more appropriate for the most important social function of the century."

This was all going way over my head. I could only guess that my father's vision of southern hospitality extended further south than we had thought.

I left the great cottage, with its small storms brewing inside, and found Maggie at Ensign Bill's. She stood with one palm pushing toward the clouds, the other toward the sand at her toes, reversing them in the slow breathing pattern I had, by now, come to know quite well.

We lopped off at her usual pace and her usual nonsense rhymes drifting into the air. After a minute she asked me a typical Maggie question. "Drew?"

"Hmmm?"

"Have you ever tried to really feel the sand with your feet, feel the energy in it?"

"Like around noon when they're sizzling like barbecued wieners?"

"I'm serious, Drew. You can, you know. You can feel it."

"Well, I think I felt something coming into them the other day when I was practicing on the deck. Wasn't in the sand though."

"It doesn't have to be, but it's good that you felt it."

"All right, I answered your question. Now I've got one."

"Good. I always like your questions." And that made my morning brighten as if the sun were actually shining.

"How about two then?"

"Let's see if I can answer the first one; if so, I'll try the second." I knew she was grinning wickedly up ahead of me.

I had been thinking about both of my questions for nearly a week, and the first one I was pretty sure she wasn't going to have an answer to, but I had to ask it anyway. "Maggie, why do you think people do mean stuff just cuz somebody's different?" It was not yet apparent to me how much my parents had shielded me with their own force fields of invisible protection.

Maggie didn't hesitate, and I realized she'd pondered the same question often herself. She had her answer ready. "Well, I'm pretty certain they're scared, Drew. And that's what makes 'em mean."

"Scared?" That didn't sound right at all. "What would they be scared of?"

"That your second question?"

"No. My second is… what's all this called? This breathing and The Six Winds and all."

Maggie stopped at the entrance to the bamboo curtain and whispered back to me, "Well. The answer to both your second questions is that people are scared of bein' hurt and want to make themselves feel bigger and all those people they're hurting feel smaller. It's their way of creating power. And the Chinese name for what we're doing is chi gung."

Between mariachis, margaritas, and chi gung I was adding on a lot of foreign words to my vocabulary that morning. "What?"

"Chi gung. Energy work. That current you feel in your feet and hands? It's called chi. It's in everything."

"That's sounds a lot like how my mother talks about God."

She contemplated this for a moment as we slipped through the passage into the garden. Then with a little hiss she said, "Well, maybe that's what it is, but it sure as hell isn't the same as what my Momma calls God."

"Chi flow in water and air, and in good tea." Mai had overheard the last part of our conversation and was standing on her back porch with her arms outstretched like a picture of Jesus. For the first time since I'd known her, she was dressed in something other than shiny black pajamas. She had on the most beautiful long dress and short jacket I'd ever seen, with the brightest reds and greens found on the planet. There were dragons, a tiger, a tree with tiny blossoms, and something that looked suspiciously like an egret with long legs. It fascinated me because I had never seen ornate pictures on cloth before. "Chi in everything." She swung her arm above her head and then motioned us quickly up the stairs and out to the back deck. "Six Winds open streams in body, let chi flow free."

I looked at her jacket and asked, "Mai, why are you so dressed up today?"

She grinned teasingly. "No reason, Mr. Professional. Who knows? Maybe we have company. Ask questions later. You ready to put pieces together?"

"What pieces?"

"Six winds become one today. You do Rising Hands and then Pushing Tree, and so on. Make one out of six. Same big stomach breath. You ready to do that?"

Slowly I said, "Yes, I am." With patchy confidence I hoped that I was.

"Good, remember no think, just feel. You show me now." I nodded, closed my eyes half way and began. At first Mai instructed me softly, correcting small errors here and there, loosening my shoulders and straightening my back. Then I was floating through the six cycles of inhales and exhales merging them into one fluid movement.   Like a young bird, I was on my own. My eyes slowly closed.

Mai told me later that it usually took twenty-one days. A person had to work at it that many times before the energy flowed freely like it did for me that morning. Perhaps, as Mai had said, I had less doodles being young. Perhaps it was the strength of where we were, the movement of wind and water and sand. Maybe I was just lucky, but for whatever reason, my fingers fluttered like leaves with it that morning. My legs and arms filled with it, and I stopped thinking and drifted fully into the streams.

The jingling of sea glass and tin, of hollow bamboo, the waves, the wind, and shrills of birds, and the rustling of reeds all blended into a single song. My feet, hands, and body melted into the river around me. I drifted with the current.

Slowly, ever so, I became aware of different sounds--noises that I dreamily felt weren't issuing from Mai Lin's garden or the water or surrounding air. They were unsolicited echoes, memories calling hazily from places in the past. They were wrong, and they were ugly. Then I recognized the all-too-familiar desperate wheezes, the agony of struggling breath.

"Donny!" I screamed. My eyes flew open. The deck was empty. Mai Lin was nowhere to be seen. I raced into the kitchen and looked into the side room, then out to the back porch. In the garden below I saw all three of them. Mai was kneeling, her red dragons and green tigers all bunched up around her knees. Maggie was kneeling on the far side, and in the middle, my brother Donny was thrashing like a pinned serpent on the gravel path, his face an ugly blue and purple.

"Sit him up." Mai ordered evenly, no hint of distress. They lifted together, and Donny was sitting.

Mai lifted his chin and looked carefully at his face. Then she began pushing her fingers into places along Donny's shoulders and neck in vigorous, tight circles. I stood paralyzed for the moment. "Daughter, remember Kung tsui?"

"Yes, Mai," Maggie's reply was nearly as calm as Mai's question, but not quite. She began massaging and pressing her own fingertips into places on Donny's left forearm and above his elbow. She moved across to his right arm.

"Good, good." Mai's fingers were now flying like a concert pianist's, pushing deeply and precisely into locations around Donny's shoulders and chest. Hearing me leap down the stairs two at a time, she turned and smiled as if we were casually sipping tea on the deck and said, "Ah, Drew, you back?"

I was terrified. "Mai, we've to get him to the cottage. He's needs special medicine." Mai continued unheeding. I pleaded again and then yelled frantically, "We've got to get him to the doctor."

"No, we don't." It came quietly. It came from Donny. His head was hung low, his chin resting nearly on his chest, but the wheezing, liquid gurgle of breath, the horrible sound that had crept in among all the celestial sounds of the Six Winds, had ceased.

"I'm okay, Little Guy." Donny pulled a full breath into his lungs, raised his head, and looking around at the garden, stole my best vocabulary word of the summer, "Wow!"

"Okay, we have tea now."

Somehow, she had worked magic. She had known exactly what was needed and how it needed to be done. Donny's breath had returned in a few short moments. There had been no medicine, no inhaler, no long hours of lying quietly and waiting while the liquid that filled his lungs receded like a slow tide. There had been merely the pressure of her fingers, and for a couple of Outer Banks boys, that was pure magic.

I believe that Mai Lin's tea that particular morning was the best any of us had ever tasted. It was accompanied by drifting flights of pelicans and gulls, shore waves, and a warm wind. No one said a word until our cups were completely empty. The sun began to break through the grayness, and Donny sat watching every shadow and shaft of light. I think he was even more impressed with Mai's face and her dress than the view over the water. I saw him secretly glancing at her. In his eyes I saw astonishment and a lot of questions. I also saw respect, as much as if he was sitting right next to Y.A. Tittle himself.

Finally, Mai patted his knee. "So, you Drew's brother? Donny? He tell me about you." My manners had lapsed entirely in the excitement, and I'd forgotten the introductions.

"Yes M-Ma'am. D-Donny MacLaren." That was a first in a long time, my older brother stuttering from nervousness.

She grinned, patted his knee again, and said, "Not Ma'am, Donny, also not Mrs. Lin. You call me Mai Lin, or just Mai if you please."

He smiled back--a little uncertainly--and said, "Okay, Mai." Then rubbing his palm in a slow circle around his chest, basking in the absence of congestion and pain, he said quietly, almost in a whisper, "Thank you, Mai."

She clapped her hands together excitedly. "Oh. My joy, Donny. Not good to be without breath. Your Fei ching all blocked up. I clear. Medicine very old, but still good you see. I forget to tell you that I'm doctor?" At that, the dam burst and all of us began laughing and talking at once.

Like a magnolia unfolding into soft, fragrant petals, Mai opened small pieces of herself that morning, stories that she hadn't told any of us before, even Maggie. We learned that she had been a doctor in two worlds, taught the traditions of her country by her mother, and by way of the British she had become a student of Western medicine. We learned, in total astonishment, that her parents and sister had been killed by Japanese soldiers in a field next to her home. She had watched from a hidden place in the trees. She told us how she had fled to Taiwan, to Baltimore, and eventually to the little cottage where she now lived alone. My view of Mai changed that morning. She was no longer the petite, eccentric woman who spoke rapidly and taught me about birds and breath. She was still Mai who prepared delicious tea, but she grew somehow larger and sadder, like a furrowed field that filled slowly with green shoots.

I often wonder what tumbled about in Donny's mind that morning as we sat on her deck. It was obvious that he was astounded that I was so closely connected with the likes of Maggie Silver and the imaginary Chink Lady. It was, in reality, the image of Mai Lin as a sinister witch that had induced his most violent asthma attack yet. It was, as Maggie had spoken of earlier that morning, the fear of the unknown. He had snuck into her garden steeped in curiosity and terror, and that fear had caused his lungs to constrict.

For me that morning there was a peculiar blend of delight that our triad was now four--and a smidgen of resentment that our secret circle had been penetrated. In due course I realized that it was as it should be.

After receiving a warm hug and kiss from Mai, Maggie returned alone without complaint on the path that morning. Her obligations called. Donny and I sat in Mai's kitchen while she bustled about, pouring and mixing from jars and vials in a steadfast whirlwind. She consulted her books, and I saw my first examples of pictographic language--the script looking like elegant bird scratchings to me. My questions really percolated when she told me that it read in the opposite direction. The result of her bustling was a tincture of dark liquid that she poured into a small bottle, corked with an eyedropper and presented as a gift to Donny. Two drops a day he was told and his asthma would stay suppressed. Just before Donny and I walked back through the dunes together, Mai talked to us about the foods that we liked to eat.

Mai never told me how she knew Donny would be there, but she did. Later I suspected that it had come to her in a dream, but that day it was a mystery. She was waiting for him patiently, standing on the back porch, looking, as Donny later described, like a short, fiery sorceress in her red and orange silk. It was that very sight that caused his breath to shorten and the fluid to enter his lungs.

***

In the end Jean Gray's party of 1958 was the best yet. The Mexican mariachis got a flat tire, no doubt due to the weight of four very large bodies and the most amazing array of instruments, sequined pants, jackets, and huge hats anyone in that part of North Carolina had ever seen, but they did arrive. The music was loud and wonderful, and only outdone by my father's now famous grilled snapper with Vera Cruz sauce, chicken mole poblano, and blended margaritas. The best part still lingers. I can picture it easily in all its innocent elegance. Right there on the front porch of the great cottage, with the sun shining into fiery waves, and all the adults chattering away in little groups, Donny danced with MaryEllen Brewster. It was a slow Mexican love song, and it was almost as sweet as the seamless sounds of The Six Winds. Almost.

I sat quietly on the bench in the corner with my legs tucked up under me and watched it all. It seemed like most of the adult population of Nags Head was in attendance, all the people who influenced my life and the lives of my peers. The Morleys, the Tyners, Widow Harris, Zach Jensen, Mr. and Mrs. May, and Miss Millie. They congregated on our porch or mingled under the huge tent pitched in the sand out front. The tent fascinated me because it hadn't any walls and was supported only by pipes that looked just like the ones under the cottage. Everyone laughed and talked and spewed opinions like politicians. Recipes and points of view were exchanged like baseball cards. Even Captain J. arrived late in the afternoon. He moved about, shaking everyone's hand, making most of the men wince with his grip. He yelled in Spanish to the mariachis and called out to each and every person in his booming voice, patting them heartily on the back and only grew quiet when someone handed him a beer and a big plate of food. Later he came and sat with me.

With a mouthful of fresh strawberry ice cream—and a motion with his spoon towards the waves-- he told me, "You know, Lad, that sea gives us our weather. It is a mystery of God, no? The water out there heats and cools and stirs the clouds like a giant propellers all around the earth. There is a desert in Africa, the biggest on earth…" and I learned that afternoon how hurricanes came to be.

When the mariachis were at their loudest, when everyone was dancing and conversations had built to a swollen crescendo, Father handed me two towering plates of food and two big casseroles to carry to Skeeter and Maggie's. As I made my way down the front steps on my third trip across the sand, I heard Mrs. May whispering to Sean Tyner's mother. They were standing just inside the tent near the skirted table with all the bottles of whiskey and gin and other drinks I didn't know a thing about. The barman was dressed in a white jacket and bowtie and had on little white gloves, which I thought was pretty funny because I knew he was barefoot behind the bar. Father had rigged up a long electric cord and written instructions on how to blend up all the drinks the barman had no clue how to make.

Just like her son, Mrs. Eliza May seemed to be looking down her nose at things pretty much all the time. She had on the biggest necklace of green stones I'd ever seen and more colors of paint around her eyes and mouth than my flying sheets. She glanced towards the cottages on the north side and set three jeweled fingers on Mrs. Tyner's arm. It was a little movement of snobbish confidentiality. I heard her whisper, "They're trash, Marcy. Soil up this nice beach front property in my humble opinion." Sean's mom looked in embarrassment from Mrs. May to the barman, who was pretending not to hear. Mrs. May kept on, "It's because of that man of hers. He was a piece of work, wasn't he? Hated her through and through. Detested her the moment he returned from the war. He knew that child wasn't his. Can you imagine? I mean, I know he was pure trash. Drank himself stone cold every night, but he had his reasons. Wouldn't touch her after that. That's what I heard. And that, Marcy" she tapped her fingers on Mrs. Tyner's arm and declared with snooty authority, "that is the why she's gone insane."

I pretended to fiddle with the foil on the casserole in order to linger and eavesdrop a bit more, but the only added part was Sean's mom saying quietly, "Well, he must've touched her at least once more, Liz, because they had the boy. I think that little one is as cute as a button; he always waves to me when I take my walks. I feel sorry him sitting up there by himself. They seem to do well enough, but I really think that child ought to be a ward of the state."

As I walked north I thought about those purloined words. They seeped in and pestered me. I didn't know it then, but they would tag along next to me like bothersome

siblings until I solved the mystery behind them. I also
wondered as I trudged north, what a ward was.

The three of us, Maggie, Skeeter, and I, sat on their
front porch and watched the sky change slowly over the
water. We didn't talk about the party or the peculiar notions
of adults. We just listened to the songs of the mariachis and
staccato laughter rising and falling with the breeze. The
songs were in a language none of us understood, and we
tasted foods none of us had ever eaten before. We decided,
without actually saying it, that we would talk about what
was going to be right and good in our futures. The three of
us contrived ingenious ways to get Skeeter his own surf rod
and a good spot by the waves. Maggie promised to teach me
the Eight Strands, and we all made promises to each other
that made us feel warm inside.

That night, when the tide was low, and all the guests
had drifted away with so many "Thank Yous" and "It was
glorious, Darlings," my family sat together in the living
room. Alex wasn't there, of course, and we missed him
terribly, but I think for the first time Momma was okay with
it. She seemed happy for the right reasons, not because her
party had been the most successful event of the season, or
that margaritas were now her favorite cocktail, but because
she was there with two of her three boys. And I believe she
finally recognized were going to grow up, no matter how
much she tried to blockade it.   Momma had also seen
Donny dancing with MaryEllen Brewster.

For a few minutes the only sounds to be heard were
the light winds and the heartbeat of the ocean, and then
Donny and I made our pronouncements. I stood and

announced that I was going to be eleven in less than two weeks, and it was high time that everyone stopped calling me Little. Then both of us politely demanded to be vegetarians.

Later that night, when all the lights in the great cottage were out, Donny came to my room and sat on my bed. We talked about a lot, about things we knew the answers to and those we didn't. I told him about what I had learned, about my new friends, and even how Charlie looked as he left Skeeter's bucket and swam home. I told him about Maggie and Mai, and about Clarisse.

He told me he was proud of me for being Skeeter's friend, and he told me about himself. I listened and found out that we were still brothers. As he rose to leave, I asked, "Donny, how'd you know where I was today?"

"Hell, that was easy, Drew. You been smellin' like 'em for ten days straight. Tangerines peels."

***

Father, Donny, and I performed a short re-christening ceremony on The Hopeshefloats and then took her for a second maiden voyage the afternoon before we were going to leave for the summer. We'd all decided that it would have been a sin--or maybe just really sad--for her to just sit in the garage all those months and not feel any water pushing past her hull. We'd also decided she needed a new name because she wore two new coats of oil and varnish about her woodwork.

We were also certain Father had never really liked the original name anyway. Donny and Alex had thought it up when Father had bought her from Miss Millie's friend,

Clara, before she'd died. Donny shook up a can of soda for three minutes and sprayed the bow with a dark, sugary mess. Then he christened her in his most official voice while Father decorated the new name on the stern with a small brush and stencil. <u>Our Aliento</u>. It was a combination of Father's and mine, and meant our breath in Spanish.

Getting <u>Our Aliento</u> rigged and into the water required rolling her down on the old trailer that had more rust than paint on its surface. Father kept it stored under the right side of the cottage, and salt had frozen all the moving parts like Elmers, so he and Donny spent the better part of the morning taking the wheels off and re-greasing the axles.

By the time we were ready to raise the sails, it was past lunchtime, so Momma brought us a tackle box full of fruit and sandwiches for our voyage. We didn't receive that box until she'd instructed us in complete detail on how to avoid storms, sharks, ships, fog, and a variety of other maritime perils. We assured her we would be extra vigilant, and then set to the final preparations of <u>Our Aliento's</u> maiden journey.

There was a wonderful precision with which we left the shore that afternoon, something we knew was important. We couldn't see them, but we could be certain the eyes of Nags Head were watching us from inside all the cottages along Cottage Row, observing our launch like Olympic judges. But, to our credit, it was the best yet, ten of ten. The wind was warm and steady, coming from three points of our port bow. I hauled on the jib, Donny the main, and Father pushed us off and hiked himself easily into the stern to take the tiller. <u>Our Aliento</u> heeled over lightly and sped away from the beach on a perfect tack. We rounded the sandbar and set a course south. The wind was off our port stern. A five-foot swell rolled abeam. Donny and I fed out both sheets, the sails filled evenly, and we skipped across the lines in swift, rolling motions.

"Well, that was a launch to be proud of, men." I loved it when Father called us that. "She likes the new name. That's certain." He was leaning against the cushions in the stern, pilot sunglasses set low on his nose, patting the tiller. "Feels like she handles better than I remember. Donny, want to take over while I get us something to drink?"

Donny leaped to the task.

Beyond the jib I watched the sky. It had been a humid morning with a heavy mugginess settling in thick layers over the strand. In the west, the sky looked hazy, almost yellow, with an electric tension to it. I knew there would be a storm sometime during the afternoon; it was simply a matter of when.

Our objective was the opening at Oregon Inlet. Father had estimated a little more than an hour to get there with the good wind at our backs, an hour of picnicking and exploring, and then an hour and a half to return. That was without any unusual circumstances.

After a while I began to see the black and white spiral of the Hatteras lighthouse poking up in the distance and the ferry docks inside the inlet closer by. Hanging above the spiral of the cupola, I could see a dark wall beginning to form. With the wind coming from behind us, I expected those clouds would be moving in the opposite direction.

We dropped the sails and the small anchor just inside the inlet. It felt smooth and peaceful after pitching through the swells the previous fifty minutes. The sun--milky in the sky—made the air warm. Father opened the tackle box with our lunches, each wrapped in paper napkins with notes written in Momma's perfect cursive--mine reminding me not to dip my hand in the water lest it be bitten off. Within seconds all three of us looked like hamsters with egg salad and apples ringing our mouths. Father let Donny have half a beer with his sandwich. I was allowed two sips which I turned into gulps. We didn't have to remind each other not to let any of that get to Momma's attention.

It was a fine picnic of men on the sea, a banquet of masculine indulgence and relaxation. The uncertainties of our other world slipped away. Nature, however, as the unpredictable Mother, has ways of changing attire rapidly in that part of the strand. She transforms with a twinkle of her eye. It occurs in noticable, and too often, in unseen ways. Her powerful currents reshape the seafloor in a matter of hours making depth charts obsolete before they've left the store. Winds change and waves rise quickly as if her huge hand is stirring them in a kettle.

As I was swallowing the last bites of lunch, the sky took on an eerie texture. I felt it ripple along the back of my neck and looked at Donny and Father, wondering if they felt it, too. Father was looking towards Hatteras at the wall of thickening clouds that were supposed to be moving away. They weren't, and I knew Father had seen it, but I also knew how much he loved adventure. He could've decided to wait it out inside the inlet, but that was not his way. He popped up, grinning like a schoolboy, and said, "Well, men, what do you say, are we ready for a little race? I think Our

<u>Aliento</u> needs a good challenge. Let's see what she can do with her sails full."

The sunlight disappeared entirely before Donny and I had the anchor hauled aboard and the sails raised. The wind began gusting in short, sharp bursts ahead of the squall, and because Donny had forgotten to tighten and cleat the main sheet, the boom snapped violently from port to starboard as the wind filled the sail. We all ducked just in time, and Donny said, "Sorry" twice as we turned to the north.

Then we were flying in a full run with a powerful wind directly behind us.

There are times of inexplicable magic on the ocean, times when the rare and unusual occur. Both sails were open fully on either side of <u>Our Aliento's</u> mast when Father called out through the spray slicing off the bow, "Gentlemen, we've got company." He was pointing forward, laughing at our companions. "Porpoise!"

I looked east and saw dark streaks speeding parallel to us, thirty or more of them, flying through the waves. They were playing, racing, crossing in front of us, leaping and twisting like men and women on the high trapeze. Suddenly, from some stirring in her great kettle of sky and sea around us, Nature sent a single shaft of sunlight and lit up <u>Our Aliento</u>. The leaping porpoise looked like dancers on a stage. The spotlight held all of us in its beam, while all about us the sky was an ominous gray. Around us a spectrum of colors filled the air. We were inside the rainbow, or at least so close I could have gathered in a cupful of indigo with a sweep of my hand.

We raced in that light until the porpoise veered seaward and we jibed to port and headed toward the cottage. The rain began to pepper us just as we stepped onto the sand. Father announced proudly, "Well, Gentlemen, I think we won. Let's get her on the trailer."

***

The closing of the great cottage at the end of each summer was never a joyous affair. That year for me, especially, it was a somber ritual of sweeping and scrubbing and storing of folded sheets. I said good-bye to Pooh and others friends, spent my remaining time with Mai, and took a wonderful, last Holy Communion with Father. Now the blue Chevy Nomad was laden with suitcases, the doors and shutters of the cottage bolted, and everything sealed like an ancient vault of pharaohs. The final act was always pulling the knife-switch in the garage, severing the lifeline of electrical power. After that, it was done and there was only the rechecking of mechanical items on the car. Like the brass dinner bell, I had one minute.

I ran across to the back side of the Silver cottage. Skeeter and Maggie weren't on the side porch where we usually met. I ran to the front and saw no one. I sprinted desperately to the north side. It was empty also. I stood there for a moment, and all I heard was the wind.

I had never called out for either of them. Mostly because one or the other had always been there, standing or rolling on caster wheels on that side porch. I suppose it was also from the genuine fear that I might have--with my voice--roused the wrong person in Clarisse. I was not about ready to call out this time, even though it was torturing me not to. I turned and walked slowly towards the waiting car.

As I reached the corner of the Harris cottage, I heard Maggie's voice call out softly, "You're not thinking of leavin' and not saying "good-bye" are you?" I spun on my heel. They were there, both of them. Maggie was standing with a brown paper bag in her hands, in the same purple shirt and denim shorts that she had worn the first time I had seen her. Skeeter was on the side bench, legs tucked up in his usual way. I ran to the front steps and down the side. The horn on the Nomad blared once.

Panting from the sprint, I gasped, "I gotta go, and I don't want to."

"We know, Drew. But you go on now. We'll be here waiting for you." Maggie held out the paper bag. It was folded and rolled with a thin pink ribbon tied around it--her hair ribbon. "These are for you. Open them later. They're not much, but..." she smiled that deep smile again and said, "maybe they can be a small part of you."

I hugged Skeeter, who was looking as sad as could be, so I said, "I'll bring us some good comics, Skeeter. We'll read em all together and we'll fish every day next summer, okay?"

He brightened and replied, "Maggie's gonna buy me some new comics, too, when she goes shopping. We can swap when you get back."

The car horn sounded once more, and I stood awkwardly facing her. I had seen her standing in the same place with a tear rolling onto that same purple shirt just four weeks ago. It seemed so much longer than that.

She leaned in towards me, waves of hair brushing my face, and whispered, "Remember what she's taught you, Drew. Practice and use it." She kissed my cheek and it felt like a million sparklers were dancing around that spot, and I wanted to stay right there with her lips on my cheek until the oceans dried to salt. The horn blared a final time.

In the back seat of the Chevy, just before we got to causeway over the inlet, Nina May fell asleep. She began snoring lightly between Donny and me, so I could now do my unwrapping without the whole car watching. I turned myself towards the window and untied Maggie's pink ribbon. Inside I found a carved piece of wood. It was a simple fish shape, but the gills and tail at each end were long and smooth, and wrapped around the center, was a neat ball of brand-new kite string. I imagined Skeeter carefully carving off bits of wood with a kitchen knife that he had searched through kitchen drawers to find.   The gift from Maggie was a tangerine.

I thought about what she'd said about them, "Maybe they can be a part of you." One so durable, the other so fleeting.

I peeled the tangerine and heard Donny start to laugh to himself as the odor of citrus filled the car. I popped one of the segments into my mouth and took a deep breath down into my stomach. I closed my eyes. The juice slid down my throat. I tasted the essence of tang and sugar and understood right then what Mai had tried to teach me about molecules. I felt each one, each atom and charged particle of energy as it flowed through me. Perhaps it was not so fleeting a gift as I had thought. I leaned forward past Nina May's stomach and tossed Donny a section. I took another deep breath and smiled. The air felt full.

Interlude

It wasn't that the events between those two summers were in any way insignificant. They were not, but placed in relative positions within the scale of my young life, they were simply a little less noteworthy, and besides, a full recounting of them adds little to the narrative of Maggie and the course of events that altered all our lives.

The episodes that occurred during my hiatus from Nags Head were more like the assorted items in a certain kitchen drawer that we had in Burlington. Objects were tossed into that drawer in spontaneous ways. Some were more useful than others. Some were hardly used at all. But they all took up their space and added to the general hodgepodge within. So it was with the eight and a half months of my life between those two summers. The experiences were gathered and added to my medley of awareness. And some were clearly more useful than others.

By that autumn I had learned to keenly dislike the phrase "school year," as it seemed to define--or confine like a chain link fence--that entire period of time to the routines and minutes within the classroom. It was as if the school had become the central hub of my existence, and the personal explorations I took so much pleasure in were to be decided upon and designed entirely by others. I had graduated to Burlington Day Middle School, a name forbidding enough in itself, and had to learn quickly to adapt to a hasty schedule of diverse teachers, subjects, and classmates. I was no longer to be guided and comforted by a single mentor. Graham crackers and small cartons of milk were replaced by raucous cafeterias. The familiar cubby that once held my pencil box and thin books was replaced by a misshapen metal locker that, as hard as I tried, never seemed to open easily or remain neat.

Into my drawer of experience I added authentic school dances with crepe paper decor and naked gym showers with older boys, both of which were equally terrifying initially. I added scarred desks with foul language carved like hieroglyphics into the surface. I learned how lunch cards worked and that it was pretty much impossible to be a vegetarian with a rotating menu of Sloppy Joes and fish-sticks. I found out that I was better at math than I thought and that I liked track, because I could do it all on my own. I learned to stretch the muscles of my body. And I learned a great more about bullying.

But always I returned to the Six Winds of the House. I would come home in the afternoon and snack on my own grahams and milk, shuffle up to my room with all my books and close my door. It was there, inside that space and inside my breath, that my reality became manifest. Just like Maggie, that time was precious and it was mine.

I spoke only to my father and, occasionally, to Donny about the fact that I was continuing what I'd been taught. Father, as was his custom, set to researching the subject, because as he'd told me more than once, "the more you understand about something, the better off you are making a decision about it." His readings lead him to the conclusion that I was unquestionably doing something good and thus encouraged me at every step.

I spoke to Mother about it on occasion, she taking a small interest in it, but I sensed that it was not an area she thought was as beneficial as Father, or that it was not going to improve my social position in the small circle of future Yale graduates she selected as my friends.

The events of those eight months slipped by, separated by family celebrations and holidays. My eleventh birthday arrived a week after leaving The Banks. That was a miniature golf excursion with six classmates that bore enough resemblance to total chaos that Mother swore such an event would never occur again in her lifetime. Alex came home from George Washington University for Thanksgiving. Mother doted upon him for five days, asking him all sorts of questions about his girlfriend whom, it appeared, he was quite serious about. Her name was Sarah, and Mother was ecstatic to learn that she was from a refined, and wealthy, Protestant family.

As a result of his one morning with Mai Lin, Donny became very serious about what he ate. Although neither one of us were quite able to adhere to strict vegetarianism, we did eat less meat, and my brother, to everyone's surprise, removed wheat entirely from his diet--it happened to be in the negative column of a short list Mai had written out for him. Nina May's beaten biscuits, he stated, were the only thing he truly missed. Whether it was from his dietary changes, the potion that Mai Lin had prepared, or his mind simply willing it, his asthma became a thing of the past.

I was convinced it came from each and every one of those things.

Unfortunately, Donny was now attending the local high school, leaving me to fend for myself at Burlington Middle. Perhaps because his legacy of indelible coolness still hovered like a specter in the hallways I was not taunted overly much. Not so with many of my classmates. Sixth graders were the youngest and subsequently easiest targets for the ever-present bullies. I kept a low profile and developed the best defensive tactics any boy could, a good sense of humor and fast legs. That was where track came in handy. I ran well. In the beginning it was the half mile. Then I graduated to the mile itself. I found unmistakable similarities between the solitude of long distance running and my practice of Chi Gung. The dominion of breath was essential to both. They complimented one another and each flourished accordingly.

Christmas Eve was overshadowed by Nina May's sudden rush to the hospital. At first the receptionists weren't willing to admit her, and I added the perplexing word segregation to my vocabulary that season. Father grew steely, and the doctors ultimately told us that a minor heart attack had occurred. I sat by her raised hospital bed while most other Carolina boys were proudly gazing at new bicycles and skates. She kept apologizing, and it was the first time in my life that I felt like I took care of Nina May instead of her taking care of me. We talked on and on about past Christmases and how they had felt.

Springtime brought early flowers and the promise of lots of ripe pears on the giant tree in the backyard. I was certain there were more buds than any previous year on that old thing. Mother, seeing the early thaw, jumped at the opportunity to dig in the soil. She donned her gardening gloves, baggy jeans, and wide brimmed hat, cleared the detritus of winter and set huge amounts of bright annuals into the earth about our house. And because Nina May was soon moving about her Burlington kitchen with relative ease again, the world felt as it should be.

Towards the end of April, when the celebrations of May Day and Mother's Day commenced and continued for many days, according to Momma's creed, I gradually began to feel the inexorable pull of warm dune air and salty skin. I saw porpoise leaping weightlessly into the air. On those spring nights I saw all of the intricate details of Nags Head, and they became etched into memory. It was at that time, when life seemed to swell up from the ground and pulse in massive waves into the atmosphere, that my energy work truly blossomed.

Undoubtedly there were other notable pieces that were added to my drawer of experience that year, but like thin coats of patina they were merely supplementary.

The only other item worth noting was Maggie's single page letter. It arrived a week after the New Year. The envelope had been set on my homework desk, propped up like a picture frame for me to open after school. I'd never seen her cursive before, but just like the hand that created it, it was the most beautiful script in the world to me. The letters were smoothly curved with an elegant tilt to right, and for a few moments, I just stared at my own name on the front, and hers on the back.

The letter was written on white, lined school paper and consisted of three paragraphs, short and succinct in Maggie style. The first told of a cold winter with big storms and Clarisse improving a good deal. The second told me that Skeeter was well and that a small bus now took him down to Manteo for school, making her routine much easier. The third paragraph I read a dozen times. She and Mai missed me and set an empty cup on the tray each day in expectation of my return. I was sent hugs and kisses, which prompted me to touch the place on my cheek that Maggie's hair and lips had graced at our parting. That single page was the most wonderful gift of the season, and I folded it carefully and placed it next to the pink ribbon in the M section of the big dictionary on my desk. It told me so much, and yet it was the omissions of that letter that eventually I questioned, why she never mentioned the increasing, and unwanted visitations of the impolite Deputy Curry.

Waves

Most of the folks in Dare County decided immediately that she'd done it. Like inattentive jurors they'd gathered shreds of evidence, right or wrong, and delivered their premature judgments. Momma had also meted out a guilty verdict. I think Skeeter and I might have been the only ones who were dead set positive Maggie hadn't done anything wrong.

Folks reasoned that because Maggie had asked if Skeeter could stay over during the storm, she'd wanted to be alone with her mother, and that struck them as far too convenient. They didn't know that Skeeter and I had been planning sleep-overs for a while. As it turned out Skeeter would need to sleep over for a lot of nights.

That was how we began to figure it out. The night after Big Leo tore up everything, we talked about it in my room. Then I snuck across for the letters.

After Donny had gone back to his room, and everyone in the great cottage was asleep, I went to the Silver cottage and into Clarisse's room. Going into that darkness was the hardest, most terrifying thing I'd ever done in my life.

Skeeter kept his own comics hidden. He had to. It was because Clarisse had come to believe there was something pure evil inside those drawings. She'd gotten it into stuck in her brain somehow-- like all those ideas that slipped in like unwanted thieves to steal her sanity and replace it with madness. Wonder Woman had looked too lascivious one quiet afternoon while Skeeter had been reading on the porch. Clarisse had seen that sexy costume

and ample bosom and promptly flown into a violent rage.
She'd torn the comic to shreds and, proclaimed Wonder
Woman to be a wanton slut, never to be allowed with any of
her Super friends in their cottage again.

So Skeeter secretly pried up two planks behind his
sofa in the living room and made a hidden space for his
collection.

He'd reasoned that if Clarisse could do that, he
could too.

It was what I found under Clarisse's bed, in her own
secret hiding, place that Skeeter and I read together.

There is a curious exception in the annals of comic
book heroes. There is a strength missing amongst all of the
numerous and awesome powers. None of them, as I recall,
ever attained it. They each had their methods of brawn and
speed, weapons of every type, and force-fields of every
form of protection. They had the ability to see within
objects, breathe fire and ice, and they always seemed to be
able to move in some manner through the air with ease. But
none of them had the one power that would give them true
dominance over evil. None of them had the ability to see
into the future.

At the beginning of the summer of 1959, one iota of
that power would have made all the difference in my world.

We never tarried in Burlington once school was out.
Everyone, even my parents, who directed our loading like
dock masters, were anxious to leave. Our departure day
arrived two days after Donny and I finished classes, just
enough time to close up the house and arrange all the food,

clothes, tools, assorted toys, and people into and atop the
Nomad. Off we rolled, looking like an overloaded bus in
Bangkok. That summer I added a bright green hula-hoop to
the packing riddle. It rested on top of the boxes on the roof
like an emerald crown and proudly signaled to every other
car on the highway that we were emancipated and heading
for fun.

My suitcase held fewer clothes that summer than
those items I decided were truly important--my assortment
of new Super Hero comics, two new novels, my gift of
string from Skeeter, and my knife. I also packed the
Instamatic camera I'd received at Christmas and the journal
I had taken to writing in each week. I'd decided, in a
moment inspired by Jimmy Olsen, cub reporter, to chronicle
the continuing adventures of Drew MacLaren, Superhero, in
both film and pencil.

The drives through the tidewaters were always
interminably long for every member of the family, though I
believe it became easier each year for Mother and Father, as
Donny and I grew to ages where we didn't need constant
reminders to stop bickering or ingenious car games to keep
us amused.

We eventually neared my spot. I elbowed Donny and
pointed to it--the invisible line anticipated at the beginning
of each summer. It was where my world of rules and
demands slipped away, where I crossed into the realm of
salty skin and liberated adventure. It was that point,
precisely, where we left the mainland on the ferry and
chugged across the inlet leading to the strand. I knew
exactly what the cracks in the cement looked like, how the

bumps in the big metal plates felt when our wheels rolled over them onto the deck.

Salt air poured in, and looking at my family, I saw each of them settle into their own dreamy transformations.

The great cottage appeared exactly as we had left it. The outside, however, looked altered, as if the sands and grasses there had been re-shaped by enormous, messy children enjoying unmonitored time in the play box.

The engine stopped, clicking on in cooling relief, and I yearned for immediate adventure. Knowing the expected routines, however, I suppressed my longing. We had to unpack the Nomad--a chore requiring far too much patience for any creature cooped up in a vehicle for six hours. I was ready to tear across the sand, scream, jump, and swim, anything but unload boxes.

I lifted and fetched without complaint, however, until all was stowed, and the shutters and doors of the great cottage were open anew. I tossed clothes into drawers, set my camera and journal on the table, and then stood silently at the ocean side window for a moment.

I closed my eyes and let it settle upon me like marigold petals. I was back. In deep breaths I inhaled it. I stretched my hands towards the horizon and drew them slowly in, feeling every particle. I looked at the vastness of ocean, the clean horizon with swells marching in like cavalry regiments against the shore. Then I was ready to run. I was ready to do it all at once. I wanted to see everyone all at the same time, go fishing, swimming, build forts, climb dunes. I might even have joined in a game of football had I been asked.

It was late afternoon, when I touched the sand below the front porch. It appeared narrower to me, as if the winter storms had stripped away more than their fair share. I sprinted north and immediately found Skeeter in the exact spot where we had launched our balloons the previous summer.

I knew he'd been waiting the only way he knew how, patiently. He'd probably seen our car pull into the drive and sat there gazing south while I'd finished my chores. I pulled up short and started grinning, almost laughing, because he was sitting in a wheelchair, upright and proud as a ribboned soldier. The metal was rusted, the rubber tires were chipped in places, but Skeeter was sitting in it with a look like he had just landed the biggest fish anyone had seen in those parts. He seemed taller, even though he was sitting. His hair was longer, and he was less skinny, but his eyes hadn't changed one green speck. They were grinning right back at me.

"Hey, Skeeter. You look good in that, Son, and I'll bet my best comic you got a name for him."

"Hey to you, too, Drew. And sure he's got a name. Meet Pegasus. I call him that 'cuz I can fly around here on him." I thought his mouth was going to split, he was grinning so hard.

"Where'd you get it?" I wondered if the old caster wheel board was still around.

"Well, I got me a nice teacher down in Manteo, Miss JuneAnn, and she raised money last year with cake sales and stuff like that, and the school folks bought it for me. It'd been used a bit, but they cleaned it up and adjusted the pedals and all, and it works great. Watch this." He tilted back, pulled sharply on the wheels and balanced on the rims like a circus bicycle act.

"Whoa, that's neat." I was impressed. And happy for him. "You still have your old board?"

"Have to. I can't roll around inside of the house with this so well, so I still have to keep Lizard close by."

"Lizard?" I was starting to laugh.

"Well, yeah, because he's so low to the ground."

There was a simple ease in the way we caught up with each other's lives that afternoon. It was the unpretentious chatter of boys. We never ventured beyond the pleasant episodes of our time apart, never talked of hardships, or nightmares, or meanness. It was just the recounting of accomplishments of pride and laughter.

"Is Maggie around?" I asked trying to sound casual. I had to get back for dinner and hoped she was close by.

Skeeter frowned just a shade, just enough for me to notice and wonder about it. "Naw, she's up at Jensen's shopping for the week. Ought to be back in 'bout half an hour I expect."

"Dern. I've got to get back for dinner now. Can you tell her I'll see her tomorrow?

"Sure thing, Drew. Say, do you think we'll get to do some more fishin' this summer?"

I popped him gently on the shoulder with my fist. "We're gonna catch 'em all this year, Skeeter. You wait an' see."

I hopped over the railing.

"Drew." Skeeter's voice called after me.

"Yeah?"

"I'm glad you're back."

"I'm glad to be here, Skeeter. I really am."

***

For the first time in many years, Donny didn't arrive at the dinner table right on time. Mary Ellen Brewster had gotten a lot prettier over the summer, in his estimation, and he lingered just a bit too long conversing with her, causing him to be late to our first Nags Head feast of the summer. He paid the price without complaint, however, and washed and dried all the dinner dishes with an undeviating smile. Donny was clearly as happy as I was to be where we were.

I came in to help him put the last of the plates away, and we shared the information we'd gathered in our first hour of homecoming. Donny told me his most important news first. MaryEllen had grown breasts, and according to him, they rivaled Jane Mansfield's. That didn't interest me as much as it did him, but I think he considered it to be one of those batons of image refinement to be passed along to me.

It wasn't that I didn't know about such things. I was certainly more knowledgeable than the previous summer when it came to parts--girls' and boys'--and what they were supposed to do. I'd been imprisoned in the school auditorium, along with all the other sixth-graders, and forced to watch "the film." There were more uncomfortable, squirming bodies during those two reels than a full showing of Psycho, and I was sure I received more accurate information on the subject listening to what older boys talked about during gym class.

As we were finishing up on the dishes, I learned that Georgie Marovich and his family were coming in from

Richmond the following day, and that the Morley twins were already here. Pooh Hutton caught a King Mackerel in April all by himself, and it was so big they put his picture in the paper.

The most interesting news MaryEllen told Donny was that Wink May had gotten arrested and thrown out of school for a week. She didn't know much about it, but he'd been caught in a car with some older boys and gotten into some kind of trouble just before Christmas.

Later that evening, in the solitude of my room, I did my energy work, slipping with more than the usual effort into the sounds of my breath. It was more difficult that evening, because my brain was far too busy planning the minutes of the following day.

In the morning I woke before the sun crept above the horizon, but I lay in bed until the first rays crossed my sill. I wanted to feel the air around me. As that summer began, a subtle change had begun to seep invisibly into my life. In tiny degrees I'd simply become more aware of things around me. I didn't question it at all. I mistakenly assumed that it was a part of my growth, something every boy experienced at the ripe old age of eleven. Mr. Driscoll, my science teacher, had said something similar. "You'll be experiencing lots of changes in your bodies over the next few years." That was right before we were all marched off to see the film. I figured that's what it was, one of those mysterious changes that all the adults had hinted at with furtive smiles. Eventually I realized that it was something unique, a keenness of the air around me. It was connected, in its way, to my ability to feel the changes in the winds and cloud. I'd always had it, and by that summer, it had merely multiplied in the agar of my experience. Eventually I realized that it had only needed a catalyst--the very powerful one that Mai Lin had added.

Lying in bed that morning, all my senses were open. There were whispers, and fragrances, and a dancing of dust motes. I tasted mist and salt and felt the radiance of sunlight playing about my room. I lay there for long moments just being in it, and then, as the sun lit up my room, I threw back the covers with a flourish. I was going to see Maggie.

It was a quintessential Outer Banks day. There were no clouds, and the air was warm and fresh on the skin. I trotted south along the beach towards the turnoff to Ensign Bill's, carrying my small package carefully in my left hand, trying as hard as possible to keep sweat and sand from staining the wrapping. I crossed the highway near the Beachcomber and climbed the low rise above the shack.

For a moment, I was puzzled. The old house had vanished, not completely, but almost. Where it had teetered precariously the previous summer there were now just a few gray boards laying horizontally and three rotten steps entombed in drifting sand. Maggie was nowhere to be seen.

I jumped down the bank in giant strides and stood on the top step like an athlete accepting a ribbon, and then, without turning, I felt her behind me. She must've hidden behind a mound of sand and waited for me. She stood at the top of the rise with both hands on her hips, grinning like she had just won a race. She looked at me as if she were trying to identify every little change that had occurred in our time apart.

She was, if possible, more beautiful than the previous summer. Her hair was longer, nearly to her waist, and she already wore a summer tan so deep it made the blue of her eyes contrast against the background. And I also saw something else there, a deeper pain etched in the eyes; it was there in the pupils like tiny flaws in otherwise perfect gems.

Before I could speak she said, "Well, you look like you've gotten somewhat taller, and I do believe a bit handsomer, too." That melted me right at the knees and had me beaming like a king's fool.

"Momma always says Brussels sprouts and good sleep will do that for you," I replied. I leapt off the steps and part way up the slope. She stepped down to meet me. We stood there for two heart beats just looking at each other, I feeling awkward, she seemingly at ease, and then we hugged.

She pulled me gently back by the shoulders and looked at my face carefully. A slow smile came to her lips. "You kept up with it. I can see it in your eyes. Mai's going to be proud as a momma duck."

I nodded shyly and said, "I couldn't find any reason not to. It sort became a part of my day, like lunch lines and homework, but a heckuva lot more fun. How is she?"

"She's as good as ever, keeps saying she can't wait for you to get back. Wants to show you the next exercises and talk about birds and things." She looked around and with a hopeful voice said, "It's going to be a good summer, Drew."

She noticed the wrapped present in my hand. "What's that?"

I grinned teasingly. "My secret, and you'll find out soon enough."

We started along the familiar trail, with one exception. I was so excited to be on that path again that I took the lead for the first time and stretched my stride out like a camel's, so Maggie had to hop to keep up with me. From behind I heard her. "Yep, those legs have definitely gotten longer over the year." And then the nonsense rhymes that she always sang going in that direction started up.

"Maggie?"

"Hippity, hippity hop, the winter rains won't stop." She either hadn't heard me or was lost in her world of rhyme."

"Maggie?" I called back again.

"Hmmm?"

"How's your Momma doin? Your letter said she was getting better."

The humming stopped. It took a second longer than it should have for her to reply, and I knew it wasn't good. "Well, she was. Seemed like for awhile she might be just like she was a few years back. You know, normal like." Then she added with a sarcastic tone, "but I guess her God just didn't have it planned it that way." Her voice trailed off, and she must have known what I was ready to ask, because she started up again. "Somethin' went bad with her back in May, Drew. One morning she was standing in the kitchen, doin' her cooking like she'd do when I was a little girl. She started starin' out the door, just starin' and starin', and then that look came back. She began swearing something awful and hitting the counter with her frying pan like she was gonna kill it. She gets awful strong when she goes off like that. I can't figure that one out at all. Anyway, I went to try to calm her and she swung it at me."

"The frying pan!"

She sighed deeply. "Yep, hit me right in the collarbone and busted it clean through. I finally got her to calm down and into bed and then got myself up to the market. Mr. Jensen called the sheriff. It was bad, Drew. It'd never gotten so bad before." Maggie's voice faded, and then said, "The sheriff was ready to call the state people. Somethin' about her bein' a danger to Skeets and me."

"Why didn't he?"

"By the time he got to our place, Clarisse was sleeping as sweet as could be, and Skeets had a sandwich and iced tea made for himself. He was sitting in wheelchair at the kitchen table with his homework in front of him. That boy could've fooled a detective. I guess it all looked peaceful enough, because Mr. Brennan let it be."

I was trying to picture it, Maggie stumbling into the market up near the pier, the usual people that were always there, staring at her. There would have been whispers, and maybe one or two who thought of trying to help, but never did. Mr. Jensen would have been the only one who did anything. "They take you to the hospital?" From Nina May's collapse at Christmas, I knew how these things played out now.

"Millie Martin heard about it somehow and got over 'bout the time the sheriff's deputy arrived. Those two got into a big argument about who was going to take me down to Manteo. I guess Millie won. She's the toughest short lady I've ever known."

"Was it that Mr. Curry?" I suddenly saw his face, smeared with chocolate pie, sneering at us in Miss Millie's diner.

"Only deputy there is, Drew, and I don't call him Mister or Sir or anything at all. He's a worm, and that's the truth."

I started giggling because I instantly pictured Mr. Curry crawling along on his belly and a big hand scooping him up to slide him onto a rusty hook with a bamboo pole attached to it. "I guess you don't like him much either?"

She almost growled. "Hell no, I don't like him. He started drivin' that damned deputy's car of his up to Jensen's just about the time I'd get there on Friday afternoons, very convenient like. He'd come in and start talkin' to me near the comic rack, and then, when I wouldn't talk back, he started whisperin' ugly things an all. I ignored him, and I think that made him even more set on botherin' me. Now I'm doing my shoppin' on Thursdays."

"What kinds of ugly things?"

"Nothin' I want to repeat, Drew. Stuff about how he wants me to touch him. He's got a mouth filthier than a sewer."

Most likely from the way she said it, angry or maybe a bit frightened, I was suddenly enraged. Mr. Curry was now arch-enemy number one of Drew MacLaren, Superhero. I just couldn't think of how I was going to defeat my evil nemesis. He seemed to have all the super weapons at his disposal and I had none. The only thing I could think to say was, "Well, my mother and father pretty much think he's a worm, too," hoping that might ease some of her hurt.

We arrived at the corridor between the bamboo walls, everything appearing as familiar as before. I smiled back at Maggie mischievously and skipped through. Immediately Mai's voice called out from above, "Ah, Drew, you back. You been away too long. Tea cup sit empty, very lonely all this time." I ran through the garden, up the stairs, and directly into her open arms. I was almost as tall as she was now. I stepped back and proudly held out my package wrapped in bright yellow with tiny green Christmas trees. "I brought you a Christmas present, Mai," Then stated the obvious. "It's kind of late."

With a big smile she said, "Presents always on time, Drew, never late." Maggie followed me up the stairs, where Mai hugged her and kissed the side of her face tenderly, asking in a concerned voice, "Daughter well?"

"I'm fine, Mai. It's good to have my Drew to walk through the dunes with again." In both of their voices I heard a fraction of uneasiness, as if during my absence, the world outside had gotten harsher.

"Open your present, Mai. It's really for both of you. I would have sent it at Christmas, but I didn't really know how." I was proud and excited. It was the first contribution that I was going to make after so much had been given to me.

"Not to worry, Drew. I not celebrate with Christmas tree anyway. Celebrate other holidays. Big holiday in spring. We celebrate that."

It was another one of those Mai surprises. I only had one other friend who didn't celebrate Christmas. He lived in Burlington and celebrated Jewish holidays. These were more puzzles that I made a mental note to ask my father about later that day.

Mai handed the present to Maggie, saying, "We open together. My glasses in bedroom, Daughter read card for us."

Maggie unfolded the small paper and read my left-handed, all-capitals print out loud. "To Maggie and Mai Lin, from your friend, Drew MacLaren." Like our Moravian blessing, it was short and to the point. Instead of shredding through the wrapping as I would have, they took agonizingly slow turns peeling the tape off in stages. Maggie eventually lifted my gift out, and just as I had hoped, the light from it danced instantly about the garden. It was a small spiral of crystals, cut in prismatic tear drops, that my mother had helped me find. Now in the garden rainbows spun like carousels.

Maggie watched the revolving colors and then smiled at me like a child. "Drew, it's the most beautiful thing I've ever seen." Mai squeezed my hand and said, "Okay, we have tea now."

That morning the three of us sat on low cushions and talked about the year and the migrating birds that had returned punctually this cycle. The water sounded like heartbeats, as it lapped against the band of shoreline. My world was as it should be. Mai told me twice how proud she was that I had kept up with my practice. She kept reading my face and hands, smiling. She patted my knee and said, "You ready for next breath, Crane movements and Eight Strands. We start tomorrow." I figured that I had received my diploma.

Before we left, Mai massaged Maggie's neck and collarbone, and then together we hung the string of crystals in the garden. And of course, there were tangerines.

***

My first swim in the Atlantic that summer left me with honeyed memories and a sizeable new scar. The sweetness came from the three men, I now included myself in this lofty category, Donny, Father, and I all riding the surf together. The scar came from a combination of a long, narrow shell that I never saw and a wave that needed only a few more inches in height to have washed clear over to the Sound.

Donny and I had both seen that the swell was large the previous afternoon, and the hollow echo of big waves had pounded through my dreams during the night. That morning we saw that they were lifting across a newly-formed sand bar easily thirty yards further out than the year before.

The three of us stood for longer than usual at the water's edge that morning. We cautiously noted the size of the waves, which were well over my head height and pitching from top to bottom like cement mixers. I could tell by Father's expression that he was considering a veto of our Holy Communion, but his belief that we needed to do such things together, and his inherent sense of adventure, outweighed his reluctance. Donny, being thirty pounds larger, was eager to plunge right in. I was a tad less enthusiastic, but still ready.

After the customary retying of trunks and probing of water temperature, we dove in. It was chillier than normal from the swell's stirring, and we each came up sputtering from it, but after a strong swim out to the bar, our blood was heated properly, and we were ready. We moved a few feet beyond the crests and Donny immediately provoked a water fight with me that soon drew Father in, and all three of us ended up laughing like six year olds.

There was with me that morning an intense feeling of companionship and family, of growing up. For the first time I understood why Momma and Father encouraged our experiences together. I knew that I had changed, and that Donny had changed, each of us for the better--even though it wasn't quite how Jethro had described it, both eyes still being in the same place on Donny's head. So, for a few minutes, while Father and Donny stroked into the biggest waves they could get, I just bobbed and launched myself upward through the peaks, leaping like the porpoises I'd seen the previous year. I felt the air and water about me, the movement and motion, and then I slid into my first wave. It was a medium-sized peak, still large by comparison, coming in at the proper angle. I pushed off the bottom, rose into the pinnacle and dropped flying and whooping across the wall to the left. As I sped across the bar I saw the color below me shift to a lighter green. The coarse sand was just six inches below the surface.

Donny, not to be outdone, took the next one, a big wave that took him far inside. Father and I were drifting lazily beyond the bar.

"Father?"

"Drew?" He sensed I had things on my mind and waited in his patient way.

"I gave Maggie and Mai Lin my present this morning."

"They like it?"

"Yes, Sir, very much. I wish you could've seen it. There were rainbows everywhere. It was as perfect as could be."

He smiled thoughtfully. "Then you make sure to give a special thank-you to your mother. She always seems to find the perfect gifts doesn't she?"

"Yes, Sir, she does." I paused. "Maggie's mom's sick again."

"I know, Son. Dellie Harris told Momma yesterday evening."

"Can't anybody do anything? Maggie told me Mrs. Silver hit her with a frying pan, and Maggie had to go to the hospital."

Father sighed and twisted his head side-to-side to stretch his neck muscles. "I hadn't heard that one. When did it happen?"

"Back in May. Miss Millie drove her from Mr. Jensen's market down to Manteo." Then, because I believed Father might actually able to do something about it, I told him how Frank Curry was pestering Maggie whenever she went to the store. I told him all the pieces that I knew, and when I was done, I saw his jaw tighten. Having been aware of them throughout my life, I knew most every shift in my father's expressions. Rarely did his eyes show the expression that I saw right then. It was unmistakably grim, and I was glad right then that it wasn't aimed at me.

"Drew?"

"Yes, Sir?"

"You do me a favor, Son. You tell Maggie not to fret too much about Frank Curry." And as was his custom, nothing else was said on the matter, but I was pretty certain that morning that Drew MacLaren, Superhero had unleashed something more powerful than x-ray vision or flying shields--his father.

I misjudged my fourth wave. It looked to be a moderate-sized swell with a smaller companion a few feet in front of it. I was standing in shoulder-depth water, deep in the bowl where the peak would rise, a little too deep. As the wave rose, I spun over and swam into it in one smooth motion.

What I had not anticipated was the smaller wave a few feet in front. The bigger wave sucked the smaller one up, and I was now dropping diagonally across the largest wave of the morning, and at that moment I was certain the largest of the decade. There was no pulling back. For an instant I was suspended, peering through the prettiest cascade of curving water I'd ever seen, and then I felt the ocean take control. Slowly I was lifted upward and flipped like a flapjack and then tumbled with all the force that tons of water and gravity could provide. Had they witnessed it, the barrel-riders of Niagara Falls would have written it proudly into the history books. The explosion that followed shot through every muscle and bone in my body, and I bounced across the bar and swirled about underwater like a leaf in a storm.

I finally managed to find my feet and push upward through the foam into the air, again grateful for how it felt pouring into my lungs. Father and Donny, having watched my spectacular tumbling from further in, were now sprinting towards me. Father came up quickly and reached to pull me out of the way of the next wave. As calmly as I could I told him, "I'm okay. Really, I am." Good training, good breathing, and a little size had all added to the fact that I was just fine, a bit shook up, but fine. As we made our way to shallower water, however, I discovered that my right knee had met up with what was, by the shape of it, a hefty razor clam shell. It was neatly sliced and bleeding profusely. That caused Donny to conclude that I needed to be carried up the slope to the cottage in a fireman's hold. I politely declined.

As much as I wanted to, I knew I wasn't going to be able to avoid my mother's intense fostering. The tiniest nicks sent her into medical emergency mode, and sure enough, before I reached the porch steps she was there shrieking orders and calling for bandages, tape, and the dreaded bottle of denatured alcohol. Nina May came out clucking her displeasure at yet another mishap to one of her MacLaren boys. As packets of gauze were being shredded open like Christmas wrapping, I heard Momma delivering her predictable reprimand in short, terse phrases. "You could have been killed." I started to protest, and she interjected, "Those waves are simply enormous and the three of you ought to know better than to be fooling around like that. This is worse than that stunt you pulled on that damned boat last year." Then Donny started up only to be cut off, "There is absolutely no sound reason to be challenging danger every minute the way you three do. John, this cut needs immediate attention."

There ensued a lively discussion between Father and her about whether I was to be taken down to Manteo for stitches. I'd never had them, and if I had any influence in the decision, wasn't going to that morning. Father, fortunately, won out, and I was patched up instead with Bactine, gauze and the largest Band-Aids Johnson and

Johnson ever manufactured--Where my mother purchased and concealed these items in the cottage, none of us ever knew.

The alcohol dousing of my knee that morning is a memory that I prefer to keep subdued.

"Great way to start the summer, Knucklehead." Donny's new name for me was a step up from last year's. He was smirking, but I could see his brotherly pride about my stoic reaction to it.

"Was it a big one, Donny?"

"Maybe the biggest, Little Guy. You didn't quite clear the tunnel though." He popped me lightly on the side of the head.

"Yeah, I know," I said, looking at him puzzled. "It's a weird feeling. You know, when something else takes control and you can't do anything about it."

Donny took a breath into his asthma-free lungs. "Yeah," he laughed. "I know."

Momma made the unilateral decision to thwart my tendencies to get into all forms of water. She crowned herself head nurse and decreed that I was not to enter anything except the outdoor shower—and that only with my wound sealed tightly in plastic wrap. My injury had grounded me, literally. It was going to be a long two weeks on land. But as I learned, often when the door closes, a window opens.

Momma asked what most of the folks of Dare County were asking. It was right after dinner the same night the sheriff took Maggie away and Skeeter and I found the

*letters. I was clearing dishes. The shutters were still pulled
shut against diminishing gusts. I heard her ask Father as
they stood on the porch looking at the damaged boards.
"Do you think she did it, John? Killed her own mother?"
There wasn't enough doubt in her voice. It was Father's
anguished reply that started me crying once again that year.
"I don't know Jean Gray, I really don't, but she sure
would've had reason to."*

    *Skeeter told me exactly where to find Clarisse's
hiding place. "She's got everything tied in bundles under
the two boards below her night table," he said. "I found
'em last summer just after you left, Drew, but I never got the
nerve to take anything out and read it. She was always in
there and I just couldn't do it." My heart started pounding
because I knew what he was going to say next, "But you
could get it all now." The trouble was, exactly how to get
down the stairs, across the sand, and back up without
anyone hearing me. I switched off the flashlight under the
blanket that draped over our heads and took a deep breath.*

    *We swore a promise to each other. No one would
find out what we were going to do. As Skeeter had said,
"What if it's bad stuff, Drew? Stuff they'd use to take
Maggie away forever? We've got to find out what it is first."
I knew that thought terrified Skeeter more than anything--
the idea that Maggie might be taken away forever. His
mother was gone now, but he was less upset than one might
expect. After all, she'd already been gone a long time.*

    *As I stepped onto the board next to my bed in the
precise spot to keep it from squeaking, I decided that my
entire life had been a preparation for the task I was about to
perform. I knew every inch of the great cottage. I knew the*

stairs in the front creaked like old cupboards and the secret
passageway was the ideal direction.

There was a reason I'd snuck down that corridor
every summer for eleven years, a reason I could breathe and
move with the silent deliberation of Batman and Cat
Woman. As I silently pulled the string that lifted the inner
handle, I thanked once more the children of the contractor
who created the secret passageway.

***

After lunch I began to feel a throbbing radiating
about my knee. It always puzzled my why my injuries
waited so long to reveal their true severity. This one had
waited patiently and was now pulsing about my leg with a
sweet vengeance. With all of her bandages, Momma had
made me look like I was a purple heart candidate, and
normally I would have been off somewhere nonchalantly
showing Pooh Hutton or the Morley twins how tough I was
about the wound. By the afternoon, however, I didn't feel
much like walking around to find them or anyone else.

I had nestled myself into one of my favorite spots,
the big canvass hammock hung from the first two posts on
the front porch. Earlier Nina Mae had shuffled out with an
iced tea, a sandwich, and soft sheet to tuck under my legs,
and then everyone, sensing my need to be that way, left me
alone. The old hammock, from years of salty spray, was stiff
and mildewed in places, but it was the most comfortable
spot on earth. The ancient rings that gathered the cords at
both ends were rusted to dangerous thinness in spots. I
didn't care. I was swaying dreamily with the breeze,

fascinated by how a simple twitch from my butt muscles could keep the whole thing moving.

I drifted off and dreamed of riding giant waves of air, and when I opened my eyes sometime later, I saw two of Jethro's longboats bobbing in the swells, their bows turned to shore like horses heading to stable. The cork lines were floating like giant leashes behind them. The third boat, untethered, rocked to the side, ready for the unforeseen events that occur with too much frequency on the ocean.

The boats were motoring slowly in along the south side of the pier. It seemed a little unusual for them to be beaching on that side, but not overly so. Jethro had been setting his nets in his locations and hauling them to shore according to his own superstitions for too many decades for anyone to question it.

Two adults and a child were watching the last stages of the process from the shore. I didn't recognize them, so I immediately placed them in my all-inclusive category of unfamiliar people, tourists. A family that I did recognize was walking from the pier towards the spot where the boats would be coming ashore. People were gathering, and I wanted to be down there. I wanted to watch the net haul, maybe help Jethro and his boys.

Behind me, the screen door creaked open, and I looked over the folds of the hammock to see my mother peering across the porch. She had that concerned look on her face as if she were reading the red line of a thermometer that wasn't where it was supposed to be. She came and sat on the bench beside me and stroked my forehead with one hand and rocked the hammock slowly with the other. "So...how's my little patient? Feeling better?"

"Yes, Ma'am." I scrunched up my nose. "It kinda aches."

She nodded, still stroking the side of my head gently. It felt nice, warm and soothing. She looked at me and I could see she was happy, like it was the most natural thing for her to be making me feel better using just the touch of her fingertips. "Well, it should," she said. "You cut it deeply." There was a slight frown and admonition with her statement. "But it's a good sign that it's feeling achy. That means you're starting to heal already. It's probably going to hurt a bit when you set it back down."

I didn't like the sound of that. "Why?"

"You've had it elevated all afternoon, and the blood's got to flow back and that'll make it ache some more." She smiled reassuringly at me. "But not for long."

I looked down the shoreline to see the first of the longboats slide high up onto the beach wrapped in a wall of white water. Momma looked towards the pier, then thoughtfully at me. With a sly smile she whispered, "Do you want to walk down there with me?"

The MacLaren sons, and Father as well, knew for a fact that Momma had special gifts. Donny and Father called it ESP. I just knew she had a certain sense of things and could tell what any of us was thinking by a mere look at our faces. She could sense prohibited activity an hour before we set to do it. She also had the most acute sense of smell of any human in that part of North Carolina, knowing precisely when our shirts were too smelly to go another minute on our bodies. Right then I was glad she knew exactly what I was thinking.

"Yes, Ma'am, I do. I haven't seen Jethro, or Pooh, or anyone yet."

She put her finger to her lips and whispered, "Well… why don't we go on down there for a bit. A little exercise will help the circulation. No further though, just there and back." She lifted my leg carefully over the edge of the hammock, and sure enough, it began to ache like the dickens by the time my feet touched the porch. She held out her hand as we stepped onto the sand, a gesture I might have shunned on any other day, but that afternoon it felt right. We walked slowly, and just like we did when I was five, we searched for sand dollars.

The air smelled of diesel and brine. Jethro's three boats were lined up about twenty yards apart with their bows and sterns tilting upward at angles from the sand. They were sturdy, wide and stable, custom made from planks of heavy Carolina fruitwood. In the center of the two closest to us, large winches were grinding slowly, pulling the dripping rope back from the sea. The bows were staked with thick poles and heavy line to prevent them from sliding back towards the water.

Jethro's method of catching fish was simple. Passed on from his father and grandfather, it was also effective. Two of his boats would spool out one net apiece in the morning, well away from each other, but usually not more than a half mile from shore. The bottom lines were weighted with lead, and the upper lines had fat cylinders of cork woven into them with heavy cord. In the afternoon the lines were reattached to the giant winches and wound up as far as they would go.

Watches could be set using his orbital schedule.

As the catch came to shore, Jethro and his boys would step like booted giants into the middle of the silvery mass and hook the fish, separating them by type and size into coffin-like boxes which were then topped with crushed ice and driven the short distance to his market. Finally, the balance of net, line and cork would be folded into the stern like furled sails and the whole of it washed down thoroughly with hose water.

By the time Momma and I made our way down the shoreline, a group of nearly fifteen had assembled to watch the final part of the haul. Children raced through the crowd, while two of Jethro's boys heaved on the lines snaking into the boat--their corded muscles strained hand-over-hand to relieve the pressure on the groaning winches. Within moments the great semi-circles of cork and net had tightened to small ovals near the shoreline. The water inside was bulging with frothy flashes of silver and black. Captain J. stood dead center between the two boats, inspecting each net carefully. His high boots were spread wide in the sand, massive hands set firmly on his hips, the ever- present fisherman's cap set even more firmly on the back of his head.

Immediately I had the urge to call out to him, but I'd long ago learned that until those big winches had stopped chugging and the catch examined, Jethro wouldn't say a single word to anyone but his crew.

After a quick nod from Captain J., Bertram Sein, the youngest, and by all accounts, handsomest worker of the group, leapt heroically into the mass near where Momma and I stood and began the hazardous task of disentangling and tossing the stingrays back into the waves. They weren't edible by human standards, and for that conflicting reason were allowed to reclaim their freedom. The rays always thrashed about in unpredictable motions, and the barbs at the roots of their tails could slice through the thickest of boots and gloves, leaving behind a painfully poisoned gash. That was a good reason in my book, especially with my own aching cut, to jettison them promptly.

I watched squeamishly as Bertram bent to grab them by their wings and fling them one by one into the breakers. The rays whipped their tails in wild efforts to slash the unfamiliar hands, but Bertram merely smiled at his audience, held on a bit more firmly and threw the rays further into the breakers.

Eventually, after the rays, sand sharks, and other inedible life were removed, Jethro's boys lugged the crates down. I watched the web tighten and slip higher onto the sand. The life inside was ebbing now; fewer and fewer spasms of fins and gills could be seen. I saw the curved tail of a yellow fin twitch and then stop.

Momma looked at me as I stared into the web and gave my hand a little squeeze. She knew—with her talent for such things—that I was seeing the dying in that net, aware the lives inside were slipping into some unfamiliar place. I had wondered often, since that afternoon when we men had patched Our Aliento, where something went when it died. I had caught my own fish, seen the hauling of life to shore, but the implications of it, the mystery of it, tugged at me.

Right then I wished all those fish could be, just like Charlie, heading home.

After most of the fish had been packed into ice crates, I stuck my head out from behind the fanny of a very large tourist and called out, "Captain J?" Jethro turned, and seeing me, bellowed, "Ahhr…Who's this? First Mate MacLaren! Well, now, it's been a long a time since we've chatted, eh? You're a fine one to be hanging back with these landlubbers." He beamed mischievously at the thinning crowd. "Come 'ere, Lad. Let's have a look at you." I hobbled over and Jethro lifted me like a toddler, instantly embarrassing me and making me feel like the luckiest boy in The Banks.

"By my beard, you've grown as big as pilot whale." I was plumped back down, and seeing my excessively bandaged knee, he added, "Oh…now what's this? A nasty saber wound, eh? I hope the other fellow lost a bit more of his leg." If I'd been a tad taller he would have elbowed my ribs along with his joke. "You know, Lad, in the old days, scars like that were something we seadogs wore with pride."

"Jethro!" Momma was wagging a finger at Captain J.

"Ah… Jean Gray, didn't notice you there, which is extremely unusual considering how dazzling you look this afternoon."

"And you also, Jethro." She smiled charmingly. "Drew had a little encounter with a razor clam this morning. Sabers were not involved in any way."

"A razor clam, eh? There's a tough adversary for you, a little slow in his movements, but plenty sharp." Jethro grinned at the double meaning of his joke, which I hadn't gotten. "By the look of all those bandages, it must've been a tough fight."

I nodded sternly, trying to appear the durable first mate. He clapped me lightly on the back. "Well, the catch is on ice, as we say, Mr. MacLaren. Day's work is nearly done. Do you think you'd want to join me on a short walk to the lot to fetch the truck?" He looked to Momma for approval. She nodded at me with a smile.

"You bet, Captain!" I was nearly hopping up and down. We turned towards the pier and heard Momma's lecture voice from behind me. "Jethro?"

He spun us both around to face her. "Yes, Jean Gray?"

"Drew's eleven. He doesn't yet know how to drive. Please make certain to remember that when you two get into that truck. And Drew…"

Yes, Ma'am?"

"Be at the dinner table on time."

"Yes, Ma'am." I paused. "Momma?"

"Yes?"

"Thank you." With that we turned back towards the pier.

Jethro and I walked slower than usual in deference to the stiffness in my knee and his own limp. I knew that if he wanted to, he could move pretty fast, but I was doing everything to keep my own leg from bending at the joint. We made our way to the pilings at the edge of the water. The tide was at its lowest, revealing more than the usual quantity of shells and pebbles. From habit, both of us searched the surf as we moved slowly along the shoreline. Jethro talked about mollusks and explained what invertebrates were. In exchange, I told him about Sloppy Joe's and the unusual events at Christmastime.

I reasoned that Jethro wouldn't mind my question, because we shared one that afternoon. "Jethro, how'd you get the limp in your leg?"

I was a bit worried that he was going to tell me it was from a razor clam and that I would have my limp for the rest of my life, but to my relief, he looked sideways at me and said, "It was my knee, Mr. MacLaren. It had a mind of its own one morning. Just about the year I was your age it decided to place itself in a location all fishermen know is a very dangerous place, between a dock and a boat. Mine got itself between my father's boat and the wharf, and that wasn't a good place for it to be with the waves being as big as that ridge of sand over there."

We'd arrived at the spot where we were ready to turn left to the boatyard, and I was going to ask how it had happened, when he surprised me by asking, "So, how are your visits with our Chinese friend and Margaret going?"

I was surprised, having thought only my family, Maggie and Skeeter knew of those visits. Jethro seemed to be looking at the water, waiting patiently for my response, when suddenly he pointed and whispered, "Eh? Now, Lad, what do your young eyes make of that?" He was pointing ten yards further on, a few feet into the surf. I peered at the spot. Just as a small wave drew itself up from the shallows in front of it, I saw what appeared to be a metal box, or part of one. It looked like the corner of a television set sticking up eight inches out of the pebbly sand. Then it disappeared, covered by the next wave.

Jethro took six big strides, and with one of his wading boots, stepped right on the corner. It wouldn't shift an inch that way, but Jethro needn't have worried about it moving. It wasn't, as we soon found out, going anywhere. I caught up with him and was ready to wade out when I remembered that for every drop of water on my bandages, I could add an extra week on dry land. Momma was her strictest when it came to her patients' recovery. "What do you think it is, Captain J.?"

He reach down with one massive hand to lift whatever lay buried at his feet, only to find that it didn't budge a trace. "Well, it's metal, Mr. MacLaren, and it's a lot bigger than this piece we see sticking up here. Hold on a minute." He called down to Angelo, who was furling the last of the netting into the <u>Santa Maria</u>, and motioned for him to fetch the truck on his own. Angelo signaled back and trotted up the rise toward the lot.

The waves eased back, leaving our mysterious object a bit more exposed in the waning light. I strained to see. Jethro was fifteen feet into the surf, bent over and scooping with his huge hands like steam shovels. Wet sand flew in thick clumps through the air, flying in every direction.

Ten minutes later I knew I was going to be washing dishes for being late to supper--assuming I even got supper. Jethro had cleared three feet of sand in a wide circumference around the box. A much larger piece of metal lay buried below it, and on the left side--I could barely see them--were a string of numbers and letters. Stenciled in white blocks were U-S-N.

Three more minutes and Jethro was laughing and hooting like a madman. "Mr. MacLaren, I'm not sure, not absolutely, but I believe we've discovered ourselves a duck."

Now I knew ducks, and like egrets, hadn't yet met one made of metal. "Captain?...Uhmm. What kind of duck?"

Jethro stood up from his digging. Breathing heavily he clapped his hands together. "A duck, Lad! A navy duck. D-U-K-W. They're amphibious boats used during the war."

In addition to teaching us about our own bodies parts the previous year, Mr. Driscoll, our science teacher, had taught us about amphibious critters. That was right before we were partnered up and politely forced to dissect a very ugly frog. I still didn't make the connection. "Amphibious? What…"

Jethro answered before I could blurt it out. "It's a boat, Mr. MacLaren, one that can drive on land and in the ocean. Six wheels, big propeller, and more space in the hull than all of my longboats combined. She's got six cylinders, two hundred and seventy horses, five speeds, and a mighty fine winch for hauling. And depending on how long she's been buried here," he thumped the metal with his fist, "she'll be the finest fishing craft in these parts when I'm through with her." He walked towards me with a huge smile and added, "after a bit of sanding and painting, of course."

Explaining how triangles were used to locate things, Jethro lined up the exact spot with the corner of his fence and the third piling from the end of the pier and we headed up the beach towards the boatyard.

On the way up Jethro pointed with a salty finger at the first of the stars twinkling through the sea-mist, "You know, Lad, you can't tell it by looking at them, but those stars aren't the ones moving around. We are. It's like a carousel in the park." Then he decided that it was probably a better idea for him to drive me back to the cottage. I liked that idea as it would save me the walk, but more importantly, his explanation of why I was later than I'd ever been to the dinner table would be more believable than mine.

It was a big, beat-up pick-up truck that was so pungent with the odor of fish I expected gulls to be floating in the air behind it, but I loved sitting there in the front seat with Captain J. Except being with Mai Lin and Maggie, I don't think I'd ever felt so proud.

We were rolling out the front gates of the lot when I asked, "Captain, how'd the duck get there. You know, buried like that. Where'd it come from?"

He looked down to the water and started shaking his head with an odd sort of expression, thoughtful and tender. "It is mystery of God, eh?" He looked at me in the dark, and I could just make out his eyes shining like diamonds. "I believe it is a gift, Drew. So many small miracles, all connected together, were needed for this gift to be given to us. Think of it. The grains of sand and drops of water that needed to be moved. The winter storms swept away more than most years. The spring tide and the new moon all happened precisely at that moment..." He stopped and sighed. "Precisely as we walked along together. Everything had to be set just so. It is a gift of divine intervention"

I didn't get the chance to ask what that was.

We pulled into the drive and Jethro beeped the horn in a short blast that I prayed didn't sound like an alarm that would send Momma into a startled panic. Both she and Father came out. Jethro carefully explained why I had not been punctual for crab cakes and corn on the cob. It seemed the discovery of a U.S. Navy DUKW, inexplicably buried in the sand, was justifiable reason for my tardiness. I was pardoned from washing dishes.

As I closed the screen door ever so softly, it occurred to me that Jethro had called me Drew for the first time in my life. I wondered if that meant I was an adult.

Treasure

Had I been asked to explain in words the lessons that I was gleaning those first weeks of the summer of 1959, I would have failed. It wasn't that I didn't understand them, I'm quite certain that I did, but I understood those lessons on a different level, one that involved feeling rather than intellect. It was really a matter of not having the adequate instruments to put it into words. Now, it is simple. Life has provided the catalysts. What I was beginning to sense that summer before my twelfth birthday was that everything occurs for a reason. And it is all connected.

As I washed the grit from my face, I thought about what Jethro had told me, how it had taken so many finite actions to reveal the submersed duck to us that evening.

Previously my comprehension of cause and effect had been limited to being punched in the arm and feeling pain, or gagging on a particularly disgusting vegetable, but that evening I began to create my own chain-of-events: My knee had stumbled upon a razor clam because the winds had formed two waves that had traveled across thousands of miles of ocean. They had joined as one as they rolled over the sand bar in front of the great cottage. The razor clam had moved purposefully into position--that one confused me a bit. My mother knew somehow that I needed to be at the nets that afternoon. Her ESP had allowed me to fetch the truck. Jethro and I discovered that duck because a hundred events had transpired to help us. We had been directed to find it.

That evening at the dinner table, Father clarified some of the mystery with a few additional facts that I quickly added to my list. "The area off Oregon Inlet was known as Torpedo Junction during the war, Drew. By most counts, more than a hundred ships were sunk by German submarines along this stretch of coast. It's pretty likely a few of those ships were carrying assault boats, ducks, even a tank or two."

I immediately pictured myself in charge of finding every ounce of that salvage. I especially liked the notion that I might locate and restore one of those tanks. I pictured the damage I was going to inflict on Deputy Curry's patrol car when he pulled into Mr. Jensen's lot to bother Maggie.

The rest of the evening was dominated by speculation of how the amphibious duck was going to look and ride, and then just before bed, I spent time writing in my journal—organizing how my daylight hours were going to be divided.

The next morning Maggie was quieter than usual as we started out. She seemed remote and weary. By the time we reached Mai's, I'd told her all about the duck. The only time she brightened was when she explained how she'd received a letter from the state tax people. She'd filled out some forms in January, gotten their doctor to sign them, and now she and Clarisse didn't have to pay taxes on their cottage or the little bit of money they received from Clarisse's inheritance. Maggie explained how it all worked, but taxes were as confusing as chemistry to me.

When we arrived at the cottage, Mai chattered away and re-bandaged my knee with one of her magic concoctions and then set to teaching me what she called The Crane Dance. It was a glorious morning of new lessons.

As soon as I returned from the sound I walked without stopping past the cottage and up to the thick cable that now stretched like an enormous snake up the sand on the far side of the pier. To say that Jethro understood some about machinery would be an understatement of vast proportions. His life depended upon them. He tinkered continually with them, polished them, and talked to them in a sweet voice from an unstated belief that they would respond in like manner. Often enough he could be heard whistling love arias to his motors or winches, as he topped their fluids and cleaned their parts like newborns in diapers. So no one was surprised when he had his machinery working so quickly to dislodge our grand discovery from its watery encasement.

Before dawn Jethro waded out with a diving mask and a coil of the best nylon rope in his shop. By the time the sun had risen, he had a steel cable and a hook larger than my head attached to the chassis of the duck. That was the easy part. It was buried almost perpendicular to the shore, on its side with its back end tilted downward. The hard part was clearing the sand, which could only be accomplished when the tide was right and delicately, inch by inch, tugging it out. But, by the time the Nina, Pinta, and Santa Maria returned from their morning run, the duck was dripping quiescently above the high tide line on its rubberless metal rims, all six of them.

Also, by that hour, every person in that part of The Banks had come to inspect and offer comment on what ought to be done to fix her up. With each suggestion Jethro replied that the best material he'd ever found was elbow grease. No one questioned his wisdom at all.

Angelo and Bertram called the statehouse in Raleigh to inquire about salvage laws, and the proper papers were now in the mail. The Navy, Jethro found out, could care less about their boat, but they were still sending an officer to make certain no weapons or ordinance were still somehow on board.

Jethro had a lot of helpers right off, most of them eager children who tired within minutes of scraping the crusted marine life from the hull. Even Donny and Georgie Marovich arrived and helped for awhile. Only Pooh Hutton and I lasted through until lunchtime.

Pooh looked exactly the same as the previous summer. Where I had grown three inches over the year, he hadn't sprouted at all, but those kinds of things never affected our friendship. Very little did. Thinking on it, I don't know if I'd ever seen him get mad at anything but a snapped fishing line, and that was being madder at himself than anything else. Even our secret handshake felt exactly as it had for three years. We talked about our time apart, as we scraped away and sweated into our shorts and oversized work gloves Angelo had loaned us.

I chipped at an unusually immovable barnacle and said, "Hey, I hear you caught yourself the granddaddy of Mackerel; got your picture in the paper. I guess your famous now, huh?"

He looked at me through foggy glasses. "Well, I ain't famous, but you should've seen it, Drew. He nearly busted my arms trying to lift him. I was out with Poppa off of Kill Devil, up past Kitty Hawk. Poppa wanted to check out a new bank that'd formed over the winter, and you know, I believe it was the coldest dern day of spring." This took about a minute to come out. Pooh undoubtedly communicated slower than any boy in North Carolina.

I asked the appropriate fisherman's question. "What were you using?"

"Poppa's big trollin' rod with the heavy line and a six-inch diving lure. We'd caught a few punkies, mostly throw back stuff, and all a sudden my line bent so hard I nearly lost hold." I looked at his hands, the gloves covering them were spattered with flecks of shell and dried algae. Pooh was small and kind of pudgy-looking, round and soft. His Momma had taken the shears so close to his head, he only had bristles there, but the longer you stayed around him the more you began to realize that underneath he was like a chunk of heavy iron. I imagined him in the stern of their charter boat with the tip of that pole pulling into the water like a divining rod and him not budging an inch.

He went back to his scraping. "I played out the line almost to the end of the reel, and Poppa strapped me into the bucket seat. I worked him slow an' easy for over an hour. Poppa knew it was a King, so he backed up the boat just like he does when the tourists catch somethin'. It took so long I thought my arms were going to drop into the water, Drew, but I landed him myself. Only help I got was from Poppa using the net when he came close." Pooh looked up and smiled in his slow way. "And I don' think neither of us felt the cold out there at all."

By late morning I was ready to devour six sandwiches and eight sodas. Jethro'd been clanking away on the engine the entire time, whistling and chuckling with delight. He would peer over the side every few minutes with updates and encouragements like, "You're the best, Lads.

The best. We'll have her cutting foam in short time, you'll see. She's going to need these cylinders re-bored, that's for certain, and new rings on the pistons, and new cables..." He listed about ten more engine parts that I didn't know at all, then leaned way out to look at the corroded rims and grinned at us. "And a new set of rubber all around, but she'll be the best craft in these waters." He looked at Pooh. "Except maybe for your dad's Sweet Ann, Mr. Hutton. Sam keeps that boat in fine shape. Fine shape." Jethro was as animated as either one of us had ever seen him and that just prompted us to work harder for him.

We'd scraped about half of one side when my arms told me they were going to mutiny if I didn't stop. Pooh had just left for his own lunch, so I put my gloves and scraper inside the hull, and said goodbye to Jethro. He jumped down into the sand and looked me directly in the eye and then shook my hand, pumping it up and down six or seven times. "Mr. MacLaren, you and I found this beautiful lady together. That means part of her is yours to keep. Laws of the ocean, Lad. I would be honored if you'd give her a good name. I'll abide with whatever you decide upon."

I was thunderstruck. Part of the duck was mine. I figured it was probably going to be a pretty small part since I didn't have a nickel for any of the replacement parts Jethro said she'd need. But that fraction, no matter how small it was, was huge to me. "I'll think up the best name ever for her, Captain," and immediately ideas for lucky names began popping out of the woodwork in my brain.

"I'm sure you will, Lad." He looked at me quizzically, and said. "You never answered my question the other night."

"What question's that, Captain?"

"I asked you, just before we found our treasure here, how your visits were going with Margaret and our Chinese friend. Are you finding her to be a might kinder than you expected?" He looked at me slyly.

I still couldn't figure out how he knew, but I answered, "She's the kindest lady I know, Jethro. She's teaching me all sorts of things. Things from China."

"She treats you well then? You and Margaret?"

"Like special guests, and she healed Donny's asthma last year." Then, without thinking about it much, I added, "and Captain J., she makes the best tea in the history of the world."

Jethro looked at the waves lapping against the sand at the water's edge and said, "I'm sure she does, Lad." He patted me on the back and said, "Remember, I'm towing the duck up to the lot this afternoon, so that's where she'll be if your arms feel like they want more work tomorrow. They have a way of aching on the second day, so if you don't show up, I won't worry why."

"I'll be there, Captain. I promise."

Between my bandaged knee and my sore arms, my body was wondering if I should have made that promise.

***

After I finished a double-sized peanut butter and jelly sandwich, fried potatoes, and two chocolate cupcakes, Nina May hobbled off to her room near the garage. I washed my dishes and thought to stretch out onto my bed upstairs to read, but Father had other plans. He came in through the back door and made me sit down at the

breakfast table, while he took one of the other seats and
turned it around to sit in it backwards. He could see my
obvious fatigue. "You feeling okay, Son?"

"Yes, Sir. I've been working with Pooh and Jethro
on the duck, so I'm a little tired. Guess what?"

Father looked at me and waited a flicker. I could tell
that his mind was on something serious. "Hmm?"

"Captain J. told me that part of the duck is mine, and
I get to name her. He's already got the engine apart and
knows all the things she needs, and she's gonna to be fixed
and ready real soon."

He nodded, but I could see that my enthusiasm and
the importance of what I'd said was lost in whatever he was
thinking about. "Well, I know you'll come up with
something special. You're good at that sort of thing, just
like your Momma. Listen, I want you to take a drive with
me down to Manteo in a bit. We'll drop by and pick up
some barbecue on the way back. Visit with Miss Martin for
a spell. You can nap on the way if you like."

I didn't really want to go anywhere but upstairs to
my books and bed, but replied, "Yes, Sir. Can I get washed
up first? I've got a ton of shells and paint flakes still sticking
on me."

"You take as long as you need. Just call me when
you're ready."

"Yes, Sir."

On the drive down to Manteo I fell asleep before
we'd gotten a mile down the road. I nodded off where
Ensign Bill's steps were buried on the right side of the
highway and woke up with Father calling my name and
gently touching my shoulder. We were parked in front of the

sheriff's station in Manteo, and I didn't want to be there. That building frightened me. It really didn't look that scary, but since being at Piggly's last summer and hearing Maggie talk about the Frank Curry, I wasn't too keen on sheriffs or their deputies.

"Come on in with me. You don't need to speak unless you want to. I just want you to hear what I have to say. Okay?"

"Yes, Sir." The sleep was beginning to fade. I rubbed my face with my knuckles and followed close on his heels as we went through the door. Inside, the front room was made of old dark wood that smelled like furniture polish. There were benches and a tall counter separating the entry room from the desks in the back, and a swinging gate over on the left. It reminded me of an office Father had taken me to once where his books were made.

Sitting behind the counter there was a big woman with a microphone on a low stand near her elbow. Seeing Father and me, she smiled at us as if she knew who we were, but I didn't know her. "Well, I'll be, John MacLaren." She looked Father up and down appraisingly, and I thought I heard a low whistle. "You look as good as you did twenty-five years ago. I don't think you've gained one ounce on that body." She glanced down at her own stomach. "Unlike a few other Tar Heel alumnae around here. What brings you down to Manteo today. Alpha Tau Omega boy come to ask a Sigma Chi girl to dance again." I was beginning to suspect that this woman knew Father pretty well.

"Good to see you, too, Jenny. Has been a while, hasn't it? You still go by Bristol, or has some lucky man come to his senses and taken you to the chapel?"

"There've been too many lucky men, John, but none of them have taken me to the chapel; most of 'em seem to prefer a crappy hotel room."

I saw father smile at that and say, "Well there a lot of fools out there. A smart one would have settled down with you in a heartbeat. I do have a little business with Jack this afternoon. He knows I'm coming."

"Well, hold on a sec. I'll fetch him. If he's not in the office, he's in the can, so he won't be hard to find." She set a pencil down and went through a door on the left.

After a short wait Sheriff Brennan came out, and for the first time I saw him in his uniform. He had a gun, a nightstick, and handcuffs, all of which fascinated me immediately. He was bald as a flagpole, and his shirt hung over his belt from the bulge underneath, but his badge looked just like the ones I'd seen on TV. He had his hand stretched out to shake Father's before he'd gotten through the swinging gate. "John, good to see you, Come on in. This must be…let me guess. Donny. No. Andrew. That's right, isn't it?"

"Good memory, Jack. This is my boy, Drew. He's been working all morning with Jethro on that duck I expect you heard about, so he's somewhat tuckered right now."

"I did hear about that. What a crazy thing that is, right in the sand and all. If anybody can fix up something buried in the sand, Jethro can. Well, come on in."

I wanted to blurt out that part of the duck was mine, and that I wasn't that sleepy, but the serious quality of the station kept me quiet. We went through the swinging gate and the big woman named Jenny kept grinning at me like I was her closest friend, which irritated me. In the inner office there were two seats in front of the desk, and behind there was a big leathery one that you could lean way back in. Mr. Brennan eased himself down, and we sat in front.

"So what can I do for you, John?" Mr. Brennan seemed awfully willing to be helpful, but I saw his smile wasn't that big. He picked up a letter opener on his desk and began twirling it in his fingers.

Father leaned forward. "Jack, my family's owned our cottage for fifty-two years now, and you and I have known each other for a pretty long time, long enough that I know I can talk straight with you. I know we haven't always seen eye to eye and probably register our names under different parties, but I'm going to get right down to brass tacks here. I know a lot of people in this state. Some very important people. We still get cards from both senators at Christmas, and Jean Gray's father is still circuit court judge up in Alamance County. I grew up with a lot of understanding of the law, and I know when it's being followed…," Father paused and set both hands on the corner of Mr. Brennan's desk "and when it's not." Mr. Brennan stopped fiddling with his letter opener and set it down. "My boy here tells me Frank Curry's been spending too much time trying to get the attention of Clarisse Silver's daughter. You might say he's choosing off one of the weakest of the herd. You and I both know that family doesn't have a whole lot of clout around here, but if that girl doesn't want to talk to him, Jack, she doesn't have to. It's going to stop."

"John, you sound a might threatening."

"No, Jack, threatening is when harassment charges get filed at every level of government, and when my publisher calls in a few chips and some timely articles come out in newspapers and magazines around the state. That's threatening."

Mr. Brennan leaned back in his leathery chair and stared for a two-count at Father. He nodded. "I take your point, John. It's well-made." He tilted the chair back down and said, "You know, that boy Frank's got a head like New Hampshire granite and he sure wouldn't have been my first hire. Hell, I wouldn't have hired him at all, but I owed his daddy a favor, a big one. I can't tell you how many times I've come this close to kicking that boy into the sound with something heavy wrapped around his waist. Hell, I almost canned him last year after that ugliness at Millie's, but I can't let him go, John, not unless he does something that breaks the law bigger than flapping that damned mouth of his." He glanced at me with his weak smile. "Sorry, Son." I really didn't like him calling me Son, but I nodded nicely. He took a breath and said to Father, "John, I'll tell you what I can do. I'll come down on him. Hard. Get him to mind his "Ps and Qs" a bit more. That sound fair enough?"

Father stood up, indicating his agreement and stretched his hand out. "That sounds fair enough, Jack. Just to be straight, though. If I hear he's even winked at her without her wanting him to, I'll be making six calls right after I call you. That sound fair enough to you?"

Mr. Brennan released Father's hand and replied, "I respect that. You and your words, John. I always like a man who says his piece and says it straight out without any…" I saw him look at me again and knew he was ready to swear but he said, "mincing." Speaking of that family, you're close by. Tell me how Clarisse is doing. I'd heard from one of my gals that she was getting better, and now I hear she's getting worse. We had that accident back in May and I haven't been up there since."

I wasn't sure if I'd heard Mr. Brennan correctly. Did he think Maggie getting hit with a frying pan was, an accident?

Father looked at me, and I knew he didn't want me to hear what he was going to say, but he said it anyway. "She's slipping, Jack. You might want to drop by and check up on her sometime. You've known her since you were kids. It's a nice part of the county. Not a bad drive at all." He looked kind of thoughtful and said slowly, "You know, I believe it's our old families, the ones that have been out here for so long, that are the strongest. They're the foundation for us. They stick out the storms each year while we come and go and the tourists pour in and buy up more and more sand."

As we left, the woman Jenny, who'd been behind the counter, was now standing near the front door. She opened it for us with a little bow and then leaned over to kiss Father with a wet smack on the cheek. I heard her whisper, "John, you ever have a big fight with Jean Gray, you come on down and dance with me again. We danced pretty well together if I remember correctly."

"I'll think real hard on that, Jenny, but don't quit breathing while you're waiting." He squeezed her hand and we were out the door.

"What did Mr. Curry's father do for Mr. Brennan?" We were driving north on the highway towards Miss Millie's diner.

"I see you were listening pretty closely."

"Yes Sir, you told me to."

Father smiled. "I'm glad you were listening. I wanted you there to hear all that. There's ways to do things, and ways not to. Sometimes the law doesn't quite cover all the people it's supposed to and you have to get a little..." He hesitated for a moment, searching for the right word, "persistent."

"So what did Mr. Curry do?" I was being my own form of persistent.

"He saved Mr. Brennan's life. It was during the war."

"Wow. How?"

"They were both on the same ship together. A lot of boys from this area ended up in the Pacific. It was during the war with the Japanese, and Jack Brennan and Will Curry served on the same ship together."

"What kind of ship?" I was an expert on navy ships. I'd made every model Revell had ever packaged. Donny and I had dozens of them, and an entire shelf of my room in Burlington was covered with an armada of gray plastic replicas of three different nations.

"It was a destroyer, Son," Father slipped into his slow, somber voice. "They were struck by a torpedo plane, a kamikaze near Guadalcanal. Mr. Brennan got trapped, and Mr. Curry pulled him out and got him into a life boat. The navy gave Mr. Curry a medal. He saved three men's lives that night."

Right after Father explained what kamikazes were, I asked him what Estrella y Luna meant. I figured he knew enough Spanish to hire mariachis, he'd probably know what the name of Jethro's imaginary Galleon was. As we pulled

into the sandy lot in front of Piggly's, I looked at the sky
above the water and knew exactly what I was going to name
the duck.

*Like all of parts of machinery that drove the shaft
and propellers and wheels on that boat, like all of the pieces
that fit together and connected the lives of the people who
lived in those cottages, I knew I was as important as any of
them. I knew what I was; I was the catalyst. I was the
ingredient in the mixture, the drop in the center that would
change it all, and there was no way I was going to fail.*

*The sand at the foot of the back steps of our cottage
was cool when I stepped onto it, the sky moonless. Slipping
across the space to the Silver cottage, I breathed so softly
only the faintest of molecules moved.*

*What I knew of my own cottage-- the creak of every
board, the length every door spring would stretch before it
squeaked--I didn't know of the Silver cottage. I remembered
that Skeeter always slept in the front room on the couch,
and I knew from my two visits how to find Clarisse's room
beyond the kitchen.*

*I stood shivering on the side porch in front of the
torn screen door, too frightened yet to enter. The darkness
inside loomed like the black hull of a sunken ship. I heard a
thumping, a pounding and realized that it was coming from
my ears.*

*As I inched the door back just enough to slide myself
through, I exhaled into darkness and it came to me right
there. Maggie couldn't have taken Clarisse's breath away
the way so many people were whispering she had. It was
what she had told me as we walked through the dunes that*

second morning. "I can't imagine not being able to breathe. That's our gift, Drew, our key." And I knew Maggie would never have taken that gift away from anyone.

Clarisse's hiding place was exactly where Skeeter had described it, two loosened boards beneath the very bed where her breath had ceased sometime during the previous night. That thought set me to shivering so hard I could barely lift the boards.

***

Miss Millie was bobbing like a buoy on her peach crate behind the counter. I could tell by the way she held on to it that she had already been sipping from her Mason jar a lot by the time we got there. She had that impish look and smelled like Coca Cola and what Momma splashed on my cut. I'd known about her jar since I was really young, because Miss Millie didn't care a nickel if any of the locals knew about it. She just kept it hidden out of some deference to the tourists. Other than being a bit rounder than the summer before, she looked pretty much the same. Her new helper-- Rindy they called her--was talking to a young couple that sat close to each other and didn't stop looking into each other's eyes when their food was set down.

As we entered she called out, "Well, hello boys, welcome back. I always know summer's arrived when the MacLarens walk through my door." MacLarens came out sounding like Muglaarins.

Father walked behind the counter and kissed Miss Millie on the forehead; afterwards she stepped down with a plunk and wrapped me into a ten-second hug replete with alcohol whiffs that would have staggered a horse. With her off of the peach crate, and my three inches of new height, I was an inch above her. I liked the feeling, but I still hopped up on one of her bar stools for a good spin. "Hello, Drew Drop. I am not pleased in the least that you're taller than me now. Every year I'm looking up at someone else who used to be shorter. Always reminds me that I'm getting too damned old and shrinking with age."

Without missing a beat she shifted into one of her favorite subjects. "You boys missed a couple of big storms this winter, but all of us are still here. Look at that one. I got a new addition to my collection." She flipped a finger towards a color photograph on the wall to the right of the door. Water was rolling over the bank at the foot of the pier, and I suddenly realized why the sand around the cottage had looked so different. "Lot of surge in that blow, but the waves weren't so much. Nothin' like what we've seen before, eh, John?" She paused for a breath. "So how are ya'?"

"Fine as can be, Millie. Jean Gray's well. Nina May had a rough time of it last Christmas with her heart, but she's doing better now. We're seeing to it that she does a lot less around the place and gets more rest."

She smiled a little sadly. "You're a good man, John. This ol' earth needs a lot more of your kind."

"Yours, too, Millie. Not half an hour ago I was telling Jack Brennan that it's people like you who've been here the longest, the ones who look out for each other, lend a hand when it's needed. You're the ones that make the fabric tight while everything's trying to unravel it."

"Coming from you, John, that's a special compliment."

"The truth always makes for good compliments."

"You tell Jean Gray and Nina May to come on in and visit. We'll have some girl talk and catch up. So what can I get you? If you're here for food I expect I know most of your order already, exceptin' the drinks."

Father nodded, smiling and said, "Let's see, we'll have...," He fished into his shirt pocket and opened the note. "Five orders of barbecue with hush puppies and slaw, two chocolate shakes, and three teas."

While Father and Millie discussed national politics and the deficient qualities of a host of current politicians, my counter spinning began to slow. I looked at the new photograph of the winter waves and noticed another picture, an older one, near it. It hadn't been there the year before, I knew, because I made a point of studying every picture in Miss Millie's diner over and over. It was part of my way of learning history, look at Miss Millie's pictures and ask her about them.

I hopped down and walked over to it. It was two photographs to the right of the one where she was holding the King Mackerel when she was seventeen, but this one was different. It was of her and Clarisse. She looked a few years older in it. The two of them were standing with their arms draped over each others shoulders at the entrance to the old dance hall that no longer existed. They were smiling sweetly into the lens with their hair drawn back by wide hair bands, and they looked like they were ready for mischief. I could tell because they looked just like the sixth-grade girls who stood in clusters at recess and whispered in giggles when I walked by with any of my friends.

At the bottom of the matting, printed in fancy letters was The Pavilion, March, 1942.

"Miss Millie? When did you get this one?" I lifted it off the wall because I knew she never minded that. She liked me to bring them over to her so she could point out details in them.

Miss Millie looked at me strangely. "I got that back in May, Mr. Curious."

"Where'd it come from?"

"It was a gift, Drew Drop."

I asked from whom, but she had just turned away from me to the blender, so I re-hung it in its place on the wall. "Is that you and Mrs. Silver?" I hopped back up on the stool as the blender started up in a racket of whirling chocolate ice cream and milk.

"Yes, Child, it was taken some years back, not that many, but enough. That was a night we went dancin'."

"And that's Mrs. Silver with you?"

Miss Millie sighed at my persistence. "Yes, Child, that's Clarisse and me." She smiled at some drifting thought from the past. "You can't see it there, being black and white and all, but we had big green ribbons in our hair because it was a Saint Patrick's Day dance."

"They still had special dances like that during the war?"

She poured the chocolate shakes right in front of me and snapped the lids on with a fanfare. We both knew it was on purpose, because I'd have to wait until I got home to taste them, and she was demonstrating my need for a tad of patience. "Drew Drop, you've more questions inside that head of yours than a TV detective. Where'd you get all that curiosity?"

I wagged my head and wiggled. "I don't know, Miss Mille. I guess I just like questions."

She slid the shakes into a bag and towards me with her big smile and whispered, "Well, why don't you come on back sometime, and we'll sit and I'll try to answer all of 'em. Deal?" Her hand shot out and we shook.

"Deal!"

On the drive home I told Father my idea for naming the duck. He nodded, patted me on the back of the head and smiled in a way that told me he really did like it and wasn't just being nice. "That's a perfect name, Son. It's just right, and I expect Jethro will love it." The rest of the way home he kept smiling and repeating it just to hear how it sounded rolling off his tongue. "<u>The Rising Star</u>. <u>The Rising Star</u>."

***

Liberation. That was what it was; the autonomy to select where I wished to be, and with whom I wished to be during those warm months. My commitments to Mai, Maggie, and Jethro were my own, unlike my time on the mainland. Not that I truly detested the dissecting of frogs, or the pushing of cracked cafeteria trays in front of the cranky woman who always scowled if I asked who made the salads, but it continually felt as if someone else was making my decisions for me, some invisible time thief.

I had taken to writing the events of my days into my journal before I went to sleep and had arranged my schedule in that book like an architect of time. I woke before sunrise, chatted with Nina May, helping her if she needed things beyond the perimeter of her kitchen. I walked with Maggie, sometimes in silence as she hummed and sang her way along the path to Mai's cottage, sometimes with easy conversation, or questions we both sought answers to in our mutual world. We would joke and giggle, and I tried to do everything that I could to make her look at me and smile, because that always made my insides tingle and feel like melted butter.

Afterwards I would stretch my arms and legs in a sequence of new movements and flutter them slowly with profound inhale upon Mai's deck. And I sipped tea.

One morning, while the air whipped through the curves of the lower dunes and the sky hung like brushed lead around us, I asked Maggie, in my recurrent need for more of her story, about her grandparents. For my part, I told her I'd only known Father's parents through vague memories and photographs, but my grandfather Donnell on my mother's side, I knew well. I was always proud to talk about him because he was an important man, a judge and retired brigadier general in the Army. He and my grandmother Dorothy lived in a rambling old mansion on Main Street in Graham, a short drive from our home in Burlington.

Maggie confided, "Well, I only knew my momma's daddy, Simon. He died when I was three, but I remember him well enough. I got taken to his church a couple of times."

"Was he a priest?" My understanding of denominations and their terms was limited to Episcopalians and Catholics.

"No, he was a minister, a Baptist," she smiled to herself, "and a loud one at that. I remember him yelling down at us like there was a fire in his church. Damnation and sin, all that kind of stuff."

"That all you remember?"

She looked ahead. "It's about all I can remember, but I still hear all his words. You listen careful enough, you'll hear 'em too."

"How's that?"

"They're coming out of Clarisse."

Jethro, Pooh, and I worked tirelessly on The Rising Star. All of Dare County now called her that because each of us yelled out the name to every passer-by. Then we'd point proudly to the lettering and the Portuguese colors arcing across the stern. Each successive day brought more shine to her hull, more luster to her hardware. Parts arrived. Sanders, large and small rotated about her body. More people stopped by, more hands found work. We became loving cosmeticians, layering oil-based primer like eye shadow and lipstick. The Star gained elegance and beauty with each stroke, and I kept a record of the entire process with my Instamatic camera.

On the last day of my tenure on dry land, the day before I would take Holy Communion again with Father and ride the waves across the bar, Mai took me through the final set of the Dances of the Crane. Those movements had, for some reason, been easier for me to execute than any others she had taught me. They were like natural extensions of all I had learned before, a graceful curving of fingers and outstretched limbs fed by the rhythms of my breath.

Afterwards, as she had done so often before, Mai would take my hands and looked at the palms carefully. I was beginning to understand that she could interpret signs there that she didn't always tell me about.

"My Drew beginning to improve. Good student, more and more like a strong river, nothing stopping flow now." She looked at my face and asked seriously, "What you hear inside this morning?"

I thought on it. It had sounded like the whistling of wind. "I guess it sounded like the wind, Mai." I joked, "Heck, maybe it was the wind. Kind of sounded like a song." Then I remembered what it had soundest closest to. "It reminded me of being in church at Easter with Momma last year when the choir sang really high."

Mai held both of my hands inside hers and smiled perceptively, as if she was closely acquainted with whatever music I was trying to describe. Rubbing my hands warmly inside hers, she said seriously, "Listen to that sound, Drew. Listen to the song. The more you listen, the more you will hear." With those few words Mai lead me up another rung on her great ladder.

Maggie and I had never walked together beyond the tumbled boards of Ensign Bill's. We met there and parted there each morning. I didn't ask why, and she never offered a reason, though I presumed it came from her not wanting anyone to see us that way. Or maybe I didn't want folks to see us together. Nonetheless, until that morning none but a select few saw where I went, or with whom.

I had crossed the highway at a trot and was skip-hopping between two cottages toward the ocean, thinking of my imminent freedom in the waves again, when something popped raggedly against my left ear. A bottle cap, flattened and sharp, spun into the sand in front of me. A snicker followed.

The cottage on that side was boarded up with heavy ply, signifying its vacancy.

There were rules about that kind of cottage. As children we'd learned them at early ages, most of us from threatening parents. A vacant cottage was an acceptable and fabulous hiding place, the shadows below providing superior concealment in the games of hide-and-seek. No adults yelled at you to quit fooling beneath the pilings. Even the porches were fair fields of play, but never, ever, were we to enter the forbidden territory inside. As I looked to the source of the bottle cap, I saw the plywood that had covered a side window was now lying splintered upon the porch below it. Another snicker. "Where ya been, Squirt?" The instant I heard the voice, I recognized it. Winston Ewell May III was standing inside the illicit shadows.

I started to walk towards the ocean without answering, hoping to get far enough beyond the cottages to be seen by anyone along the beach. "Hey, you little fuck, I asked you a goddamn, fucking question." His voice had a snarl to it that set my skin to crawling. I knew I had to say something quickly, but it came out with more tremor than I wanted. "Hey, Wink, is that you? Couldn't see you. When did you all get back?"

I wanted to keep moving, keep treading a path out in front of Cottage Row, but as I took a step toward the opening, a figure appeared in front of me. A boy who looked monstrously large blocked my way. Wink leapt over the railing into the sand behind me.

"I asked you where you been." His eyes hadn't changed over the year. His hair was crew cut, and he looked bigger than I remembered A lot bigger.

"Oh…well, you know, dune walking an' stuff, Wink. Hiked up Old Faithful this morning."

Wink spit a glob of gooey mess into the sand between my feet. "That so." The other boy stepped up next to me.

I knew my voice was revealing every shred of fear I was feeling; I hoped it wasn't giving away my untruths. "Yeah… I met Pooh Hutton up there real early…and we had a can race. You remember Pooh, he played on our team last year." I was trying anything.

"You're fucking lying, you little sack of shit. I saw you. You came over from Bill's place. And you know what else I saw, I saw that Silver girl with you." My heart clawed its way into the upper part of my throat, and my knees sagged. If I'd thought it would have done an ounce of good, I would have succumbed to that sinking right onto the sand and begged forgiveness for my fib, but all my experience whispered to me that it would have been totally in vain.

A thin, wicked smile spread across Winston's lips. "Whatcha been doin' over there with Raggedy Ann?" He glanced at his companion, and the unspoken signal was sent. The other boy's leg went in classic fashion behind my heels while Wink popped me in the chest from the front. I tripped flat onto my back, and then I saw Wink musingly turn his ring, the one with the over-sized purple stone on it, around on his finger. Without warning he knelt on one knee and whacked me just above the ear, the spiky point cracking just above my left temple. Pain burst in a sharp explosion, and I cried out, my hand flying to the spot. I tried, fought with all my strength, to keep tears from rolling out. "Know what I think? I think you been putting your fingers in that trash girl's pussy. You sure can't be sticking that little dick of yours in there, 'cuz you'd need a microscope to find it." Monster boy giggled right on cue. "Course, maybe she does know how to find it. I bet she likes it when you stick your fingers inside her, huh? Let's see what we got here."

Wink was straddling my knees like a rodeo rider now and was reaching for the knot on the rope belt around my waist. Monster boy stepped on my sleeve, pinching the flesh on my arm, while Wink held my other arm submerged it into the sand. With his free hand he tugged at the knot on my belt. "*Oh, God.*" The rope pulled free.

Out of the corner of my eye I saw a flicker of movement, a ghost on the porch opposite the vacant cottage. The porch was screened, so I couldn't be certain what, or who, it was. I prayed I was right and yelled out, "Good morning, Mrs. Sezinsky." Mrs. Sezinsky, I knew was more than eighty, with eyesight worse than Nina May's, but it didn't matter, and I knew she had cats, about thirteen of them. As Wink was trying to smother my mouth with his hand, I squirmed my head to the side and yelled as loudly as I could, "Are you feeding your cats."

"Good morning…Who…who is that." Her voice sounded so weak, I was sure my tormentors were going to ignore her completely. Wink's hand cupped tightly over my mouth again, and I struggled to breath.

Because I'd talked to her a few times on my returns from Mai's, and because I had always taken a polite interest in her feline friends, as she referred to them, she recognized my voice.

"That sounds like Andrew MacLaren." The side screen door creaked open and suddenly the hand over my mouth was gone.

"Yes, Ma'am, Mrs. Sezinsky. It's me, Drew. How're cats doing?"

Wink and his companion were standing now, shifting further away from me and turning their faces towards the vacant cottage. I took the opportunity and bolted to the bottom step at the foot of her side door. "Yes, Ma'am. It's me." I was breathing like a diesel engine.

"Well, how are you doing this morning, Andrew?" She stood curved like a little conch shell with her hand pushing the screen door back against its frame. The yawning porch beyond looked like the nave of a warm chapel. My sanctuary.

"I'm fine, Mrs. Sezinsky. Fine as can be." My heart rhythm slowed from a racing gallop to a canter. I hopped onto the middle step and glanced over my shoulder. There was nothing across the divide. "How're your cats doing?" If you wanted conversation with Mrs. Sezinsky, there was only one subject.

"Oh, they're just as chatty as can be this morning. Sir Lancelot was arguing with Rudyard at breakfast, and Eleanor, she's named after Mrs. Roosevelt, you know, she didn't show up with the others. I don't think she likes to eat with them. She's sort of prissy sometimes. And Mr. Churchill's acting like he expects second helpings again."

"Yes, Ma'am, I remember you telling me how he does that." I looked down the divide between the cottages, towards the highway, and saw two figures sprint across heading south towards Hatteras. My heart slowed. I could have hugged Mrs. Sezinsky, and I was definitely changing my attitude towards her cats, two of which were now curling around my ankles like large caterpillars.

A few minutes after I'd told her how I'd love to help her feed them all one morning, I decided to attempt a personal best on my one-mile run. I reached the cottage in less than six minutes.

Fear is a form of emotional mildew. It grows like thick mold on all the shiny impressions of freedom a boy develops, a mold that slips invisibly across all the sweetness of liberation. I learned that peculiar lesson all too clearly that morning. And more than any single moment I'd yet experienced in my life, that moment when my mouth was held shut and the knot was loosened on my belt, when helplessness saturated everything, that moment stole my freedom.

I sat as far as I could under the pilings of the great cottage, completely out of breath. I crawled below the maze of galvanized pipe and old wire to the very center and would have dug my way under the sand if I could have. Completely clothed, I felt naked. I sobbed and clutched my own body in the shadows, as if to console it with my own arms. I cried and rocked like a baby until there was only numbness inside. Around me the air had a different appearance, a sharpness that stung my eyes, and I didn't know at all what to do. I didn't know who to talk to.

My mind was scattered into portions of embarrassment, fear, and the need to tell someone, anyone what had occurred. In the middle, I had no idea what to do.

Even though Father had intervened on Maggie's behalf, this was something I knew he or Momma couldn't know of. I thought of Donny, how he might help. As brothers our relationship had evolved to a place where his teasing was now innocent fun, and we had a good mutual respect for each other. Donny looked out for me now. Perhaps he would know what to do. I wasn't sure.

I didn't work on <u>The Rising Star</u> that morning. I made my way quietly to the upstairs bathroom and washed myself twice, then lay face down on my bed and wrote in my journal until my fingers ached with the task. I wrote things I didn't want anyone to ever read. I wrote about the choir that sang inside my head on Mai's deck that morning. I wrote about the people who had confided their deepest fears to me. Sixth-graders pinned against lockers, Pooh crying in the sand, Maggie, Nina May, and Mai. My list grew. Then I re-read Super Hero comics all afternoon and wished just for an hour that I could bend steel.

Donny eventually figured out what to do. I guess it was because he'd been around it longer and had more experience in the politics of cruelty. I told him what happened, of course. It was right after an uncommonly quiet dinner where I hoped none of my family would notice my silence and miserable expression. Over chicken cacciatore and summer salad, Mother and Father exchanged more than a few questioning looks, and I ended up perjuring myself at least six times with statements that everything was just fine.

Eventually I was able to excuse myself from the table to follow Donny up to his room. I sat on the bed, and within minutes, was sobbing into a pillow, because I had to repeat all the ugliness of Winston May's words. It was the darkest blasphemy I'd ever uttered when I forced myself to repeat what he'd said about Maggie and me. Donny listened without a word. He waited until I had spilled it all out, and afterwards all he did was ask me to describe Wink's companion once more. Then there was a look that came into his eyes. A look that came directly from Father, and for a second I became worried he was going to rally an army that included my parents.

"You can't tell Momma, Donny." I pleaded. "You just can't. Father neither. They wouldn't understand. You know Momma'd go stompin' down the beach to jump all over Mrs. May about it. You can't, you can't." I started crying again.

"I know, Drew. This is guy stuff, and guys always have to figure out what to do about each other. Momma won't know. Nobody will. I promise, but listen here, I've gotta think on this for a while. Okay? You get some sleep and quit thinking about it yourself. All right?" I just shook my head weakly up and down.

My eyes were puffy red as I opened the door and peeked into the hall to make sure no one was there before I snuck to my room. One final, fearful thought came to me. "Donny?"

"What?"

"What if he's there again? What if he follows us?"

"He won't, Drew, and I'll think of something. I promise. Go to sleep now."

***

Nina May had pancake batter with chunks of peach and hazelnuts swirled into it sitting on the counter next to the griddle on her stove. Butter, syrup, and a small glass of fresh orange juice waited in front of my placemat on the table in the breakfast nook. It looked suspiciously as if she knew I needed extra affection that morning, and sure enough, before I could sit down or even say good morning, I was pulled into her massive bosom for a lengthy hug. Somewhere inside that sweet aroma of flesh and peach, I realized there had been a discussion of some sort the night before. The adults in the great cottage were pondering why the youngest MacLaren was so down in the dumps.

"You must've slept well, Master Little." Nina May couldn't seem to let go of the title she had used for me since birth, even though I had politely asked a few hundred times. "Cuz your eyes are shiny and bright as buttons this morning."

I figured that was because my tears had cleaned them pretty well the night before. I wasn't ready to get into any of it yet, so I responded simply, "Yes, Ma'am, I went to bed early last night."

"Well that's the way it should be. Where're you off to today? You still goin' over to the sound to see that Missus Mai?" She couldn't let go of that title either.

My family, by that time had taken my daily excursions across the strand as an expected, and accepted, part of my mornings. Father still asked me about all the physical parts, the exercises and breathing. Momma, after our first week back, asked if Mrs. Mai Lin wouldn't like to come over for hors d' oeuvres and cocktails some afternoon.

I told her I would extend her invitation, but that Mai pretty much stayed put, unless she needed her groceries.

A steaming pancake slid off Nina May's spatula onto my plate. "Yes ma'am. I'm going there this morning, then I'm taking off this pile of bandages for the last time, and I'm going swimming with Father, and I'm gonna paint on <u>The Rising Star</u> and help Jethro. An' maybe later I'll climb in the dunes with Pooh or go fishin' with Skeeter." I always knew that it gave Nina May some sense of peace when she knew where I was going during my day. Though I never said so, it gave me a warm feeling knowing that she knew where I was, too.

"Well, you'll be running all over the strand with that set of plans, but I guess that's the business a boy your age should be in." She flopped another pancake onto my plate and said, "Master Little, you do us all a favor, your Momma especially, and keep from getting yourself hurt again." Then she looked at me with a questioning smile, tendering a silent offer to tell her what was bothering me. I couldn't tell her. Not yet.

"Yes, Ma'am. I don't need anymore time on dry land. I'm healed and plan to stay that way." After two more pancakes, which I knew were going to make me late, I hugged Nina May, this time of my own volition, and flew out the back door.

I didn't walk along the sand in front of the cottages or along the highway either. I threaded my way through the low dunes on the west side, well out of anybody's sight, and only here and there had to run across open spaces where I might be seen. I kept seeing Winston's face sneering at me from the dark shadows of every window. I saw his face above me, the purple stone of his ring dripping with my blood. I saw my pants down around my ankles and my hands tied with my own belt rope

Maggie was sitting on the last of the sunken steps at Bill's Spot. That was our name for it now. The Spot. For me that place had been ours for two summers, secret and ours, and now I wondered if Winston Ewell May III was watching it like a sniper with a rifle, camouflaged in some unknown position. Maggie was sitting cross-legged, Indian style, her hair braided in a single cord down her back. Her hands were folded neatly upwards in her lap, and as usual with Maggie in our Spot, her eyes were closed and she was drawing in the air in deep, slow cycles. I stopped and watched her for three breaths. I believe I could have stood there watching the contentment in her face until the sun set. I silently cursed Wink May and Frank Curry.

"I've been waiting for you, Mr. Long Legs. You have a nice big breakfast this morning?" A teasing grin curled at the corners of her mouth. Her eyes were still closed.

"How'd you know that? I had peach pancakes for your information, Miss Margaret." I'd taken to calling her that whenever she called me something other than Drew. "And I kind of walked in a different direction from the cottage this morning." I hadn't meant to let that slip out, or maybe I did. I wanted desperately to talk to her about the afternoon before, but I couldn't tell her, for all the gold in the sea, what Wink had said about us.

She eyed me curiously. "Why's that?"

We started walking, but I knew her question wasn't going to be left hanging on Bill's rotten steps, so I had to answer, "I just didn't want anybody to see me is all."

"Who's going to see you, Drew? It's not like anybody's going to care? You worried about bein' teased?" She looked over her shoulder with a teasing look herself. "You know, being with a girl."

Maggie's was in a feisty mood. She was all set to joust with me and didn't recognize that she had by mere chance tapped into the tenderest hollow in my heart. I stared at the burs as we rounded the curve, saying nothing, and she instantly knew that was what it was. She kept on. "That's it, isn't it? You're worried somebody giving you a pile of trouble bout bein' with a girl." She started singing the timeless taunt, "Drew and Maggie sittin' in a tree, K-I-S-S-I-N-G. First comes love then comes marriage...,"

"Maggie, stop it!" I kicked into the sand and bit my upper lip so hard it split. An uninvited tear rolled far too slowly along my cheek. She spun right around and stared at me.

Like a finely cut jewel, Maggie Silver had a thousand facets. Most of them were covered by the dismal grime of Clarisse's slow descent into madness. They were obscured by her inability to prevent the awful decay in her life, and by her resolute commitment to her brother. For short, fleeting moments with me, she had been mischievous, childlike, even blissful, and a few of those facets had been granted fractions of time to shine in their natural states. Maggie had been as compassionate and protective as an avatar, a caring shepherd, a loving mother, and a first-time lover. She was none of those to me, but her compassion rose from those places.

She stepped towards me. "Oh, Drew! I'm sorry. Something's happened. I should've seen it. I didn't know. I'm so sorry. Tell me what it is. What's happened?" Then she had her hands on the side of my face, her fingers lightly finding the exact place that amethyst and blood had mixed. She pulled me inside her arms and I cried. I didn't want to, but lately my tears had been dropping from the end of my chin like a leaky faucet, and I had absolutely no ability to curb them.

Through a blurry mist I hiccupped, "Wink and some…he was so big, Maggie…they saw me…they saw us…and they beat on me yesterday…said I was…" I hiccupped into silence.

"Said you were what, Drew? You tell me now."

"I can't, Maggie. It was… horrible…"

"You listen to me, Drew MacLaren. We haven't kept any secrets from each other since the day we met. I've told you my whole rotten story whenever you've asked. Wink's a damned worm just like Frank Curry, an' if he's talkin' with an ugly mouth, it's just the same as air coming out. Nothin' but air, Drew."

In a hiccupping voice I threw it up like vomit, ugly sprays of vomit. "He said I was putting my fingers inside you and you were playin' with my dick."

Maggie had the sense not to laugh, but she did grin. "Well…that's pretty ugly air, Drew. You're right about that. But it doesn't mean crap. Ugly words. Ugly, but…well, it isn't half as bad as what Frank Curry said I ought to do to him." She laughed a bit and shook her head. "What is it with you boys?" She wiped a tear from the side of my eye with her thumb. "Always trying to impress us girls with how tough you are?"

In a sulky voice I said, "I'm not trying to impress anybody, Maggie."

"Then I guess you've never had a girlfriend, 'cuz that's most of what you do when you have a girlfriend. The other half bein' tryin' to figure out whether she likes you or not."

"You ever had a boyfriend?" My hiccups were subsiding slowly.

She pinched her lips together like she was trying to decide. "I don't know if he was what you'd call a real boyfriend or not. It was back in tenth grade and we went to the movies twice, and the second time he bought me popcorn and tried to put his hand down the top of my sweater just before the end of the movie. He spilled soda on his crotch tryin' to reach around my shoulder, and when lights came on everybody thought he'd peed his pants." Finally, I smiled.

"Any others?"

She sighed heavily. "I went on one date a little over a year ago. That was with Mark Hemmet from Elizabeth City, and he had a black Ford Fairlane." She slipped into the memory of the boy with the shiny convertible. "But the second time he came down,…Momma. Well, damn if she didn't came out onto our deck in her nightgown. It was four in the afternoon an' we were sittin' in the driveway getting ready to go to bingo and dancin' afterwards. Momma screamed at us. Screamed like she was looking down from her daddy's pulpit. Said God Almighty was going to turn

Mark Hemmet's skin into big open sores for taking me dancin'. 'Putrid pustules,' she called them. Mark didn't drive down from Elizabeth City anymore after that. I guess that's when I knew for real Momma was having trouble in her head."

As the bamboo of Mai's garden rose at our approach, all the misgivings I'd had of talking to Maggie remained in the sand at the curve in the dunes where she had held me inside her arms and touched my wounds. We shared essential truths with each other that gray morning, created a pact-- we could, and always would, talk about anything inside our hearts, even if it was the disgusting words of Winston May and Frank Curry. After all, they were just air.

***

Mai brushed Maggie's hair as we sat on the pillows. Our cups were empty, but no one rose to clear them. Mai had unbraided the thick cord after our Chi work and now sat drawing long strokes through the satin strands with a wide brush. Every few minutes she would gather it into a bundle to lift so she could brush the underside. The hair glistened like oil in the sunlight and Maggie would have purred with each stroke if she were feline.

I had never seen a woman's hair being brushed that way before. Momma always seemed to enjoy it when she brushed hers, but not like this. This was done with such affection that they both looked like what I figured people must've felt when they kissed. I watched in silent awe.

My questions floated up. "Mai?"

"Yes, Drew"

"Why did you decide to come to Nags Head when you came from China? Why'd you decide on comin' here?"

Mai continued brushing Maggie's hair, but a sad kind of smile came to her lips. "It was good place to start again, Drew. I was leaving many bad places behind, places of killing and hate."

"Your home in Tantsien?"

"My home was gone. I needed a new home." It was such a simple statement, but it attached itself like resin to me.

"Is that why you stay alone?"

"It is best for me to stay alone.

"Why's that?"

She sighed. "Because too many people...sometimes they scare me. I go to store alone for food. I have my house and books, my birds. When I left Tantsien I needed place with strong energy, and this place have strongest energy ever." She smiled and looked from Maggie's hair to me and said, "Strongest chi come from moving water and air, Drew. Come from moving sand and wings of birds. Where can I find such good chi? Here it is best. What else an old woman need?"

It took a moment for that to settle in, but with a sudden revelation, I realized that I had already known that. I had felt that energy for a long time, for eleven glorious summers.

I just didn't understand about Mai living alone.

***

"She's a sight, Lads, a true beauty. Boxy lines like the great galleons the Spanish made. Now they were people that knew how to build boats." Jethro was walking along the port side of <u>The Rising Star</u>, caressing her paint job like she was a magnificent, tame panther that purred under his touch. "The pistons have new rings, her cylinders are re-bored, we're only waiting on the carburetor and a new battery for her. She'll be a fine sight on her maiden voyage, that's a sure bet."

Pooh and I were sitting exhausted on three-legged stools, one of which I was certain Jethro had requisitioned from Old Mason Farrow at the gas pump because it had a lingering, peculiar odor just like him. Our arms were streaked with ivory and sky blue, the same lacquer colors that now covered <u>The Star's</u> hull and topside. Jethro had hand painted her name in gracefully curved black letters in a half moon across the stern. There was also a small Portuguese flag in bright yellow, black, and red, and Nags Head, NC below all of it.

The boat yard had never seen so much activity. Over the three weeks, delivery trucks arrived, helpers came and went, and Jethro's boys made certain every contributor had plenty of hot coffee and pastries in the morning or sandwiches after midday.

A high transom had been welded on the stern below her name, and over those weeks she had metamorphosed from an unsightly woman with a frock of barnacles to an elegant lady of ivory and blue. She even had a new set of shoes, six large black tires that looked totally incongruous with her curving hull lines and propeller. They clearly weren't the stylish shoes one would expect of a lady in such a fine dress, looking like more functional tennies below a fine evening gown, but to all of us, she was as sophisticated as a queen.

During that period I had learned a good deal about how engines worked and which paints stood the salt of the sea. I learned about ballast and bilge, how shafts turned, and the way propellers and tillers kept a craft on its steady course. I was still working on what drove people on their courses, but boats were becoming much less of a mystery.

"When do you think she'll be ready, Captain?" I swatted at a double-winged dragonfly about to make the mistake of its life by landing on the last of the wet paint.

"Well, Mr. MacLaren, if we get the carburetor in and all the wiring done, she'll need a good tuning, of course, and some testing in the lot. We could say three more days. So that would be Friday, and if the calendar in my head is working correctly, that's the Fourth of July. A proper auspicious day for a launch."

Pooh nodded and drawled slowly, "Can I bring some fireworks, Captain?"

"I would be mighty disappointed if you didn't, Mr. Hutton."

Rockets. That's what I wanted. Big ones. No cherry bombs, no crackers, I wanted Roman candles lining the sand as she rolled towards the waves, and a hundred rockets exploding high in the sky above her. It was, after all, the culmination of Jethro's great dream, when the tides, wind, and stars were all in place for him.

After I scrubbed the paint from my arms and set a time to meet Pooh later in the afternoon, I ran to the cottage for lunch. On my way I stopped to tell Skeeter I'd come over afterwards for a decent review of our newest comics.

I'd hoped Donny was going to be home. I wanted to know if he had designed any new blueprints for solving my problems of Wink and his ogre friend, but Nina May told me he'd left early in the morning and she hadn't seen him since. He hadn't returned for lunch either.

Skeeter was waiting on the front porch with a four-inch stack of Marvels. Every Thursday Maggie would bring him any new comic that had arrived at Mr. Jensen's. His collection was bigger than mine now.

We were discussing The Phantom, who wasn't one of my favorites--he rode a horse which just didn't seem like a proper style of transport for a comic book hero. Capes and anti-gravity vehicles were more to my liking, but Skeeter had two new Phantoms, so that was what we were discussing.

"I just don't like his mask, Skeets. I mean, it's too small. Look at that. Anybody could figure out who he was just by looking at him. He looks like the Lone Ranger in purple tights." Skeeter was looking a little disappointed that I wasn't totally enthralled with his newest additions, so added, "He's still a great hero and all, and I like the way he's always in the jungle. That's some place I want to go sometime, the jungle."

"Me, too, Drew. Guess I'd need a motor-powered wheel chair, though, huh? An anti-gravity machine would be neat. Somethin' a little better than Pegasus." We laughed, because we could do that now, laugh together about his not being able to leave the porch. Still, I thought every time we were together how unfair it seemed that he lived on an island surrounded by sand, a surface where his wheels would not rotate.

"Yeah," I agreed, "we could get you a horse, just like The Phantom. You could ride a horse, I bet." Then out of the blue I asked, "Hey, is Skeeter your real name?"

Shyness wrapped about him. "No…it's Stephen, but nobody calls me that, so I guess you could say Skeeter is my real name."

I was ready to ask him how he came by it when suddenly behind us a shriek split the air. "Devil's music. Devil's music." Clarisse, or a part of her, had risen from the caverns of dreams. The shrieks subsided into an unintelligible muttering.

I heard Maggie's voice whispering softly, "It's okay, Momma. Nobody's here. There're no devils, Momma."

Then, like a chant Clarisse mumbled over and over, "Lord God, strike the sinner. Strike the sinner down." Skeeter reached across the open pages of The Phantom and wrapped his hand around my wrist. I set mine atop his, both of us equally terrified.

The screaming tapered to silence, and I whispered to Skeeter, "How'd you like to sleep over at my house some night?" It was spontaneous, but it just seemed so unfair that his island was surrounded by impassable sand and the center of it was sinking into a dark abyss. He looked at me like I wasn't serious, so I continued, "We could have dinner and stay up in my room and read comics all night. Father could get you up there real easy."

"I ain't never slept over at nobody's house, Drew. I don't know what I'd need."

"Heck, you don't need anything, Skeets. Just some PJs and your comics, maybe Lizard to get to the bathroom."

I could see that he was thinking about it, but the uncertainty of leaving his small, ordered world, where the iced tea was always at the correct height, the sofa bed so familiar, was tugging him back. The idea of venturing beyond that place was terrifying.

With some hesitation he said, "I guess I could go, but I gotta ask Maggie."

"You know she'll say okay, Skeeter. Heck, it's only two doors down. It's not like a lot can happen." Not having that most unattainable of superhero of powers, that of clairvoyance, how was I to know how horrible it would get?

In the afternoon Momma drove me up to Mr. Jensen's market. I wanted something new to add to my own comic collection after Skeeter and I had dissected the two issues of Phantom. Momma had sensed in her usual way that I preferred not to walk there by myself, even though it wasn't that far.

Mr. Jensen had a small bell on a curved piece of spring steel hanging above the door of the market. I always liked it because the jingling sounded happy to me and sort of welcomed you as you entered.

Mr. Jensen was crusty. That was the way most people described him. Donny used the term 'tough old buzzard' when he talked about him behind his back. All I knew was, I wouldn't ever have thought about trying to pocket a piece of candy in his store without paying for it. I also knew he was one of those people who, underneath all that toughness, had a heart of gold. He was as tall as my father, but the better portion of a decade older. He always had stubble spreading out like an infestation from his chin, and wore a red and blue baseball cap with a 'B' stitched on the front. Donny, knowing more about such things, told me Mr. Jensen was a Boston Red Sox fan, one who had gotten very cynical about their chances of ever winning a world series again.

Mr. Jensen's market was the greatest repository of sweet-goods an eleven-year old could dream of. As a matter of fact, everything in that store seemed to be designed for young boys. He had pizza that came directly from the oven that you could buy by the slice, sandwiches so big you couldn't get your teeth around them, cold sodas of every variety, and a candy rack that stretched down half of one side of the back aisle. But his best offering--in my young opinion--was two spinning racks of comic books. Being his best-sellers, he always kept them fully stocked with the newest editions.

"Good afternoon, Zacharius." Momma always called Mr. Jensen that, and I was certain it was because she liked the sound of the name more than the pleasant address.

Mr. Jensen grunted, "Jean Gray."

"Beautiful day outside."

"If you say it is, then I guess it must be." I scooted over to the racks to bury my nose in something, while Momma went to the back to get milk and margarine. It took me less than a minute to find the newest issues of Flash and Captain America. My day was complete.

When I returned to the counter with my bag of coins and my purchases, Mr. Jensen looked at me and said, "Looks like you've grown." That was it. No name, no 'how've you been?' Just an acknowledgment that I'd grown. The funny part was, I knew he understood how proud those four words made me.

"Yes Sir. Three inches since last summer." I pushed my comics and a pile of coins forward and he rang it up. The faintest smile curled on the sides of his mouth.

"Well, I guess you're just about big enough to handle a broom now. If you're interested, I'll pay six-bits an hour to push one through this store. Three hours a day, startin' August."

Momma set her groceries down, but didn't say anything. She looked at me and I knew it was my decision. Suddenly, all these adult decisions were coming my way.

"Yes, Sir, I'd like that," though I wasn't sure if that first employment was something I really wanted or not.

Momma drove back by herself, with a promise to place my comics with the utmost care on my bed before she put the milk away. I was free to meet Pooh as planned.

Jockey's Ridge. Of all of the great venues for boyhood adventure, that enormous, drifting mountain of soft sand was highest on the list. It was the foremost setting for a child's imagination to be set free. It rose from the lower dunes and thick shrubbery like a towering patriarch surveying its lesser relatives in a proud but disdainful manner. The elevation was high enough to see dozens of miles in any direction, and the sand at the top was pale and soft as feathers with sides wind rippled into a thousand perfectly spaced ribs. No plants marred the upper half, and from the top, a boy could run and leap and sail a full thirty feet downward before sinking knee deep into its powder.

Every game, every contest took on new dimensions when played upon its surfaces. Tag become an arduous spiral chase around and over its dome. Can races, jumping contests, kite flying, army assaults. My friends and I had done them all. We owned Jockey's Ridge. No matter what the park signs said, we knew. It was ours.

Pooh was waiting in our customary meeting place at the base. His cottage was north of the pier on the west side of the highway, and by mid-afternoon it lay in the long shadow of Jockey's Ridge, so he always arrived at our base camp before I did and waited patiently.

"I bet we can see into the boatyard from up there," Pooh said before we'd finished our secret handshake. "Too bad The Star's covered up with tarp. I'd bet we could read her name otherwise."

I looked wistfully at the peak. "Let's make a pact that we'll sit up on top some morning and watch her head out. That'll be a pretty sight to watch, huh?"

"That's a promise." Secret handshake. Then Pooh said, "How 'bout runnin' up today?"

"As far as I can before I drop. My arms and legs felt like noodles. No racing."

"No racing." Pooh started trudging at a steady pace straight up the east side and I loped along behind him. He looked like a toy truck chugging along, and I knew he wouldn't quit until he reached the summit.

Twenty minutes later we lay on our backs gasping for breath, the entire sandy world dropping away from our spines to the ocean and the sound. I sat up and looked around. The blue of the horizon whispered to me, and I took a breath deep into belly, my hands drifting up and down.

Pooh seemed on the edge of sleep. After a moment or two I tugged on his sleeve. "Can race?"

He rolled to his knees and unhooked the wire frame of his glasses to clean the lenses for undoubtedly the first time that day. His small eyes looked sadly at me.

"Drew?"

"Yeah?"

"We still best friends?"

I knew where that came from. I'd talked to him a few times about Skeeter, even talked about Maggie some. He didn't quite understand yet that it was possible to have new friends and still keep your old ones. "Course we are, Pooh; we're still best buddies. And you know what? I figure you'll probably own a small part of The Rising Star too, just like me. You've worked on it just as hard as me." He stopped looking sad, and the Pooh smile I'd known for eleven summers came back. I tossed out my question again. "Can race?"

"Full or empty?"

"Full, they'll roll better that way."

"Okay, let's find 'em."

Can races were an inherent specialty of every Nags Head boy, a skill developed from the time-honored process of testing every hypothesis, and like Edison, every available material. They required the steepest sections of the dunes, which is exactly what lay below us, and a short list of prerequisites. The first, of course, was the vehicle itself. Solid tin, the chubby cylinders that held vegetables or beans in their previous lives, we knew, worked best. Soda and beer cans were a distant second. We were pretty certain it had something to do with the physics of smaller diameters, or the softness of the metals, aluminum just seemed slower. But, vegetable cans were definitely more difficult to find in the dunes than soda or beer cans. The next item was the filler, the wetter the sand and heavier, the better. The racers then needed to be packed and stuffed tightly with whatever substance was readily available to seal them. Wads of cloth had the best staying power against the centrifugal force of the spinning racer. Nothing sent a young boy's machine to an earlier defeat than leaking sand as it rolled down the slope.

"Let's look over on the sound side," I suggested. That area was hidden from the highway and shielded from the wind, making it the ideal location for the itinerant bum or the beer guzzling teen. Pooh and I sailed in eight giant leaps down into the vale. Scratchy shrubs clawed at our t-shirts as we searched in and around them. Within minutes we had our racers filled and properly corked. They weren't the coveted tin variety, but two common soda cans, making the competition even.

Coming over the saddle at the crest, Pooh poked me in the ribs, pointed south with the same finger and drawled, "Hey Drew, ain't that your brother. Somebody's with him." I glanced at Pooh's glasses, which resembled small muddy headlights, and wondered how on earth he could see anything directly in front of him much less a mile south, but he was right. Two minute figures had halted on the west side of the highway waiting for a single car to pass. Then, right near Ensign Bill's, I saw them sprint across, one unmistakably the thickset body and stride of my older brother. The other, I was fairly certain, was an even thicker Georgie Marovich. They disappeared between Mrs.

Sezinsky's and the dark, vacant cottage from where my nightmares continued to surface.

"Wonder where they're headed," Pooh said.

I watched, waiting for one or both of them to reappear on the ocean side. When they didn't, I said, "Yeah, I wonder, too."

We drew our starting line at the top of the smoothest face of Jockey's Ridge, which happened to be on the northwest side and opposite where Donny and Georgie had disappeared. Pooh raised the invisible checkered flag, and we placed our racers cleanly on their marks. We knew the rules, no encouragement other than yelling was allowed. Our fingers rested like small electromagnetic clamps, lightly restraining the oriented racers. I counted--Pooh's drawl clearly too slow--, "three, two, one." They were rolling. Slowly. Always slowly at the start. Then, like skiers tucking into tight spheres, they gathered speed and trundled smoothly faster and faster down the slope. Two sets of parallel lines spewed out behind them in grainy jet trails.

Half way down I let out an audible groan; my can was wiggling first. Two-thirds of the way and it was gyrating wildly, its ends flipping upward in gloomy omens of imbalance. Pooh's racer rolled smoothly on. Near the bottom his winner, at top speed, hit a sizable bump and flew birdlike, in one last victorious flight, far into the bushy growth. Mine petered sadly into the depression.

"That was a good one, Drew." Pooh's head was bobbing back and forth in the only indicator of excitement he ever displayed. "Yours was going great until it hit that bump."

It had been a good one, he was right, and as usual, he was trying to make me feel better about my loss. Then, at Pooh's suggestion, we had a jumping contest, which I won.

The sun was settling slowly towards the warm waters of the Pamlico, signaling the hour we both needed to make our way back to our cottages. Below, I saw Jethro's longboats on the north side of the pier, the nets already layered neatly inside. The crew was lifting the iced crates into the bed of the truck that smelled of fish. I scanned the shoreline. Jethro wasn't on the beach with his boys or the truck.

After a moment I located the conspicuous mass of beard and hair a hundred yards from Mr. Jensen's market. He was walking alone, no children bustling about. Moments later he stopped, looked once at the market, and then turned crisply back towards the boatyard. From the summit of the ridge it looked as if he was a sentry on duty.

Coming through the tangle of bushes near the bottom, Pooh and I pushed our way out to the highway. We were saying our good-byes. I was setting to cross the asphalt and turn south, when a car, approaching from the north, slowed and pulled onto the shoulder near us. It was a black and white patrol car, its red dome centered on the roof like a cherry atop a sundae. Frank Curry, looking more authoritative and more diminutive than usual, sat stern-faced behind the wheel. He rolled the passenger window down and called to us. "You boys come on over here. Where you heading?"

I answered first, "Home, Sir. Just down the road."

Pooh looked like he wanted to crawl under the car or back in the bushes. I don't think he'd ever talked to anyone of authority before. "Me, too. I'm goin' home, too."

Curry looked at me like he was trying to remember where he'd seen me before. I saw him sizing me up as the clear ringleader of our gang of two. He asked suspiciously, "Where you boys been?"

I answered quickly, "Just up on Jockey's, Sir. We had a can race." I was hoping Mr. Curry remembered what it was like to be boy. He must've had can races when he was younger, but he frowned. "You know that's part of the park, don't you?"

"Yes, Sir."

"You ain't littering up there, are you?"

Pooh's head hung down and I thought he was going to start crying. I answered for us. "No, Sir, we found some old cans to use. They were already up there."

"How long you been playin' on the ridge."

I didn't fault Pooh for not being any help, he was terrified. I said, "Hour and a half, maybe two."

Curry peered at me closely, his eyes squinting against the last of the sunlight behind me. "What's your name, Boy."

"Drew, Sir."

A light clicked on in his squinty eyes. "You John MacLaren's son?"

"Yessir," I whipped off proudly.

Curry looked at me harshly, like he was filing my face into his card catalog and would know just how to retrieve it when he needed it. He thought hard for a second, and I could see he was trying hastily to think of one last thing to frighten us with, but all he could come up with was, " Okay, next time you boys bring them cans out with you and throw 'em in the garbage, you hear."

"Yes, Sir, we would've done that too, but they bounced right into the brush and we couldn't find them."

He shielded his eyes and pulled his official rank a final time. "All right, you get on home now."

I didn't answer impolitely; I just didn't answer, and with a nod trotted across the highway while Pooh headed north.

Mr. Curry watched me until I was out of sight.

The Deputy would live. His skull was fractured, four ribs were cracked, and there were enough bruises and cuts on his face that he likely wouldn't be sneering at anyone the same way ever again, but he would live. It took two days for him to come out of it, three days to regain enough dexterity in his jaw to tell Jack Brennan who had put him in the hospital at Manteo. By that time, it didn't matter. What he wasn't prepared to tell his own sheriff was why his assailant had battered him nearly to his grave.

It took two terrifying trips across the sand to Clarisse's hiding place to fetch the letters Seventeen dozen is large number. Each bundle of twelve was tied neatly with red silk ribbon and marked with a number. The first envelops were yellowed with age, the last were shiny white.

Skeeter and I tucked all but the first beneath my bed. I draped the blanket over both our heads and flipped the switch quietly on my flashlight. Skeeter untied the silk cord on the first stack and I lifted the top envelope; it was thin and cracked with time and had been opened and re-sealed

*with glue. The other eleven looked like they had never seen
light nor air.*

*Under the pale glow of the beam I ran my finger
across the inscription. It was scrawled in strong lettering on
the outside. "For The Light of My Life. The second envelope
was addressed the same, and the third...*

*I lifted the single page, neatly folded into thirds,
from its antique resting place. My hands trembled and
neither of us made a sound. I unfolded it tenderly, sensing
that inside secret keys had been stored. A single green leaf
fluttered and twirled onto my knees.*

Skeeter gasped.

Redemption

"Eat your Brussels sprouts, Drew. They'll make
your eyes strong and your teeth white." She popped one into
her mouth like some disgusting green jawbreaker.

"Momma, please! I hate Brussels sprouts. My eyes
are strong as can be already. I can see fly's wings a mile off,
and these things are like little green..." I was so close to
saying putrid pustules, having learned what that actually
meant from Maggie. Frustration and annoyance was pushing
me right to the edge. I held off.

"I thought you wanted to be a vegetarian. You can't
be a true vegetarian and not love these precious emeralds.
They've got every vitamin and mineral your body needs,
every one."

I'd eaten everything else on my plate, fish cakes,
potatoes, salad, and I was now pushing three oversized
green marbles around the perimeter with my fork. Couldn't

she see that I'd eaten everything else and didn't need any additional vitamins and minerals? Didn't she remember that I was going to be gainfully employed in a few weeks? That I wasn't a child? The only way those 'precious emeralds" were going down my throat was by force. Violent force.

Donny and Father had already excused themselves from the tortuous scene. Momma sat primly, watching me suffer like a prison warden. It all felt like some repulsive leftover of my toddler days when I wasn't released from my high chair until some variety of malcolored mush was completely consumed. I'd eaten one layer of one of those nauseating balls when I was seven and wretched. Never again.

"Just try one, Sweetheart. I know you'll like them." Another one popped into her mouth.

"Here, you eat mine. I hate them."

"Don't say hate. It's not a nice word."

"Okay, I very, very much detest them."

She smiled. "Much better choice of words, Darling." She sighed deeply, and intuitively I knew I'd won. "All right, Dear, we'll save them. I'll put them in the refrigerator for later."

"Yes, Ma'am, that's a fine location, maybe even in the freezer; they'll stay much longer that way." I slid my chair out, the tray was removed from my highchair, the prison gate was swung open, and I was a free man. Boy. Whatever. I lifted my plate to the kitchen and bolted up the front stairs to Donny's room before any reversals of my pardon were handed down.

Donny, like me, had two single beds in his room. I sat on the one furthest from the window, looked right at him and started right in. "I saw you running across the highway when I was up on Jockey's Ridge today. You were down there." I didn't even want to mention the location out of some fear of dredging up demons that would haunt my dreams later that night.

He surprised me by answering, "I know. I saw you, too. Funny how you can see everything from up there, and you forget that everybody down below can see you too." Then he added as reinforcement, "You were with Pooh."

"We were can racing. So why were you down there?" I was tired, my battle over Brussels sprouts was behind me; I wanted answers.

Donny smiled as slyly as I'd ever seen him, and I cautiously hoped that he had discovered some resolution to the terror of Winston and ogre boy stalking me all over The Banks. "You remember MaryEllen telling me Wink got arrested at Christmastime?"

"Yeah, what's that got to do with anything?"

"A lot, Drew. He got caught trespassing, busted into a house in Greensboro and trashed it up pretty bad."

I frowned, not getting the connection. "And…"

"So, Georgie and I…let's just say we slipped a few things out of the cottage next to old lady Sezinsky's."

I was thunderstruck. "You went in there? You guys broke into the cottage?"

"We didn't have to really break in; we went through the same window Wink had busted."

"And you took stuff."

"You keep this quiet, Drew. We grabbed a couple of candle-sticks, nice brass ones." He puffed up proudly.

"Candle-sticks!" I came way too close to screaming it; as it was, my voice had already risen well above any intelligent levels for secrecy.

"Shush…damn it, Drew. Keep it down. You can't say shit about this to anyone. They're buried in a sack 'neath Georgie's garage."

I still couldn't figure out how this petty crime was going to help my situation.

"Right after we buried the pirate's loot, as Georgie called it; we went and had a chat with Wink and his butthead friend. Brandon's his name. Anyway, we explained how it's going to work from now on. Georgie phoned the sheriff's office. You should've seen him; he talked through a sock, with his mustache full grown he looked like Groucho Marx." Donny laughed like it was the funniest thing anyone had ever seen. "He told them 'bout the cottage being broken into, and guess which deputy went over to Winston Ewell May III's."

Frank Curry. That was where he was headed, probably why he questioned Pooh and me. "Damn, Donny, Mr. Curry talked to us, acted like we were doing something wrong!"

"Hell, you guys are too small to be suspects. Besides, Wink's already got himself a little history, if you know what I mean."

I was a little disappointed that I might still be too small to be considered suspect in petty crime. I asked, "So what did you say to Wink."

"Georgie and I told him that if we ever heard he was fucking with you or anyone else, something would show up right there on his property. Something valuable He wouldn't know when or where, but if he ever fucked up, he was going to get his sorry ass thrown in jail until he was well old enough to buy a six-pack."

For the first time in my life I was beginning to understand the value of carefully selected cuss words. I was also getting my first lesson in extortion, but didn't realize that at the time. I asked optimistically, "Do you think it's going to work?"

"Hell, yes. Wink was pissing he was so scared. Georgie's got a streak of tough in him a mile wide, and he's never liked ol' Wink acting like he owns the rest of us. Georgie made certain he and Butthead understood. He made 'em understand real well. Neither one of those boys'll ever stir up anything with you or anyone else again." It was such a simple solution, but one that I knew could work. I wanted to hug my older brother but remembered that brotherly solidarity came in more carefully planned increments.

My brother had been right. It was the rudimentary method of guys taking care of their own. "Donny…?"

"Nope, don't even say it, Drew. I know you. Someday you'll do something like this for me."

I sank into my breath that night without the fear of amethyst stones cutting into my face, without fiendish smiles and horrid words, without the fear of hands stretched like tape across my mouth. I released the deep exhales of relief and breathed in the deep inhales of my brother's protective friendship. The chi flowed smoothly.

***

The Rising Star rolled like a juggernaut, a bright, beautiful, irrepressible force of metal and shiny paint directly towards the open arms of the Atlantic. Bottle rockets and hundreds of larger varieties exploded with embers and brilliant colors in the sky over the ocean and its new traveler. At sunset Mr. Jensen brought down his entire stock of unsold fireworks, and the celebration continued far into the night. You couldn't count the people along the shore, on the pier, or in the food lines, only the ones who hadn't come, and that was on your hands.

It had become an extraordinary, impromptu festival, a combination boat christening, Fourth of July picnic, baking contest, and implicitly competitive potluck. Patriotic bunting festooned the pier and along the folding tables stretched across the sand. Father spent two days preparing large quantities of his mouth-watering crab cakes with mousseline sauce. The aroma itself inspired six women to flirt brazenly with him and demand the recipe. He answered with a slow smile that it could all be found in his second cookbook, which had sold three times as many as his first. There were more flavors of homemade ice cream and pie that afternoon than anyone thought existed. Music blared from the pier, and young and old danced and ate to exhaustion.

Jethro boarded twenty-two people for the maiden voyage. It was a short trip, just to the other side of the pier and back. Pooh, Momma, and I were in that privileged group, along with Miss Millie and a lot of people from the established families in Nags Head. He stood proudly at the wheel while the engines puttered smoothly, and every passenger marveled at how amazing it was that they could step into <u>The Rising Star</u> from dry sand and return to that exact spot without even taking their shoes off. We all got a loud lecture from Captain J. on the engines and linkage and how the propeller and wheels revolved.

Father went out on the third excursion, and when he returned he searched and found me racing around in the chaotic frenzy of the crowd. The Morley twins had started a small game of tag which had rapidly swelled to enormous dimensions. Children of every age and size were running, screaming, and weaving like barrel horses through the crowd. And most of those involved couldn't determine who was "it."

He raised his hand like a traffic cop, and I came to a screeching halt in the soft sand in front of him. "How about a little break, Son?" That was the message that he needed me to slow down and join him on one of his missions. I looked up the sand and saw Momma setting an over-sized arrangement of cattails and pussy willows on the dessert table--another mysterious and out-of-season procurement on her part.

"Yessir, what kind of break?"

"You don't need your shoes; just walk with me for a spell." That was an incomplete answer if I'd ever heard one.

We turned south, and as we walked through the pilings at the pier, he wrapped his hand around my shoulder in a long-established gesture of fatherly love. "First, you need to know that I'm proud of you."

That felt beyond good. "Thank you, Sir." I wondered what was bringing this parental candidness on.

"You've made a lot of good decisions recently, Drew, been true to others when most would have taken an easier route. That takes heart and a special sort of talent.

Makes me feel fortunate as your father. I wanted you know that"

"Thank you, Sir." Now I was really wondering what was behind this.

We walked along for a few minutes. Father skipped a flat stone like a miniature discus that skimmed and sank into the blackness. I tried to out-skip his rock with my own, but managed only four measly jumps. We neared the section of beach where I thought we were going up to the cottage, but Father surprised me by turning towards the Silver's. He surprised me even more when he said, "Everybody ought to be at that celebration tonight, Drew, including Maggie and Skeeter." I knew then that my father's innate sense of fairness was at the heart of our mission. "I thought you might be able to sit on their porch for a bit while I carry Skeeter down there on my shoulders. A boy ought to see fireworks like that up close."

As we strolled up the rise of sand, Maggie came out looking puzzled. She was barefoot, in the same dress that reminded me of the evening sky. She looked tired, more so than I'd seen in a long time. "Good evening, Mr. MacLaren." She looked at me questioningly. "Drew?"

Father walked steadfastly up the steps, sat on the bench and looked her right in the eye. He spoke in his slow, decisive manner. "Maggie, I want you and Skeeter to come on down to the picnic with us for a time. I'll carry Skeeter on my shoulders. Most of Nags Head's down there, and it's not right you two can't join in. There's enough food on those tables for everyone, so you won't need a thing, just yourselves."

Maggie's eyes brightened, then like a curtain being drawn slowly across a window, they dimmed again. "Mr. MacLaren, that's the sweetest offer I've had in a year, but I can't. I just can't leave Momma this time of the day."

I piped up cheerfully. "That's why I'm here, Maggie. I can stay. I'll get Clarisse anything she needs." I was secretly praying Clarisse was sound asleep and wouldn't need a thing. Maggie looked unsure, then gradually more cheerful. She looked like she wanted to kiss something, and I hoped that something was me.

With a fading reluctance she said, "Well, I guess we could go on down for awhile… I've been listening to the fireworks and music; it all sounds so fun." She looked appreciatively at both of us.

Father stood and held out his hand just like he did when he taught me to swim. "Well come on then. Let's get your brother."

With their backs to me as they strolled towards the pier they looked like a typical family off to a parade, a man, a woman, and a boy laughing deeply from his vantage point on the high shoulders of the man.

Later, Father described it to me, and being a writer, he described it in perfect detail. A few people stared in the beginning when the three of them strolled into the crowd. There were breathy whispers, but when they moved to inspect The Rising Star, Mr. Jensen came up to say hello and inquire respectfully about Clarisse. Then others approached, and gently, gradually Maggie and Skeeter were absorbed into the invisible circles of Nags Head society. Father told me how Maggie greeted each one like a shy, but durable rose, and Skeeter endeared himself by laughing at everything and everyone. Father told me how Skeeter stroked the sides of <u>The Rising Star</u> like it was a live animal. The three of them watched the fireworks together and even swayed just enough to the music blaring from the pier to call it dancing.

Maggie told me it was like a dream, one she didn't want to wake up from. There were only two things wrong she said. Mai Lin and I weren't there to share it with her, and Frank Curry was serving potato salad. Sheriff Brennan had forced the deputy into the duty as a civic responsibility, or some form of penance, nobody was sure. He didn't even attempt to hide his disgust at the servitude and stood with the surliest expression possible pasted on his face. He served everyone the same way, with disrespectful grunts and a sloppy smack of the spoon against the outstretched plates.

Maggie had pushed ahead to get Skeeter and her big plates of crab cakes and salad. She didn't see Frank Curry until she was directly in front of him with her plate stuck forward. Perhaps, as Maggie had said, his meanness came from being scared. Maybe, like she said, he wanted others to feel small and himself bigger, but he made a cruel mistake when he saw her. He launched right into a vulgar remark. "Well, I'll be damned. If it isn't Miss Maggie tight-twat. You know, I got a better idea where we can put those long legs when I get through sloppin' this…" In that instant he saw Father with Skeeter on his shoulders, and his mouth shut like a trap.

Jethro, by that time, had more ale in his belly than he was accustomed to. Each round trip with his passengers warranted a fresh bottle of stout—that was a Portuguese custom for maiden voyages, he proclaimed--and being on his ninth maiden voyage he was enjoying the tradition more than was customary, even for a sailor. But instead of imprudently accelerating his departures and landings with all that horsepower in his hands, he slowed it to a meticulously unhurried pace. His speech slowed, the propeller slowed, the wheels rolled in inches, and then with a final gulp, he turned over the last three runs to Bertram Sein. The Rising Star was then decommissioned for the evening. The engine shut down to a long round of applause.

Jethro stepped proudly, if not a bit wobbly, from the transom onto the sand, and seeing Father and Skeeter looming above the crowd, he reeled with concentrated care over to them. With an outlandish grin and a noticeable effort to keep his words in the correct order, he announced, "John, I'm proud to have had your son work on The Star with me." He listed slowly to port, then starboard, in the sand. "Best boat I've ever set to sea in and the best lad I ever had working with me, and that's the truth. I meant what I said about him owning part of her. He deserves it, and I'll make sure the papers show his name as well as mine."

Father smiled at Jethro's gregarious, if not inebriated, speech and replied, "Well, thank you for taking him on, Captain. She's a fine boat, and Drew's proud as he can be to say he's had the opportunity to work with you. It's been a good education for him, and that's important for the boy."

Maggie appeared from inside the crowd at that moment. She carried a heaping plate of food and a dismal expression. The offensive remark of Frank Curry had done exactly what it was intended to do. She was chewing on her lip, breathing deeply, and for the first time since arriving at the celebration that she wasn't smiling radiantly.

Skeeter guessed immediately what had happened. "He's botherin' you again, isn't he, Maggie?"

Maggie looked uncomfortably at her feet and sullenly handed her brother his lemonade. "Wasn't anything, Skeets." Father glared across the crowd at Curry, who was studying the handle of his potato salad spoon.

"Then why you looking like that?"

"He didn't say anything, Skeets. You leave it be."

It had been an unusually harsh response, and Skeeter suddenly looked as sad as she did.

Jethro watched her silently. He had his huge hands buried in his overalls, his mouth set firmly, hidden in the tangle of beard and moustache. His eyes followed her moves, his ears heard every word. And he said nothing.

Father was still looking at Mr. Curry when Maggie said, "Mr. MacLaren, if it's all right with you I'd like to get on back after we finish this food." She smiled radiantly again. "I don't think I've ever had so much fun." That was the best thank-you Father could have received.

Very few people had ever seen Jethro cry, and that was only when one of the aria of the great operas was filling the mainsail of his heart, but Father, Maggie and Skeeter noticed him that evening with tears in his eyes. Everyone who noticed it passed it off to stout and the great celebration, but as he left, Jethro looked almost shyly at Maggie once more and spoke the same words to Father as he had the previous summer, "You are a fortunate man, John." He walked back towards his <u>Rising Star</u>, the salt of his tears melting with the spray of the ocean.

***

The sky was thick with a dense smoke of acrid cordite that rose into the clouds and smudged the horizon. I sat nervously on the bench, bouncing between the delight of Skeeter, Maggie and Father sharing in the celebration together, and a fear that I was anchored alone on the Silver porch with the darkness dwelling inside. At the onset, Father's idea had seemed considerate and compassionate and I'd been an eager volunteer. What I hadn't fully considered was the effect of having to wait in that solitary place for them. I was scared. I looked towards the pier. How long had I been waiting? A brilliant rocket curved outward over the ocean, rising with a screech into a jeweled explosion. From the pier The Drifters wafted across the sand. "There goes my baby, movin' on down the line." Laughter. A couple, arm in arm, strolled south past my post. When would Father return? I waited.

Behind me the click of a switch sounded and an odd polygon of yellowish light and obtuse angles lit up the boards below the kitchen window. Clarisse was up. "Maggie? Honey? You out there?"

For two seconds I considered not answering. If I stayed very still, if I didn't say anything at all, perhaps Clarisse would fade back into her cave. "Skeeter?" A face appeared at the screen, yellow radiance framing the long hair. I jumped from the bench. With a stumbling voice, I said, "No, Ma'am, it's me, Drew MacLaren." I nearly ran to the screen wanting her to see my face, recognize it, and prevent her from coming out.

"Drew MacLaren?" There was a moment of confusion, an instant of panic. "Where's Maggie?" Her fear was rising. "What's all that noise?"

"It's okay, Mrs. Silver. Maggie and Skeeter went down with my father to the Fourth of July celebration. That's the fireworks you're hearing." I waited, hoping desperately she would understand. "They'll be right back. I told them I'd sit here with you. I met you last year. I'm Drew. I live two doors down."

That one worked. Recognition trickled into her voice. "Drew MacLaren. John and Jean Gray's son? Why are you sitting out on the porch, Child? Come on inside." She pushed on the screen door with an effort and it creaked outward. I stepped across the threshold and saw how incredibly thin she now was. She looked like a stalk of sea grass, gray, wispy, sea grass. Her hands were like bits of fragile china, and her face sallow, drawn taut like cello strings. Of all her features, her eyes had changed the most, they were old and weary like a tired foot soldier's, but I saw that they held, if only temporarily, a spark of coherence. "It's dark out," she said, recognizing for the first time the lack of light on the porch. Then, with an inspired thought, she asked, "How about a cookie, Drew? Would you like a cookie?"

"Yes, Ma'am, that would be fine. A cookie sounds fine."

She turned and with feeble movements began tugging open drawers, and then she stopped as if realizing the cookies weren't supposed to be in drawers. I asked, "Would you like me to help you look, Mrs. Silver?" She looked confused and self-conscious. "Yes, Child, that might be best. I just…" The sentence hung there.

"Yes, Ma'am. I know. Let's try this cupboard." I reached for one away from the sink, thinking that Maggie would have stored dishes in the nearer one. It held pots and cooking utensils. Then I remembered how Maggie told me she arranged the kitchen for Skeeter. I opened the lower cabinets near the refrigerator. The Oreos were set right in front, clamped shut with a weathered clothespin. "Here we are, Mrs. Silver."

"Well, bless me, that's right where they're supposed to be." She smiled, and the very movement made her wince from effort or pain. "Drew?"

"Yes, Ma'am?"

"Would you mind calling me Clarisse? Silver was Buck's name, and Clarisse is mine. It's no one else's, just mine."

"Yes, Ma'am. I like it better myself. It's pretty name."

"Do you think so?" She clutched the remark like a warm mantle and bit into a soft Oreo.

"Yes, Ma'am. One of the prettiest." Hoping, like a seasoned ferryman, to guide us into protected currents of conversation, I asked, "Clarisse, would you mind awfully telling me about Miss Millie?"

I struck the perfect chord with that request. "Oh…Millicent." She smiled warmly with a black veneer of Oreo crumbs flecked across her gums. She paused to gather the bits of memory floating like dandelions in her brain. "Well, let's see… we were good friends growing up, best friends in high school, even though she was older by three years than I was. Millicent Danover she was called." She framed the face in her mind's eye. "Millicent had spirit, Drew. She was different than the other girls. She was small, but she had fire. And you want to know a secret?"

"Yes, Ma'am."

"Millicent actually taught me how to swim. Can you believe that. No one else ever thought to do that. But Millicent did." Clarisse pushed the second half of her cookie into her mouth and continued. "She taught me all sorts of things, how to laugh at things I'd never have thought were funny. Brightest girl I ever met. She knew all about books and paintings and music. We'd walk over to her house after school and sit on her bed and read, and look at magazines together. I think I learned more sitting on those pillows than all those years of listening to teachers. She just knew what a girl needed to learn."

I pictured Miss Millie now, standing on her sagging peach crate delivering sermons on incompetent politicians to any poor soul that walked through the door at Piggly's. "I think I can see that." Seeing Miss Millie, I remembered the photograph of the two of them in front of the Pavilion. "Clarisse?"

"Yes, Child?"

"Did you and Miss Millie go dancing at the Pavilion much before it got torn down?" I had the impression that I was inserting a brass key into an ancient lock, testing the direction of the turn.

"Oh, Lordy, yes. We'd sneak down there and dance 'til our feet were blue. I remember 1939, or maybe it was 40, they had a dance contest there and Millie and I came in second. We always thought those judges didn't score us higher because we were two girls. I think they thought we were peculiar dancing together like that." The delicate smile returned and then disintegrated. "My papa found out, though."

I turned the key a few more degrees. "What about during the war?"

The latch opened. "Oh, yes. We had less dancing partners then, of course. I met Buck Silver down there in 1942. He'd ridden the bus down from Newport News, and we fell in love right there on that parquet floor. Leastwise, we thought we were in love. He was a handsome boy in that sailor suit, and I think that was more than half the reason we got married. It seemed like a chance to do something different, but it wasn't much later that everyone got shipped out around here, including my new husband. Did you know that I knew your mother back then?"

That took my by surprise. "No, Ma'am. I didn't know that."

I saw one of her bony hands move in jerky motions into her lap, then the other. "I walked around this cottage wondering all day where Buck was in that big ocean." Her eyes looked out the screen and twitched. "Other side of the world is where he was." Her voice rose a notch. "Other side of the world, and I was in this cottage all by myself. Right here, by myself." For a brief moment Clarisse's eyes locked with mine, and suddenly I was scared. They had changed. Where there had been awareness a moment before, there was now only an unfocused flickering. They were the eyes of a fish in the nets. Her short voyage into reality had returned to the comfortable harbor of insanity again.

"Did you still go dancing?" My question was-- except asking if she would like another Oreo--the only one I could think of. I couldn't tell if she didn't hear me or the idea was too difficult to deliberate on, because she didn't answer. She just let out a long, deep moan that set me to shaking so hard I dropped my half-eaten cookie onto the floor.

"Beelzebub's footsteps!" Clarisse screamed in the same shrieking voice I'd heard too often. Oatmeal and demon raisins smashed against the wall of my memory. "Dance with him in Purgatory." She smacked the table with a force far beyond what her frail arms should have mustered, her robe parted to reveal a thin nightgown and drooping breasts beneath.

"Clarisse? Please don't," I begged.

"Into Purgatory," She mumbled. She whacked the table again.

"How about bed? Can I help you get into bed." She stood, and for a moment I was terrified she was going to exit through the screen door. I imagined her walking down the steps to the sand while I vainly tried to turn her back, but she looked merely looked at the opening, made tight fists with both her bony hands, and shuffled towards the darkness of her room.

I scooped the remains of my Oreo off the floor.

From the front I heard a soft laughter approaching, then footsteps padding across the planks. "Drew?" Maggie's voice floated in from the porch.

"In here." I tried to keep the panic from saturating my answer. I wasn't sure if it had worked.

The screen door swung outward and, Skeeter's legs poked through the opening wrapped inside Father's arms. All three of them entered the kitchen looking flushed with sea air, smiling, laughing.

Maggie hadn't gotten completely inside, before she asked, "How's Momma? Did she wake up?" She looked at me with concern.

It was a choice. I could explain how Clarisse had wakened, how she had told me about Millie and dancing with a sailor who was no longer here, and how she had frightened me to the core with her slide back into madness. Or I could say, "She's fine, Maggie. She came out for a while, then went back to bed." I chose the latter. They looked so happy, and it was such a small fib.

Father tucked Skeeter onto the lumpy sofa, and we said our goodnights. Maggie hugged both of us with true gratitude, her brief freedom still shining like fireworks in her eyes.

We sat in the rockers on our porch before going to bed. The music and rockets had drawn to an anticlimactic finish, and the only residual signs of the celebration were our full stomachs and the smell of cordite that lingered in the air. I knew Father was proud of me for staying alone at the Silver's. It was then that he told me about their time at the picnic, and I felt good that it had been so enjoyable for them.

My yawns were growing bigger and coming with more frequency. My curiosity, however, was still wide awake. "Father, what's a Beelzebub?" He looked at me with an odd smile that I could just see in the darkness. I could also see that he knew that my conversation with Clarisse had been somewhat more elaborate than I had let on.

"Beelzebub's a who, Son. It's another name for Satan... Where did you hear that? It's an old name."

"Clarisse... Mrs. Silver said something about a Beelzebub tonight. I was just wondering what it meant."

"Well, it's a different use of the name. To be honest, the only times I ever heard it was in stories."

"Or church?"

"Sometimes, though it's more colloquial, certainly old-style."

Rather than extend things by asking what colloquial meant, I asked, "Like the way Maggie's grandfather might have talked?"

Father looked quickly at me as if I had slapped him with the question. "You referring to Simon Cotton, Son?"

"Yes, Sir, but I didn't know that was his last name. Maggie just told me he was a minister. Said he was kind of loud." Father smiled at that.

"He was loud. A bit too loud for most folks tastes. Momma called him an obnoxious Bible thumping son-of-a-bitch, if you'll excuse the phrase. You'll stir up a wasp's nest if you ask her about him. He ministered a church north of here for quite a few years."

"What happened to him?"

"He died about fourteen, fifteen years ago? Where're all these questions about Simon Cotton coming from? Something you need to talk to me about?"

"No, Sir, Maggie told me a little bit about him, and Clarisse said he didn't like her listening to music or dancing at all. She said she caught lashings from him."

Father grew quiet. "That doesn't surprise me much. He was a pretty harsh old bird with a temper like a snake, and most people knew it. The word was that for a man of the cloth he beat on Clarisse and her mother a whole lot more than he should have."

I was getting so sleepy I had to force my eyes to stay open, but Father was in a fluent mood, willing to tell me the pieces that he knew of Simon Cotton, so I pressed on. "Did you hear about him hurting her while Buck Silver was in the Pacific?"

Father looked towards the ocean as if it was 1942 and he was on the other side of the world again. "I wasn't here, you probably know that. Your grandfather Donnell was in England, but Momma and your grandmother Dorothy were here. They stayed in the cottage for close to two years. It was a hard time for us, Drew. We were young. Alex was only three, but war is like that. It has a rotten way of separating people when they should be together, sometimes permanently. It's how Mrs. Harris lost her husband. Anyway, your mother tells it better than I do, but Simon Cotton lived with Clarisse's mother, Ruth in a parish house about twenty miles north. Clarisse was living alone down here after Buck Silver shipped out. I guess old Simon came down here one night and found some reason to beat her nearly to death. Momma and your grandmother tried to take her down to the hospital, but Clarisse wouldn't have any of it. They helped her as much as she would let them, and she mended herself pretty much on her own. It hurt your momma that she wouldn't take more of her help, but I think she understood why. Clarisse was just a solitary type, and proud." He laughed to himself. "And I'm pretty sure remembering Simon Cotton is where a part of your Momma's anti-Baptist feelings come from."

"Why'd he beat on her?"

He shook his head. "I don't know, Son. I expect only Clarisse knows that, now that Simon's dead."

I slid into the softness of my bed late that night, the bright tumblers of lemonade and games of tag fading like sparks into the ocean. The Rising Star had risen from the depths to traverse the waves like royalty. Wink May was vanquished. Skeeter had seen fireworks, and Maggie had graced us all with her smile. All was well. No storms loomed on my horizon, or so I thought.

Wind

Now that my refurbishing skills were no longer needed on <u>The Rising Star,</u> and my concerns of Wink May were phantoms of the past, I had more time to devote to the important activities of riding waves, trying to make Maggie laugh, and learning new things with Mai Lin. Always pushing to the surface was my need to solve the puzzle of Clarisse that I'd raised with my incessant questions. It was like an engrossing comic that I was half-way through. I needed to know the ending. Incomplete answers floated like gossamer threads in the air around me, and I couldn't seem to grasp and connect them.

I suspected that certain adults were holding back on me, a natural suspicion for any young investigator. I also wondered if I simply hadn't asked the right questions of them. There were two people I definitely wanted to interview. One was Miss Millie, the other, strangely enough, was my mother. Momma was the easier route, at least in proximity. She had returned from a Woman's League brunch around eleven on the morning after the Fourth-of-July picnic, and Father and I had just finished our Holy Communion in the ocean.

Talking with Momma about most subjects, but especially sensitive ones, required more cautious maneuvering and consideration than with Father. Momma could misconstrue my intentions for just about anything, or worse, view something as being totally unsafe—an all too frequent event--and that would shut down any further discussion and have her watching my moves like a bird of prey. She also could opine at length on any subject and ignore what I really needed, facts.

The first basic requirement was a proper setting without any distractions, a place where her comfort level was highest and familiarity firmly established. As soon as I heard the Nomad lurch into the space behind the garage, I ran to the outdoor shower, soaped and rinsed, then leapt up the secret passageway to my room to comb my hair and dress in a fresh shirt. Any dirt or malodorous clothing would suspend my interview instantly. I jumped back down to the kitchen and prepared two iced teas with lemon and a measured teaspoon of sugar. Another distraction contradicted. Glasses in hand, I knocked gently on her bedroom door. "Momma?"

She called out from the inner bathroom. "Hello, my Sweet. Come in. I'll be out in a jiffy." She was in a good mood, which I suspected came from a constructive Woman's League meeting. I pitied the vice president and secretary that worked under her administrative hand.

"I brought you some iced tea."

She came out in a thick terry cloth robe and her hair tucked into a towel so she looked like someone from another country. "How thoughtful, Dear. How did you know that was what I needed?"

I smiled sheepishly. "You always like tea after your meetings."

"Well, thank you for being such a little gentleman." There was that word 'little' again. She took the glass and sipped it experimentally, smiling as the exact proportions struck her taste buds. "And you mix a perfect drink, too."

"Did your meeting go well?"

"Like clockwork, Dear. I had agendas typed up for all of us, and we stuck right to our timetable." I imagined the timekeeper with a whip keeping all those ladies right on task.

"Did everyone like your idea about the stop signs and writing letters to the governor about the traffic?" Momma had been on a crusade for a few years to get summer traffic, if not eliminated physically, at least slowed to a snail's pace with every available form of obstacle.

"Of course, they did, Dear. It's just common sense. Who wouldn't like that idea?"

"Well, I think it's a great idea." I was nearing the transition to my subject. "Traffic has gotten so much heavier over the years."

"Yes, it has, and it gets worse with each summer. It used to be that we could walk along the highway and see a single horse carriage go by each day. I'm joking, of course, but it was so much better just a few years ago."

"I'll bet there was hardly any during the war. You know, with so many people gone." I sat on the bed, and Momma pushed her towel-encased hair further onto her head. She sat next to me and took a long sip. I sensed that we were now safely into the territory I desired.

"Drew, there was hardly anything out here then. Oh, there were the big cottages, like ours, and some of the others along the beach. Mr. Jensen's was here, and the casino and Beachcomber, but all the tacky houses hadn't been built yet." Momma was now opining on the decline of the local architecture, and I knew I needed to guide us into a different area.

"Was it lonely being out here with Grandma Dorothy?" Momma was looking out the window now.

"Yes, it was. When your father left, your grandmother came out here to live with me. She really wanted us to be in her house in Graham, but I'd grown up in that house, and it didn't feel right going back there with Alex. So I told her I wanted to be here, and she came out to help. It just made sense with your grandfather off in Europe."

"I guess people had to look out for each other back then, huh?"

"Just about everyone."

I had skillfully arrived in serpentine fashion at the doorsill. "Was Mrs. Silver out here, too?"

Momma was now ensconced in the war years. She took another sip of tea. "Of course, Dear. She, and Dellie Harris, and I were all by ourselves. All our men were off fighting."

"And grandma was with you?"

"Yes, thank God."

"Did Mrs. Silver or Mrs. Harris have anyone around?"

Well, let's see…Mrs. Harris had relatives up in Wilmington, and Mrs. Silver's parents lived up north. Not too far away."

"What were they like?"

"Mrs. Harris's?"

"No, Ma'am, Mrs. Silver's parents. What was her father like?"

Momma leaned back against the pillow of the headboard and looked at me sadly. "Drew, I believe Mr.

Cotton, Clarisse's father, was the meanest man to ever step on this earth."

"Why's that?"

"He was just a cruel man. Biggest hypocrite I've ever known."

"What's a hypocrite?"

"A hypocrite is someone who says one thing but does the opposite."

"Father told me he was a minister, but that he beat Clarisse, one time pretty badly while you and Grandma were out here." Momma looked at me oddly, as if she was surprised that I knew that secret item of Nags Head history. She nodded.

"He did, and that is probably the best example you will ever find of a hypocrite."

"Do you know why he beat her?" My pivotal query.

She shook her head, not as a negative answer, at the memory, and then looked directly at me. "You're probably old enough to know about such things." That was a first in my life. "Clarisse wouldn't tell your grandmother or me why her father beat her so badly, but my guess is she simply got lonely and went on a date with someone after Buck Silver left." Momma drained her glass.

"You think Mr. Cotton found out about it?"

"Yes, I do, Dear." She patted my hand, a signal that our history lesson was drawing to a close. Then she said quietly, "It was such a lonely time for us all."

"Momma?"

"Yes?"

"Have you ever heard Clarisse when she's not right in her head, the way she screams?"

Momma looked at me with the sadness and awkwardness that came from having shut Clarisse's screams and all other aspects of Clarisse out of her mind for seventeen years. "No, Honey. I guess you could say I've kind of closed my eyes and ears to most of that. I expect it's been just too painful for me to listen to."

I nodded. I think I understood why, for her at least, it was a rock she wanted left unturned. "She sounds exactly like Simon Cotton. Maggie told me."

I stood and one last question came to me. "Do you think it would be all right if Skeeter spent the night tomorrow night?"

Momma handed me her glass, and with a smile of atonement said, "I think that would be marvelous, Dear. We'll make him feel like one of the family."

***

The following week started with a ragged, tumultuous sky. Wind sheared across the upper layers of Jockey's Ridge from the north, and before I had finished my breakfast, rain was pelting the sand outside in indecisive but forceful bursts. I considered, for a brief moment, not setting off to Bill's Spot to meet Maggie, but she had appeared so tired and quiet the previous morning—even her nonsense rhymes had ceased--that I felt an almost moral, if not supportive obligation, to be there. So after discussing opinions of pork chops versus fried chicken for dinner with Nina May, I wrapped myself into one of the big yellow slickers hanging by the back door and treaded south along the beach.

Maggie was wearing a Duke University sweatshirt with a threadbare hood pulled tightly around her face. The whole messy thing was soaked through to her skin. She had her arms wrapped around her middle like she had a stomach ache, the effort not doing a bit of good to warm her or ward off the rain-drenched wind. She looked miserable, and I couldn't determine if she looked that way from the foulness of weather or a clear lack of sleep. As I crested the dune and jumped down next to her, she turned and smiled with a gray weariness. "I wasn't sure if you were coming this morning." She looked at the brush whipping wildly in the wind, suggesting that it would have made a perfect excuse to stay home.

"Wouldn't have missed it for the world, Miss Margaret Silver. What's your middle name anyway?"

She brightened slightly with my question, and my insides warmed for the first time that morning. "I'm not telling you, Mr. Curious. You'd just laugh," but I knew she wanted me to pursue it.

"I won't laugh. I promise. I'll tell you mine, if you tell me yours." That sounded a bit funny to us and made us smile at each other again.

"Jackson," she exclaimed. "Your father already told me yours." I felt mildly betrayed, and now had no way of calling her hand.

"I'm not the first boy to have that name around here, you know."

"I like it. Andrew Jackson MacLaren. Has a sound of authority to it."

"Come on, Maggie, what's yours? It can't hurt that much to tell me. I won't laugh. Remember what you said.

We don't have secrets from each other." That was my ace. Maggie and I didn't keep things from each other, and both of us took comfort, even pride, in our pact, and for her more than me, it was a way of handing off some of the pain when we talked.

She sighed and blew her breath out through pursed lips. "Okay, it's Martine. It's French, I guess, but I've never liked it that much. Sounds too much like a boy's name."

"Well, I think it's beautiful. Margaret Martine Silver. Sounds like the name of famous person, like an actress or royalty or something. Even more so when you just say Margaret Martine." I thrust out my hand and said, "It's a pleasure to meet you, Margaret Martine Silver. Andrew Jackson MacLaren, at your service."

She turned away, leaving my hand untouched, and from the side, in the shadows of her hood, I saw tears rolling onto the highlights of her cheeks. She didn't say anything, just stood there in the rain with a slow stream of sadness trickling down. Her lips parted as if she wanted to explain it, but she knew that I understood. Nothing came out. I reached out and found the end of her sleeve, and then her hand, curled up tightly inside. She started sobbing, and like a dam of clay and straw, the crack appeared and broke.

"Oh God, Drew. I can't keep on. I can't. I feel I'm gonna die before I've done anything at all in my life. It's smothering me. I got nothin' left inside, nothin' left to give. She's gone almost completely over to the other side now, and I can't pull her back anymore." I looked at her bare feet and cold legs with goose bumps and rain water splattered on the calves, and my own tears came. I didn't fight them, they came and I welcomed them. I squeezed her hand.

"Drew," she sobbed, "I'm almost eighteen and I've never danced with anyone."

There were no secrets left between us.

"You've still got Skeeter and Mai and me, and I'll dance with you, if you want." I sniffled. It didn't sound like a whole lot right then, but it was all I could offer.

She raised her eyes to meet mine, both of us looking through a mist of salt and rain. "You're the only friends I've got, Drew, outside of Skeeter. You and Mai. The only ones I've got."

"Well,… I guess that's a proper reason for us to be good ones, then." The wind gusted and dropped, and then Maggie leaned forward, and with a sniffle, kissed the drops that had gathered at the corner of my mouth.

Every man—one who has a been boy at some point in his life--can recall his first kiss in detail. From memory he can taste the honey of caressing, the tingling of four parts of flesh as they touched. For me, though so much less conventional than others, my first kiss was Maggie. Salt and rain and Maggie's trembling lips against the corner of my mouth, and like so many of the memories of that summer, I merely close my eyes to feel it again. Now every time I do, my mouth turns as if by magic to meet hers.

Maggie brightened one last time and said, "Come on, Andrew Jackson. Let's get out of this damned stuff and go have some fun."

That small storm, just like the smaller wave that had traveled in front of the giant that had pitched me onto the razor clam, was merely a forerunner. Its big brother was not far behind.

It was to be a day of sad revelations for all of us. We didn't have the expected fun that Maggie anticipated. We stepped through the bamboo of Mai's garden, and for the first time, she wasn't in her usual place on the back deck. I supposed that with the rain she had moved inside to the warmth of her kitchen, but when we climbed the steps and walked in, it was also empty.

We found her sitting on one of the flat cushions inside the screened-in porch. Her legs were pulled up, crossed over with both of her feet on her thighs. Her hands rested in circles against her upturned feet. She was in her black pajamas, motionless, eyes closed, and like Maggie and me, there were traces of tears on her face. The screen door creaked as we entered, but her eyes remained shut. "Sit with me, Children."

Maggie lowered herself, but I, out of shock or concern, asked, "Mai, what's wrong?"

For two deep breaths she didn't answer, then slowly, she opened her eyes and gazed at me with such profound sadness and love, that I thought I might start crying all over again. In a quiet voice she said. "I am ashamed to be from my country today." I sat facing her, not understanding or saying a thing. She took one Maggie's hands and then one of mine in hers, connecting us in a triangle. Looking of us she said, "It is the children who will lead us out of the dark and into the light. It is you who must be the guides."

Maggie whispered, "Mai? What is it?"

"They have taken the land of the holies."

"What land of the holies?" Maggie asked.

Mai looked at the rain and began quietly, "I will tell you another story. I think that it is the best way to explain.

The story begins with a boy, a young boy. His name is Tenzin Gyatso. Tenzin was a bright gem, with eyes that always laughed. He was born in the land west of my village, a land of deep rivers, and high mountains, higher than any mountains in the world..." Her story spun out like a chrysalis, a long tale of beauty and sadness. It had all the components of one of the fantastic fairy tales of my childhood, all the while whispering to me that it was a story of truth, of events happening just then in a world far away, but very real. Mai recounted all of it in a lonely voice, and as she told it, all three of us began to weep. We wept for a land on the other side of the earth, a land called Tibet.

"...and the Dalai Lama fled his beloved home to live in another country."

I didn't understand. "Mai, why...?"

"Shhh. Who can tell why people do such evil? There is a reason. Somewhere."

We had only a few minutes of practice that morning. They were gentle and pure moments, rid of any of the wickedness and insanity beyond our closed eyes, and yet there rose in me an irrefutable ripple along my spine that the sky was changing.

Meteorologically it was an insignificant event for most of its two short weeks on the planet. It was born in the great desert of North Africa, a small spiral of wind and dust that, like a hungry calf, instinctively sought the warm, nurturing waters of the Atlantic. Once outside the stockade of the Atlas Mountains, it drifted lazily south and west and eventually, as it neared Dominica, it was bestowed the official title of tropical depression. Unlike so many of its

*older and larger sisters who had been granted notable
women's names over the decades, the storm never gained
enough force to warrant the full title of hurricane. But it
had significant force, more so than anyone imagined, even
the veteran observers of such events.*

*Someone said it was near Grand Turk Island that the
storm decided to take charge of its own destiny and change
direction. It moved with certitude along the eastern edge of
the Bahaman archipelago, past Eleuthera and Abaco, until
it encountered the 77th line of longitude. There, it sped north
as if drawn like a kite along an invisible cord directly
towards the Hatteras shoreline. For three days the watchers
predicted it was moving out to sea.*

*Most of the Outer Banks residents were indifferent to
the approaching storm, either from enduring dozens of more
powerful events, or from the lack of specific information
concerning wind speed and the location of its landfall. Like
many of the assessments made during those hours before
and during the storm, they were wrong, quite wrong. As
many declared when they viewed the damage afterwards,
"Yep, Big Leo fooled us all."*

It took a very short time, all of three minutes, before
Skeeter felt totally comfortable being in the great cottage.
Everyone involved made certain that he was. Father set us
up on the front porch for the afternoon. We strung blankets
to make a wild-west stockade. Lizard idled beneath the
hammock, ready if need be. Donny fetched all the comics
and fishing poles. Nina May prepared us a snack of grahams
and milk, which I carried out to our corner fort. Momma
came down and sat with us for a surprising long time and

read us a short story called "The Happy Prince," by a man named Oscar Wilde. The story was beyond beautiful, and afterwards Momma gave Skeeter a gift wrapped in purple paper, a book about another prince who was lame, just like Skeeter. He had all sorts of magical adventures on a flying carpet. It was the perfect gift.

Later, Donny and I set up beach chairs and together we lifted Skeeter in the fireman's-hold Donny had always wanted to try. We fished from the shoreline like portly adults, with coolers of drinks and tackle boxes full of bright lures. I taught Skeeter how to cast on his own, and we caught mackerel and perch and laughed at the seagulls.

In the late afternoon Maggie came down to chat and shed her weariness for a few minutes. She looked exhausted and bore four new scratches from her left ear down across her throat. Already knowing the cause of both, I didn't ask about them. It was like watching a flower with no water in the vase.

Eventually Skeeter and I got her giggling. I told her how my father was planning to dig a pit in the sand and cover it with a blanket to trap a jeep that kept racing up and down the beach illegally. It got us all laughing so hard we knew Father was serious.

I understood somehow that the best tonic for Maggie right then was seeing Skeeter laughing, sitting by the waves with fishing poles and sodas, just being a boy. With that small water-color in her mind, she could climb the bank to her cottage and go through the screen door once more.

Father arrived, hugged Maggie tenderly, and hiked Skeeter to his shoulders for the royal ride back up the sand. I walked with her up to her cottage. On the far side of the pier, a half a mile up the beach, <u>The Rising Star</u> rolled out of the surf and came to a rumbling stop near the lot.

"Maggie?"

"Yes, Andrew Jackson?"

"It's going to be all right. I know it." I couldn't stop picturing her standing in the rain with tears on her cheeks.

Almost as if she hadn't heard me she said, "Drew?"

"Yes, Margaret Martine?"

"Thank you doing this for Skeeter. It's such a sweet thing you all have done."

"I'd do more if I could. Father's always asking me how you are and what we can do to help."

"Well…it's nice feeling knowing he'd be okay if something happened."

I looked at her eyes and the scratches along her neckline said as reassuringly as possible. "Nothing's going to happen, Maggie." Then with a grand gesture I bowed and added, "Andrew Jackson MacLaren will make sure of it." She answered with a short-lived smile and then I watched once more how her hair swished as she went through the side door.

Skeeter and I had a grand time. Shrimp and corn, and card games filled the first part of our sleep-over schedule, then pick-up sticks that he had an uncanny flair for. He had never played the game, and I reasoned that his natural patience had steadied his strong hands enough to make him virtually unbeatable at it. Later I took some revenge at Parcheesi and showed him how to work my Instamatic camera. Finally, we settled into the twin beds to critique our latest comics. Just before I turned out the light we read advertisements on the back page and devised ways to sell enough tins of medicated rubbing salve to get ourselves a pony, or at least a book on ventriloquism.

Tempest

My curiosity was drawing me into the mystery of
Clarisse's early years like a ship across the shoals. It
beckoned me like one of the pirate's lanterns of old, pulling
me towards some collision that I couldn't recognize or
predict. It was like my questions had uncovered slivers of
mirrored crystal that I could see individually, but couldn't
piece together. I sensed that buried somewhere was one that
lay like a fulcrum. I needed only to loosen it for the others
to tumble into neat positions, creating a whole reflecting
glass again.

Miss Millie knew something, of that I was certain.

Piggly's was just far enough away from the great
cottage that walking there required some planning and a few
provisions. I needed a sandwich and a canteen of water.
Oreos rounded out the requisites nicely, so I packed
everything into an emptied knapsack that we used for
extended fishing trips and tucked my knife in the inner
pocket. I snuck out the back screen door, but as I reached
the bottom I heard Nina May call, "Master Little?"

She stood at the top step. "Yes, Ma'am."

"You gonna be gone a long time?" She was eyeing
the knapsack.

"Most of the day, Ma'am. I'm going picnicking."

She nodded with an indulgent smile. "You know,
Child, I think it might wise for you to tell me what you're
up to one of these days. I've always had a knack for being a
right good listener."

"Yes, Ma'am. I know" I turned to leave, thinking
that she'd somehow gotten hold of some of Momma's ESP,

and then turned back. Nina May looked older than I remember standing on the top step. I walked up and hugged her. "You're the best listener I know, Nina May."

"You be safe, Master Little."

"Yes, Ma'am, I will."

The walk was long, easily twice the distance to Mai's. I ate my sandwich prematurely and thought of stories Nina May had told me as I'd grown up in her kitchen. Then I polished off most of my water just before I spied the fat pig dancing on the roof of Miss Millie's diner. I struggled with the idea of hiding my pack somewhere before walking through the door. I didn't want Miss Millie to know that I'd walked there all by myself, but I knew she would find out anyway, so in it went with me.

It was mid-morning and the booths, and tables were nearly empty. An older man was sitting on one of the stools, waiting on two quarts of barbecue to go. Rindy stood behind the counter punching the big keys on the register which opened with a loud ding. Seeing me, she gestured toward the rear with her head and said, "She's out back at the oven, Drew." She said it sweetly, and I guess she'd been paying more attention than I had thought, because she'd remembered my name. I thanked her and walked through the side door near the restrooms.

Miss Millie turned from the brick oven as the screen squeaked and smiled when she saw me. She pushed the cast-iron door closed with a stick that had seen a lot of use and proclaimed, "Drew Drop, you resemble your daddy more and more every day, and that's a damn fine way to look. Not that looking like your Momma would be a bad thing either.

You could've gotten the worst of both their genes and still look like Cary Grant."

I'd become more adept at fielding compliments in that year. It was something you absorbed through some invisible form of osmosis in the South back then. "Thanks, Miss Millie, you're looking mighty pretty yourself today."

"Hmm… Well, I'd say the disadvantages of owning a barbecue place has caught up with me." She patted her stomach with both hands. "But thank you anyway. So where's the rest of your family?" She eyed my knapsack skeptically. "You walk here by yourself?"

"Yes, Ma'am, I did. Donny's learning how to drive this summer, so he and Father are up at the casino lot with the car. It's empty right now and they're practicing how to turn the Nomad around."

She laughed and shivered visibly. "Whew. Well, I guess it's a good thing that lot's empty. Probably good that it's as big as it is, too. God help your father. He's going to need it." She looked at me quizzically. "And what do I owe the pleasure of your visit today, Drew Drop?"

I didn't need to tread as carefully with Miss Millie as with my mother when it came to sensitive questions. I could ask candidly, and I knew she would tell me what she could. "I wanted to talk. Actually, I wanted to ask you a few questions, if you don't mind."

"Hell no, I don't mind. It's not like the place is spilling over with customers right now. Rindy can tend to things inside. You just remind me to add my hickory to the fire in a few minutes."

"Sure thing, Miss Millie. I can help you if you want." That went without saying, but saying it was the correct thing to do.

"I accept that offer. Now what's on your mind?"

We'd arrived at the threshold of my inquiry so quickly that I had to pause before asking, "Miss Millie, you were good friends with Clarisse during the war, weren't you?"

"Oh…so this is about Clarisse" Her voice curved off, and she looked sad, an unusual disposition for Millie. "Probably something to do with Maggie, too." The last part came out as a statement.

"Yes, Ma'am. Maggie's my best friend." I realized how proud I'd sounded saying that.

"That's a proper thing, Drew Drop. If anyone needed a best friend, it would be Maggie Silver." She reached behind the stack of wood to the left of the oven and pulled out her Mason jar. "Guess I'll need some vitamins to answer what I expect you're going to ask."

Millie smiled for the briefest of moments, and then studied my face with the sadness of memory weaving delicate threads in her eyes. She took a long pull of rum and coke. "Drew, you've got to understand that adults…well, sometimes we don't act like we're supposed to. I guess some children don't either, but they've got better excuses. During the war there was a lot of behavior that we just had to chalk up to wartime foolishness. People's lives got spun all around and they did things differently. Sometimes they did things that now they wouldn't do for all the money in the world; sometimes they did things on their own because they wanted to. And yes, Clarisse and I did our share of foolish things back then. Hell, maybe they weren't all that foolish, but they changed our lives. We did stuff that we've had to live with for a lot of years. Maybe some of it we regret, but most of the time, I think we'd do it all over again."

"What did Clarisse do that Simon beat on her so badly for?"

Miss Millie looked surprised, but then nodded. "So you know about that one then?"

"Yes, Ma'am, my Momma was living here and she told me about it."

"You're Momma *was* living here, and she was a damn fine friend to Clarisse and everyone else in this area. She didn't hold any judgments about what anyone did and helped everyone who needed it. She was right there when Dellie Harris learned her husband wasn't coming back. Your momma held Dellie for a long time, until all that shaking stopped. She's a good woman through and through, Drew Drop, never forget that."

I thought of the smoothness of Momma's fingertips as I lay in the hammock with my cut knee and said, "Yes, Ma'am, I know."

Millie took another pull on her Mason jar and seemed about ready to offer me a swig, then realized with a little jolt, I was still just shy of twelve. She sat on the wood pile and crossed her ankles. "I'll tell you what I know. Mind you, I don't know all of it. Clarisse never would tell me everything that happened. Don't ask me why. I guess it was too close to her heart, or maybe she didn't want me to know who it was so she could protect him."

I asked, "Who what was?"

"The man she was with, Drew. Simon came down and found Clarisse with someone who wasn't her husband."

I nodded. "Momma said the same thing, said she'd gone on a date with someone while Mr. Silver was off at the war."

"Your Momma was putting it nicely. It wasn't a date, Child" She fixed me with a bold stare. "Simon came in while they were in bed together, and afterwards he beat her near to death. Somewhere during that beating Clarisse yelled that she didn't care and she'd been seeing him for weeks. That was the first time she had ever stood up to that old coot. She told him it was none of his business, which made him even angrier."

"And you don't know who she was with?"

"No, I don't. I have my guesses, but I won't say, because they're just guesses, and I don't want to make the mistake of stirring any of it up again. It's done and over with. Now it's just a sleeping dog that I let lie."

"But Clarisse is going crazy from it. She screams about dancing with Beelzebub in purgatory."

Miss Millie set the jar at her feet and patted the log next to her. "Sit down here next to me." I did as I was told. "Listen carefully, Drew. Clarisse is going crazy because her brain is falling apart with a disease. It's going rotten like an old log in a swamp, and it's nothing to do with her past making her crazy. Only God knows why it is, but the past wants to keep coming back to her as she's going crazier. It's haunting her like a ghost, but that's not the reason she's going crazy. Do you understand the difference?"

"Yes, Ma'am. I think so. It just seems so sad." I could feel the flush of tears starting to rise. "And it's going to kill Maggie!"

Millie shifted her bottom on the log and wrapped a soft arm around my neck. "That won't happen, Drew Drop. It won't. Don't you worry those pretty curls. God has ways of fixing these things." She kissed my neck.

"Did you get that picture of you two at the Pavilion from her?"

She looked thoughtfully at me and replied, "Actually, no. Back in May, when I came from the hospital with Maggie, I saw Clarisse again. God, I hadn't seen her for over a year, and she was someone else, someone I didn't know. I asked Maggie if I could have the picture for my wall. It was the way I wanted to remember our time together." She looked at the Mason jar between her hands and said, "I guess it was how I wanted to remember both of us."

"She told me you taught her how to swim."

"Yes, I did, and that's exactly how I want to hold her in my head."

One final question tugged at me. "Miss Millie, what did you do during that time, you know, foolish stuff that you were talking about?"

"Something I've never regretted, Drew. Not once in my life." Her eyes filled slowly with tears. "I met Clara and fell in love."

I didn't understand entirely what Millie meant by that, but I helped her stoke the fire in the oven and she packed me a pint of barbecue for my walk home. We topped off my canteen with cold water, and I shouldered my pack again. Millie followed me out the front door. "You go carefully home. Best walk on the beach side. There's gotten to be far too much traffic on this damned highway during the summer. Good for my business, but truth be known, I'd have it the way it was thirty years ago."

I shuffled in the sand. "I guess I'd just have like it was eight years ago."

"Like when you spun on my counter stools?"

"Yes, Ma'am, just like that." My history lesson was over.

***

I had been thinking a lot about Mai in addition to all my investigations of Clarisse's life. Upon asking, Father provided me the appropriate vocabulary word. He then directed me to consult Mr. Webster for the correct definition. Recluse, one who lives a secluded, solitary life. I liked the sound of the word. It seemed to have decent variety of good consonants, with its esses and kays, but the meaning left me shivering with its inference of loneliness. I was trying to separate the connotations of solitude and loneliness. I personally liked being alone for short periods of time, but couldn't imagine being that way all the time. Mai Lin had always been so cheerful and gracious in ministering to Maggie's or my needs that I had never really thought of her as being lonely. That had changed the morning we found her with tears on her cheeks.

I considered the details of Mai's life, as Maggie and I walked quietly through the dunes to her cottage the following day. Her family had been murdered. She had fled her own country, just like the boy in the story she'd told us about. The world of her childhood had been destroyed, and at my age that seemed incredibly sad. I began to sense that she must have, with that solitude, also been lonely. She rarely went out, walked once a week to a small market near Manteo, arriving just as it opened to avoid being seen. She bought meager supplies--rice, fish, fruit, spices, and teas that the owner ordered especially for her. She walked alone along the shoreline and took her only contact with the rest of the world through our daily visits. And now, even those seemed in jeopardy of drifting away from her. Maggie was more remote with each passing day.

Mai greeted us with smiles and kisses and concerned looks. Maggie brightened slightly from her warmth. As we stepped onto the porch, Mai took Maggie's hand and said, "Daughter stay outside today. Big day for Mr. Professional Student. He graduate to new class. Today we all practice together. First part of Eight Threads of the Colored Cloth."

Thrilled at the idea of this arrangement, I asked, "Didn't you say it was called The Eight Strands of the Brocade?"

"Same thing, Mr. Student. You just listen and watch."

The first movement was called The Triple Burner, and by the time I had learned enough to continue on my own, I understood why. From somewhere just south of my belly button right through the top of my head, I felt as if liquid heat was churning inside me. Mai explained that, like a powerful magnet, the energy was pouring in from the stars and planets above, and had I not felt it so plainly, I might have been skeptical. There was no need to convince me.

At one point, I shifted my eyes to both sides and saw Maggie and Mai framing me like columns. All our palms were pushing in synchronous fluidity towards a bright sky, our faces turned serenely towards the cosmos. For a moment I imagined the three of us in a big house in China. It was where, from the moment I'd first stepped on that deck, I'd imagined we should be.

After tea we sat silently. Mai tucked Maggie's head onto her lap, and with splayed fingers, massaged the thickness of hair and gently stroked her brow. For the first time in weeks, a small sign of contentment settled into Maggie's eyes.

"I have strange dream last night, Children. Dream of waves." Mai continued working her fingers along Maggie's scalp and smiled at me, knowing my new-found respect for large swells. "Big waves, like mountains. They tear up trees and toss them into the air. People running and screaming like dogs and ducks. But then the three of us were there like magic. We held hands. Tightly, and no waves could break us apart. We sang and called the sun to come out and shine. Good dream in the end."

"Wow, I like that dream."

Like a strident buzzer that heralded the end of an exceptionally agreeable recess, the moment came when Maggie and I needed to return to the opposite side of the strand. She rose to don her suit of mental armor, and I went to the kitchen to fetch us tangerines. Mai accompanied us to the steps above the fishpond.

"Everything has reason, Daughter. This, also." She kissed Maggie gently on both eyelids and then stepped towards me. I was on the first step, and as Mai came to kiss me good-bye, she missed it. She stumbled and fell, and with a small cry struck the railing sharply with her forehead. Her leg corkscrewed beneath her. She slid down into my legs, and I managed to grasp the handrail just in time to prevent both of us from crashing violently to the bottom of the steps.

To our credit, none of us panicked. Maggie and I carefully lifted Mai from the crumpled position at my feet, up the stairs, through the kitchen and onto her bed. Like every person that has ever caused others to be concerned about them when they are hurt, she began expressing regret. "I apologize. I sorry, no need to do anything for me, Children. I'll be fine." She started gasping from the pain and reached to clutch her ankle. By the time we had her settled as comfortably as possible on her bed, I could see the physician inside Mai's head assessing the damage and designing cures for recovery. Her head had a sizeable lump forming that, from personal experience, I knew would bruise brilliantly, be tender for a week, but wouldn't require more care than a washcloth filled with crushed ice. Her ankle, however, was a bigger concern. She had turned it solidly underneath her full weight, and the ligaments were sprained badly. All three of us knew that walking on it was out of the question.

Maggie, from the desire to stay and comfort Mai, cried as she left. I lingered and fetched all the things that I supposed Mai would need until we returned the following morning. She had me fetch jars and liquids, and a sturdy wooden mixing bowl. From memory she mixed a pungent paste that looked similar to the one she had put on Maggie's eye, but with a stronger odor. She instructed me how to fix a cup of tea from jars of twigs and powder. It would help her sleep, she said. While she sipped and shook her head impatiently at the nuisance of her propped-up leg, I sat on the edge of the bed. She took my hand and laced our fingers together.

"No worry, Drew. Like all pain, this will also pass. This is good message for me. Let me know I am still like a child and can fall and hurt like one."

"I know, Mai. I've had few accidents myself recently. My mother always called them boo-boos when I was growing up.

"Boo-boos. I like that word. Boo-boos add dust to our chalkboard. Boo-boos add doodles." She smiled weakly, and I saw that the tea was already helping her sleep.

"Mai?"

"Yes?"

"Why do you stay here by yourself, not want to meet other people besides Maggie and me?"

"Oh, Drew. This question not so easy to answer." She played with our laced fingers. "Maybe it is me. But I think many people not ready for old Chinese woman to be living with them."

"Why not. I think they are." I was. I couldn't understand what she meant.

She smiled, a little slyly, at me. "I say it this way. What do the children call me?"

It caught me off guard. "You mean…The Chink Lady?"

"That is the name."

"But that's just kids. That's the way children are. They're just stupid sometimes."

"And you don't think adults are stupid sometimes? You think they would trust Chinese doctor?"

Suddenly I understood—in a small way--why it frightened her. I understood why strangers scared her. She began to drift off, and I leaned down and kissed her forehead.

I brought her fresh water, a peach, and a large handful of almonds—ready for her when she awoke.

"Mai, if I can't get back here this afternoon, I promise to be here tomorrow morning before the sun comes up. I promise." That was an oath I should have known better than to make, because even though I walked home under a sunny sky that morning, each of my six senses was shouting at me that a storm of the largest kind was nearing.

I dropped by Mrs. Sezinsky's before running along the shore to the great cottage. I owed her a lot more than a few minutes of assistance feeding her cats, so as we gathered every shape of bowl and saucer from the porches, I listened to her tell me how all thirteen feline friends, but especially Mr. Churchill, were acting nervous about something.

Skeeter's eyes caught the rotating numerals on what I had mistakenly thought was a leaf. He saw the one and the zeroes as it fluttered softly onto my knee, causing him to swear for the first time since I'd known him.

"Damn, Drew, it's a hundred dollar bill." His voice was a wound up whisper.

I picked it up and held it against the beam of the flashlight. Watermarks and linen fibers silhouetted like spiders against the blanket. I stared in awe. I'd never touched or seen anything larger than a five-dollar bill in my life. It looked like it had been washed and ironed, no wrinkles on it, just Ben Franklin with that secret grin of how he'd snuck inside those sheets of aquamarine writing paper.

The letter was old. It smelled of too many years inside the envelope, and as if to lend proof to its antiquity, March 21, 1942 was scribbled in brisk script in the upper right corner. The fountain pen had bled in places into black pools, leaving behind sentences with thick curves and heavy marks at the conclusion of the words. The lines strayed, but not much, giving an overall sensation of orderliness and efficiency, and as soon as I'd read the first line, I knew for a certainty that the author was a poet.

'Have you stolen the stars and the moon from the sky?

For I swear I see them in the evening of your face.

They dance upon your hair and lips like angels in the clouds.

Have you swindled the rose?

Taken in some clever way, its perfume to wear upon your breast.

Have you robbed the candles of their flames?

For that light, so gentle, burns only in your eyes.

Have you stolen my heart? For clearly it is gone.'

The final line was a declaration of absolute affection:

' I bask in the memory of your caress, my love.

I need nothing else, it feeds me and I live.'

The words fell in soft streams of tenderness, all of it penned by an anonymous hand. There was no salutation, no conclusion, and no admission of who had composed them. It

caused me to question why any person would refuse to
profess ownership to such declarations of love.
    The final line suspended like mist in the air beneath
our blankets. Skeeter lifted the second envelope and asked,
"What do think it means, Drew?"

***

Our Aliento had been pleading with Father; at least
that's how he described it. The boat had been calling out in
a lonely voice from the boathouse that it was far too
cramped and dry inside that space, and that Father had better
get her into some water soon, lest she expire from the arid
air. For over a month he had been ignoring the protests, he
told us with a hint of a grin, but they had gotten so loud over
the past few days that he wasn't able to sit at his typewriter
a second longer.

    I was also pretty certain that the experience of
instructing Donny how to accelerate, and more importantly,
decelerate, during driving lessons had also added to Father's
hearing of this voice. Three strong men--he whispered us in
conspiratorial fashion--were needed to release Our Aliento
from her confines and take her out for a damn fine jaunt
down to our favorite picnic spot at the inlet. There were
subtle hints of beer and guy talk, good food catered to our
individual diets, perhaps a trolling lure or two, and with the
day being as splendid as it was, not much more was needed
to convince most anyone. I, however, was hesitant.

    We all stood at the water's edge, and the air felt
prickly on my skin. I looked at the horizon. Nothing but
blueness presented itself. So what was scratching at me?

Mai Lin's dream, my own premonition of foreboding, or
Mrs. Sezinsky's nervous cats.

Mother slapped the inside of the hull like a gavel.
"Listen to me, Children." My father was apparently being
momentarily demoted from captain. She stood opposite him
with one hand firmly gripping the gunwale like a metal vice.
She was leaning slightly towards the cottage side; Father
leaned casually seaward. <u>Our Aliento</u> rested in a peacefully
neutral position between them. Her voice had the
unmistakably tone of last word authority. "If you think you
are going to test me, fool me, or do anything even slightly
dangerous in this boat, think again." Father stood politely
agreeing, assuring her that we would all be safe. I could see
patience behind his smile, or maybe it was persistence.
Another moment of her customary homily on safety and we
could raise the sails and take to the sea like men.

"This family prides itself on being intelligent," she
went on. "I want a solemn promise from each of you that
you will not try anything stupid." Stupid ripped into us like
buckshot. Our hands jumped pledge-like into the air. Oaths
were sworn, coolers of contraband were boarded, and we
were off. A final bow-shot exploded in the air, "And that
cooler better have healthy refreshments in it."

"Nothing like being held captive by a madwoman,"
Donny quipped as he hauled on the mainsheet.

"It all comes from love, Son."

"I know it does, but I'm still going to be glad when I
have my license and my own car."

I chocked the jib sheet and made my way carefully
forward to pull in an errant bowline. The swell was large,
rolling up from the southeast like a line of war elephants.

<u>Our Aliento's</u> bow lifted and dropped like a heavy pendulum. As I stood from my chore, the sloop launched skyward and plunged into a deep trough, sending a spray that showered and soaked me head-to-toe.

Father, standing proudly at the tiller, was in his element. His sons were with him. White caps were blowing directly into his eyes. A good adventure was close at hand. Our course was taking us almost diametrically into the wind, requiring us to tack with short course changes every few minutes. I picked up a towel to dry my face.

"Drew."

"Yes, Sir?"

"I forgot to tell you that Maggie came over while you two were getting the mast out of the rafters."

I glanced at him apprehensively, wondering if something had happened, if she were hurt, or there was bad news of Mai. "Is she okay?"

"She's just fine, Son. Looks tired as she can be, but she's okay. She wanted to know if Skeeter could spend the night tonight. I thought it would be okay with you, so I said yes. Nina May's baking up extra spaghetti casserole to send over to their cottage. That way she won't need to cook for a couple of days, maybe get some rest. That okay with you?"

"Yes, Sir, that would be fine." I smiled at the idea. "We can go fishing again. I've never known anyone to like fishing so much, except maybe Pooh."

A gust tore the crest of a swell over our port bow, soaking all of us with thick spray. Donny tightened the main and <u>Our Aliento</u> heeled over steeply and began to hum, the sails and keel vibrating with the speed. I squinted into the wind. Southward I thought I could see a thin, low line of dark gray. It looked like a single brush stroke of black ink, and it made my skin tingled.

"Father?"

"Drew?"

"Did you hear the weather on the radio this morning?"

"Some of it. Why?"

"I was wondering if we were getting any heavy weather today."

"Well, they said there's a tropical depression moving up, but it supposed to be heading east, out to sea." With a little smile he asked, "You nervous?" Our sloop dropped eight feet into a trough.

"A little bit, yes, Sir. Do you see anything up ahead, because it looks like a line of clouds up there to me?"

Donny scoffed, "There ain't nothing out there but blue, Drew. You're as nervous as Momma."

Father cleared his throat. "I believe I've mentioned this before, but <u>ain't</u> is not a word in the English language."

"It's in the dictionary. I looked it up," Donny responded, with more petulance than usual. Father and I were both mildly surprised at it, but more at the notion that Donny had actually flipped through the pages of a dictionary, even if it was just to validate the existence of inappropriate vocabulary.

"Did you happen to notice the word in italics after it?" My father was getting ready to make a point.

"No, Sir, not that I can remember."

"Slang. Son. And that means it's not usable, just like in Scrabble."

"Yes, Sir, I get the point, but Drew is still too nervous, and there *is not* anything out there." We tacked to starboard. Each of us however, even Donny, peered cautiously into the distance beyond the bow.

Our picnic included a vigorous, but vigilant, swim after lunch. We checked the horizon from time to time, but the waters inside the mouth of the inlet were a greater cause for watchfulness during the swim. The warmer temperature and abundance of smaller fish attracted the occasional shark, and although we never allowed fear or imagination to get the better of us, we were still cautious and always kept one person on deck as a lookout while the other two swam.

Fatigued and sated, I later crawled up to the small deck area near the bow hatch and stretched out like one of Mrs. Sezinsky's fat cats to lounge in the sunlight. The sloop rocked like a slow train. I drifted. What seemed to be minutes later, I blinked, and stared for a disoriented moment at the sky above me. There was a circular band forming around the sun. A thick, colorful halo. A shiver ripple out to my fingertips. "Father?"

"Hmmm?" A sleepy answer rose through the hatch. He was sprawled on the bunk below. I raised myself on one elbow. Donny was curled up on the cushioned bench in the stern. The wind had died to a whisper, as if a greater breath had inhaled it upwards into it.

"Father!"

"I'm up, Drew. What's the matter?"

"There's a storm coming, Sir. I can feel it." I looked towards Hatteras. A band of black hung in a low, sinister wall along the horizon. "Look!" I pointed southeast.

His head poked through the hatch like a sleepy gopher and saw where my finger pointed. He turned. "Damn! Well, that's not a baby squall, that's a big one, and by the looks of it, it's not heading out to sea. My guess is, we're going to be in for a couple of days of it. We need to get back fast. There's a lot to do." Father started into commands faster than I had ever seen him, and we were at full sail in half the time that it took the previous summer.

The return, however, was longer. No one said anything as we left the inlet. The winds were eerily light, and the air felt low and heavy as if some part of it was gathering itself in. The swells had become giants. We rolled across them like they were foothills and tacked only once, and that was when we reached the beach in front of the great cottage.

The main sail was already down and furled about the boom, only the jib and Father's keen timing brought us around the bar and into shore without capsizing. We surfed in on a wall of white water that rose in height above the lower rigging and part way up the mast. At the last instant he shoved the tiller hard to port and we heaved sideways, tilting so deeply that gallons of water spilled into the stern.

"Get the trailer turned!" Father directed our landing calmly, but with an urgency in his voice that left no doubt as to our need to move quickly. Donny and I leapt into the water and struggled through currents that tugged and pushed at us madly. We rolled the trailer backend into the waves and then all three of us guided Our Aliento, who bucked like rabid dog, onto the saddle. The surf sliced high along the hull and pounded against us.

We tugged the boat in unison, and in minutes <u>Our Aliento</u> and the MacLaren boys stood unscathed on dry sand. Momma appeared almost magically, and with little said, she helped us roll the trailer up the slope, lower the mast, and settle everything into the boathouse.

Donny and I hefted the cooler between us, while Father latched the doors. I noticed that, in our absence, Momma had already managed to bolt the shutters on all four sides of the cottage. That task was not as simple as it might seem. Each year more corrosion seeped into the hinges, and at least half of those sixty-four pins would have needed a good dose of oil and a strong arm to pull it shut.

The sky was milky and felt peculiar from the almost total lack of wind. It was like a subtle inhale before an explosion.

"Drew, you get on over and see if Skeeter still wants to stay the night with us. If he does, you come on back and get that food for Mrs. Silver and Maggie, and then I'll come over to fetch him. Don't dawdle, Son. There are things to be done. You understand?" The urgency hadn't left his voice.

"Yes, Sir. I'll be quick." I tore across the sand as Father told Donny to get the rockers and hammock stored.

Part way over to Maggie's I saw Widow Harris struggling with a stuck window in her back bedroom. I ran to her door, and without asking or rinsing my feet, bolted inside.

"Mrs. Harris?"

"Up here, Andrew." Her voice called from above. I made my way up the stairs and found her standing next to the bed pulling on the uncooperative frame.

"Let me help you with that, Mrs. Harris." Our hands worked together, and the window slid with creaks and grumbles into place. I wanted to stay and chat, ask her about the early years, but I knew that would need to come later.

With the echo of her gratitudes following me down the stairs, I sprinted out the back door and over to Maggie's. Skeeter sat patiently in Pegasus on the side porch, smiling nervously. His paper sack of pajamas, toothbrush, and comics rested on his feet above the pedals. Lizard waited patiently at his side.

Just as the sun disappeared entirely behind a streak of gray, a sharp gust buffeted through the alley between the cottages.

I was anything but naïve when it came to the big storms. I knew what they could do and had absolutely no illusions about their danger. I had listened to too many stories, but more importantly, had ridden out a hurricane in Burlington at the age of seven. We'd opened all the windows and doors on both sides of the house and taped the glass. At first it had seemed like a grand adventure, one to beat all. Then, as I watched, my favorite climbing tree was ripped like thistle weed from the ground and laid out like a cadaver. In the Outer Banks big storms were fearsome beyond measure.

As I rounded the front, Maggie came out through the screen door. She looked unruffled, almost tranquil in the rising breeze. She had loosened the braids in her hair, so it spun wildly about her head, but her eyes, in contrast, seemed oddly peaceful.

Donny yelled from the back of our garage, "Skeeter still sleeping over? Father needs to know."

"Yes," I yelled back, then looked at Skeeter. "You got everything."

"Yep. I got a double issue of Superman for us, and Lex Luther kills him at the end of the first one."

Even with a near-hurricane marching towards us, I had to respond to that. "What! That's not right; Superman can't be killed."

"Well, that's what it says." Skeeter didn't like to be contradicted much on his comic book knowledge. "We'll have to read it, I guess."

I looked at Maggie, "We're going over to Mai's first thing after this is over, right? It can't last that long or they would've had a warning on the radio."

Maggie looked distant, like I'd seen her the first morning we'd gone to Mai's. Her voice drifted from some other place, and another person answered when she said, "You didn't hear? There was a warning, Drew. It came over the radio 'bout three hours ago. Might last for days. It's a hurricane."

***

Everything happens for a reason. And it is all connected. As children we are not always provided the answers for the events that alter our lives. We are rarely handed the precise explanations we need, but in some enormous plan, some vast set of circumstances, there is a purpose. A tear falls, and that drop rises to the clouds. A sigh mingles with another's exhale and the vapor ascends. It is said that from the single beat of a butterfly's wing the course of a storm may change.

Big Leo didn't move offshore. Perhaps somewhere the molecules of a butterfly's wing changed it. Perhaps it was a teardrop. The storm charged the horn of Cape Hatteras like the lion that it was. By the time Father had lifted Skeeter up to my room and I had toted two casseroles over to Maggie's, the wind had intensified so much that I had to lean into it to walk

There wasn't a single car on the highway—that would have pleased Momma on most days—and along the shore, in every occupied cottage, there were single-minded preparations taking place. Every resident knew what had to be done. Most of them were experts. Candles were laid next to matches. Food and water was stocked. If shutters couldn't be fastened, thick plywood was nailed across windows, and if that wasn't possible, the last defense of masking tape was stretched geometrically across the glass. Flashlights were tested, boards and hammers set at the ready, and every loose object smaller than a truck was secured. And then everyone waited.

I had wondered at times during my first eleven years and eleven months why adults always gave names to the big storms. Hurricanes, during those years, had appealing appellations like Flora and Dorothy. My grandmother was a Dorothy, and certainly not the windy beast that tore up the hackberry tree in my backyard. It puzzled me. Then I met Big Leo and I understood. We needed to chuckle at it, shake our heads and personify it. Then we could lay blame at its feet. During the pinnacle of all that chaos, when it roared and snarled around us, we had to give it a friendly name. Only then could it become little bit less terrifying to us.

Skeeter and I played cards and ate jelly sandwiches and chips. Momma came up and was prepared to move us to her room on the lee side. The wind, in her opinion, would then be less likely to lift us out the window and deposit us somewhere over in the sound. I managed to talk her out of it with a promise that if we got scared we would shift our fort without delay.

I was glad to have Skeeter there. Like giving a name to the storm, it softened the fear just a bit to have him as a companion. We played 'War' and 'Slap' and tried to ignore the tempest growing outside, but I was curious about the ocean. I wanted to see all that movement of air and water, but the shutters that protected all our windows also sealed out the view.

"One, two, three, War!!" We turned cards like wild croupiers. Outside, the wind smashed a small, unseen object against the shingles next to my bed. A bird? Uprooted sea oats? Perhaps I would find it when it all stopped.

"It's getting stronger, Drew. I hope Momma and Maggie are okay." In his voice I could hear the same fear that was stirring up inside me.

"They'll be fine, Skeets. They've got everything they need, and Maggie knows how to take care of anything."

"I hope so. So, you wanna read the first Superman together?"

**

Inside the shuttered fortress of the great cottage, we amused ourselves with games and food and tried every ploy to reduce our fear of the waves that were mounting the sand.

Father left one shutter, the one below the ship's bell in the dining room, unlatched for the first hour, so he could monitor the situation outside. Every few minutes he would peer out the window, nod and tell my mother that it was going to be just fine. It took a lot to convince her, but Father was practiced in such things.

What happened outside I learned of later. Eventually all of Nags Head learned of it. Stories were shared, details were added, everything was compared, and all the events eventually became clear. The reasons for all of them, however, remained unclear for a longer time.

The northern part of the strand was Deputy Frank Curry's responsibility. It had been for three years. He patrolled his section of highway and considered that area to be his dominion. He liked that part of his job, because it allowed him to tell people what to do. There was a good feeling of power associated with his rule.

As the storm approached, he made his way slowly from the filling station beyond Kill Devil Hills south along the ocean. First, he stopped and inspected the doors to the casino. He made sure the lot was empty. At Kitty Hawk he barked at a few residents who still had last minute preparations to see to outside. He told them with his most condescending voice of authority that they'd better hurry it up.

Frank Curry, like too many residents, was convinced the storm would be weaker. It was just going to graze the coast like a flesh wound, he thought, and certainly wasn't going to be life threatening. But Frank still liked to intimidate people with the potential danger. He ordered folks to get inside, close their windows and secure everything. He tried to make it all seem more perilous than he secretly thought it was going to be. Most people believed him, though. After all, he was the deputy.

He stopped in at Mr. Jensen's market and bought a few supplies for himself. There wasn't much left on the shelves after the locals had bought the provisions they supposed they would need for the next few days, but Frank did get the beer and the last of the frozen dinners he wanted. That was a plus. He brusquely told Mr. Jensen to lock up and get himself into his own cottage up the road.

Mr. Jensen looked right through Frank with eyes that told the deputy to go to hell. Mr. Jensen had seen two wars and had stared down a lot more in his life than a foolish youngster with an over-sized head. He told Frank as much. "I'll be locking up my store when I damn well please, Frank Curry. I seen more wind and waves in my time than you ever will, and I know exactly when it's going to get bad and how bad it's going to get. You understand. I feel it in my bones, so you get in that damned car of yours and go do what you been told to do." The rejoinder stung the deputy like a slap on the cheek. It was an affront to the rule of his domain.

"Listen here, Zach. I'm supposed to make sure people are doing what they're supposed to be doing. It's my job, an' I'm telling you to get on home."

Mr. Jensen set the beer and food into a sack and replied, "Your job is to help people, Frank, and I don't see you doing that often enough. You seem to like bullying and pushing people around, and right now I'm pushing back. Get the hell out of my store."

Curry threw a crumpled ten dollar bill at Mr. Jensen that bounced off the older man's chest. He grabbed the grocery bag and hissed, "Keep the fucking change, old man."

Twenty minutes later Frank Curry was still fuming. His fourth beer was getting warm and he wanted to call Jenny at dispatch and tell her he was heading home. His TV dinners were melting and that old fart had insulted him. He didn't call the station quite yet though. He started the ignition and drove south.

**

Maggie stood in her denim shorts and purple t-shirt on the side porch as the wind whipped in stronger and steadier bursts across the strand. She had made a decision as the hurricane had approached—one that had come more easily than she had expected, and during those first hours her answer had come to her with certainty. Now, she was unsure. The weight—the one that was pulling her under and drawing her life away--had gotten so much lighter when she had made her decision. Now the weight had returned.

Looking at the ocean she pleaded silently. *Please! I just want to be someone. That's all. I just want to dance with a nice boy. Maybe someone who likes to brush my hair. I want to be Maggie Martine* The final plea screamed inside her head.

As news of the storm had come over the air waves Maggie had been resolved to leave. She didn't know where, or how, or even for how long. Now, as she stood alone on the side porch, she didn't know what to do. With a deep breath she pushed her hands slowly towards the ocean and drew them back. Then she turned and looked down the strand, across the dunes to where Mai's garden must be. She sighed deeply. *What would Mai want me to do?* The voice came back instantly: *Be patient, Daughter. Give love, even when none given back.*

Maggie shivered in the wind. She would stay.

Deputy Curry was trying to steady the wheel of his patrol car as he rolled south on the highway. 'Fuckin' wind's getting crazy,' he grinned to himself. 'Getting a little hard to hold the road.' He smiled again. 'Or is it that fifth can over there? Knew I should've bought more. Fucking old man. Well, I believe I'll have my last one at home.'

Curry radioed Jenny Bristol at the Manteo station that he was done for the afternoon, and if they needed him he'd be sitting in his chair in front of the television, but don't call unless someone was dying. He signed off and said out loud, 'Well, Hells Bells, I gotta piss.' With those words lingering in the patrol car, he saw Maggie Silver step onto her porch. Frank pulled to the side of the highway and watched her for a moment. Her long legs tapered silkily down from her shorts, and for a moment he just watched her. It looked like she was trying to push over a tree. 'What the hell is she doing? Girl's crazy as her damned mother.'' Maggie opened the screen door and disappeared inside. Like a homing shark Frank turned his patrol car into her driveway.

Maggie was in the kitchen when Curry came to her door. She was pulling on her long jeans, the shorts ones that had made her legs shiver lay rumpled on the floor.

Frank saw those legs. He saw the pants slide over her underwear, and he hitched up his own belt and sniffed. Maggie spun around as Curry walked into the kitchen. For a brief moment they just stared at each other. Proud defiance stood facing vicious arrogance, dignity watched small-minded power.

"Get out of my house, Frank. You got no business here."

Frank swayed forward. "You always act like such a bitch, Maggie. Why is that? Huh? I ain't going to bite you. And anyways, I'll go when I damn well please."

"Frank, you get out of my house. I don't want any trouble right now."

"Now what trouble would that be, Maggie? I'm not causing any. What the hell you going to do anyway, call the police?" He gave her an untidy smile. "An' if I remember right, you don't even have a phone in this dump."

"You sound drunk, Frank.'

"No, I'm not drunk. You'd know it if I was drunk. I couldn't get hard if I was drunk, and I'm hard as billy club. See" Curry grabbed his crotch and stepped to left of the kitchen table. Maggie moved to keep the table between them.

In a moment of oddly-timed madness Clarisse started singing. Refrains of an old gospel song rose from the back room to mingle with the howling winds circling the house. The cottage had become an eerie chapel. "Take his hand, Children, take his hand. Take his hand, Children, take his hand. Let him lead you, Brethren, to that land…"

Maggie's head turned from habit at the sound of her mother's voice, and Frank Curry, in a motion that contradicted the clumsiness of too much alcohol, reached across and grabbed a thick handful of her hair. Maggie screamed.

"You just never been taught how to act like a proper lady, Miss Maggie. Nothin' to it, really. You just need to be shown how." She yelped as he yanked her head backwards and fumbled with the wide buckle at his belt. "Shit!" Maggie had swung her fist with a thud into his ribs and screamed again. The blow didn't seem to faze the deputy. Her scream died in the wind. His belt, with cuffs and gun and nightstick, dropped to the floor. He pushed his left hand under her t-shirt up to her breast. "Nothin' to it, really."

"Take his hand, Children, take his hand. Let him lead you, Children, to his land."

"Just a little lesson in manners." Curry yanked his hand from her breast and slapped her sharply across her cheek, knocking her backwards onto the table. Maggie screamed once more.

Time slowed like separate frames on a movie reel. Below the wind, below her mother's voice and Frank's grunting, Maggie heard only one thing, the slow ticking of the mantle clock in Clarisse's room. A lonely thought slipped in. How foul his breath smelled.

She felt his hand tearing at the buttons of her jeans.

"Let him lead you, Brethren, to his promised land."

She closed her eyes and drifted like a ghost to Mai's porch where she stood gazing at a long vee of drifting pelicans.

. *Skeeter and I barely breathed. The second letter poured out as the first, a record of adoration so profound*

that even two boys reading it in the pale light of a hidden
flashlight could feel its haunting passion

'With each breath and step I ask

Why have I been sent a gift so precious?

There has been no jewel yet carved, no metal yet
forged,

No ivory so perfectly smoothed, as the touch of your
kiss.

I lay, the contented, in your arms.

I dream, the contented, on your thighs.

I wake to see Eden curved upon those pillows

And realize it is not a dream.

Why has God given this to me?

What acts have I committed to deserve such bliss?

I ask of Him, nay beg, with every breath

That I may lay in that Eden forever.'

It wasn't until the fourth letter that we began to
whisper questions to each other once more. April 21, 1942.

'I feel my heart shall dissolve like salt in the sea.

I implore you to tell me. Have we created a gift of
God?

Is it ours together?

Like rain upon the soil, a blend of heaven and earth.

Is it ours together, yours and mine?

I listen for your voice,

Taste the air for a scent of your breath,

There is nothing.

I hear the whispering of my heart.

I taste only the salt.

You are not there.

Will you not answer?'

"*Why isn't she answering him, Drew? Is he writing to
Momma?" Skeeter sounded almost as desperate as I felt. I
lay the letter on top of the others, beside the four green bills.
Neither of us had ever seen so much money. I reached under
the bed.*

"Let's read the last one."

*I turned over the final envelope, shiny white with
newness, and with my pen scribbled calculations of
multiplication. Then I did it again. I looked at Skeeter, saw
him following the algorithm with fascination. 'Twenty-one
thousand three hundred,' I whispered.*

'Dollars?"

I nodded in astonished agreement.

'Gawd, Drew!'

*I read the last letter slowly in barely audible
whispers. It was a desperate cry.*

June 21, 1959

'What little I had of you,
What little I held in my loneliness,
Has sailed beyond my reach.
The horizon is empty now,
As it has been so long for you.
We are left alone, marooned.
The nectar of my soul has dried to dust,
My thirst is no longer bearable.
Pain cuts me as a rusted blade.
Why, why, my love, has God, taken back
The only gifts I have ever asked of him?'

'The only solace I take in this world
Is what we have created together.
But even that is too little to sustain me now.
Can you understand what I must do?'

The final question tolled. I whispered it twice, trying
to understand its meaning. Deep in the caverns of my mind I
heard a refrain. It rose like a whisper, a song. The choir
was chanting, and as Mai had so often told me, I closed my
eyes and listened. Then, with a flood of fear, I knew who
had written the letters in my lap.

When Maggie opened her eyes seconds later she was
certain she was having a vision. Beyond Frank's shoulder
she saw a hand. It looked like a picture in her <u>Stories from
the Bible</u> book, the one where God, with all that electricity
ready, was reaching down to spark Adam's finger, but the
hand she saw wasn't descending from heaven. It was
coming from behind Frank Curry's head, and then it
smashed into him like a wrecking ball. It sent the deputy
sprawling against the kitchen counter like a sack of
potatoes.

Things happened consecutively in that moment.
Frank Curry, dazed and throbbing, slapped at his hip,
searching for the pistol that was supposed to be belted to his
waist. It wasn't. It lay on the floor along with the stiff billy
club at his victim's feet.

His own billy had softened.

Maggie jumped up, pulled her shirt down over her
breasts. Shivering violently, she tried to button her jeans
with trembling fingers. When she lifted her head she was

staring into the dark eyes of her rescuer, Jethro Maximillian Sorrini. For an instant she saw something in the pools of blue she had never seen before. Love, an intense, glorious love.

"You fucking, son of a bitch," Curry screamed. "Aaarghhh.." With a roar he charged Jethro, his shoulder lowered, arms spread. The fisherman spun and brought his elbow down with the massive power of decades of hauling tons of fish-laden nets. Curry crumpled to floor, as the elbow landed like a sledge in the center of his back. He rose wobbly to his knees. The fingers on his left side were on fire and didn't seem to be working correctly.

Through a dense fog drifting around him, he heard the fisherman whisper in an eerily calm voice, "It's okay, Margaret. It's okay. It's all fine now." Curry heard Maggie weeping softly. His brain screamed. Where the fuck is my gun? Above him he heard the Portuguese ask, "Can you go to her, Daughter?"

Then from her a simple, "Yes."

"You should go before the wind gets worse." There was quiet concern in his voice.

Clarisse's voice rose from the back room. "Let him lead you, Children, to that land."

"Go to Mai. She's waiting for you." The wind ripped a shingle from the front side and smacked it sharply against the side door. "She will be there for you now. Always."

Maggie's weeping grew louder. Frank Curry slowly pulled one foot into a position below his leg and felt for the table edge above him.

Sobbing desperately Maggie begged, "You've got to tell me, Jethro. Please God, tell me."

Jethro pulled her in his arms and gently rocked her like a newborn. They swayed together and seventeen years of watching, seventeen years of separated love slipped away in a single moment. "You are a gift of God, Margaret, a gift given to Clarisse and me. You've always been ours." And then Frank Curry heard something unexpected; the big fisherman started weeping. "She wouldn't let me," he sobbed.

"She wouldn't let you what?" Maggie's wept the words.

"She wouldn't let me near you, Margaret. It was my wall of glass. I couldn't be there. I begged her. Time and again. All these years I begged. I wanted just to touch you, to hold you. All I could do was watch."

In that hour Big Leo rose to just below hurricane strength and began to drive the ocean in a rampaging wall before it. With each new offensive, it sought higher sand, and with raking fingers, it tore at every object as it sucked backwards. Then it rose and smashed against the sand again. The rain turned horizontal and sought to flatten anything it encountered upright on the strand.

A wall of water surged up the slope of the beach and crested the lower steps of the porches along Cottage Row. Inside the front rooms, on planks of pine five feet above the swelling waters, people trembled. Those with religion, and many of those without, began praying with an earnestness they had never before expressed. Terrified, they questioned the miscalculations. Big Leo was bigger than anyone imagined, and it was angry at something.

As the wave ripped an eight-inch board from the first step of the Silver cottage, Frank Curry pulled himself painfully to his feet and made a concentrated fist with his right hand. Then he made the last nasty remark he would make for a very long time. He looked at Jethro Sorrini with seething eyes and screamed, "You fucking wop, I'm going to tear the goddamn face off your head." At that moment, the electricity and all the lights from Buxton to Kill Devil Hills went out.

Jethro whispered, his voice barely audible in the shrieking wind. 'You must go now, Margaret. Go before the waters get any higher.'

He looked at his daughter. Her hair was his. Her eyes were his. Her pain was his.

He looked at the evil crumpled on the floor. Six blows from each fist and it had been done. Even in the dark he had known exactly where they landed.

'But what about you?' she whispered.

'I have my chores. But I will be by your side, Margaret. Just listen for me. Go to Mai.'

She looked once more at his eyes. Pure love reflected back, and the she was gone.

The fisherman wept. He sang his favorite aria. O Terra Addio. Good-by Earth. We leave you now as lovers. The pillow lifted slowly--like a dancer's mask. Good-bye Earth. Good-bye my Sweet Aida. He sang and wept, touched a drop of perfume upon the softness below her lobes. He brushed her hair and settled his face into it. Gazing at her, he saw that something was still wrong. She was so beautiful. She had danced like the morning breeze. He changed her dress and ivory belt, her shoes. Now, now she could dance again. He lay there next to her, and deep rest settled upon him for the first time in seventeen years.

The fisherman awoke and stood slowly. The candle had melted into a pool of soft wax on the mantle. The wick flickered once and went out. She was gone.

He looked around the room, bowed and stepped into the kitchen. There were chores to be done. The mess needed to be cleaned. It would be a bit of a lift for his arms, but everyday brought that, didn't it? He just needed the keys.

Jethro waded across the highway from the parking lot at Jensen's and turned north. The water was nearly to his waist, pulling violently at his legs, but he knew the tides. They were the rhythms of his life. He knew it was at its highest, and soon it would be turning out to sea again.

He started to whistle a tune, but the wind ripped the air from his lips, reminding him that it alone would whistle that night, so he sang the fisherman's song his father had taught him.

'Round the cape of great fortune come with me.
Where the sails fill with sunlight endlessly.
And the moaning of the whales
And the beating of their tales
Bring us home to our lands beyond the sea.

Jethro started the engine and listened to the smooth growling with pride. He opened the door above the transom in the stern, and fastened the chain through the helmsman's chair. It wrapped about his waist like a saber sash.

The Rising Star, his Estrella Y Luna, was under his command again, top gallant, mizzen and main all hoisted fully to the sky. He pushed her into gear, and she rolled like a beautiful irrepressible force of oak and canvass directly towards the open arms of the Atlantic. O Terra Addio. The sails filled, and she slipped smoothly across the waves.

Beyond the pier Jethro Sorrini sank slowly to the floor where Clarisse waited in her flowered dress and ivory belt. She caressed his face, kissed his smooth cheeks, his lips. He bowed, and they began to dance.

Lantern

Father found Clarisse.

The morning after Big Leo inflicted its heaviest damage, he struggled through the receding waters and gusting winds to check on our immediate neighbors. That was his way. Next door he found Dellie Harris sitting in her kitchen reading by an oil lantern. She was fine, and of all the cottages, hers had faired the onslaught better than any. He brought her a gift of Nina May's biscuits and a thermos of tomato soup. Then he returned to our cottage, restocked with biscuits and soup and ventured back out into the winds to check on Maggie and Clarisse.

The damage to the outside of their cottage was obvious as he came closer. The front steps had been swept away completely by the waves, forcing him to climb onto the porch using the splintered railing and balusters. Boards were buckled up all along the front and side porches. Shingles and screens had been torn away from the façade, and the side door that led to the kitchen was twisted and held weakly in place by a single hinge. He knocked sharply and called to Maggie. Silence answered.

"Clarisse. Hello? Anyone home?" Nothing. His first thought was that they had evacuated somehow and gone to one of the shelters. But none of that made sense. They had no way of leaving, except by way of neighbors or the sheriff, and Father would have known about that. He turned the handle and pushed the door inward. The kitchen was a wreck. The center table was tilted, with two legs snapped and scattered into the living room. Shattered plates and corn flakes were strewn across the floor. It looked like a bar-room brawl had taken place inside that confined space.

"Hello?" He stepped over a chair leg and moved towards the closed door in the back. To the right, in the front living-room, he noticed the tattered sofa where he had tucked Skeeter in after the Fourth-of-July party. It was pushed up sharply on the right side by the buckled boards beneath it. "Hello?" He pushed open the door to Clarisse's dark room.

For a few seconds Father breathed more easily. She was asleep on her bed. Then he saw that she was in a flowered dress with an ivory-colored belt and black sequined shoes. Her long hair was neatly brushed and pulled back with a wide, green band. Her arms stretched languidly by her side. She looked like she had just settled into repose after an evening dance, and had it not been for the gray waterfall of hair across her chest and the ancient appearance of her skin, she would have looked like a beautiful twenty-year-old going on a date. Father didn't call her name again. He had seen the look of death before and knew it was pointless. He just whispered, "Oh, Dear God." Clarisse was singing her gospel songs with the angels.

He left things exactly as they were, and gathering up the meaningless biscuits and soup, closed the side door tightly. He returned quietly, and certain no one would hear him, dialed from the only phone in the cottage. He spoke with Jenny Bristol at the Manteo office. Jenny had endured one of the longest nights in recent memory, having relayed messages and instructions to the sheriff for twelve hours straight, and to make it all worse, their lazy-ass deputy wasn't answering his phone or the radio in his car.

"No, John, Jack's still out," she replied to his question. She sounded worn to a frazzle. "I can probably get through to him when he gets back into his car. It shouldn't be long. He's looking into another problem right up near you. Are you all right?"

"We're fine, Jenny. But I need Jack down here as quickly as possible. I can't go into it right now. Just have him get here as fast as he can."

***

Zacharius Jensen returned near midday to check on how his store had held up during the night. Being on the opposite side of the highway from the ocean didn't always ensure minor damages to a property. Zacharius knew that luck had more to do with it than anything else. He looked at the place in the sky he supposed the sun should be. 'You sure wouldn't know it was noon,' he said to himself. 'Still damn near as dark as last evening, damn near as windy too.' He turned to the ocean and tipped his faded Red Sox cap respectfully. 'One helluva storm, Missy' he said.

As he pulled his keys from his pocket and stepped towards the front door, he noticed the chrome of a heavy, rounded bumper protruding beyond the edge of his garbage pen. The fence stuck out four feet from the back of the store and housed six metal cans and enough space for flattened cartons. The bumper stuck out a foot beyond the fence. Mr. Jensen got angry. He didn't like teenagers using his lot for drinking or smooching. If they felt the need for that, they could take it up the road a piece, but he didn't want it in his lot. He'd cleaned up empty beer cans, cigarette butts, and a few too many pieces of underwear over the years. He'd tired of it after the first damned time.

He stepped out further and saw the markings and license plate on the rear of a patrol car. Jensen got angrier. 'What the hell is Curry doing back here?' He took another step and saw the back of a tilted head. For a brief moment his feeling softened slightly towards the deputy, thinking that the young man had patrolled throughout the night and was now getting some deserved rest. But then Zacharius remembered that Frank Curry was just too ornery and lazy for that. 'He's sleeping off that goddamn beer is all.'

Two more steps and he saw the side of Curry's face. Even from ten feet it appeared purple and misshapen. Zacharius walked towards the car and started to worry because the deputy didn't seem to be breathing at all. He bent his stubbly chin down next to the window and peered in. Curry was nearly unrecognizable; his head was battered and lumpy like clusters of purple grapes and his face was rested against the window, but the store owner knew instantly that he was alive. The faintest condensation of breath pulsed onto that window, and that fine bit of respiration sent Zacharius running for the phone behind the register in his market.

Sheriff Jack Brennan had been a whole lot busier than his unconscious deputy. He had spent the better part of the previous night assisting terrified people and a good variety of animals through swirling water and howling winds. As soon as he was positive the storm was going to be worse than predicted, he had made certain three places were open and readied as shelters and that a crew was prepared to bring phone lines back up the moment the weather allowed. The county did have decent contingency plans and enough people who had seen every form of storm. The seasoned ones knew precisely when they needed to get to shelters. The newer ones would learn.

The high school auditorium in Manteo had been opened with a single phone call and was now half filled with older and younger refugees wrapped in wool, navy blankets. The information center at Kitty Hawk was the second shelter, and that was where he happened to be helping people when he received a message from Jenny Bristol that Zach Jensen needed him at his store immediately. Jack Brennan knew that meant trouble. Zacharius wouldn't call anyone unless there were problems he couldn't handle.

As he pulled into the front side of the parking lot, Zach was on his steps waving him around back with his baseball cap. He saw his own deputy's patrol car parked at an odd angle and his first thought was, 'What's that stupid son-of-a-bitch kid done now.' He was angry as hell, because they'd all been trying to raise Frank at home and in his car the entire night.

Ten minutes later he was waiting on the ambulance from the hospital. He was worried. He thought once, just once, about pulling those beer cans out from the passenger side and throwing them into Zach's trash bins, but it was out of the question. Besides, whatever Frank had gotten himself into, and it looked like he'd tussled with a bear, he most likely deserved. He'd just have to face his own music on this one. If he lived.

He had just settled himself back into the warmth and protection behind his steering wheel when Jenny's voice

crackled over the radio again. "Jack, John MacLaren just
called. He needs you at his place ten minutes ago." There
was another man who could take of himself, he thought, and
just about everyone else for that matter. He had a bad
feeling. The one that was already rumbling through the back
of his weary head got suddenly worse. He asked Zach to
wait for the ambulance and to call Jenny after it left.
Nothing else could be done. Then he turned south onto the
highway and began threading through the debris.

Fifteen minutes later Sheriff Brennan weaved around
a wide section of missing tarmac and pulled into the short
drive behind our boathouse. Father went out to meet him.
Minutes later, the patrol backed into the wind and re-parked
at the Silvers. Afterwards, he and Father spoke on that porch
for a very long time. Inside our shuttered cottage none of us
were aware of any of the events unfolding outside.

Father made a deal with Sheriff Brennan while they
stood at the foot of Clarisse's bed. They had known each
other a long time, long enough to be able to trust each other.
Father would call the office in Manteo as soon as he saw
had any information or saw any sign of Maggie, and the
sheriff, in turn, promised that they would provide her every
protection the law afforded.

The sheriff asked if Father had any idea where she
might have gone. He did, but he didn't tell Mr. Brennan
when he was asked. Out of some innate faith in the way
humans acted, he knew in his heart that Maggie would come
back. He always saw the good in people. He hoped for her
sake that she did return. If she were caught trying to hop the
ferry, it would look bad.

In twenty-two years of service, minus his war time, Jack Brennan had never investigated a homicide, and that was what he was guessing this was. The scene looked like an explosion had ripped through it. The kitchen looked like a barroom brawl had taken place, and the girl was gone. But the oddest part was Clarisse. She'd been laid out on her own bed with some very apparent tenderness. The sheriff had to reason that the girl had killed her own mother.

When the coroner arrived with the ambulance to remove Clarisse's body, Father returned to our cottage, and after quietly telling Mother, he knocked on the door to my room. Skeeter and I had re-strung the best blanket fort possible across our two beds and were inside playing pickup sticks on the top covers. We had been spending the last hour discovering how difficult that was with the wrinkles and bulges shooting tremors along their fault lines. We were just making the frustrated decision to switch to Parcheesi when Father entered.

"Drew?"

From inside the fort the tone of his voice struck me as odd. "Yes, Sir?"

"Could you go downstairs and speak with your mother for a few minutes? Fix a couple of sandwiches and some of that soup to bring back up here. I'll call you in a bit."

I left without saying or asking anything; Father's tone had scared me. He sounded too much like he had to do something he didn't want to do, and that always meant trouble.

Downstairs, Momma told me in a calm voice that Clarisse had died. I stood forlornly in the kitchen. It was my first true encounter with the mystery of human death, and I had no details, nothing to help me understand what had occurred or how she had died. I wanted to ask where someone went when they ceased to breathe. For a moment I pictured Clarisse slumped lifeless against the headboard in her room, her last arrow launched somewhere into the dunes.

Then I felt a secret relief that Maggie might now be happy again, and that thought made me feel a little guilty. It didn't seem right to be glad that someone was dead.

Father didn't tell Skeeter any details, either. He merely held my friend while his tears came. Later I came to understand that it wasn't as difficult for him as we might have expected. He hadn't wanted Clarisse to die, but eventually we all understood--she had been lost to him already for a long time. What Skeeter did want--and asked for over and over again--was Maggie, but no one seemed able to say where she was, or when she would come for him.

It was a strange day. We were cooped up inside the cottage, the shutters still latched like rigid armor against the wetness that continued to pound in from the ocean. All of us were sheltering our own individual emotions when, in truth, we needed to be releasing them outside in the open spaces.

I felt tortured inside my room. I was desperate to know how Maggie was, how Mai Lin was, but that information wasn't being offered by any of the adults, so along with Skeeter, we waited the best way we knew how, playing like boys, so the hurt was held at bay.

That night Maggie returned. A single light shone through the side window and just before midnight Sheriff Brennan arrived in his Pontiac to take her away.

The day after Maggie was arrested the sun rose through scudding clouds. In the great cottage we all helped to push the shutters open and lift the windows wide to let the air and light sweep through the rooms and into our hearts.

I looked out my window. The ocean was still raging angrily. White caps and froth tattered across the surface. Directly in front of the cottage the pocked sand was littered with debris of every imaginable size and source--much of the refuse had been trapped in the low hillocks along the right side of the cottage as the water had washed back to sea. Pieces of board, asphalt, shingles, plants, and rusty cans appeared to be sprouting inside the mangled sea oats and dune grass.

I went to find Father, to tell what we had done the night before. I had to tell him about the letters and the money.

One of the supports on the side below the post where the hammock hung, had been shattered during the storm. Father was kneeling underneath the corner inspecting the top piece that drooped down like a jagged stalactite. The bottom was probably washing ashore somewhere in Maryland. Two of the front steps were cracked and pitched up at sharp angles.

As I stepped carefully across the first board, Father stood and looked curiously down the beach towards the pier. I followed his gaze. A large crowd had gathered at the end, and one of the longboats was lifting and pitching roughly in the waves.

In the distance I heard the long wail of an ambulance rising and falling. It was coming north.

I hopped over the last board into the sand, I saw him grab his sneakers and begin to jog towards the pier. Like a can racer down Jockey's Ridge, he started slowly and then built up speed. I ran after him calling, "Father! I have to tell you something." Frustrated, I screamed it again at his retreating back.

He was near a full sprint when he yelled, with an unusual impatience, over his shoulder, "Not now, Son." He kept running. I followed.

When I reached the foot of the pier and scrambled up the embankment I heard whispers. In the water I saw the longboat and Angelo's short frame draped in a blanket in the bow. He looked like he was crying. Words and phrases from people around me began to sink slowly into my recognition. 'Tragedy.' 'He was such a good man.' What was he thinking being out in a hurricane?' I saw Mr. Jensen standing next to Marcy Tyner and Angelo's wife, Pirena. All of them, even tough old Mr. Jensen, were weeping. I started slowly down the walkway and Mr. Jensen grabbed my forearm.

"Drew, you can't go down there."

My stomach began churning. "Why not? What's happened? What's everybody crying for?"

And then I started screaming, because suddenly I knew. I knew the answer better than any person standing on that pier. It shouted at me from one of his letters-- *'even that is too little to sustain me now. Can you understand what I must do?'* I screamed and screamed, and kept on until Father found me and wrapped me in his arms and held me.

The last sliver of glass had fallen into place and the picture was whole.

It took all of Jethro's boys and a few other strong volunteers, to lift him into the longboat and then up the beach to the ambulance. For a long time I couldn't talk, not that anyone would have paid me any attention. I was simply an hysterical child. What light could I shed on such tragedy? I wept and hiccupped and watched Captain Jethro's body slide away from me.

Angelo and Bertram were good first mates. They saw to things in the correct order for their captain. When Angelo resurfaced the first time, he didn't say anything about the chain wrapped around Jethro's waist, or the transom door latched open. He whispered to Bertram to fetch the key, and then he dove down into that cold water one more time. Bertram began hooking up cables and winches to attach to the back axle. They did things in the right order, because they sure as hell weren't going to pull the duck onto the beach the way Angelo had first found it.

By seven o'clock the entire community had gathered along the shore and pier. Within two hours most of the county had heard the news. When the ambulance left, people began to drift away. There were damages to be repaired, lives to be lived.

Had I been a few inches shorter, perhaps a few pounds lighter, Father would have carried me back to the great cottage in his arms. As it was, I walked with him. He kept his long hand around my shoulder; my breath still came out in gasps and hiccups. He kept saying "He was a good friend, Son. We owe it to him to keep him in our memory that way. It's the best that we can do."

By the time we reached the broken steps at the front of the cottage, my breathing was coming easier. In truth, I had let Father guide me along while I inhaled deeply. I pictured trees and mirrors, and cranes. I saw egrets and the reflected waters of the sound. I saw Mai and Maggie, and Clarisse. And I saw Jethro. Father reached to lift me over the splintered board, and I stopped him. "Father...I need to tell you something."

Skeeter, Momma, Father, and I sat on the beds where our blanket fort had been, and my parents read the letters, every one of them. We told them what we had done—what we had discovered the night before. My parents read the letters and cried like children, or maybe just like adults seeing a very sad tragedy for the first time. I'd never seen both of them crying and it made me feel funny, a little proud that they could be that way. Momma put the money in one of Father's manuscript envelopes and organized all the letters by dates. Then she called Mr. Brennan. There was a look in her eye, sad, but full of resolve, and I knew Mr. Brennan, no matter how tired he was, would be at our house as quickly as his patrol car could get him there.

Just before she hung up I slipped down the secret passageway, ostensibly to help Nina May with our lunch. I listened to the last part of her conversation. "And Jack, bring Maggie with you." There was a moment of silence while she listened, then she replied, "Not one bit of that matters right now, just bring her." Click.

Maggie had been in a cell for fifteen hours, and that was fifteen more than she would ever spend in one again. She was swept into four sets of arms at once like one big octopus. Her eyes were puffier and redder than mine, and I knew that she had been told what was being talked about throughout the entire county.

Mr. Brennan stood off to one side, frowning at the whole scene. He had squeezed in just enough time at his own house to shower, slick his eyebrows, and get into some cotton pants and an ugly Hawaiian shirt.

"Jean Gray, you ready to tell me what's going on here? I really don't like the idea of driving back without getting to the bottom of something today. I've got a headache a mile wide, a deputy in the hospital, two friends in the morgue. And, I've got enough questions to choke an elephant about every piece of it."

Momma smiled so politely at times. "Jack, why don't you stay and have a nice late lunch with us."

It was like a play. People were called in and out, went to the wings, reappeared, and left again. First, Father, Maggie, and Mr. Brennan went upstairs for a long time, presumably to look at the letters and clarify their significance. Momma, Nina May, and I set out plates of every kind of sandwich makings we had. There was a huge Waldorf salad, and when they returned a tureen of clam chowder was brought out, and we all ate together. Donny and Father lifted Skeeter down the stairs.

While fresh cherry pie rounded off the menu, Momma and Maggie went out to the back porch. When Maggie came back in I saw she had been crying some more. Momma then spoke with Mr. Brennan outside on one of the side decks. Later I learned that she became the consummate mother that always she was in those moments. She had talked to Maggie about the details of Frank Curry's attempted rape. Maggie couldn't have told it on her own. Momma sensed that with her psychic—or as I now suspected they were, her intense female--intuitions.

Donny took it upon himself to keep Skeeter company and play pick-up sticks while I lay on my bed and wept again. He told me later that he kept losing to Skeeter and was happy when Mr. Brennan said we could all come back together again.

Father walked me out to the front porch so we could be alone.

"Drew.'

"Yes, Sir?"

He hesitated for a long time. I knew what he was going to say wasn't good. "The letters don't get Maggie off completely." My lip started to quiver, and I knew I was ready to start crying again.

"But Jethro wrote them, and Maggie said he was there. She said that."

"I know, Son. But it still doesn't prove she didn't...kill Clarisse after he left. Mr. Brennan said she doesn't have to go back to Manteo tonight, but..." He stopped and looked directly at me. "If we can't find something, she will." I wanted to start screaming all over again. What was the matter with adults? Why couldn't they see what we saw?

Truth

For the first time in three days I got to sit alone with Maggie.

Skeeter and Donny were working on a five-hundred-piece jigsaw puzzle that Skeeter was showing more skill at than pick-up sticks. A picture was slowly taking shape of two pirates pulling an old horse, a nag, along the beach. Around the nag's head was a lantern that beckoned, like a buoy. A storm-tossed ship veered towards it.

We sat in the rockers on the side porch away from the corner with the broken pillar. There was so much I wanted to ask, so many parts to gently probe, but for a short time we just looked silently at the first stars rising above the ocean.

"You went to Mai's, didn't you?"

She sighed, and her chin dropped slightly. She whispered, "Of course."

"Is she okay?"

Maggie knew what I meant. "She's Mai Lin, Drew." She looked at me and smiled for the first time in a very long time. "You know what I mean, don't you?"

"Yep, I expect I do."

"She did like the peach and almonds by the way." I smiled, and watched as Maggie reached across the space between us. She took my elbow in her hand. "You know, I got to thinking when I was coming up here with Mr. Brennan. Something so strange. It was like I lost a mother, a father, and added another mother all in one night." She looked thoughtful a moment. "Come to think of it, I guess it's going to change what Skeeter and I have to call each other. You know, half-brother and sister now"

I nodded. "What did you and Mai do?"

"You'll laugh."

I tried to see her expression in the fading light, hoping she was smiling, even slightly. "I won't. I didn't laugh when you told me your middle name, did I?"

"Well, we played checkers. Mai said she was pretty sure checkers were invented in China, so she lit an old oil lantern and we played until we both got so sleepy we couldn't slide the pieces any more." She squeezed my elbow gently. "We lay down and she wrapped me up in her arms and we slept through the whole night and whole lot of the next day. After the winds all died down the next night, she sent me back."

"I figured as much. Maggie?"

"Hmm?"

"We've never held anything from each other."

"I know that."

"Were you there …You know, with Jethro when he did it?"

I heard her breathe out like a valve releasing pressure. With a whisper she squeezed my elbow and said, "No. He made me leave. I'd decided to leave earlier in the day, but then…well, Mai's voice told me to stay. I guess in my way I was ready for it to end. It just wasn't how I thought it would be. But…no, I left just after the lights went out. It was before …" She stopped. I had to ask that question, and I knew that Maggie knew she had to tell me.

I whispered, "I read all of his letters, most of 'em anyway. He loved you so much, Maggie. He loved you and Clarisse all those years."

I heard her begin to weep very softly. "I don't understand it, Drew. I guess I won't ever know now. Why didn't he say anything to me? Why wouldn't she let him near me? I would have liked it."

I nodded, and then realized she couldn't see me in the dark. "Do you think maybe it was because he wouldn't go against her wishes? Couldn't go against what she wanted, because he loved her so much?"

"Maybe. But why would she tell him to do that? Why didn't she want anything to do with him? He was such a good man. Heck, she didn't even open the letters. She could have spent the money he sent. We sure as hell could have used it."

I thought for a long time, the silence settled gradually around us, but as always never uncomfortably between Maggie and me. Finally I said, "I'm not sure. I guess only she knew the answers to those, but you know something? I got to thinking it was because of Simon. It sounds strange, but somewhere, way back inside herself, I think she was more like him than she wanted to be. It was like you told me. His voice kept coming out of her. Maybe he just scared her too much to go against his wishes, even after he died."

I heard Maggie sigh deeply in the chair next to me in the darkness. "Maybe," she said. "Maybe."

I looked at the night sky. The stars flickered like a million bright pins. The air was cool and fresh with just enough chill in it to raise the goose bumps on my arms. Maggie's hand still rested lightly around my elbow.

Suddenly I remembered what Jethro had said about stars. He'd explained it to me the same evening we discovered the duck. I hadn't understood it then. Or hadn't thought much on it with the excitement, but right then, sitting with Maggie on the porch, I realized then that we spun in the circle, and not them.

***

Being the catalyst has its responsibilities. It is up to you to agitate all those other ingredients and get them doing what they are supposed to be doing. That night I lay in my bed listening to the great cottage. I heard Skeeter puffing in his sleep. I heard Father's light snoring in the nearby bedroom, and Momma's exhale next to him. I heard Donny. I even heard Maggie's breath from the sofa in the living room. The entire cottage seemed to be filled with breath. Very quietly I lifted the covers and lowered my feet to the floor. Mai had told us that the current flowed better when our heads were skyward and our feet touched the earth. The Song of Rising and Falling Hands. Like a balloon filling slowly.

The pattern filled me. It rose and joined with the ocean. Then it circled into the breeze and fed into the sand and mist and salt. I listened. Mai had told me to listen. The voices, hundreds, thousands of them, whispered around me. They sang, came together like all the stars in a celestial harmony. There is another, they whispered. There is one more. There is another, they sang.

The following morning the ocean looked as if it had never gotten angry at us at all. It lay flat and placid like a huge sheet of bright, green wrapping paper. I had slept later that morning than any other that summer, and the entire household was already up and moving about. I stood at the window in my pajamas, looking out at the sun now well above the horizon. I might have been embarrassed by this singular change in my waking pattern, especially since Maggie was in the house, but I wasn't. There was too much to be done.

I didn't wait to change into my shorts, to wash, or even eat. I found Donny first. "Where's Father?" I demanded.

"You're looking a bit scruffy there, Little Guy. Hairstyle could use some work." Then he looked at me with brotherly concern and asked, "You okay?"

I ignored him and repeated my question. "Where's Father?"

"He's out in the boat house getting some tools to work on the front side. You need any help?"

I didn't answer. Without as much as a good morning to anyone I ran through the kitchen and out the back door. "Father!" His head poked around the corner of one of the big doors. "There's another one!" I yelled.

"Whoa, Son. Slow down. You look like you've forgotten something, like your clothes and some water on your face." I ignored that.

Gasping, I ran up to him. "There's another one."

"Another what?"

"A letter. There's another letter. I know it."

"Okay, Drew. Slow down. Take a breath." I did just that. "Now tell me what you're talking about." I explained what I knew and how I knew it. I was certain.

Father looked at me and then nodded slowly. "Well, it makes some sense I suppose. Let's hope you're right."

Sheriff Brennan came back to our cottage around ten o'clock. Father had called him at the station, but it wasn't necessary. He was already on the highway coming up the coast. When he arrived he looked a lot better than the day before, though his shirt was uglier, if that was possible. He did seem to be in a better mood. Father started right in.

"Jack, Drew's got something you ought to hear."

So I told him. "Sir, There's another letter. I'm positive of it." I took a deep breath and added, "And I think it…" I stopped. "I am positive it has something we have to read."

I told them how all the others were written on the twenty-first of the month. Jethro had to have written one on July twenty-first, and we just hadn't found it. What I didn't mention to Mr. Brennan was how that particular idea had come to me in a celestial song during the night.

Jethro's cottage was searched from top to bottom. Mr. Brennan found pens, writing paper, and envelopes that matched the ones upstairs. He searched Clarisse's room, her hiding place, the mailbox, every logical location. There was no letter.

By the time Father and Mr. Brennan returned, I had gotten cleaned, dressed, and had eaten a huge breakfast. I felt like I had ants crawling on me I was so jumpy. I told Maggie and Skeeter what I was so certain of.

Maggie asked me to repeat exactly what I'd heard the night before. She looked thoughtful as I told her about remembering to listen to the voices—one of Mai's constant reminders. Then she went for a long walk by herself down past The Beachcomber.

I found Donny sitting in the breakfast nook in the kitchen, reading. That was odd enough, but he was reading a book of Momma's poetry. His eyes were misted over, and that was even odder. He told me that he'd just read The Ballad of the Harp Weaver, one of the really sad ones that Momma used to read to me. It brought us to talking about all of it, Clarisse and Jethro, and the death of people we loved. I discovered that he didn't have any more answers than I did.

I went back out to the porch and looked south. Maggie was far down the shore, standing alone at the water's edge. Her arms were curved like cranes' wings, lifting and dropping in graceful, sweeping motions. Her feet lifted in almost perfect harmony. She looked as if she were flying on the breeze. It was most beautiful movement I'd ever seen her do. Though I couldn't see them from the distance, I knew her eyes were closed. I supposed she was saying good-bye in her own way.

"There is no letter, Son." Father's voice came from behind me in sad, slow measures. I looked at Maggie down the beach. Her arms drifted gently down to her sides, and she turned and started back towards us.

"There has to be." I'm certain I looked exactly like a small soldier refusing to cede a strategic hilltop. Father silently patted my shoulder and went to discuss things with Mr. Brennan again. I waited.

Maggie came up the rise of sand wearing that deep smile, the one that bubbled up from that infinite well inside her. With two hops she stood next to me on the porch, bent to my ear and whispered, "They told me, Drew. Both of them. We've got to look under the clock."

She had listened as Jethro had told her, as Mai had told her. She'd let herself slip into the song of her breath and listened.

I turned and ran to the back through the house screaming for Father.

***

All four of us stood in Clarisse's bedroom. Nobody spoke. Mr. Brennan, being the sheriff, did the searching. It wasn't hard. He took a pen from his pocket and pushed against the top of the mantle clock to rock it back without touching it. The envelope was pressed there. It was different than all the others except the first one from March of 1942. Like that one, this had been opened. The sheriff used a handkerchief to lift a single aquamarine page and unfold it. There was no money inside. There was, however, a small photograph. A young Jethro, clean-shaven, with short, combed hair stared at us again with those amazing eyes.

Father read from Mr. Brennan's side. He read it quietly, respectfully like a venerated poem.

> *O Light of My Life*
> *How dim your flame has become.*
> *It flutters unsteadily in the breeze*
> *And crackles now with nightmares.*
> *It is no more your light, my love,*

It is the light of a ghost.
It glows black and scorches.
Burns all those around you, Clarisse
It burns us, Love, consumes us.
It is destroying our Gift of God.
Your flame is so dim, and so dangerous.
Do you understand what I must do?

I think of the time we met.
I watched you swimming as I walked upon the sand.
Your grace and beauty filled my heart,
You took my hand and asked me.
'Will you not come with me and dance?'
I was ashamed, but you laughed and paid no
attention to how I walked.
You laughed at everything, the clouds, the wind,
The shells that we collected and let fall into the sand
again.
And we danced. We created life.

Clarisse, your flame is deadly now.
It is killing that life. Do you understand?
It burns and cannot be.
I alone must take its breath.
Shall we dance once more?

No one spoke. Our heads were bowed, and we all
wept. Tears fell, especially Mr. Brennan's. Father, in a
choking voice, finally spoke. "There is something else." He
stretched his hand forward, and Maggie and I saw what he
meant. There was an oval of crimson circling the word 'we.'

At the bottom of the page, in the last line, Clarisse had kissed that word. It was her acknowledgment, her acceptance, given in one diminishing moment of sanity. It was there for us to see. *Do you understand what I must do?* She did.

***

In the time following the storm there were words and phrases that seemed to have been eliminated from the vocabulary of Nags Head. It was as if they suddenly didn't exist. Even in private, unregistered conversations they were omitted. Words like murder, suicide, mercy killing, guilt, and even death were sucked away by the salt air and replaced with love, passion, and eternity.

The crowd that gathered at the shoreline was larger than anyone thought imaginable. There were no priests or ministers and little was said. All heads were bowed and then raised high. No one needed to speak in lengthy discourses about God and the souls being remembered. Most said short, kind statements, and then Angelo and the boys took both urns so far out to sea that the ashes would not return with the tides. They would be caught in the great Gulf Stream and circle the globe. And then the people on the beach smiled at each other warmly and made their way back to their homes.

Life was for the living.

I took the job at Mr. Jensen's market. It was the first gainful employment of my life, though how much I actually gained and saved is a matter of question. I added to my comic collection substantially and consumed far too much sugar. I became skilled at sweeping and learned how to ring up small orders for customers with a big smile. I was Mr. Jensen's public relations specialist. I bodysurfed and did Chi Gung. I walked with Maggie, and little by little I got her laughing pretty much just by opening my mouth. Skeeter and I fished a lot, and Pooh joined us. The two of them became fast friends, which didn't bother me a bit. And of course I sipped tea with Mai Lin and watched egrets above the sound.

The Rising Star was refurbished; Angelo and Bertram did most of the work on it. Pooh helped some--but I couldn't. It was as if there was too large a hole where that boat had risen in my heart. It wasn't the same for me; our captain wasn't there. My part of her was relinquished to his boys. I did love watching her set to sea each morning, though. That always made me feel good.

Momma helped Maggie and Skeeter a lot, and I sensed that she was taking up a new crusade of sorts. She set up a bank account and deposited their money. She talked with a lawyer and had Clarisse's inheritance shifted into their names, and then she helped with their cottage. With Maggie being almost eighteen they worked on her guardianship of Skeeter. She walked with Maggie on the beach every afternoon and listened a lot while they collected seashells together. Like a skilled surgeon she excised the guilt, hers and Maggie's.

Father labored on two cottages at once, conscripting Donny and Georgie Marovich to help him with the rebuilding. He even got Skeeter hammering from a deliberate position on Lizard. Donny grumbled at first about the forced enlistment, but once he inspected the results of his saw and nails, he decided he had a great future in cabinet making, if not rough construction. It was a cool profession, he announced.

In small steps we all moved forward, changed by the winds, but forward.

One afternoon, a few weeks after Mai Lin was walking with ease again, Maggie and I convinced her to come see what the birds looked like on the ocean side. It was a glorious day. Sunlight streamed down in warm pillars as we marched through the curves of the dunes. Maggie sang and hummed the entire time, even across the highway and along the beach. Mai Lin was the only one who was quiet.

We set up three pillows on the porch of her cottage and Maggie made tea, the sweet kind we all liked. Mai Lin looked at the waves, quietly taking it all in with deep breaths. A line of pelicans graced us with a low flight over the crests. She smiled and clapped her hands and then took each of ours in hers. "Oh this is good, children. This is good. Just like my dream."

I grinned at Maggie. She grinned back. "You know Mai, if you stayed here long enough, I could teach you to swim. I'm a pretty good teacher, you know." And she did stay.

Epilogue

A woman told me in passing, at some decorous, non-essential social function that I was anxious to exit, that she saw life as a series of lessons. There were lessons that we learned the hard way, she said, those that we accepted easily and embraced in our lives, those that we rejected, and finally, those that we didn't recognize when they were presented to us and therefore never learned. Some months later I picked up the telephone next to the photograph that stands at the corner of my desk and thanked her. Life is a series of lessons.

The summers of '58 and '59 return to me often. I merely look at that photograph and they return. I think of those who lit the lanterns to light my path, even the bad ones like Wink May, and I hope with all my being that I learned what I was supposed in those two seasons. I feel I did. Those lessons arrived exactly on time, like deliberate waves on a pebbly beach, and each had its select teaching. They were the lessons of growing up.

I did not return to Nags Head the following summer, nor the one after that.

Nina May took ill that winter. Her health was failing quickly, so Momma and Father took her where she wished to spend her remaining days, with her sisters in Raleigh.

And we moved to California.

Father was asked to be the chief editor for the best gourmet magazine in the country, and he accepted without hesitation. It didn't take me long to adjust. We arrived in La Jolla during the early summer months with a moving van filled to the ceiling. The Nomad was now a shiny new

Impala, which Donny drove rather erratically in the southern California traffic. The Pacific was one block away.

Surfing with a board, I discovered right off, was an even greater Holy Communion with God. It became a passion, along with The Beach Boys, sailing and scuba diving. I was still good at track, and better at math than I thought. Every evening I returned to The Six Winds of the House. There wasn't any reason not to.

Eight years is a magical length of time. It changes a boy into a young man. It narrows the gap of two ages in some mysterious algebraic formula. In 1967, just before my twenty-first birthday I loaded up a Volkswagen camper van with a few pairs of shorts and a lot of tangerines and drove east. I made solemn promises to preserve my student deferment and return to college in the autumn. I had plans to be a meteorologist. I drove leisurely and saw the Grand Canyon and the Painted Desert. I saw Niagara Falls. Eventually I saw the ivory softness of Jockey's Ridge rising up from the shoreline.

The boy at the filling station, who looked like he was just about ten-years-old, told me that the best restaurant in all of Dare County was Martine's. "Just down the road, Sir,' he said. I smiled to myself and told him that I would be sure to try it out.

People were waiting to be seated. The view of the Atlantic was spectacular. Waiting would be a pleasure. They hadn't heard of Corona beer in Martine's, so a club soda with lemon would be just fine.

Along the wall behind the bar three photographs were hung. The first was of two young women with wide hair bands in front of a large dance hall. The second showed a handsome young man, cleanly shaven, dark hair neatly parted, staring into the lens with strong, passionate eyes. The third was a series of four in a single frame, a barnacle encrusted boat becoming a thing of beauty.

I looked out at the waves. Small peaks were rolling across a familiar sandbar down the beach. A breeze wafted through the window. The air was full. Then I felt it. Maybe it was a ripple of movement from her fingers or her breath, but I knew she was there. I turned and saw Maggie Silver with that deep smile, the one that rose up from a well inside her.

"Well, you look like you've gotten somewhat taller, and I believe a whole lot handsomer too."

ABOUT THE AUTHOR

Mr. MacNair spends his time between San Diego and Costa Rica. He has been married to his beautiful and patient wife, Lynne, for twenty-nine years, and together they have two stunning daughters who are making positive changes in the world.

He is convinced that writing is a part of his genetic make-up, a pesky strand of DNA that rattles his sleep with niggling thoughts until he renders them into physical form.

8115763R0

Made in the USA
Lexington, KY
08 January 2011